LOVE IN FRAGMENTS

KIT MASON

Love in Fragments

Published by The Conrad Press Ltd. in the United Kingdom 2022

Tel: +44(0)1227 472 874

www.theconradpress.com

info@theconradpress.com

ISBN 978-1-914913-96-9

Copyright © Kit Mason, 2022

All rights reserved.

Typesetting and Cover Design by: Charlotte Mouncey, www.bookstyle.co.uk

The Conrad Press logo was designed by Maria Priestley.

Printed and bound in Great Britain by Clays Ltd, Elcograf S.p.A.

EROS

January 1997

Turning, Ralph Edwards, who had been the barrister for the prosecution, caught the eye of one of the defendants who had both just been imprisoned for five years.

'A particularly unpleasant assault committed by two callous thugs with no compunction or remorse,' the judge had remarked during sentencing. Ralph saw, rather than heard, the defendant mouth the words at him, 'You cunt. Our friends know who you are and will see to you,' before the man was hustled away by the warders. Smiling, he continued picking up his papers and then left, unperturbed, as it was a common enough reaction. His mind was on other things. He was thinking of the previous evening and the encounter in the kitchen.

When she reached towards him, took his left hand and pulled it gently to her breast, pressing it firmly against her, turned her head up, opened her mouth, wiggled her tongue slightly and, looking straight into his eyes, murmured, 'Kiss me,' he experienced immediate arousal.

'My God,' he thought, 'at thirty-eight my lower body still behaves like that of a sixteen-year-old.'

He did not know this, but these invitations always took place in there, where she had established, to the second, the time lapse between the opening of either the sitting room or dining room door and someone coming in. She had adopted the same routine, with almost invariable success, at many of the dinner parties they had given in their new house. If she liked a man enough and considered he might respond, at some stage when everyone was engrossed in conversation and as hostess she could quite naturally slip away, she would ask him to help her. Once in the kitchen, two doors safely closed behind them, she would lean against the wall, take his hand, right hand if left-handed, left hand otherwise, she made a point of checking before she started, press it to her opposite breast and murmur, 'Kiss me.'

Her view was that she was doing no harm. At worst, and this had never happened, he might refuse but, at best, she would have what she thought of as a jolly nice grope. Men almost always, and so very predictably in her opinion, reacted in one of two ways. There was either a quick kiss, with an occasional slightly embarrassed excuse or, more usually, they leaned down and started to kiss her, at the same time moving the non-breast hand round to her back. Then she would sigh and sink, moving her feet about twenty inches apart. She hoped his hand would, and it usually did at that point, drop down her back, move round her waist and start to journey towards her pelvic region and, when she made no protest, end there sometimes rubbing, sometimes just resting tentatively.

Again, her routine never varied, she would now exhale sensually and sink a little lower at the same time moving her feet further apart. This pushed his hand more firmly between her legs, at which point she would sigh, a low sibilant, 'Yes,' and rub herself gently against him.

Men then did one of two things. None, having got to this point, had ever stepped back or withdrawn from the embrace. If she was wearing a long skirt or dress, the same hand would go round to her back, encircle her bottom and gather the loose material of the dress, drawing it upwards at the same time.

Once the hem was reached, the hand would then feel her bottom before going towards her pubic region again. If she was wearing a short dress, the man would simply drop down a bit and move his hand from outside her skirt to underneath it.

Either way, their reaction was invariably identical. 'You're wearing stockings, not tights,' they would exclaim with barely concealed interest. She regarded herself as an expert at measuring the extent of their interest by pressing herself against their lower bodies.

Her husband always asked her why, when they were dressing for dinner, she was wearing her 'tart's knickers and stockings.' Sadly, at least from her point of view, he was a man of limited sexual appetite who derived more pleasure from looking at pictures of women with no clothes on in magazines, preferably the open crotch shots, than the warm reality of his wife. 'I'm putting them on for you darling,' she would reply, and he would give a non-committal grunt.

She knew however that at the end of any dinner party in their own house, or anywhere else for that matter, he would have drunk so much that he would be to, all intents and purposes, comatose. It was sometimes as much as he could manage to get to their bedroom and into bed (although on nights such as that she did not share these with him) via the bathroom without wetting himself.

Their marital sexual activity was confined to either Friday or Saturday night, and then only on the rare occasions when they were neither out nor entertaining others. She found it all perfunctory and unsatisfactory. It was not that her husband was unattractive: it was just that he no longer seemed to find her so. She was not sure why she even bothered. She would not let him adopt the missionary position, as she did not want his total proximity, so she would straddle him, rocking backwards and forwards until she heard the grunting noise he made during an orgasm. This generally did not take long and usually he fell asleep very quickly afterwards. Then she stroked herself, thinking of her kitchen experiences, until she came, quietly choking back the little panting sobs that accompanied her orgasms.

Having got to the outside of her knickers, but under her dress, men again divided into two different camps. Some preferred to put a finger through her knicker leg and into her from the side. Whilst she wore underwear on dinner nights that facilitated this, she far preferred the more direct approach of sliding the hand down her lower stomach, into her knickers from the top and then down into the wet intimacy that awaited him.

What she actually wanted was for him to put one, or even better, two fingers into her as the mere fact of insertion would bring her usually immediately to a small orgasm that always delighted her with its intensity. She would, however, never reveal that she had had one to the man, she had become adept at disguising them, and having achieved her purpose, would finish the kiss - it had continued until then - and say with complete innocence that they had better take whatever it was through to the dining room, delivering herself of a half-smile that seemed simultaneously to suggest that he had gone too far but also that she would not give him away.

She aimed to complete the whole process in less than two minutes and her tally to date was no refusals to kiss, five touchings only and nine orgasms.

She did not regard it as cheating on her husband, nor did

she see it as infidelity. On the one occasion when a man had managed, she was wearing one of her shortest skirts, to open his flies, taken his fingers out of her, and tried to insert himself, she had immediately drawn away, she had already had her orgasm, and put her finger to his lips and said, 'Shh,' and he had meekly, with some embarrassment, done himself up again.

The nature of the setting and the encounter, she was sure, would mean that men would not reveal what had occurred but, in any event, with that in mind, she only chose safely married men who would be unlikely to admit to any such behaviour.

If her husband was ever to learn, she would deny it vehemently but in a sense she was unconcerned. It was the only sexual fulfilment she could find in her marriage without being unfaithful.

She already knew what had attracted her to Ralph. They had met once before and she and he had seemed to find each other mutually attractive. She had certainly found him amusing and intelligent, two of her prerequisites for being drawn to anyone. He was eight years older than her husband, stood about the same height and was much the same build as him, although a bit leaner perhaps.

She had also decided that he was more sensual than he would probably publicly admit. She thought there was something about the way in which he chose and wore clothes that suggested that there were hidden sexual depths. That, to her, was in a sense irrelevant as she had no intention of otherwise than perhaps the usual encounter.

However, she had registered one of his throwaway lines over dinner about sex, paraphrasing Chesterfield he later told her, that whilst it might look ridiculous, it certainly need not be expensive and could be great fun. His wife had looked at him at that point and she had seen her smile, a small but very satisfied wry smile, and as he had noticed the gaze, his wife had, well-nigh imperceptibly, raised one finger to her lips before pretending to brush away a piece of stray food.

The evening had been a success so far. Four couples, all professional middle class, the only unifying social glue being that she and her husband knew each of the other three pairs.

As she said, 'Kiss me,' to him, she opened her eyes wider and looked at him appealingly.

He paused. There was nothing he wanted to do more than to lock the door, ignore the world, his wife, Christina's husband and to simply succumb. He had thought of next to nothing but her since they had met and her invitation to dinner had been an eagerly anticipated highlight in his calendar.

He remembered his wife taking the call and, putting her hand over the mouthpiece, saying that it was the couple they had recently met, asking them for dinner a fortnight ahead. His wife had looked slightly cross when he nodded and said, 'Accept, it might be fun.' Fun it had been.

Simply looking at Christina and talking to her, inconsequentially across the dinner table, had been enough for him. He had not anticipated, let alone expected the situation he found himself in. What harm could it do? He had no idea. He was highly sexually aroused and found this bewildering. She had pulled him towards her and would be aware of his excitement. He removed his hand and said sadly, 'No, I think you are gorgeous but...'

She looked as though she had been slapped. She started and bit her lower lip before replying, 'Oh well, never mind,' and pushed him away from her, turning towards the surface with the cheese board.

'Why so...' he began but she cut across.

'I wanted you to, I wanted to and thought you would. So what. It doesn't matter. Let's get the cheese in,' she replied, pointed to a green salad, motioned to him to pick that up and went through the door carrying the cheese dish and leaving him to follow.

He stood for a moment and thought what a fool he must have looked. He was not sure of his response or the reasons for it. Rationally, he supposed, it might be because he was worried that he would look guilty or furtive when he went back into the dining room had he taken up the invitation.

However, he was already full of regrets and chagrin and aware of the possibility that he might have offended her in a way that would be sufficient to prevent any further attempts at even a closer social relationship. He extrapolated and imagined a wonderful clandestine affair, although he had been totally faithful to his wife since their marriage fourteen years earlier.

He realised his sexual excitement had subsided, he would and could not have entered the room a few minutes earlier because of this, and adjusted himself, rearranging everything more comfortably, before following her through. The others must have assumed he had been to the lavatory for no comment was made. The rest of the evening passed uneventfully and unmemorably, but he was uncharacteristically quiet, contributing little to the subsequent conversation.

Christina's husband more than made up for any reticence on the part of his guests, holding forth with a stream of salacious jokes, some of which were very funny indeed. It depressed him to see her laughing at some of the most risqué, in contrast to his wife, who was doing her best to disguise what he thought of as her stony-faced look. He knew that later that evening she would say, 'I told you so. I told you it would be a dull evening among shallow people,' and he had already decided upon a response. The wife of one of the other couples was a solicitor who had, he knew because he had talked with her, a litigation practice and he thought that she might well instruct him as a result of their conversation and thus the evening could be justified.

They were the last to leave. Christina stood at the door and said a polite goodbye to his wife who started to walk towards her car. They had left Christina's husband sitting at the dinner table, eyes glazed, yet another very full glass of port clutched in one hand. He had mumbled goodbyes rather incoherently but had been pleasant enough. Watching his wife walking towards the car Ralph bent towards Christina, kissed her very quickly on both cheeks saying, 'I've been wanting to do that all evening.'

'What, say goodbye?' she enquired mock sarcastically.

'No, to kiss you,' he whispered.

'Goodnight,' Christina said and smiled as he followed his wife.

They had first met at what Ralph felt promised to be an extremely dreary dinner given by a large firm of solicitors to celebrate some anniversary of interest only to the partners. Nevertheless, the invitation had been accepted and eight people found themselves sitting at one of many tables each hosted by one of the firm's partners but here also with an assistant solicitor and an articled clerk.

There were name cards, but her husband was first to introduce himself.

'I'm Crispin St John Fortescue. My friends call me St John. This,' he gestured towards her, 'is my wife Christina.'

She smiled and said, 'Hello everyone.'

The partner and articled clerk introduced themselves, as did the other couple. Finally, his wife introduced herself saying,

'I'm Virginia Edwards - my husband Ralph.'

Crispin St John Fortescue immediately said, 'Rape Edwards. Funny name,' and laughed loudly. There were some suppressed nervous titters as the hosts and guests looked at Ralph expectantly, but he replied very simply, 'Ralph, spelt Ralph and pronounced Rafe, Crispie.'

St John looked irritated but laughed, wine was poured, and conversation started.

Ralph was sitting next to Christina and paused, before saying, 'I know your husband by name and sight but curiously we've never met.'

'Why curiously?' she asked.

'We're both barristers on the same circuit but in different cities. I operate out of a set in... Oh God, that sounds so pompous, and I don't really mean to sound like your average self-absorbed barrister.'

'No, self-absorption to the point of narcissism seems to come as standard,' she said and looked at her husband who was expatiating rather loudly on what sounded to be his last court room triumph. 'What kind of law do you do?'

'Me? I'm just a knock about common lawyer.'

'What, crime, injury, divorce, family law, that sort of thing?'

'Yes, in the early days, but now I suppose it's mainly crime and injury.'

'St John does Chancery.' She seemed to invest a certain contempt into the last word. 'He takes his work frightfully seriously and intends to be a High Court Judge. No, doesn't intend to be. He knows he will be. His father was one, so he's convinced, whatever his abilities, he'll get there, by right of succession.'

'No harm in optimism, even if it may be a triumph of hope over experience. What about you, what do you get up to?'

Christina thought for a moment and made a moue with her mouth, before replying, 'Well, I'm not a lawyer, although I did a law degree. He decided,' a nod towards St John, 'that I was better suited to a career in the retail industry. I actually manage a mother and baby shop.'

'You seem too young to be a manager.'

'I'm twenty-eight - it's not unusually old or young.'

'Do you enjoy it?'

'It has its moments.'

'What, like closing the doors at the end of the day?'

'Yes, but it pays the mortgage.'

'Successful Chancery barristers can more than pay a mortgage.'

'Well, he has some rather extravagant hobbies including extremely fine wines and extensive entertaining. The two together are enough to see off most of what he brings in. He's still pretty junior.'

'Does he cook too? For these dinner parties, I mean.'

'No, that's very much my department.

St John, between the female partner and the articled clerk, seemed to have embarked on another anecdote, although this one sounded rather dubious. Ralph looked again at Christina and realised that he found her very attractive. She had dressed with care; he did not know much about clothes but what she was wearing suited her and, he guessed, had been expensive. She was, he judged, an inch or so shorter than him, had large eyes, a very expressive mouth and, he suddenly noticed, a rather daring décolletage. He looked away as she turned her face and hoped she had not thought of him as eyeing her cleavage. She seemed amused and smiled enquiringly at him.

'I was admiring your dress.'

'Jaeger. I treated myself.'

'It's a lovely colour and, if I may say so, looks good. Christ - pomposity again. It must be second nature.'

'What does your wife do?'

It was an abrupt change of subject but, as he wanted to keep the conversation going and was terrified that she might dismiss him as just one more barrister she had met at yet one more function, he replied, 'She's a doctor.'

'A proper one or just medicine?' It was the same joke that he sometimes made and he told her so. This seemed to establish an intimacy and they both laughed.

'No, medicine. A G.P. A partner. Very happy and no

ambition to do any more than she does.'

'Where did you both meet?'

'At University. Like so many. Married directly we could and ran our training side by side. 'What about you?'

'What about me?'

'Where did you and Crispie meet?'

She giggled. 'He'd go berserk if I called him that. He takes himself so bloody seriously. At University. Like so many. Married directly we could and I supported him through his training. Have done ever since,' she added, with what seemed a trace of bitterness, and laughed again.

The meal was drawing to a close. Coffee had been served. Port was being poured and speeches had started. They were all silent at their table, although there was a hum of conversation from some of the others.

When it was time to leave, Ralph suddenly felt desperately anxious that he might not see Christina again. Neither he nor his wife had had any conversation with St John enough to justify an invitation to dinner. He was not likely to bump into him again having spent many years on the same circuit already and never having met, and Christina and Virginia had not exchanged a word.

'Where do you live?' he suddenly asked.

'Rodhanger. Why?'

It was, he thought, a lovely coincidence.

'I simply wondered. But' and he knew he could only be rebuffed, 'that's about six miles beyond our village. We're practically on the way home for you. Would you and St John like to stop and have a drink, coffee or something?'

'I'd love to. Tell me where your house is.'

'Don't you have to ask St John?'

'Don't you have to ask Virginia?'

'No, she's polite. She'll live with it. What about him?'

'He's got to that stage of the evening, and that state of mind, where his worst enemy could offer him a drink in a pigsty, and he'd accept with alacrity. We'll be there.'

He gave her the address and a description of the house and said, 'See you later then.'

'Yes, very soon.

In the car he told Virginia.

'Christ, haven't you had enough of boring lawyers for one evening?'

'Come on, we meet so few new people, it makes a pleasant change.'

Virginia had drunk slightly too much of the cheap red wine; her cheeks were flushed, and she was annoyed. She actually had other plans for the rest of the evening.

Theirs was not an unhappy marriage and most certainly not loveless. In fact, Virginia ran a sexual regime that was, by most standards, eye-poppingly rigorous. Her preference was for an orgasm at least once a day and Ralph had long since abandoned the pretence of actually wanting to do it that frequently.

She had had an early morning call which meant that she had missed the Friday morning orgasm and was looking forward to one on Friday evening instead. Ralph knew that she would probably have a large gin and tonic and then disappear to bed. It had happened many times before, the only variable being whether she was still awake when he came up and feeling, in her words, randy and ready.

'Perhaps, they won't stay long,' he added, patting her knee.

She responded by sliding down the seat, so that his hand ran up her leg and he found himself with his hand amongst her pubic hair.

'Why aren't you wearing knickers?'

'Because I was hoping you might stop the car and do it to me. I took them off before we left' and she laughed.

She also had a penchant for making love in places other than the bedroom. It was not exhibitionism, far from it, for she only liked doing this in the dark and privately. No matter how often Ralph told her that even she, not easily discomposed, and certainly he, would find it excruciating to be discovered by a policeman and taken to court for an offence against public decency, she would still periodically surprise him, as now, making overtures that would have to be contained until they arrived home or were immediately satisfied by stopping the car and, if warm and dry, going into a wood or field, or if cold and wet, staying in the car and risking, as he saw it, spinal injury.

'Well?' she said.

'We haven't time,' he replied, 'they'll only be a few minutes behind us.'

'If we turn off the road at Forest End they can pass and wait. If they can't be bothered to wait, it doesn't matter. I imagine they'll still be arguing about who should drive and we've plenty of time. Come on, you know you'll enjoy it.'

In truth he knew he would. He also enjoyed the unexpectedness and there was an indescribable frisson to the idea that there was a possibility that a respectable barrister and his respected G.P. wife might get caught in flagrante delicto - with each other. He carried on driving and said, 'Why not later, inside the house - I mean'.

'Why not outside now? And please, keep on stroking me.'

Suddenly he wanted her very badly and said so.

'Stop then,' she muttered with her eyes closed and he turned into a lay-by formed by a section of the old road, driving a hundred yards or so down it, and then, after checking to see that there were no other parked vehicles, switched off his engine and lights. She leant back in the now fully reclined passenger seat and said, 'Come on. Fill her up.'

He wriggled over the gearstick, murmured a prayer that there were no police cars in the vicinity, and entered her smoothly and easily. Soon, he heard her short breaths start turning to moans.

'Not far now, not far now,' she panted.

This was her mantra to indicate that she could now hold herself back until he came at which time she could let go and they could have what she called an HMO or 'hugely mutual orgasm' - which she always regarded as much more satisfactory than joint orgasms even if only separated by seconds rather than minutes.

'Now,' he cried, totally taken aback by the intensity of his own, only just aware of her kissing his neck and writhing beneath him and she, repeating over and over again, 'God, I love you so, so much'.

He kissed her on her mouth, at length and then said, with a conviction that frightened him, 'I love you too.'

He walked round to the driver's side, got in, started the engine, engaged gear and was just about to pull away when she said, 'Ralph?'

'Yes?'

'Will you always love me, do you think?'

'Why ask?'

'I feel scared.'

'What of?'

'I've no idea. Angels have just walked over my grave. Trampled over it. I'm all goosebumps.'

'Don't be silly. It's cold. We've just done it in the car - you've been drinking etc. etc. And yes, I believe I shall.'

'What?'

'Always love you,' he replied and, leaning over, kissed her again before setting off.

They were in her Porsche, and he drove quickly, reflecting on how the sudden urgency of his passion for Virginia had displaced all thought of St John and Christina. Only minutes before he could think of nothing but his anticipation of prolonging and perhaps consolidating a very shallow, but enjoyable, intimacy.

As the Porsche turned into their driveway, the headlights illuminated the Fortescues' car and Ralph had the impression that the two occupants might have been arguing. There appeared to be at least cross glances as they got out when the Porsche came to a halt.

'Been here long?' Virginia was more affable now that she was feeling satisfyingly sticky in the knickers she had slipped on again before they got home.

'No, a couple of minutes only. We came into the village and then missed the opening of the driveway.'

'Yes, Ralph knows the opening well but came pretty quickly anyway,' and, chuckling at her own joke, Virginia opened the door saying, 'Come in.'

She led the way to their sitting room as Ralph turned towards the kitchen, bottles and glasses. Christina looked about with unconcealed interest. It was an old house, more house than cottage, and certainly medieval. The room was low, beamed and there seemed to be pictures everywhere. Each was individually lit and, as she started scrutinising one, Virginia, who had adjusted a woodburning stove, asked if she was interested in art.

'I loved the subject at school and would have liked to have learnt more about it really.'

'Pictures are Ralph's thing. He collects. Illustrations for books mainly. Don't get him started. He's enthusiastic as well as knowledgeable but can get dull. Here he is. Darling, I was just saying don't get started on pictures.'

'Why not?'

'Because few people share your enthusiasm for them.'

'Well, I know you don't. You'd prefer to spend the money on holidays wouldn't you?'

'Not really...'

The exchange suggested a practised conversation between them, and they both seemed startled when Christina interrupted, saying, 'Is that a Rackham over there?'

Ralph immediately looked interested. 'Yes, one of the Ingoldsby Legend pictures. Do you like him?'

'I've always adored Rackham and Dulac and the others of that time,' Christina replied.

'Then you might be interested in seeing the pictures properly,' he said.

'Oh God,' Virginia said, 'etchings time. Except that all women are safe with him.'

This was true. Theirs was held up among their friends to be a model marriage. They never disagreed or argued. They admitted to one small argument before they were married. It was a fairly trivial matter. Virginia had been staying with Ralph and his parents at the family 'home' as his parents called it. His parents were really rather old fashioned, Ralph was quite happy to respect their values, so he and Virginia were to occupy separate bedrooms. After his parents had gone to bed Virginia had undressed and climbed into his bed saying, 'Come on into bed and me.'

This was fairly early on in their relationship, and he still found the prospect of sex with her, wherever and however she wanted, exciting enough to be immediately stimulated. After they had finished, she announced her intention of staying in his bed overnight. He was unhappy about this, but she was insistent. By marital argument standards it was insubstantial, but she got her way. He pushed her out in the morning and then, when she met Ralph's mother on the way to the bathroom, Virginia, who was naked and carrying her clothes under her arm, merely said, 'Good morning' and went on her way. Mrs Edwards coloured and never referred to the incident again.

The next time they stayed, they were shown, with some obvious nervous hesitation on the part of his mother, to the guest, twin-bedded room. Virginia had won, a very small point, but then she was accustomed to winning. They had never had another argument. Ralph usually found it simpler and easier to agree with her and, more often than not, since she was usually right, he was pleased to have done so.

'What would you prefer to drink' he asked Christina and St John. 'I've got a bottle of Sauvignon or a malt or gin.'

'A whisky would be pleasant, old chap', St John slurred. He had been looking around the room from where he sat in a deep and ample armchair. He had noted the obviously expensive but very 'tasteful' modern furnishings, considered that he knew enough about fabrics to appreciate that the soft furnishings were top quality and although he did not have an eye for a picture, could recognise that these were very certainly originals and valuable.

Ralph handed him a very large tumblerful and turned to Christina who simply said, 'A white wine would be lovely.'

Virginia asked for a large gin and when he had poured these and handed them to the women, Ralph poured himself a glass of wine, looked round, noticed that St John's glass was empty and refilled it with another very large whisky. St John looked up and said, 'Nice malt.'

'Bowmore,' replied Ralph.

St John, looking round the room, indifferently rather than with any obvious envy, said, 'You do yourself rather well then. Nice house, surroundings, car and everything.'

'Well, there's always something else one wants,' said Virginia.

'Like what?' asked St John.

'Oh, another picture for Ralph. A bigger house. A newer car. I'd quite like the latest Porsche, but it costs twice as much as mine's worth,' she replied.

Ralph reflected that it was not perhaps the most tactful remark his wife had ever made. Surely she had noticed that their guests were driving a five-year-old Ford?

St John thought for a moment and then asked, 'Have you got children?'

Virginia replied, 'No, and they don't figure in any of our plans at all.' She was, of course, right. She had decided so and Ralph's contribution to that particular discussion some years previously was mere acquiescence.

St John then said, 'No need for a bigger house then,' and, as though satisfied that he had disposed very convincingly of a major problem, drained his glass and shut his eyes.

Christina thought him rude and was concerned that her hosts might consider it time to call it a night. She actually very badly wanted to look at the pictures and had been genuine in her enthusiasm for the Edwardian illustrators. However, she felt that to ask once more might look a little obvious.

Virginia had filled both wine glasses again and had given herself another gin. The room was warm and comfortable and the conversation, whilst not continuous, was sporadic to the extent that it reflected a long evening.

Suddenly, and seemingly simultaneously, both Virginia and St John exhaled noisily, and Ralph and Christina realised that their spouses had fallen asleep.

'I should have asked if you'd like some music on.'

'I'd love some, but what about them?'

'I don't know about yours, but once mine's like that, it takes a rocket to wake her. I could play Led Zeppelin at full volume, have half the village complaining at the door and she'd only murmur something about it being too early to get up.'

Christina laughed, 'St John is as bad. If he wakes up, all he requires is a steadying drink in his hand, which he can sip and then he falls off again.'

'I'd better fill it up for him then,' and did so before going over to a cabinet, opening it and revealing what looked to Christina to be a very sophisticated music system and more CDs than she had ever seen.

'What would you like? Pop, classic, jazz?'

She felt he might be testing her, although this was not true. He was genuinely interested and seemed relieved when she said, 'Classical but you choose. I don't know what you've got.'

'Most of the well-known pieces, some of the less well known and a few of the really obscure. Try.'

'Mahler, songs, any,' she said.

He put on *Der Abschied*.

'Oh, what a lovely choice, I adore *Das Lied von der Erde*. Just as well you didn't ask him or we'd all be dancing to Abba. If you have Abba that is. I sound disloyal. It's just that I don't like Abba, I like Mahler, he doesn't and so we don't listen to Mahler. We listen to bloody Abba.'

'Well, someone's got to,' and he smiled at her.

'Yes. I suppose so. But,' and she stopped.

'What?' he asked.

'I really would like to look at your pictures. I felt a bit as if Virginia would have laughed at me if I'd asked before.'

'Of course,' he said and motioned her towards the door and the hallway. He took her for the full tour, she was delighted by the little Rackham traditional fairy picture and was visibly impressed by an original Mervyn Peake for Hunting of the Snark.

'My God,' she gasped, 'that's absolutely exquisite. I read him when I was seventeen, loved the writing, especially Gormenghast and loved the illustrations even more.'

'I read him when I was that age too. Not sure how his writing would stand up now. To me, at my age,' he added when she looked puzzled, 'but he's still one of the best illustrators of the twentieth century.'

'You're lucky to have that,' she said.

'Well, lucky only to the extent of being in the right place at the right time and having a friendly bank manager who was prepared to advance the best part of four month's earnings so that I could buy it.'

'Is it worth so much then?'

'No, but I bought it in my second half of pupillage.'

'Ah, I understand. Little money coming in.'

'Very little and Virginia was rather cross - we'd promised ourselves a trip to India that year and had to cancel.'

'So what - you've still got that beautiful drawing.'

He looked at her and said quietly, 'You understand, don't you?'

'Oh Lord, yes,' she said reflectively. 'I'd love to collect beautiful things. To surround oneself with objects, pictures or whatever created with love, to endure, to speak to others. But,' and she blushed, 'we can't afford it at the moment. Maybe one day.'

'I started buying bits and pieces before I went to university. Odd things. Still got one or two.'

She was intrigued. 'Like what?'

He pointed to an iridescent green vase, small, with appliquéd silver. 'I bought that at auction when I was in the sixth form. I paid three pounds for it.'

'What is it worth now?'

'I suppose a thousand or so.'

'How did you get it so cheaply?'

'I thought I knew what I was looking at and no one else noticed it.'

'Have you got an eye then?'

'Well, only to the extent of knowing what I like,' and he

looked at her directly and grinned.

She wondered what he meant and was slightly disconcerted. 'We seem to have some tastes in common though,' she blurted. She was very aware that she found Ralph rather attractive and discovering that he and she shared an appreciation of some music, art and literature, was enormously exciting. She had spent the last few years in St John's circle of friends for whom the word cultured was akin to a term of abuse.

They were standing in the dark red dining room and the only lighting was that on the pictures which glowed like little theatre stages. She was in shadow, and he could not see her face.

'Well, I like you and I don't like the fact that you are unhappy.'

'I'm not unhappy,' she muttered.

'Well, let me write your divorce petition.'

'I'm not getting divorced.'

'No, but I'll write it for you.'

'How?'

'Listen. First, the Petitioner (that's you) has a gentle, warm and affectionate nature and the Respondent (that's your husband) fails to acknowledge this to the distress of the Petitioner. Second, the Respondent is preoccupied with himself and his career to the extent that he will always put these first, often cancelling family and other engagements if necessary. Third, whilst both the Petitioner and the Respondent have full time jobs, the Respondent will never take any part in the domestic chores leaving all household tasks including shopping, washing, cooking, cleaning to the Petitioner. Fourth, and now I suppose I'm guessing, the Respondent is a creature of limited sexual appetite and when satisfied will not consider the needs or gratification of the Petitioner.'

He stopped and said, 'Sorry. The last, to use the idiom, was out of order. Forgive me. I'll not carry on.'

'No,' she sounded pained. 'How do you know? I mean, how do you know?'

'I've watched and listened to you most of the evening. The last I apologise for. It's not based on anything other than the fact that I used to have a very extensive divorce practice and invariably we could put that in a woman's divorce petition. Men are like that I think, nearly always.'

You're not, she thought to herself but said, 'I'm just horrified at how well you already seem to know me. There's nothing left for you to discover or learn. You perhaps know too much already.' She moved towards a picture, and he could see that she was smiling again.

'No, don't be silly. Life's fun. Let's enjoy it,' and saying that he went towards the door, went out and came back with the bottle of wine.

'There's a bit left. They're still asleep in opposite chairs. I guess they'll have a terrible shock if either wakes up. I doubt that they'd remember each other to begin with. It might be amusing to try it later.'

Later, she heard. He wants me to stay longer, she thought and said, 'No, after you.'

'There's not a lot left. Should I get another? What would you like?'

'What's the choice?'

'Do you want to see?'

He opened a doorway beside the fireplace, switched a light on and started going down a narrow staircase. She followed him and found herself in a small, but obviously clean, dry and recently white painted cellar racked on three walls and with what she thought must be hundreds of bottles.

'I wouldn't show St John this,' she said, 'he'll be on your doorstep forever. He'll be unstoppable. He'll be your best friend and bosom chum.'

'Anything you'd like in particular? White, red, German, French, I don't go in for New World much.'

'What about a red, lightish, cheerful...'

'You mean a Beaujolais obviously - and we can drink it cool. What about a two-year-old Fleurie?'

'I bet you've got a choice of other appellations?'

'Well,' he felt somewhat taken aback, 'yes, a couple of bottles of each and a few more of my favourites.'

'Let's try a St Amour.'

'God, a woman who knows the Crus, likes Mahler and has read Peake. You're such a rarity, he shouldn't let you out of the house, let alone his sight.'

He went to a corner, selected a bottle and indicated the stairs. 'We can go back to the dining room or the sitting room, wake the others or not, whichever you prefer.'

'Let's just sit in the dining room.'

They sat at one end of the long table, and he poured the red wine into a fresh glass.

'Cheers. Tell me, why don't children or babies feature in your plans?'

'Virginia has never wanted any - brats she calls them - and whilst I don't really think of them as brats, I don't think I could bear the emotional responsibility.'

'What do you mean?'

'The worry, the anxiety, the will they be alright, the how are they, the upsets, the disappointments, the sense of parental failure...'

'That's pretty negative,' she said quietly.

'I suppose I see having children negatively. It's much less to do with their preventing us having a good time - no, the appalling dread fear of what might become of them just terrifies me. Or worst of all, having to go to a morgue to identify them.'

'I'd rather like children. They give life a meaning and a purpose I suspect. Imagine being old and alone.'

'And not wanted by them. Visited on sufferance only. Then waiting for you to die to inherit something they should have worked for.'

'You're too cynical.'

'Probably, but I think having children is just monumental vanity. A memorial to egotism. Unnecessary.'

'Possibly, but they'd be fun. I'm sure. More fun than a dog anyway.'

'And a bloody sight more expensive emotionally as well as financially. Do you know how late it is?'

She did not, had not in fact even considered the time, but had so enjoyed talking with Ralph that she had momentarily forgotten her slumbering husband and, she remembered, Virginia.

'We'd better go,' she said, 'I think we've probably outstayed our welcome. I've enjoyed meeting you and talking to you. I'm sure I said too much but never mind.'

'Christina', he began, 'really...'

'Oh, by the way - it would probably amuse you to know that I wasn't christened Christina. My name is really Tina. St

John thought it sounded common so decided when we married that I'd not only change my surname but also my first name.'

'How extraordinary. I think Tina is a lovely name. What an odd fellow. Should I call you Tina in future?'

'No, it would only annoy him unnecessarily,' but her spirits soared as his question necessarily implied that they would see one another again. They went through to the sitting-room in silence.

'Come on, let's wake them,' and so saying she knelt and rather roughly shook St John who, opening his eyes, said, 'Good show,' and closed them again.

'Come on,' she said, shaking him again.

'What? Where?' he asked blearily.

'To the car and home now.'

He rose unsteadily and she steered him towards the door. At the same time Virginia was starting to sit up and said briskly, 'Lovely evening. Must do it again. Sorry you have to leave so soon,' obviously completely unaware that nearly two hours had passed since they had arrived back.

The Edwards followed their guests to the front door, waited as Christina expertly turned and twisted her husband into the passenger seat, pausing when she had shut the door, saying to them both, looking at them very intently, 'We've had a lovely time. It was very kind of you to ask us back. I hope we can repay the hospitality. Come and have supper with us next Saturday, we've a few others coming at eightish. It's the little house beside the pub.'

Virginia was about to speak but Ralph said immediately, 'Delighted to accept. We'd love to see you again.'

Christina got into the car, waved through the open window

and set off. Ralph gave a friendly wave before turning to follow Virginia inside and wondered how often Christina drove after she and St John had been out together. He guessed every time. He and Virginia said little to each other as they tidied up, went upstairs, undressed and got into bed.

He lay, as he always did, on his right-hand side facing the window. She lay, as she always did, curled up into him with her left arm over his hips and her hand firmly holding him between his legs. Since he nearly always and inevitably as a result, neither moved much during their sleep and, if they did, the position would always be eventually resumed, woke up sexually aroused, and since she seemed to have some sexual antenna that immediately made her stir, quite often his first sensation in the morning, as he regained consciousness, Virginia having turned him on his back, would be her rocking herself backwards and forward on top of him taking them both towards a hugely mutual orgasm.

He fell asleep thinking of Christina.

Virginia and Ralph were planning their annual party. The format seldom varied, only the guest list. As far as Ralph was concerned, it was also an opportunity to network with solicitors and Virginia regarded this as a sacred duty. They had a large number of friends and acquaintances and Ralph quite enjoyed hosting the event; they did the food preparation together and he nowadays served a decent wine. They were going through last year's list, striking the odd name off and occasionally adding a new one.

'Why not the Fortescues?' Ralph suggested. He had thought of little other than Tina since they had been there for dinner three weeks earlier. 'We owe them an invitation.'

Virginia had written a polite, but rather distant, note of thanks and had not mentioned them since.

'I'm not sure I'm that keen on them. We've already got sixty and there are other people who are more important to you in terms of work.'

This was said with some finality and Ralph was aware that to try and persuade her would only arouse suspicion. She knew him well enough to know, although he had not said so, that St John was not really the kind of person he would make a friend of and, whilst not rivals at the Bar, St John could not be of any use to Ralph professionally. Thus she would deduce, with accuracy, that Ralph's interest lay more in Tina. Virginia was not a jealous person. In fact she trusted Ralph implicitly but she was essentially practical. If she had thought matters through, having been alerted, she would simply have concluded that there was no point in putting temptation in front of him.

Ralph had been faithful to her, in conventional terms, insofar as he had not formed any kind of romantic or sexual attachment or entanglement during his marriage. He had been tempted by a couple of old girlfriends a couple of times, one when he had been in London for a case and he had been at a loose end and another, a mutual University friend he had gone out with before he had met Virginia, but declined their offers of sex, rationalising that he had enjoyed this with them in the past and that there was no point in prejudicing the present. However, he seriously doubted whether Virginia would actually have minded too much as she took a very pragmatic and business-like view of the functions of the human body. He was not willing to test this assumption though in case he was incorrect, and he certainly did not want to jeopardise the marriage.

He did not pursue the question of the Fortescues and they agreed on a final set of invitations. As they were doing this, he paused to consider Virginia and Tina. They were, he thought, extremely different. Virginia was a classic Aryan. Blonde and rather heavily built, large bosomed, a bit jolly hockey-sticks. She was the granddaughter of an Earl, the daughter of a younger son and her father, the Honourable George, had been left just enough not to have to work but not quite enough to live in the style both Virginia's parents would have preferred. Their two daughters had been the beneficiaries of a trust fund which had been exhausted by payment of the considerable fees that their very select and well-known public school had charged to educate them.

His parents-in-law had decided that the girls would have to marry well, by which they meant a fortune and, whilst pleased that Virginia had married a barrister, never concealed their disappointment that she had not married old, or even new money and that Virginia had decided to pursue a career, albeit as a doctor.

Ralph usually managed to conceal the sensation of being diminished but had once burst out that at least he and Virginia were doing something with their lives, rather than living as drones on dead peoples' wealth. His mother-in-law merely remarked, raising one eyebrow, a trick Ralph felt she had perfected only in order to put him down, 'Yes, Legal Aid work,' and had gone back to her needlepoint supremely unconcerned.

Tina was very different. She was a couple of inches shorter than Virginia, but was slimmer, more genuinely feminine and, he considered, much more sexually attractive.

He was not sure whether Tina was aware of this, but he knew that were he to be given the opportunity to sleep with her, that he would take it, even if Virginia were to find out and there was to be a horrible argument. He was fairly sure he could talk his way round her. He found it difficult to decide exactly what it was he liked about Tina. It was not the idea of the sexual conquest that attracted him. He had refused, very courteously, when single, to sleep with some girls, even though it would have added to the 'tally'.

He remembered that John Betjeman when asked, towards the end of his life, whether he had any regrets, had replied that he wished he'd had more sex. Ralph had wondered, at the time, whether his refusals might later be regretted but knew that he would not refuse any invitation that Tina might extend again.

He thought that it was perhaps the sexuality of Tina, as opposed to the heartiness of Virginia, but he was acutely aware that the attraction was a real one, and that it was also powerful could not be in doubt. He knew next to nothing about Tina and had been slightly appalled when she had taken his hand on the second occasion that they had met, at dinner at her house, and pressed it to her breast. He had made a quick calculation then that if she was drunk, it was not the time to take things further, but if she was not, then the opportunity would surely present itself again.

'That's that then,' Virginia said with finality. 'Sixty-three people. Quite enough. Let's go to bed,' and held out her hand to him. 'I'm feeling randy,' and smiled broadly.

'I'll come up when I've finished the bottle.' Ralph wanted some time on his own and hoped Virginia might be asleep when he went upstairs. She left and he went to the window, standing for a long time simply looking out into the dark night, feeling faintly disgusted with himself and vaguely repulsed at what he considered was Virginia's mechanistic view of sex.

Christina and St John were arguing again. The arguments generally started about money. She felt that there was simply not enough to fund the lifestyle that St John thought was his by right. She paid the mortgage, the household bills and bought the food and necessities. He ran a smart car for himself and an older Ford for her but often said that she should pay her motor expenses. He was essentially a man's man, preferring the company of other barristers, or the members of his County Club, to staying at home with his wife.

She wanted to be made more fuss of by her husband and still looked forward to their nights together. These however, generally consisted of a rented film, which he always chose and was nearly always an 18. He preferred a diet of horror and war to sex but was not averse to the occasional pornographic movie, provided that it was explicit, and which she watched out of boredom. It always seemed to arouse him and she had begun to dread those nights, usually a Friday, when the film had finished and he stood up, apparently leering at her, saying, 'Friday night is shag night. Let's go up.' He was slightly drunk tonight and the film had been unusually sexually unpleasant.

'Come on,' he mumbled. 'Let's go and have a shag.'

She snapped at him that not only was she tired, she had a headache, a period on the way and simply didn't want to. He said nothing but pulled her up, which he was physically well able to do, and carried her upstairs. She had tried shouting and he had simply ignored her, started to undress her and when she struggled, put her on the bed, pulled her knickers to one side, forced himself in, holding his hand over her mouth and thrust until he came to orgasm with a grunt. Only then had he taken his hand away and said with a pleased grin, 'Do you want one now?'

She had slapped him as hard as she was able, a cracking shot across his cheek. He had looked baffled then furious and had punched her, a hefty stinging blow that was going to leave a bruise on her face for days. She started crying.

'Oh Christ, not again,' said St John. 'I'm going to bed in the spare room. I can't stand it any longer.'

She had followed him in there, shouting abuse at him until, with another drunken sigh, he had said, 'If you don't shut up the neighbours will hear and I don't want the neighbours to hear. And if I don't want the neighbours to hear, and the only way to stop you is to hit you again, I will.'

She stopped and looked at him. She knew he would. It was not the first physical violence in their marriage. It was not frequent but episodic. She had told no one, not even her mother, as she was so ashamed of herself for putting up with it and of him. She reflected on the fact that to the outside world he was St John Fortescue, up and coming Chancery barrister with ambitions to become a judge, whereas at home he behaved like any common or garden lout, knocking his wife about and enjoying rough sex. She bit her lip, she knew she was going to start crying again, and she had resolved a long time ago that, if nothing else, she would try and maintain some kind of dignity.

'You're a bastard,' she managed to say before turning and leaving the room. As she did so, she saw him smiling a complacent and self-satisfied smirk that redoubled her overwhelming regret that she had ever married him.

She went downstairs. She was wet from him, a cold dampness

that felt unusually unpleasant. She could not be bothered to clean herself up, she thought a hot bath preferable but only after she was sure he had gone to sleep. She poured a glass of whisky, not her usual drink but she wanted the rasping heat and quick alcoholic kick, and thought back to their engagement and marriage.

They had met at university where he had been two years her senior in the Law Faculty. It had been at a law dinner, she suddenly remembered that she had also met Ralph at another law dinner, and St John had been drawn to her by the fact, he said later, of her being very much the centre of attention of a group of men. He had secured an introduction from someone and then had, for reasons that still remained mysterious to her, decided that he was going to take her out.

She had been flattered at the attention. She was in the first term of her first year and still highly impressionable. He had been regarded as a good catch by her girlfriends, who pointed out that he was obviously moneyed, he drove an open topped sports car, was predicted to get a decent degree and had already mapped out his future as a barrister, QC and judge in due course.

She had been going out with someone else in the rather uncomplicated and uncommitted way people did at university. A very casual relationship that was based more on friendship than on sex, in all events she had no intention of marrying the boy, but St John made plain, from the outset, that he was thinking long term.

'God, why, why, why,' she muttered through clenched teeth. 'Why didn't I just turn him down flat? Why did I accept? Why didn't I realise on the second date, dinner where we'd gone halves the first time, the fact that he had no money with him, and I would have to pay, was significant? La plus ca change, la plus c'est more and more the same bloody chose.'

She decided that he would probably have gone to sleep now and went upstairs to run a bath. She looked at herself in the mirror. A nasty blue bruise was already forming on her upper cheek. She wiped her face and stepped into the bath, lowering herself and stretching out before luxuriating in the scented water, taking great care to wash between her legs but very gently. It was only then that she saw him in the doorway.

'Playing with yourself again? You should be ashamed of yourself. You've got me for that,' and he went to the lavatory, took off his trousers and had a long noisy pee aiming for the water with the trajectory. When he had finished she saw with horror that he was stroking himself to another erection. She shuddered to herself, feeling very defenceless in the water. When he was ready, he stood over her and said, 'Suck it.' She felt physically sick.

'You know I don't want to do that.'

'Well, you are going to, like it or not,' and he bent down, lifted her head and shoulders up and pulled her face into his groin, felt around and then pushed it into her mouth, rocking her head backwards and forwards. She wondered how hard you had to bite before the pain was so intense, or perhaps it would have to be severed before he would stop. When his semen hit the back of her mouth, she gagged and spat out what she could. He held her in place and said, 'Swallow.'

She could hardly breathe, his smell was obnoxious to her, the fluid repulsive and for the first time in her life, she found herself wanting to die. She swallowed, gagging again as she did so. He seemed satisfied. He let go of her hair and, not even looking down at her, walked out of the bathroom. Humiliated and alone, she washed again in the bathwater, contaminated she thought with his globs, stepped out, decided on a quick shower, cleaned her teeth and went to the spare bedroom. She did not lock the door because in his present mood, if he decided he wanted to get to her, he would probably break through.

As she lay there, in the dark, with the streetlight throwing only a pale glow into the room, she wondered idly if the neighbours had heard anything. St John was very concerned to give the right impression and one day she thought she would just scream and scream until the neighbours called the police. Perhaps she should have done that tonight but, since she had not, there seemed little point in regretting not having done so. She was sure it would happen again and thought with envy of what seemed to her to be other people's happy marriages before, racked by small sobs, she fell into a fitful sleep.

'Tina.' She looked round. It was Ralph. 'What are you doing here?'

'Same as you. Been invited to the party. How are you?'

Ralph wondered if he had blushed. He wanted to say, I've been thinking of you, and of nothing but you, oh God, continuously since I saw you at your house last week and you put my hand on your breast and I want you and I to make mad passionate love and can we leave together now. He contented himself with a non-committal, 'Cheered up immensely by seeing you here.'

There were about forty people spread through the sitting room, dining room and kitchen. Ralph and Virginia had just arrived and he had noticed Tina immediately, deep in conversation with their host, Henry. He had wandered over, a drink in his hand.

'Sorry to intrude Henry,' he said. 'How are you? Business good?'

Henry was a chartered surveyor who Ralph had represented in a negligence action brought by a dissatisfied client. Ralph had won the case and Henry had been extraordinarily grateful; he had, in fact, expected to lose and to lose substantially. Henry told Tina all of this before commenting on the fact that Ralph and Christina already knew one another.

'And how did you and Henry meet?' Ralph asked.

'Oh, Frances, my wife, was at school and university with Christina and they've kept in touch since.'

'Which school was that?' Ralph asked.

'Whybrow,' said Tina. Ralph recognised the name as an

expensive public school with an extremely liberal reputation.

'I didn't know you had been there,' he said to her.

She laughed. 'You never asked. I've no idea where you went to school either, and won't know until you tell me.'

'Oh, a pretty undistinguished old fashioned grammar school.'

'Co-ed?' she asked.

'No. Kept locked away from women. Why?'

'Just wondered.' She had in fact been wondering whether Ralph had had many girlfriends before he had met Virginia.

'I don't suppose you were kept locked away from boys though, were you, at Whybrow?'

'No not really, although there were rules against being too close and not being alone and that sort of thing.'

At that point St John walked up to them. 'Hello, Ralph. How're things? Didn't know, don't suppose I should really anyway, that you knew the Sinclairs.'

Tina, who Ralph had thought looked momentarily pained at St John's arrival, even grimaced slightly, told him how Henry and Ralph had met.

'Good cases win themselves, old boy, don't they?' St John smirked.

'That's not what you say when you think you've got a good case and you lose it though,' Tina said icily.

'No, what he means is that...,' began Ralph, hoping to defuse the obvious tension.

'No, I know,' interrupted St John. 'I was only making a joke.' The conversation continued indifferently. Their host moved away and St John turned to Ralph. 'What drives you then?'

'What do you mean?'

'Keeps you going, keeps you interested?'

'What, in life or in work?'

'Well, both or either.'

'I suppose I'm losing a bit of interest in work these days. I'm still far too general but at least I have managed to give up family and divorce. Still do some crime though which I find less and less appealing. It gets very difficult to mitigate for obvious lowlife villains, callous, calculating, psychopathic, utterly without remorse...'

St John interrupted. 'I've never done any. Crime, that is. Wouldn't know what it looks like. Rough and tumble though, I guess. Prefer using the old brains,' and he tapped the side of his head.

'I used to think of it as helping the underprivileged, the underdog. Lost that a bit now. Everyone is a loser in their own particular way. Got one next week. The man who killed his two daughters and then tried to kill himself. Failed. Faces a lifetime in prison. What can you say for him?'

'How sad,' Tina suddenly commented. 'What happened?'

'Oh, slight variant on the usual story. Father had custody of his two daughters. Mother challenging him. He smothered the two girls and then put a shotgun in his mouth and pulled the trigger with his foot. Barrel moved and blew most of the left side of his face off rather than his brains out. Survived by dint of medical science and will now spend the rest of his life in prison at great cost to the taxpayer. Being watched all the time of course, as an obvious suicide risk.'

St John looked thoughtful. 'What on earth can you say for him? What's he pleading?'

'He wants to plead guilty to murder. Not manslaughter

by reason of diminished responsibility. We could have found a couple of tame psychiatrists to say he's bonkers but he's adamant that he isn't. Murder it was, he says. So guilty m'lud to murder, it will be.'

'Have you met him?' asked Tina.

'Yes, a couple of times. All he says is that his daughters are now safe. No one can harm them or hurt them in any way, ever. And that next time he won't use a shotgun.'

'So that's the mitigation,' she said.

'Yes. But what's the point? Mandatory life sentence. You can't really explain in rational terms. A tragedy of that kind. The judge will have his own views on length of time recommendations. I suppose I'll have to say something but I'm not very enthusiastic.'

St John suddenly asked, with startling inappropriateness, 'Do you shoot, Ralph?'

'No. Why? Can't immediately see the relevance.'

'My uncle has a shoot on his estate. I'm allowed two guns. I was just wondering if you'd care to join us one day.'

'Not my thing at all,' replied Ralph. 'I'd just get in the way but most kind of you to ask.'

'Are you interested in any country pursuits - you live in the country so presumably like the countryside? You know, riding, hunting, dogs, that kind of thing.'

'No, my kind of countryside is walking, leaves, sunshine, views, autumn,' and he thought of Virginia. She was incapable of passing a barn, when out on a walk, without wanting to go inside, climb up the hay bales, take off her coat and jeans or tights and pull him towards her. He sometimes wondered whether her first real sexual experience had taken place in a stable hayloft and she wanted to relive it again and again. Then there were also the cornfields she liked slipping into, as well as disappearing into woods, especially at bluebell time.

'It's my wife who likes country pursuits more than I do, really.' He was conscious of an unintended and unpleasant pun, one Shakespeare made as he remembered, but it went unremarked.

'St John only shoots though,' Tina said. 'He doesn't actually, you know, ride to hounds.' She affected a kind of superior disdain as she said this. 'Like to though, wouldn't you dearest? Just a bit too expensive.'

'In time, in time,' he said.

'Yes, when your parents die and you inherit and that may be another thirty years,' she retorted.

'Come on,' and he remembered to say 'Christina', rather than 'Tina', 'he'll be a hugely successful and thus rich QC sooner rather than later because he uses this,' and Ralph tapped the side of his head and smiled.

The tension receded and Ralph asked if Tina like riding. St John replied, 'Only one kind,' and laughed crudely.

Tina reddened and said, 'No, not really. Not done much at all. St John always said I didn't have a good seat.'

She realised immediately she had left it open for him to make another crude remark, as did Ralph, but each was relieved when St John ignored the obvious cheap jibe and said, 'Isn't that Jenkins over there? I must go and talk to him about shooting next week. Excuse me.'

'Phew,' said Tina with obvious relief. 'He'd had several before he came out, has had several more and no doubt is going to have still more before bedtime. Heavy hangover time again.'

'What happened to your cheek?' Ralph asked this with obvious concern. He had noticed the bruising immediately and had wondered if his instinctive feeling was correct.

'I walked into a lamp post.' She looked down.

'It sometimes seems to me that all marriages are happy or unhappy in similar and different ways.'

'What do you mean?'

'We all have the ability in a relationship to make things work if we choose to. If both people want to, it can always be successful. If either one or the other stops trying or stops wanting to, then no matter what the other does, it's finished. And long before then, there is the most terrifying capacity for cruelty. Random, thoughtless, heartless cruelty. Or deliberate. It's life, I suppose. A paradigm of pointlessness.'

'You sound so bleak.'

'Looking at you, and thinking about what I suspect really happened, does make me feel bleak as well as cynical.'

'Why, what do you think happened?'

'I suspect St John was drunk. I suspect you had an argument about money. I suspect he hit you.'

'Not quite 100 percent right. He was not really drunk. And we do argue. Quite a lot. Quite a lot about money, I suppose.'

'A lot of people do. You know the old line, 'Money doesn't talk, it swears.'

She immediately said, 'There's an older one - Nothing comes amiss, but money comes withal'.

'Taming of the Shrew,' Ralph said quickly.

'Yes, a play for reasons that I find difficult to fathom I rather like.' Tina responded, continuing, 'I suppose I identify with Kate. She should never have given in to Petruchio.'

Ralph said thoughtfully, looking at her, 'She didn't really. She just appeared to. But sometimes the appearance and reality are close enough not to be significantly objectively different. Can we always tell the difference? Can we ever know what is the truth? Subjectively I mean. Petruchio wouldn't have known that Kate was merely appearing to give in. He thought she had and he'd won. And in his terms he was right. Does St John really knock you about?'

'Yes. But not frequently and not much.'

'You know the last time I heard that sentiment it came from a woman for whom I was in the County Court and getting an injunction against her boyfriend. On the grounds of his violence. I'd read the proof of evidence.'

She looked puzzled and he said, 'I keep on thinking that since you did law at university and are married to a lawyer, you know the language. The piece of paper that has what she was going to say typed on it, it's prepared by the solicitors. Anyway, my flesh had started crawling - it was an emergency injunction, so I'd only been handed all the papers outside the courtroom door. It was unspeakable - so I said to her, 'The violence. Is it bad?', and she said, 'Not that bad.'

I took her through what she'd said to her solicitor, and she said that it was nothing to what some of her friends suffered. My God, I thought. There's a whole world out there, of men beating up their women and their women thinking it was OK and just putting up with it. And you're another one. Why? Why?'

'Why did your flesh creep?' Tina asked.

'Why did my flesh creep? I'm not sure I want to tell you. You and I are mixed company.'

'Come on. I'm a grown up. There isn't much I haven't seen or at least heard about.'

He wondered what kind of knowledge and experience that remark hinted at. She was certainly sexually attractive enough to have possibly had a varied and perhaps interesting past, he thought. Or probably had had. Or even possibly has. She might, although he strongly doubted it, be a bisexual naturist who liked to maintain at least one lover on the go all the time. If she was, as was evidently the case, unhappy in her marriage, then it was quite possible that she might want, or even already have, a lover.

Tina said to him, 'Why have you paused? Why won't you tell me?'

'I was just thinking. I was trying to remember. Basically it was nearly every weekend. Usually just, I say just, and I know I shouldn't, but it's fair in the context, punches and slaps to the head. But the final assault was particularly nasty. It was, as people say, the wrong time of the month. He wanted sex. She didn't. He went berserk. Bang, bang, thump, thump, slap, slap. She was by then cowering on the floor. He finally, to use the idiom, 'put the boot in,' kicking her all over her body. When he had finished he said, 'Are you going to fuck me then' and she said no - he pulled her dress up and her underwear off. She was bleeding down there. Not from whatsit but from the injury. It put him off the idea of sex. But he then, and this is what I found so truly appalling, went to the kitchen, came back with salt and made her rub it into her groin area. Christ. People are nice.'

'What a horrible story. Makes my life seem like a bed of roses. She must have been in pain.'

'She was, she said, screaming in agony.'

'What happened to him?'

'I don't know. We got an emergency injunction against him, that means he didn't know about it and wasn't at the hearing, but we never had the full hearing the following week because, my solicitor told me, they had reconciled.'

'Reconciled? After that? Surely not.'

'Yes, women often did or presumably still do. Better the devil you know and who only beats you up in a way you understand, than the other bastard who might really do it properly.'

At this point a woman, who Tina obviously knew but Ralph did not recognise, came up.

'This is Frances' said Tina. 'Ralph Edwards.'

'Ah,' the newcomer said, 'the clever lawyer who got my husband off the hook.'

'No, no, good cases win themselves,' said Ralph.

'My husband expected to lose and lose badly. God knows he should have done. But anyway. How are you, Christina?'

'Fine, fine but listen...'

Ralph, realising that the two friends were just about to start a conversation that picked up where they had left off the previous occasion, was about to make an excuse when Frances said, 'They're dancing next door. Why not have a go?'

Tina immediately said, 'I'll book you for numbers four and six Ralph.'

'And the last dance?' he asked.

'Depends on Virginia,' Tina said. 'She might want it with you.'

Yes, he thought. She might. But she wasn't going to. If there was one, and he hated dancing, he would rather like to be nestled against Tina. 'See you later,' he said and wandered into the hallway, filling his glass again.

The hall was a large one with a number of groups of people, talking, laughing, flirting and obviously enjoying themselves. One group, mainly of men, was laughing uproariously and he glanced over with interest. He recognised a couple of the faces and saw that Virginia was at the centre. He went up and joined them, Virginia noticing him as he approached.

'Hi, Ralph,' she said. 'Come and talk to us. I haven't seen you since we arrived,' and looking at her watch, 'over an hour ago.'

One of the men turned to him and said, 'God, she tells some wickedly funny stories.'

Yes, he thought, mainly medical ones which she invested with a droll cynicism that often reduced other people to helpless tears of amusement. He suddenly thought of Virginia in a way that he had not for some years, remembering the early days of the relationship. Recently he had found her less alluring, perhaps even vulgar or coarse even in her approach to the human body and its functions, and particularly so in relation to her approach to his and her own bodies. He had never asked her if he had been her first lover. He suspected he probably had been and suspected also that he was still the only man with whom she had ever shared both her bed and body. The nearest he had come to asking was just before they made love for the first time, lying on top of her and their faces only inches apart, when he asked her, 'Has anyone, anyone ever looked at you in your eyes like this before?'

'No,' she had replied with a direct simplicity, looking him straight in his eyes and smiling.

'I love you,' he said as he inserted himself into her and she had sighed with what seemed a kind of relief, before abandoning herself to him and reaching an overwhelmingly large orgasm closely followed by his own, when he said, 'I love you' again. She was not to know that Ralph was sensitive to the point of fastidiousness about the emotions of women he went to bed with and believed that they deserved, if he could not bring himself to say, 'I love you' then, at the very least, an appreciation of them and their bodies. 'God, you're so lovely,' was his fallback. He thought that women were pleased by either compliment and indeed deserved such. The question of whether he was her only lover had never been raised again, but, looking around him, Ralph knew that Virginia could probably have taken any one of these men present and made him her lover just by asking. Whilst unappreciative sometimes of others' joke telling, Virginia would occasionally let rip and she told another couple of stories which included one about a man and a vacuum cleaner that he thought too improper to tell in mixed company, let alone by a woman to men, that were received with howls of merriment. He joined in politely and then asked her if she'd like anything to eat.

'Not really just yet. Are you getting anything now?'

'Yes, I thought I might - just a snack or something.'

'There's dancing, come on, let's have a dance.'

He started to make what, even to him, seemed a limp excuse but she grabbed his hand and said, 'Excuse me' to the others and pulled him towards the next room. It was darkened and there seemed to be a large number of people dancing frenziedly to Led Zeppelin.

Oh God, he thought. Virginia is now going to let herself go. As she did. She immediately established the beat with her legs, started waving her arms, quite elegantly, and was shaking her head in such a way that her long blond hair seemed to acquire a movement of its own, quite independent of her body. The funny thing, at least to Ralph, was that she did not seem ridiculous. On the contrary, it was the response the music required. He did his best, conscious that it was a pale and insipid performance compared to hers, but kept up. The song changed into 'Squeeze my lemon' and she stopped; she was perspiring and her eyes glistened.

'God, I enjoyed that,' she whispered into his ear as she pulled him close and started rubbing herself against him. 'Why don't we go home soon? We don't have to stay to the end.' Her hand drifted down to his waistband and then further down until it encircled him and she squeezed him gently in time with the music. He was slightly panicked but then consoled himself with the thought that it was too dark for anyone to notice.

'Let's stay a bit longer, it's quite fun.' He was thinking of Tina but Virginia had now undone his zip and her hand was wriggling through, round his underpants. Oh God, he thought, she's going to get it out, and said firmly, 'Stop it Virginia. We'll be seen.'

'Well you could take me upstairs, there's bound to be a bathroom we can lock. I want you and I want you now.' The song had just finished and he kissed her quickly on the lips, saying, 'Come on, let's eat,' and tried to break away.

She shrugged her shoulders, gave a little frown with her mouth, opened it and teased her tongue round her lips in the approved provocative way saying, 'OK, later. But I wasn't joking about going upstairs,' and zipped him up again.

They went through to the kitchen where Virginia, who had a

healthy appetite for food as well, filled her plate, Ralph thought rather overfilled it, he just taking a few canapés and other easily transferable pieces; he hated having to balance glass, plate and use knife and fork, preferring just to use one hand for glass, deposit the plate somewhere, and pick at it rather more delicately than Virginia who would sit, on the floor, bottom of the stairs, perch on a chair, and attack her food with a heartiness that, other people had said, was rather endearing. They went into the dining room where there were a couple of spaces at the table. They knew none of the people but Virginia, ever sociable, said lightly, 'Anyone's place? No?' and sat down. Ralph said he would prefer to stand, put his plate on the mantelpiece and listened.

He suddenly found Tina beside him.

'Did you enjoy the dancing? I was watching you,' she asked quietly, seeming somewhat disappointed.

He looked at her. 'Not really to be honest. I'm not sure I'm not too self-conscious and repressed to ever let myself go. Never really have. Must be upbringing.' He glanced at the table. Virginia was in bright, lively party mode and was paying no attention to him.

'Would you have a dance with me? Perhaps just one?' Tina asked cautiously.

Ralph felt elated as he replied, 'I'd love to,' and they slipped away. Virginia did not notice. Her back was to the fireplace and her plate was still full. He calculated that there were a good five to ten minutes before she would cast about for him or more food. They went back to the main room. Fewer people were in there. It was dark, warm and rather sweaty. The music all evening had been 70's and 80's - the music that had informed the teenage years of many of the people present. 'Nights in White Satin' had just started.

She held him, her hands resting on his shoulders, closely but not pressing up against him, rather demurely and modestly. He again suddenly wanted to seize her and pull her tightly to him - inside him even - understanding that there existed, for whatever reason, and he had thought about this often already without arriving at any rational or logical answer, a sexual attraction or gravity that she exuded and that he was finding completely irresistible. He had his hand on her shoulders as well and they swayed in time to what he considered one of the blandest and most facile and clichéd pieces of music ever written. As she moved slightly nearer to him, so that their bodies were touching, he became aware that he was developing an uncomfortably and absurdly sited erection. Would she also be aware of it he wondered? Suppose she found it an offensive obscenity? He moved his hips backwards.

'No, don't,' she whispered. 'It's flattering. I think you're lovely,' and pressed herself towards him, pushing her groin more firmly against his penis.

'I think the same about you,' he said. 'Excuse me a moment,' and he quickly put his hand into his pocket and rearranged himself so that it pointed upwards.

'I feel sixteen again,' he said as she pushed her hips harder now against his, swaying and stimulating him with the gentle motion, and he wished that she would say, 'Come on, let's go upstairs and find a bathroom with a lock on it.'

But she did not and, as the music died away, he stepped back and said, 'I enjoyed that. Thank you.'

'You don't have to say thank you. Let's have one more,' she

suggested, raising her eyebrows.

The music changed to another slow one, a tune that Ralph did not recognise, but one which allowed them to resume the same close contact and Ralph to tentatively run a hand down and rest his palm against the side of her breast. She continued to push her hips against his, so strongly that Ralph was sure that he could feel her genital area actually parted around him, and then moved the top half of her body, so that he found himself to be touching a nipple and, she was not wearing a bra, he felt this stiffen as she exhaled, saying, so softly that he almost did not hear her, 'That's nice.' Just as he was considering a further move he glanced over and saw St John, to whom he had not given a thought since they had spoken briefly much earlier. He was leaning against the doorway, looking a bit drunk. He stumbled over and said, pleasantly enough, 'My turn now Ralph. My turn to dance with the delectable Christina.'

'Of course,' said Ralph equally pleasantly and taking Tina's hand in his, gave it a small squeeze and passed it to the much larger hand of her husband saying, 'See you both later,' and returned to the dining room, hands in his pockets to disguise his arousal.

He resumed his place by the fireplace. He had been gone less than five minutes. Virginia still had her back to it and was mopping her plate with yet another large piece of garlic bread. She turned. 'You're back, are you having any more to eat?'

'No, I don't think so - would you like some more?'

She nodded. 'A bit of pudding or cheese. Whatever.'

'I'll get it for you.' Ralph smiled and went back to the kitchen. He selected a few bits and pieces for her, nothing for himself, and got caught in a conversation with a married pair of solicitors and talked law for a few minutes. At a natural pause he glanced at the plate and said he was just going to take it to his wife but would come back, a promise made as elegantly as it was intended to be broken, walked into the hall where he found St John and Tina. She was obviously upset and St John looked unwell. At that point Virginia came out of the dining room. She looked at the three of them. 'Anything wrong?' she asked with genuine solicitude.

'St John doesn't feel well,' Tina said. 'He's complaining of tummy pains.' She turned to Virginia and mouthed the words, 'Drunk, I'm sorry.'

'Come on, St John,' Virginia murmured, 'sit down on the stairs here' and she loosened his top button before gently pushing him downwards. He said nothing but his forehead was beaded with sweat and he was a nasty green colour. He bent his head forward between his legs.

'Often happens,' said Tina sadly and rolled her eyes upwards. 'Probably best to get him home now.'

'Probably best to get me home now,' St John blurted out. 'Give me a hand to the car someone. Is that Ralph? Help me up Ralph, would you old chap.' He started to get up, slipped down again and slumped back.

'Come on,' said Ralph and put his arm round to raise him. He was suddenly aware of the physical bulk of the man. He pulled and Tina went to the other side. Virginia asked if they wanted her help too but Tina said, 'No, I've done it before and with Ralph, it'll be much easier than usual.'

'Right ho,' Virginia responded and watched while the three of them made an unsteady progress towards the front door.

'Do you need coats or anything?' she asked.

'No,' Tina replied. 'We left them in the car.'

Once outside the fresh air seemed to give St John strength enough to walk more or less unaided to their car where he got in the passenger seat and, fumbling for the seat belt, fastened this, turned to Tina and Ralph and said, 'Thank you old chap,' and appeared promptly to fall asleep.

Tina closed the door quietly. 'Sorry, Ralph. It happens every time we go out. When shall I see you again?'

He felt exhilarated. He wanted to throw his arms round her, to embrace, to nuzzle, to lick, to explore, but replied calmly, wondering how on earth he was going to square this with Virginia, let alone explain to her. 'We're having a party next Friday. Early evening drinks, 6.00 for 6.30. Like to come?'

'I wouldn't miss it for the world,' Tina said. 'Goodnight Ralph. Thank you. See you then,' and touching her lips with her hand, waved at him before going to the driver's side, getting in, starting the engine and driving away.

He watched the lights recede down the driveway before turning and going back into the house where he found Virginia in the kitchen. He had lost all interest in the party or the people. He made some desultory small talk with the other people there before going to his wife, putting his arm around her waist and saying, 'I'd like to go home' and lowering his voice, 'and use the bathroom?'

Virginia brightened and said, 'OK, let's go and say our thank yous and get going.'

Driving home, Virginia doing this with her usual competence, he was quiet. They lived only a few miles away and Virginia did not appear to notice his thoughtfulness. Pulling into their driveway, she got out, waited for him to do the same, before locking the doors and saying, 'I need a mega pee. I'm going straight upstairs. Will you lock up? See you in the bedroom.'

He followed her in, locked the doors and waited for a couple of minutes before going into the bedroom. The lamps had been turned off and the room was flooded with moonlight. Virginia lay on the bed, naked, her blond hair like a halo, legs apart.

'Come on Ralph. I've been looking forward to this ever since we danced together.'

He undressed quickly and he made love to her with a passion and tenderness that surprised Virginia, but then she did not know that he was thinking only of Tina and it was all he could do not to call out, 'Tina, I love you, I love you, Tina,' when they reached their mutual orgasm some minutes later.

'God, that was nice,' spluttered Virginia after they had rolled apart. 'Goodnight.'

She kissed him and lying on her left side put her arm around Ralph, nestling her hand between his legs. She hugged him once or twice before she went to sleep. Her grip on him relaxed and Ralph eased himself out of bed. He went to the window and looked out over the garden. The house was built in an L shape and from the window he could see the back door and that the kitchen light was still on. He went out, shutting the bedroom door and, entering the kitchen, took a glass and poured some wine from a stoppered bottle in the fridge.

He was alarmed. He was aware of an emotion that he had never experienced and Tina was the focus. Why had he wanted, felt impelled even, to call out, 'Tina, I love you'? What on earth was happening to him he wondered as he sipped at the glass thoughtfully. He had no idea how sexually experienced he was compared to most men of his age. He rather assumed that he was probably about average although he was aware that his first true sexual initiation had occurred at probably what was a peculiarly young age.

He had neither talked about any of his girlfriends with other males nor had he regaled any of his friends with details of the intimacies, whether full sex or not, that he had enjoyed. He believed that this kind of male braggadocio was not only bad manners but also terribly unfair to the girl. Thus, if a girl slept with him, the only way in which anyone else would or could ever have known about it, was only ever because she had decided to tell someone.

He had had a number of long-term girlfriends, a few shorter term and a couple of, what his friends and the world called, one-night stands. Whilst he had found those last rather distasteful, he had nevertheless seen the girls involved again. He had grown up in a rather small town and it was inevitable that he would. He felt that it was perhaps not quite nice, indeed had a suspicion that any girl who did it, otherwise than in the context of a longer relationship, had at least something of the loose woman about her.

Despite professing a sympathy with feminism and sexual liberation, Ralph was, deep down, rather old-fashioned. He also knew that he had never felt any overwhelming emotion that he could actually label love. He had felt desire, attraction, lust in relation to girls but not, he was inclined to believe, love - he considered whether what he felt for Tina might be 'love'. However, he knew also that there was certainly an element of lust, a high component if he was honest with himself.

Again, he had no idea why he so badly wanted to physically

possess her. Could that also be a component of love? He did not know. Tina did not seem especially different to any other girl he had ever met. He had met prettier, brighter, richer, more well-connected, he supposed that was how people would describe Virginia, and more intellectual girls. He had enjoyed sexual relationships with prettier, brighter, more intellectual girls. He had married an attractive, bright, well-connected girl. But, and this was what disturbed him the most, and he supposed it was due to his emotional inarticulacy, he had never had anything like the same feeling for any of his previous sexual partners, although he had felt himself at the time in love with Virginia, the one he had finally married and at most, one or maybe two others.

Just as he had started thinking about Virginia, she walked into the kitchen. Dressing gown on, she looked sleepy. 'What's up? What are you thinking about? Why are you down here by yourself at this time?' She seemed concerned.

'I'm just thinking about how lucky I am to have you.' He stood up, drank his wine, took her by the hand and led her upstairs where he fell asleep still thinking about Tina.

The following morning was sunny and clear, unlike St John, who was sitting at the kitchen table, looking hung-over and dishevelled. Tina was clearing away a light breakfast and was feeling cheerful. She felt she might be in love again. She knew what she liked about Ralph. One of the main things was that he was not St John. She also saw Ralph as bright, witty, well-read and cultured. She was certain that sexually he might be fun. She thought he would be a nice friend to have. She also recognised that he wanted her. She had spent so much time, in her six-year marriage to St John, feeling de trop that she enjoyed the sensation of being wanted by someone who she also desired. She knew that she had sex appeal. She had spent much of her adolescence and adult years, even still now, warding off unwanted male attention. She would only allow this on her own terms. However, she was reasonably determined not to get involved with Ralph on other than a platonic level, although she had enjoyed his arousal when they danced the previous night.

'What are you doing today Christina?' asked St John.

'Not sure. What should we do?'

'I thought I might go to the County Club and have a few hairs of the dog,' he said.

That ruled her out. It was one of his all-male bastions.

'All right.' She felt slightly relieved that they would not spend the day together.

Unusually, it was Saturday, they were not going out that night.

'I might do some tidying up here and give Frances a ring and see if she wants a hand clearing up from last night,' she said, 'and by the way, we've been asked to the Edwards next Friday, early evening drinks. We're going to your parents for dinner, so can fit the two together neatly.'

'The Edwards. Remind me who they are?' He seemed genuinely to have forgotten.

'Ralph and Virginia, the barrister and G.P. we met. We went home to their house last month. They came to us for dinner. He helped you into the car last night.' St John had drink induced short term amnesia but finally seemed to recollect who she meant.

'The rather dry barrister with the jolly wife,' he said. Tina felt this was not quite the description that she would have used but agreed.

'OK, then,' he said. 'See you later,' and left the room.

Tina heard his car and groaned, because it meant that it was a certainly he would be phoning her to pick him up and that, in turn, would mean a drive tomorrow to collect his abandoned vehicle. She pottered around for a time then phoned Frances who received her offer of help with gratitude.

Tina wanted to talk to someone. She wanted a perspective on Ralph. Tina had felt herself in love many times. She had felt in love with the boy with whom she had, and she hated the phrase as it implied something careless or accidental, where what she had done was quite deliberate, lost her virginity. She had felt in love with St John when she married him. She had felt in love with most of her lovers, some more than others. Even her only one-night stand had been as a result of what she thought was a kind of love fuelled by sympathy for the boy concerned.

She had discovered her sexuality at school when aged

fourteen. She had been going out with Alan for a month or so, just snogging, the word used at the school. She and her friends used to talk about how far they would go, as though it was only to gratify the boys, but Tina knew already that she wanted to be gratified and that she had a right to a sex life on at least the same terms as them.

Thus it was, when Alan was chastely keeping his hands away from anywhere intimate, she took one and drew it to her bosom. Surprised, Alan, who was a nice boy and really not sexually precocious at all, started to rub it and Tina said, 'Gently, gently.' Emboldened he began to undo her shirt buttons. Tina reached behind and under her shirt to undo her bra straps and Alan started stroking her nipples. She moaned, deliberately appreciatively, to encourage him. She kissed him enthusiastically and moved onto her back to facilitate his stroking and exploration of her body.

Alan was slightly bemused. The relationship appeared to have gone from one of kissing only, to something where she appeared to be offering her whole body. He was not quite right. Tina was not yet ready to enter a full sexual relationship. What Tina simply wanted was her body appreciated and her then limited sexual appetite assuaged. Alan carried on kissing her and stroking her breasts. He had not noticed that Tina was lying with her legs apart and was waiting for him to take the next step. She was getting a bit bored with his slowness. Having decided to let him, Alan, be the first boy to feel what she called her pussy, she wanted him to get on with it.

Finally, she took his hand once again and started trailing it down across her stomach. Alan felt a bit panicked. He had no idea what a girl's bits felt like or really what he ought to do.

Of course, like everyone else, he had read and talked about it often enough, had masturbated frequently thinking of Tina and what he would do given half a chance, but now that he had much more than half a chance, there was an open invitation, his courage was wavering. He let his hand carry slowly down until he had his four fingers inside her knickers and between her legs. She parted them more.

'Stroke me,' she commanded and which he did. 'Put one inside me,' and he so he slipped one into her. 'Now, rub.'

She loved it. It was completely different from doing it to herself. She hoped he might try putting two fingers in but felt that she had taken the lead quite enough. She was quite sure that she could have an orgasm, goodness knows she had made herself have them often enough, and wanted him to carry on. She felt that he might be encouraged if she, she liked the pun, took him in hand so dropped her hand to the bulge in his trousers. He stopped doing anything to her and Tina saw a look of alarm flit across his face.

'It's all right,' Tina said, 'I'm not going to hurt you,' and slowly drew down his zip before deftly inserting her hand through, down and encircling him. She liked the hardness of it, she moved her hand up and down and wondered what it would be like to have this thing stuck up between her legs and then abandoned herself to Alan's fingers.

'Rub me just there,' she said when he had found the spot. She was suddenly aware that she was close to orgasm and wondered briefly whether she would let Alan know or keep it hidden. Hidden perhaps, she decided, so Alan never knew of the wonderful tingling and rippling that he had induced.

He was just painfully aware that he had had an involuntary

and wholly unplanned ejaculation. Tina thought it rather funny and had instinctively moved her hand up and down rather faster to enhance this for him. He seemed embarrassed just as if, Tina thought, he had wet his pants, which is of course what he had done.

'Was that nice?' she asked him. He was red and panting.

'Oh, God, yes,' he said. 'Tina, I think I love you.'

Of course, being a boy and inclined to boast of his sexual experience, it was not long before the other boys in her year were aware that Tina let you put your fingers in her and was also prepared to 'wank you off'. Fairly soon, Tina was asked out by someone better looking than Alan on the strength of this awareness and Alan, who in his way had loved her, was unceremoniously dumped. Tina had started her sexual travels. Always sexually monogamous, but always ready to let her current boyfriend bring her to orgasm with his fingers, she was also always pleased to reciprocate and indeed became quite adept at masturbating cocks, her terminology, and was rather proud of her ability. It being a boarding school, it was not long before she was known as 2FT - Finger Fuck Tina - but somehow, she never learnt of this name. Even if she had, it is doubtful that it would have distressed her.

When she arrived at Frances' house, much of the clearing away had been done but she helped until they could sit down and have a cup of coffee.

'I enjoyed myself last night,' Tina said. 'Nice people, good food.'

Frances was Tina's age within a couple of months, they were close friends and Frances was aware of the difficulties within Tina's marriage. She knew that Tina was unhappy, that St John drank too much, that he was a sexual boor and that in consequence, Tina drank too much as well. She thought, and had said many times, that Tina ought to call it a day, accept the inevitable and leave St John. She would find someone better and if not as potentially well off, St John stood to inherit a smallish fortune when his parents died, well so what, if he was at least kinder and cared for her more.

Frances, a once very pretty girl, was putting on weight in her late twenties, alcohol and overeating had contributed to the problem, but had a reasonable marriage. She was not unhappy nor was she blissful; it was average, she said. No great ups or downs. Reasonable sex two or three times a week, but she would have liked more, enough money coming in to pay the bills and a social life that was like thousands of others. She was quite content with her lot and in due course looked forward to children and had already, so early on in life, plotted grandchildren and reading stories to them.

'I saw you talking to Ralph Edwards,' she said. 'He's nice, isn't he?'

'St John described them as the dry barrister and the jolly doctor. What do you think?'

'He's not dry at all. I think he's a bit cynical, but certainly when I talked to him, he came across as sincere and compassionate. I think he cares. I'm a bit envious of Virginia, you know. She's got a lot going for her. Intelligent blonde doctor and that kind of thing. It seems unfair that she has a nice husband as well.'

'It's because she's an intelligent blonde doctor that she has a nice husband,' pointed out Tina.

'Yes, but... '

'Would you have him if you could?' she asked.

Frances thought for a moment. 'For a sexual fling, I don't know. Probably. Permanently instead of Henry, God knows. Had Henry not been around and had Ralph asked me, yes. What about you?'

'I think he's going to ask me,' Tina said simply. 'But I don't know if he's serious. I know he's attracted to me.'

Frances was a bit incredulous. 'How?'

'I danced with him last night and when I was close to him he had a stiffie.'

'Might be the kind of man who gets one just by mentally undressing women.'

'Doubt it. He's a bit, not calculating, but somehow too emotionally organised for that, isn't he? I mean, he's not exactly an adolescent and he's quite a successful barrister married to a respectable general practitioner.'

Frances thought for a moment and then said, 'Not thinking of trying to get him instead of St John, are you? How on earth could you ever persuade him to leave Virginia? Henry says that theirs is the perfect relationship. She never looks at other men, he never looks at other women. They apparently have a nice house, antiques, pictures. Virginia's got her Porsche, he's got his Aston Martin or something like that.'

Tina interrupted, 'I've seen the Porsche, but I didn't know about an Aston Martin.'

'Henry says it is his pride and joy.'

Tina quite liked cars herself and very badly wanted some kind of sports car. 'I suppose he really has got everything.' She laughed. 'But I think he fancies me.'

'A lot of men fancy you, Tina. A lot more than ever fancy

me. All men are rockets - guided muscles - and you know what muscle I mean. Come with a bang and then fizzle out. They start their life coming out of a woman and most spend the rest of their life trying to get back in again. Except those who disappear up other men's backsides.' Frances could be quite crude.

'Yes, I know,' Tina bit her lip, 'but I do like him. In fact Frances, I more than like him. I fancy him rotten. I think life's unfair.'

'That's a bit much. I know in the past I've said leave him, but on the positive side, you're married to someone who is going to be well-off, even if it isn't by his own efforts. You're only twenty-eight, St John thirty. I know you have your difficulties in the marriage, but then most people have some, don't they?'

'Sure, but I can't imagine staying with St John. I don't want to go to bed with him. He doesn't want me. He'd rather be out with his bloody men friends. Where do you think he is now? County Club drinking, swapping dirty stories and talking hunting and shooting. When he comes back, or when I fetch him back, he'll be drunk. I'll cook him supper. He'll want to watch a video, probably a nasty one and then he'll think he's doing me a great favour by getting his cock out and screwing me.' Tina could be crude as well.

'I bet you Ralph doesn't call it a cock,' Frances said and giggled. 'What do you think he calls it?'

Tina thought for a moment. 'His organ. Which I bet he handles with great dexterity.'

'No, willy perhaps. It won't be any of the crude terms. Cock, prick, dick. You know, I can't imagine. But what does he call Virginia's fanny?'

Tina did not like that question at all. 'I'm not sure I want to think about it but I wonder if I'll ever find out.'

'Make sure, if you get the chance, to ask him. I'd like to know.'

They tidied away and exchanged farewells. Tina drove home reflecting on the differences between her life and Virginia's. Most of all she envied Virginia. It was not so much the fact that she was married to Ralph but that she seemed to have everything that any woman could presumably want. Her job as a shop-manager seemed very dowdy compared to being a barrister or doctor. She suddenly regretted, a kind of despair set in, that she had ever met St John, let alone married him. When she got home there was a message on the answer machine.

'Christina, it's me. Can you come and pick me up when you're ready?' He sounded happily drunk again.

All morning Ralph had wrestled with the question of how to tell Virginia that he had invited the Fortescues. He had tried various opening lines and all of them, to his lawyer's analytical mind, had sounded weak and unconvincing. He decided on a strategy. He would not tell Virginia at all. He would simply let the Fortescues arrive at their party. If he opened the door to them, he could take them in and, if Virginia opened the door, she was too well-bred and courteous to refuse them entry. He could simply tell her when, as he certainly would be, challenged that someone had been talking about their party in front of the Fortescues and he had felt it ill-mannered not to ask them as well. She would accept that at face value. It was not only the easiest course of action, and Ralph was a great believer in trying to take the easiest option, but was in fact the truth.

Virginia was on call, so she was in and out of the house. She had just returned, uncharacteristically quiet. He had asked her what was wrong, and she had told him about the last moments of a young woman's life dying at home of breast cancer, crying and screaming at the injustice of it all, watched by her terrified young children and husband. Virginia had administered the final dose of morphine, the one that had put her patient into a merciful sleep but also hastened her inevitable death.

She had stayed with the family until the breathing had ceased, the last rattle of breath, as always, incredibly distressing to her. She had comforted the ten and the eight-year-old, put her arm round the husband and made the necessary telephone calls. She felt emotionally drained. Ralph watched her as she told the story, her eyes filled with tears. She had an infinite capacity for empathy, he reflected, and was good at her job which, he knew, she enjoyed. She had never regretted her decision to qualify as a doctor whereas he had often wondered whether he should have chosen an alternative, less ruthlessly, ambitious career. He knew he would have been very happy as an academic in some old seat of learning. He would like to have written and become a world expert on some esoteric branch of law. However, he had decided very early on to become a barrister and now he was firmly stuck in what seemed a rut, in pursuit of the fruits of professional success.

'You know,' he said to her, 'we two both have rather sad lives don't we? I deal all the time with people in extremis, accidents, crime, hurt people, people who've hurt others. You deal with people in pain and discomfort. People who are dying. People who are going to die.'

Virginia paused and then smiled sadly, 'But at least we're happy.'

The phone rang. It was another patient and Virginia sighed in resignation before rushing off to a child with a temperature of 105.

After Tina had been to collect St John, having found him cheerful and relaxed, she decided that she wanted to talk to him seriously about their future together. The more she had considered the marriage, the more she knew that she no longer had the stomach to try even to make it work. It seemed to her it must be over and her natural inclination, when she thought of something, was to deal with it immediately.

'St John,' she started when they were both sitting in front of the television, 'Have you ever thought much about us? About what we shall do? Where we are going and how?'

He looked up without much interest. The programme was more engrossing than theoretical discussions about life.

'We'll have children. I'm going to be a judge. When my parents die we'll be rich. It's all right,' and his eyes turned back to the screen.

'No,' she was insistent. 'There's more to it than that. I want to be happy. I don't think that's enough.'

He looked up again. 'You've got a job you like. You want children. You can have children in a few years when I'm earning a bit more. We need your income at the moment,' and turned back in a way that signified an end to the subject.

Tina was annoyed. 'Just because you think it's all right doesn't mean that I think it is. I think our life together stinks. It's going nowhere.'

He ignored her. She got up, went to the door and said, 'I mean it,' then went upstairs to bed. She wondered if he would come to bother her but thought probably not. She was right. He finished another couple of whiskies, the programme ended and then, without washing or any attempt at personal hygiene, he climbed into bed and fell asleep immediately.

Several times the following week Ralph wanted to pick up the telephone and talk to Tina. He had little idea of what he wanted to say but very badly wanted to hear her voice. Tina thought of him too that week, many times. She was certain that she had more or less decided to leave St John and wondered if there was any possibility of discussing this with Ralph and getting his reaction. His reaction might even suggest that there could be a future for them. Tina thought it unlikely but still hoped.

Ralph spent the week working, methodically and efficiently, through his written Advices and Opinions and making a couple of court appearances. He appeared for the would-be suicide who had suffocated his two daughters and made a very moving speech in mitigation. The Defendant had pleaded guilty to murder and Ralph spelt out the reasons why he had so elected rather than claiming insanity or diminished responsibility. He moved on to deal with the moral, ethical and human dilemma. By the time he had finished, the entire courtroom appeared to be sympathetic to the forlorn, horribly mutilated figure in the Dock. The judge, noted for his leniency, pronounced a life sentence but was seen to wipe his eyes as he did so. Several people seemed to be openly crying into their handkerchiefs. As Ralph left the courtroom, on his way to pay a courtesy call on his client in the cells beneath, another barrister turned to him and said, 'Magnificent, Ralph. You should have gone onto the stage.'

Ralph smiled to himself. He had invested considerable emotional energy in the writing and preparation of the speech;

he knew it was a high-profile case that would make the local headlines and possibly even the national press. He wanted to appear at his very best, intellectually as well as forensically, and the speech had been structured to try to arouse and win sympathy. It was, in truth, a very good example of the playwright and actor's art, albeit here both were the same man. Ralph felt quite pleased with himself as he commiserated with the Defendant who, unable ever to speak again due to his injuries, there had been special arrangements to take his plea on paper, had written 'Thank you,' and nothing more. Ralph had wondered whether he would be able to retain his own composure during the hearing as he did, genuinely, find the case a tragic one but when he came to it, his had been a bravura performance.

Their party was already a success. Several of the guests had contrived, unintentionally, to arrive simultaneously and so there was no gradual social thawing; people filled the rooms immediately and the sounds of conviviality and laughter hit later arrivals as they came through the door. Ralph had decided to serve a kind of Bellini, mixing cheap champagne with peach schnapps, a combination that had worked well in the past.

When the Fortescues rang the bell, it had been Ralph who had answered. 'Delighted you could make it. Come on in.' They followed him through into the sitting room.

'I'd no idea so many were going to be here,' Tina said.

'Well,' he replied, 'it's a mixture of pleasure and duty really.'

'Which am I?'

He looked at St John, who was not listening but examining the other guests intently, turned and said, 'You two are one of each,' and his eyes rested on her husband. 'And he's not the pleasure.' She laughed.

St John turned to him and said, 'You know an interesting variety of people. I can see two QCs, a High Court judge, at least one County Court judge I know as well as...' He pointed discreetly towards a group in the corner, 'I'm sure I recognise two of the faces there as well.'

Ralph said, 'One of them you know from the local TV news I guess, and the other is Jo Collins, a Junior Trade and Industry Minister.'

'In the government?' Tina asked.

'Of course in the government,' St John said derisively. 'Where else do you find a junior trade and industry minister?'

Ralph thought the comment a little unnecessary but smiled, asked whether they would like any introductions, before saying, 'Come along,' and taking them to join the group St John had pointed out.

St John was in his element; he liked to be with well-known people and he could be genuinely amusing. The only problem was that he tended to drink too fast and too much. He had had four glasses of champagne in very quick succession before Tina said, loudly enough for Ralph and others to hear and which annoyed him, 'Come on St John. We're going to your parents for dinner remember. You don't want to...'

He cut across her. 'Neither of us really wants to go. Why don't you give them a ring and pull out?'

'Because it's rude. They're expecting us.'

'They're also expecting at least eight others. We won't be missed.'

Tina was very cross. She liked neither of his parents and knew that they thought she was just a little bit common.

'If you don't want to go, you can phone yourself.'

'No you do it, Christina,' and he turned back to the group accepting another full glass as he did so.

Ralph raised an eyebrow at her, grimacing sympathetically, but Tina felt distinctly uncomfortable and was also angry. She disliked being thought rude, a bit common was one thing, but deliberate discourtesy was not part of her social vocabulary. She decided that rather than telephone, because she knew that he would not, she would let events take their course for an hour or so and slipped away from the group. She had found the politician insincere and smarmy, the TV newscaster self-absorbed and opinionated, and their women empty fluff heads. Perfect company, she thought, for her husband.

She moved towards another group. She realised that she recognised none of them there, was just thinking of returning to her husband and the group she had just left, when she saw Frances and Henry talking to Virginia and another man. She approached them, was made to feel comfortably welcome and waited to pick up on the conversation. She was aware of Ralph fairly close by. They were talking about him and the older man she did not know, introduced to her only as Geoffrey, was saying, in slow, measured tones, 'An excellent advocate. I always used to enjoy him when he appeared in front of me. I knew the law would be lucidly explained, the case would be intelligently argued and that, since he wouldn't otherwise take a particular line, there would be more than some merit in the analysis.'

Virginia laughed, 'You're too complimentary. He agonises terribly you know. He worries all the time and gets very worked up. You know he spent hours on that mitigation he did last week and, right up to the moment he left the house, was still tinkering with it.'

'No, all good advocates should be a bit worked up. Lord Birkenhead, you know, widely regarded as the leading advocate of his generation, always used to come back to the robing room, armpits and shirt drenched in sweat. I remember seeing him once as a boy when my father took me into the robing room and it encouraged me enormously.'

Ralph joined them at this point. 'Ah, Tina, you've met Sir Geoffrey have you? Always been a great help and source of advice when necessary. My mentor in many ways.'

'Now then, Ralph. You're very talented, as you know. I understand you nearly had the entire courtroom in tears last week.'

'Well, mercifully not of laughter,' Ralph replied.

'What was this?' Tina asked.

'Didn't you see the papers and TV?' Frances said. 'It was full of the case. The one about the man who killed his children and then tried to kill himself. Ralph represented him.'

'I remember Ralph mentioning it,' Tina said. 'What happened?'

'Oh, he got a life sentence,' murmured Ralph sadly, 'as he had to.'

'Ah but Ralph made this storming, moving speech,' began Frances.

'But to no end or legal purpose,' said Ralph. 'Just to try really to make people understand that he wasn't an evil monster.'

'Yes,' said Sir Geoffrey, 'it certainly gives a new dimension to the phrase 'seeing to the children' doesn't it?' and chuckled at his graveyard joke.

People were now starting to leave, to go onto later parties, dinner or home. It became apparent to Tina that Ralph and Virginia had asked a number of people for supper. St John was ensconced in conversation with three of them, and he looked set for the evening. Tina knew the posture well.

Ralph in another room then, saw Virginia who asked, 'Why are the Fortescues here? When did you invite them? Why didn't you tell me?'

He was tempted to say that they had invited themselves but fell back on story B and how he had felt it ill-mannered not to ask them. Virginia immediately understood and smiled saying, 'Yes, of course. You had no option. I'm not sure about him though. Every time we see him, he seems to be drunk.

She seems nice enough. But a bit young for us, aren't they?'

'Good God, Virginia, they're both late twenties at a guess.'

'Well, you're thirty-eight and I'm thirty-seven.'

'Do you know, I've never thought about it? Age doesn't seem particularly relevant anymore. Anyway, most people have left apart from our supper guests. Let's go and get rid of the stragglers and set the table.'

Virginia agreed and they went into the sitting room together.

The now remaining guests, except for Tina and St John, had all been invited to stay on. Virginia and Ralph joined the group and Ralph asked, expecting a polite refusal and knowing of the invitation to his parents, 'Would you both, Christina and St John, like to stay for supper?'

Before Tina could answer, St John said, 'We'd be delighted,' and turned to him explaining that they had been going to his parents, but Christina had cancelled earlier and that they were at a loose end.

Tina turned to him and said very coldly, 'I didn't phone. I said if you wanted to cancel you should. We should have been there over an hour ago.'

St John did not look at all disconcerted. 'I'll phone them tomorrow. We'll stay. With pleasure.'

Tina did not enjoy supper. It was a pleasant enough meal, apparently Ralph had cooked the main course of boeuf bourguignon, made with proper expensive fillet steak Tina noticed, and Virginia had made a chocolate pudding. They drank what Tina recognised to be very good red burgundy and an exquisite Trockenbeeren Auslese with dessert. Ralph produced a decanter of port. The conversation had been pleasant, by turns witty, informative and fun. Tina had not participated much. St

John had and probably too much, Tina thought, to be entirely welcome again. He was still holding his own but Tina could see the signs of incipient passing out. She wondered if she ought to try and get him out of the house now but it seemed that this might compound an incivility.

St John suddenly rose, said, 'Excuse me,' and stumbling momentarily left the room, presumably Tina guessed they all thought, to use the lavatory. After some minutes had passed one of the other guests remarked on his absence.

Ralph stood up and said, 'I'll check and see if he's all right. Embarrassing to drown one's guest in the lavatory. Swimming pool is different. Somehow more acceptable,' and disappeared. He came back a moment later and whispered to Tina who left the room with him. The others, all too well-mannered to say anything to Tina or Ralph, let alone each other when they had gone, carried on as though nothing untoward had occurred.

Ralph took Tina to the sitting room where St John was stretched out on a sofa, shoes off, cushion under head, mouth open, snoring gently.

'Oh God,' Tina was mortified, 'I'm so so sorry. I don't know what to say. It's so embarrassing. It happens so often,' and started crying.

'Come on Tina, it's him, not you.'

'Yes, but I'm married to him and people judge me based on him because I presumably chose him. I didn't have to, and put up with him and have all this. Oh Christ. It's not fair.'

'What do we do, wait till he wakes? Wake him or call an ambulance?' Ralph was quite cheerful.

'When he's like this he's impossible to rouse. The most you can do usually is get him on a kind of autopilot upstairs and horizontal. I suppose we could roll him out...' she giggled.

'...and all of us lift him in a wheelbarrow and tip him into the boot,' finished Ralph.

She laughed. 'It's an attractive idea,' she said. 'No it's not, it's humiliating.' She took her husband by the shoulders and shook him so violently that Ralph thought his head might fly off but the only reaction, as far as he could see or hear, was a noise between a burp and a snore and continued unconsciousness. Tina still looked tearful but perhaps also pleased that she had convincingly demonstrated the truth of her earlier assertion.

'Never mind. Let's wait and see.'

They went back together and when Virginia asked what had happened, Ralph merely said, 'St John's giving it a few zeds in the sitting room.'

'Quite literally,' Tina added. 'He's snoring very loudly indeed.'

'All the more port for the rest of us,' someone remarked languidly, and the evening was back on course.

People had stood up and moved around while smoking and drinking the port, and suddenly Tina found Ralph beside her.

'I've had a word with Virginia. I'll try and get him upstairs and you can both stay in one of our guest rooms. Just let me know when you want him moved.'

Tina felt a mixture of excitement and apprehension. It would put her and Ralph under the same roof for the night. She wondered immediately if there might be a reprise of that first evening, when they had met, and Virginia and St John had both slept in the sitting room while she and Ralph talked.

Ralph had wondered likewise. He had actually had quite a difficult time persuading Virginia that they should stay. She pointed out that they had not really been asked to the party, not been asked to supper and most certainly had not been asked as weekend guests. Ralph had agreed with her but had simply said there was no option and he was not going to kick Tina out with an insensible husband to get home. Virginia finally accepted gracefully. Ralph, who very badly wanted Virginia to agree, had been delighted to have seen St John passed out, had hoped Tina and St John might stay for supper with that just in mind and had, for that reason, been twice as assiduous in filling St John's glass. For once it was not really St John's fault that he had drunk so much. Ralph had ensured that he had three times as much as anyone else, thinking that the cost of the cocktails and expensive Burgundy would be compensated by some time alone with Tina. Virginia, who was not on call, had drunk enough, he thought, to go to bed sooner rather than later. He had been refilling her glass more often than others with this too in mind. Going to plan he thought to himself.

What he really hoped for was to be alone with Tina and she to repeat the invitation she had extended that second time they had met at her dinner party. 'Kiss me,' she had said and taken his hand... he thought back. This time he would if asked. He would do more than that. He would probably, had not made up his mind, but probably see how far she would let him go and how far she would let herself go. He was not sure where it might lead but he found her physical presence so sexually intoxicating that he was going to take it further whatever the risks.

Ralph had nearly always let girls or women make the first move. This was less to do with his desire not to be rejected, whereupon he would have been embarrassed at his being thought to have presumed that she wanted to go further and his having misread the signals, than the feeling that if she did make the first move it was up to him to respond. He could gauge this and deal with it in his own way. If he, and he hated the word, fancied her, his response was to test whether she wanted to make love. If that got a green light then that was what would happen. If he did not fancy her like that, then he would be pleasant and polite and she would never know that she had been rejected. He did not want to be regarded, ever, as someone who pushed himself on women.

It was not a cynical approach, but a realistic one he thought, since if it did lead to bed it was because both of them wanted to be there. The most cynical he had ever been in this sense was when, at seventeen, his best friend Steven who was trying desperately to bed the current girlfriend for her first time, complained to Ralph that she had told him that she did not want to do it for the first time with him but would rather do it with someone like Ralph. Steven had told the story in exasperation, not having foreseen that the moment he left the house, Ralph would be on the phone to the girlfriend who he found very alluring, had then arranged to take her out that same evening and, later on, had relieved her of her virginity, pleasantly and satisfactorily enough to the girl to make her anticipate more encounters with him. Ralph had gone out with her a couple more times for courtesy sake, making love to her at the end of the evening again for courtesy sake, before persuading her, without her ever being aware of his intention, that she was better suited to Steven (completely oblivious of the affair) who, and he enumerated all Steven's good points, was a much better match. Ralph knew, even after that however, Steven had never actually got her between the sheets.

Ralph was feeling rather pleased with himself.

'What are you thinking about?' Tina surprised him.

'How to get your husband upstairs,' he answered lightly but thought and you alone.

'Two-person job.'

As she said this, two of the other couples started to leave. Ralph took his farewells. It left only Virginia and the last couple at the table. Tina excused herself, said goodnight and went through to the sitting room. She felt very miserable. St John was still snoring as Ralph joined her.

'The others are going too,' he said. 'Virginia is coming to help,' and so saying Virginia came through the door.

'Come on,' she said brightly, 'heave ho.'

Ralph tried to pick St John up but he was a complete deadweight. As he pulled, St John suddenly said, 'What's up?'

Tina said, 'Bedtime.'

'OK then,' and so saying St John rose to his feet. Ralph put his arm around him and led him through the house up the stairs and to the furthest guest room, where he fell on the bed, apparently once again in a stupor. Virginia and Tina had followed them.

'What next?' Ralph asked.

'I'll let him sleep like that,' said Tina. 'It's his fault. There are no pyjamas and I don't want you to have to change the bed because of his bad manners. I'll just sleep on top of the blanket or duvet.'

'Of course you won't,' said Virginia, 'don't be silly. You'll sleep in the bed. And,' she looked dubiously at St John, 'he could but not fully clothed.'

'Come on,' said Ralph. 'I'll get him undressed and to bed.

Tina, why don't you help Virginia with a bit of tidying and I'll join you when I'm finished.'

Tina looked relieved and, after Virginia had left to go downstairs, said 'You're wonderful. Nothing seems to bother you. You just get on with it.'

'Has to be done, I suppose,' he replied carelessly.

'There's just one thing I'm worried about.'

'Which is?'

'He wears contact lenses. I know he's got them in tonight. Usually if he thinks he's going to get good and drunk, he leaves them out. But tonight...'

'You were going to his parents where he doesn't get drunk,' Ralph concluded.

'No, not really, he'd probably have taken them out there himself earlier. I've never done it and don't know how to. Can you do it?'

No, thought Ralph. I've never done it and I'm not sure I can do it, but said instead, 'Of course I can, Tina,' thinking that the worst that he could do would be to blind him. He decided to leave the contact lenses until last, in case he actually hurt St John and he woke.

He wanted an opportunity to study the man Tina had married and to make comparisons between him and himself. The idea that he could also take all St John's clothes off was a bonus. Stripping Tina's husband prior to, he hoped, taking some of her clothes off later, seemed a curious coincidence. The loose jersey came off easily. The shirt buttons were tight - St John was a well muscled man. He managed them and drew the shirt back and down the arms. He noticed that Tina had thoughtfully removed St John's shoes and socks. Ralph undid the trouser belt and drew down the zip. God, he thought to himself, how many women's zips have I taken down and here's a first. A man's. He had never had any homosexual leanings at all. He eased the trousers down; it was easier than anticipated. He was left with what seemed an alarmingly large bulk with some voluminous Y fronts.

'I should leave it at this,' he thought to himself but a natural curiosity to see what it was that was presumably inserted into Tina on a fairly regular basis intervened. He, with a faint expression of disgust, took down the pants and dropped them on the floor.

He gazed at St John's nakedness. He looked at the hairy groin and envied, not St John or his penis, but the fact that that particular penis had been put into Tina, in and out, in and out, until orgasm, whenever St John had wanted and Tina had wanted him to. He stood for a moment longer. It was pretty much the same as everybody else's. Hairier perhaps, but that was all. He did not see St John as a handsome man and wondered what it was that Tina found attractive about him. He lifted an eyelid. St John groaned and seemed about to wake up but did not. Ralph felt around, got one contact lens and repeated the process with the other eye. He had not enjoyed doing this but reasoned that it was a lot worse than things Virginia did on a daily basis. He wondered momentarily why he hadn't asked her to do it but knew that it was really because he wanted the opportunity to see his opponent naked.

When he opened the door to the kitchen he saw the backs of both women. They had not heard him and were washing and drying glasses together. Ralph suddenly wished that he could have both. A ménage a trois, he thought, would suit him. He dismissed the thought as quickly as it had entered his head. Virginia had, despite her doctoring and liberal beliefs, firmly old-fashioned sexual values and would not receive the suggestion of three in a bed with any kind of amusement, let alone prospect of agreement.

He had not heard Tina's question but Virginia was answering, 'Yes, of course, I love him. He's everything to me. Always has been. I'm proud of him and he's my best friend.'

'You're very lucky, Virginia.'

Ralph decided that he should pretend to have just come in and breezily said, 'Hello, can I help?'

'No, nearly finished. Christina's been an angel - worked really hard. Two more to go and then we're done. I was going to leave everything till tomorrow but it's done now. Good.'

Virginia finished the last glass as she said this, pulled off rubber gloves and asked, 'Does anyone want another drink? I think we deserve one.'

Ralph's heart sank as he realised that Virginia was going to sit with them until they all went to bed together, in the sense of at the same time, not the same place he reflected with disappointment.

'Good idea,' and he went to an open bottle and poured three glasses, handing one to each of the women.

'Sante,' he said. 'Should we sit down?' They sat around a comfortable old kitchen table and sipped their wine in a companionable way, Tina apologising for her husband again and very anxious that they should not think her rude or ill-bred.

'These things happen,' Virginia said. 'Does he often do it? I think we've only met four times and each time - let's see, the first was when you came here, and Ralph helped him out of the house. The second was at your house, and he was all right then, the third was at Frances and Henry's drinks thing when I loosened his shirt and tonight, the fourth.'

Tina felt abject but also did not want to let her husband down in front of the formidably capable Virginia. 'He's got a lot on at work and gets pretty stressed,' she found herself excusing him.

God, it's only a few weeks ago, thought Ralph, that this girl came into my life.

He knew he was beginning to think in clichés. But, and it was a huge but for him, she had and, he knew that it was another cliché, turned his life upside down.

'Doing anything and trying to do it well is stressful,' he said.

'Don't I know it,' Virginia smiled. 'I sometimes wish I'd gone into something less tiring - both emotionally and physically - than medicine.' She turned to Tina. 'What do you do?'

Tina was aware that she had hardly talked to Virginia. Ralph had already assumed such large proportions in her emotional life that this surprised her. She also understood then that Ralph and Virginia could not have discussed her and St John at all. She was not sure whether to be pleased or a bit peeved. She decided she was pleased. It might mean that he did not trust himself not to let something out that indicated his interest in her.

'I don't want to seem rude but it's pretty late and I'm on call as of 9.00 am tomorrow,' Virginia said without waiting for an answer. 'Should we all go to bed?' She had forgotten that she had just asked Tina what she did for a living. Tina felt that she must be so peripheral to her life that the answer was of no consequence, but the truth was, of course, that Virginia was tired and had drunk too much.

'You'd better call it a day,' Ralph said, feeling irritated. He had deliberately not drunk much against what he hoped would be a different outcome.

'See you upstairs,' Ralph said to Virginia. 'You know where you are Christina, I'll show you the bathroom. I'm just going to damp down the fire and make sure it's safe.'

Tina thought quickly. 'Can you show me the bathroom, Virginia and then I'll pop out and get my handbag?'

'Of course, come on', and they went upstairs.

Ralph went into the sitting room, played with the fire, put out all the lights except a reading lamp and stood and waited. He heard Virginia's cheery goodnight and the creak of boards as she went down the corridor into their bedroom, the gurgle of the basin in the ensuite, the sound of Tina coming downstairs, going out of the front door, the flush of a lavatory upstairs, a car door being closed, Virginia settling into bed, then thought of Tina coming to him and found himself aroused. He went into the hallway and met Tina just as she was coming in the front door. She was carrying her handbag.

'She's gone to bed,' he said pleasantly.

'I know. She loves you a lot. But then I understand why,' Tina murmured and moved to pass him. He felt an opportunity slipping away but was not sure what to say. He had hoped she would make a first move, indeed had expected this.

'Tina?'

'Yes'.

'I'm glad you came this evening.'

'I'm not sure I am.'

'Why not?'

'I feel we've made fools of ourselves.'

'Not at all.'

'It's been a bit of a disaster really.'

'No it hasn't.' He wanted to reassure her. 'I've seen you again,' he managed to say.

She looked at him directly and in the eyes. 'I'm glad you feel like that. Goodnight Ralph,' and kissed him lightly on the lips before disappearing up the stairs to her comatose husband.

Tina washed and went into the bedroom. She looked down at St John and shuddered as a real feeling of revulsion passed through her. He was naked, as he had been left by Ralph, lying on top of the bed. He looked coarse and vulgar and she again wondered what on earth had attracted her to him in the beginning. She pulled a cover and duvet over him, took her outer clothing off and slipped under the cover but on top of the duvet, shivered for a moment or two before falling into another fitful sleep.

When she woke, at first she was not sure where she was; there were unfamiliar kitchen noises in the distance. She looked at her watch. It was 10.00 am and she remembered that they had stayed with the Edwards, St John had disgraced himself, that Virginia had said that she loved Ralph to bits, that she had more or less cold-shouldered Ralph, she now had a thumping hangover and St John appeared still to be sound asleep.

She then also remembered that Virginia had said she was on call that morning and, wondering whether she might be out already, thought it could do no harm to try and get out of bed quietly, get dressed without waking her husband and slip downstairs. Being by herself would look natural whether Ralph and Virginia were both in the kitchen or he was alone. She hoped the latter and, moving very gingerly, took her clothes, padded to the door, looked back to satisfy herself that St John was still sleeping, opened the door, saw no one around, went into the corridor, closing the door gently and made to enter the bathroom.

At that point Ralph emerged from round the corner. He had just come up the stairs and he looked startled at the sight of Tina in bra and knickers only.

'Good morning, Tina, slept well, I trust. How's St John?' He was determinedly normal.

Tina was totally unselfconscious. 'Fairly well, thank you. I was just going to get dressed and come down. He's still asleep. I should have woken him,' and she paused.

He took up where she had left off. 'Virginia's gone already. She'll be at least an hour. Her patient's ten miles away and...' He smiled, raising his eyebrows in a conscious imitation of her when they had danced together.

Tina did not know what to do. Was that a hint, an invitation or a simple statement of fact? She was very aware of her skimpy underwear and Ralph's enquiring expression. Should she ask him outright?

'How asleep is he?'

That suggested to her that it might be more than a hint.

'When he's like that, unless he's woken by me, fairly vigorously, he'll sleep until lunchtime.'

'Ah. Then we are, for practical purposes,' she liked his ironic legal pomposity, 'all alone. What should we do?'

This was an invitation she decided. She was right of course. Ralph had not expected the encounter when he left the kitchen to go upstairs but he was determined to make the most of the opportunity that had just presented itself. He too was unsure how to play it. He could hardly say, 'Fancy a quick bonk while my wife's out and your husband's still asleep?' but that is exactly what he had in mind as he stood looking at her.

I'm not that kind of girl was the thought that passed quickly through her mind but, that said, she knew that she wanted him more than she had wanted any other man or boy in her life. She actually thought that even a quickie, it might only be a one morning stand, would be better than nothing at all. She wondered how she could agree without seeming an easy lay.

She was nevertheless, she decided, prepared to take the risk and hoped that Ralph might so enjoy the sex that it might move things on. If it did not, then so be it. She could chalk it up to experience. The infidelity to St John did not occur to her then.

She moved towards him. 'Where do you want to go? It's your house.'

He took her hand, she very passive and unresisting, led her down the corridor, round the corner, past what was evidently the marital bedroom, Tina caught a glimpse of a large unmade brass bed, and then he opened another doorway. It was a more unostentatiously furnished spare room with just a double bed and a cupboard.

He closed the doorway behind them and turned, putting his arm round her. She dropped her clothes and put her arms around his waist. They said nothing for a moment and then Ralph made the first move. He was frightened. This was momentous. He was already sure, convinced even, that this was not a casual throwaway sexual encounter but could be an event that shaped his life. However, the desire was too strong and he bent to kiss her.

She responded with an intensity that intoxicated him. His hand dropped to her breast which he very tenderly stroked for a moment. She was kissing him, eyes closed, pressing her warm body against his and pushing against his crotch. Her hands stayed on the small of his back. He moved his hand across her stomach. She made no protest but moved her body slightly away to make it easier for him. As he slid his hand downwards, he encountered silken pubic hair, such a contrast it occurred to him, and when his fingers reached the gap, he was astonished at how wet she was. Tina was so sexually excited that she could hardly wait. He slowly stroked her and then his fingers entered her and again she gasped.

He looked at the bed, she saw this and smiled, a knowing smile of total sexual complicity. They sat down together and she lay back for a moment, undid her bra and deftly removed her knickers, before moving to the centre of the bed and slowly and deliberately, watching him all the time, spreading her legs wide apart. Ralph paused, he always felt it looked undignified to undo and take off trousers, but he did so, pulling off shoes and socks. He leaned towards her, looking at her body, every last part seemingly hugely visible and ready, and said, 'You are absolutely beautiful. You are simply lovely.'

She pulled his head towards hers and kissed him again. 'Put it in,' she whispered and he climbed on top of her and started to do so. He had always enjoyed the first part of the sex act, the anticipation of entry and then the first sensation of entry and then gently easing all the way in. As he did so, her eyes widened.

Is it all the way in yet, she was thinking? No, a bit more, there.

'Lovely,' she groaned. She was curiously still after that. Her small hands were clenched on the pillow. He used his finger to stimulate her and soon she had an orgasm, her low moans, the panting, her face contorted in an expression of what appeared grim concentration. Ralph thought, as he thrust himself inside her repeatedly but with an almost beatific passion, that she really was truly lovely in a way that had never occurred to him to consider. As he continued to kiss her, only moments later, he had a shuddering and huge orgasm that left him feeling sexually dazed. He lifted his head and, looking straight into her eyes, also whispered rather than said, 'I think that this is the most wonderful moment of my life.' She appeared to be astonished. He was insistent. 'No, I mean it.'

'Me too, but what are we going to do?' asked Tina.

He was not sure what the question meant. Do now? Get dressed as quickly as possible. Do generally? He had no idea. He just wanted to repeat the experience as often as possible.

'Do?' he asked. 'How do you mean?'

'I want you. I love you,' she said simply.

He kissed her and said, 'Tina, I love you too. God, I love you. Do? I don't know. Take short views for a time.' He thought that maybe an affair was containable and he could cope with it but anything further, he had made no contingency plans.

'Yes,' and kissed her again, 'we'll take short views.'

Tina was puzzled. She loved him and he had just said that he loved her. On the other hand, he had just had her and he might have said that out of politeness. She felt a cold bleak dread. She shivered.

'You're cold. Put your clothes on quickly.'

They both got dressed and at the doorway he kissed her

again.

'I love you Tina.' The mere words were enough to make her want to cry with happiness. 'Look, I'm going to have a quick bath - why don't you have a bath as well, there's plenty of hot water and towels and then I'll make you both breakfast.'

That brought her back to reality. She had forgotten her sleeping husband. My God, my husband. I'm married to him, and I've just done this in this house with another woman's husband. She was suddenly appalled at the enormity of the deed. She saw the wisdom of cleaning up however, for both of them, and nodded, 'I'll see you downstairs,' and then she reached for him, and they kissed for a long time, his hand straying down again to the lovely moist softness.

She pulled away and opened the door, walked quietly down and round the corner. Ralph waited for a moment, listened, heard her open and then lock the bathroom door and then, he too, left the room and went into the ensuite marital bathroom. He had just started running a bath when he heard the unmistakable exhaust note of Virginia's Porsche.

Christ, he thought. Stop bath. Not going to be able to get in it quick enough. Might smell of sex. Empty bath. Turn on shower. Get in. All of which he did. A few minutes later Virginia was in the bedroom. He was safely soaped in the shower.

'Showering Ralph? You normally have a bath?'

'We've got guests, so I thought I'd get on - I'll only be a minute.' He was just lathering his hair when the curtain was pulled back and he saw Virginia. She was naked and made to step in with him. He panicked but remembered that he now smelt only of soap and shampoo.

'No, Virginia, not now.'

'A quickie,' she said with determination and started to play with him. He was not at all excited.

'Ah, a hangover, a limp noodle, limp noodles need stimulating.' She knelt down in front of him. Could he fake an orgasm he wondered?

'Now,' she said, standing up again and leaning against the slippery wall.

Oh God, what have I got myself into, he thought. I can't do it.

'What are you waiting for? Come on Ralph, we've got to be quick,' and she guided him into her. He went through the motions, reflecting that this was not very enjoyable, and then she had her orgasm as the water steamed around them. She pulled away from him, dropped to her knees and, to his surprise, he found that he was able to have another one after all. She stood up, swallowing, grinning at him, 'They say it's good for the digestion,' kissed him, spun round and left him feeling utterly and completely confused.

He saw the farcical side of it all. He was now going down to have breakfast with the woman he had just fucked that he was married to, with the other woman he had just fucked and with whom he would like an affair and the husband of the other woman he'd just fucked. How on earth was he going to behave normally? He also suddenly realised that there was no way he could have an affair with Tina. Virginia knew his precise movements all the time and when he was not at work, they were together. To change his habits now was to effectively announce the thing. She would never believe him if he said that he wanted to spend Monday nights, for instance, at an

Art Club, or photography course, or indeed anything. In any event she would probably say that she would come with him.

He knew that Tina worked in a suburb of the city in which he had Chambers but there she was surrounded by people. He could, he supposed, 'work late' and she could visit him there; once or twice no one would comment but any more than that and tongues would wag. Cheap hotel after work? Rather sordid. He ran through possibilities and decided he needed to consider the matter more carefully and reflectively. He normally found a solution to any problem, and he had little doubt that there was some way of resolving the practical difficulties.

He finished dressing and, heart beating rather more quickly than usual, went down the stairs, having decided to affect a breeziness that he most certainly did not feel.

A scene of startling normality greeted him. He stopped short, recollected himself and continued into the kitchen. Virginia and Tina were again side by side preparing breakfast and a very sombre-faced St John was sitting at the table. He looked up as Ralph walked in.

'I'm ever so sorry about last night. I can't apologise enough.'

'He's been apologising ever since he came down a couple of minutes ago,' Virginia said, adding 'but we've forgiven him, haven't we?'

'Oh, yes, of course,' Ralph replied mechanically, wondering when St John had got up. He seemed to read Ralph's thoughts.

'I came down after Tina had finished in the bathroom. I hope you don't mind, I had a quick shower myself.'

Phew, thought Ralph. Close call. God, the danger.

He made a determined effort, had just started to enquire whether everyone had slept well, when the phone rang. Virginia answered the call.

'Hello, Daddy,' they all heard her say. 'Oh, no. Good God. How is she? Where is she? No, I'll come at once. I'll drive up today and be with you in about three hours. No, really. No. Tell her I love her and you Daddy. I'll see you later.' She turned to the others who had stopped talking and were waiting.

'Mummy's had a stroke. She's in hospital. Her condition is not good. Ralph, I've got to go up. I'll call the surgery and get one of the others to cover for me for a day or two.' Virginia would have no difficulty in arranging this as she was always ready to do the same for her partners, who in fact got the better end of the deal. 'Ralph, what about you?'

Ralph thought quickly. He did not like Virginia's mother, although her father was not bad company, and he had a trial starting on Monday and a lot of preparation to do. He had earmarked Sunday for the work without which he would lose the case.

'Virginia, I can't. I've got the Rose case on Monday. It's listed for three days and I haven't started the papers yet.'

'No, good point. I'll give you a ring when I get there. Excuse me St John, Tina. I've got to pack.' Her eyes were heavy with tears as she turned and left them.

Tina and St John seemed shell-shocked and Ralph said, 'Excuse me for a moment. Help yourselves to breakfast. It looks as though everything is out already.' He followed Virginia up the stairs. She was in the bedroom, cordless phone held to her ear, packing quickly with her other hand. She was organising cover.

'Yes. No. That's really good of you. Thanks a lot. I'll try and get back tomorrow. You really don't mind if it's another couple of days? That's great. Thanks ever so much. Bye.' He went over to her. She had started crying and he held her for a moment, kissing her on the forehead.

'Are you sure you don't want me to come with you? I can get someone else to do the Rose thing.'

'No, it's worth a lot of money to us. Isn't it your biggest brief fee ever?'

'Yes, it is. It'll pay for the Himalayan trip you booked with some over.'

'You stay. You do it and you win it.' She smiled at him through her tears. 'I'm ready. I'm off. Kiss me.'

He did and she grabbed her small hold-all and started for the door. He followed, caught her in his arms and said, 'Drive carefully.' It was a redundant comment because she always did, was indeed a safe, fast and competent driver. They went downstairs together, and Virginia touched him on the cheek.

'I love you Ralph. I'll ring when I get there,' and was gone. He waved as the car went down the drive and turned once again and entered his house. Back in the kitchen Tina and St John were silently eating but there was no unpleasant atmosphere.

'Virginia asked me to say goodbye to you both.' She had not but Ralph was courteous.

'How's her mother?' Tina asked.

'You know as much as I do. I'll be told more later I guess. Have you got enough to eat?' St John was just finishing what had clearly been a very large plate of scrambled eggs, Tina a croissant.

'Yes thank you,' they replied simultaneously.

'Coffee?' he asked rhetorically as he finished pouring boiling water into the cafetiere.

'That'd be a nice treat,' Tina said. 'I love real coffee but we only have it at dinner parties.'

Ralph suddenly felt rather sorry for the two of them. He and Virginia took real coffee for granted and in fact never drank instant, keeping a jar only for people who actually preferred this. He looked again at Tina and thought how pretty she was and sadly wondered why St John didn't make more of her, indeed why on earth he had, albeit unwittingly, allowed his host to make love to her less than an hour earlier. Ralph wondered also whether he should feel guilty. Events had rather fallen upon him, one after another and he was feeling bewildered.

'Sorry, what was that?' He looked up. 'Where do Virginia's parents live? Yorkshire. Up in the hills. Straight up the M1 and then along further to the A1, turn and drive for thirty or forty miles and you get there.' He thought of the lovely old stone manor house in the village, and how he used to thrill at the sight of the picturesque building when he and Virginia went up in the early days, always stopping en route for one of Virginia's quickies. She was unusually chaste before they married, at least whilst staying with her parents, so liked to get one in, as she joked, on the way.

'Has she said when she's coming back?' asked Tina, her eyes meeting his without a trace of guile.

'Well, it won't be before tomorrow evening at the earliest. She's arranged cover for longer if necessary.'

Tina paused as if she was going to say something but then appeared to decide against this. They had all finished drinking their coffee and Ralph murmured something about another cup which both politely refused. Tina offered to help load the dishwasher, an offer Ralph equally politely declined, saying,

'Oh, no. I can fill it very easily and quickly. I have my own way of doing it.'

Tina glanced at St John, who had turned towards the door, looked again at Ralph and said, 'I know. You do it rather well,' and her eyes dropped, momentarily, towards his groin. St John might have heard the remark but gave no sign.

Ralph laughed and said, 'It needs practice to make perfect,' and immediately regretted this comment; the words seemed to suggest that he and Virginia practised, which he supposed they did, but what he wanted to imply was that he and Tina must practice together. He thought she understood though, when she replied, 'Practice will make perfect.'

He showed them to the door, St John insisting on shaking hands. Although he did not look like a defeated opponent, Ralph was very conscious of that fact that here was a man cuckolded only an hour earlier, shaking hands in a jolly bonhomie. He turned and as he did so, Tina leaned forward, kissed Ralph on the cheek, whispering, 'I'll phone.' Then they were gone.

Ralph pottered round the kitchen, as ever methodically, mulling over events. He felt as though everything was too elusive to analyse. The enormity was still barely credible and he kept on thinking of Tina, the physical Tina, the sexual Tina. The feeling he had had when he was inside her. That sensation was nearly more pleasurable than the orgasm.

He finished in the kitchen and went through, pausing to look at pictures on the wall, the expensive antiques, the Persian rugs. The trappings of success were rather nice he reflected, and again he wanted to rail at this new banality of language that he seemed to be using. His former, articulate, fluent, vocabulary seemed to have been replaced by tabloid speak. He spread out papers across his desk in the study, looking at the clock. It was still only 11.00 am.

On the way back Tina, who was driving as usual, appeared to make up her mind. She too had been considering the enormity of what she had done. She was worried that Ralph would think of her as a little trollop and whether he was working up to making her his bit on the side. She knew that she had physical appeal and that she physically appealed to him. She believed him when he said that he thought she was lovely. Others had said it to her before. But, and it was a big but for Tina, he appealed to her in a way that St John, certainly for one, never had.

Even at the beginning. She considered the sex. Sex with St John was perfunctory. He paid lip service, but not literally, to the idea that she should have an orgasm. The problem from her point of view was that she had little, or even no enthusiasm for one with him and accordingly always faked them. He did not know any better. She was aware that she had been his first and still was his only lover. What his sexual experience had been before her Tina did not know. The fact was, however, that he had never bothered or taken the trouble to find out what turned her on, excited her or, indeed, what produced an orgasm.

Sex with Ralph was different. Even the hole in a corner, she liked the phrase in the context, sex today had been satisfying physically. She had surprised herself when she came so quickly, and Ralph had not been a disappointment. He was gentle, confident and practised. He was not rough or unpleasant. She appreciated the fact that he had waited until he was sure that she had come before he did. And when he had, looking into his eyes, as she kissed him, Tina had thought that it was the first time she had, during sex, felt appreciated for herself and not the fact of just being a female body that was getting screwed. No, the sex had been good. And there would be more. She knew that there would be. She had decided.

St John turned towards her as she drove with purposeful concentration.

'What are you thinking about?' he suddenly asked. The question was an odd one since he never asked her this, whether out of simple lack of interest or lack of imagination, she felt it made no difference.

'Supper,' she replied.

'I thought we might go out?'

'What, the two of us?'

'Yes.'

'I'd rather not. I'm tired. I'd like an early night. I'll make us something - I've got stuff in the freezer.'

'Should we stop at the video shop?'

'If you like.'

They did, and after St John disappeared and had returned beaming, with a copy of the latest horror sensation, Tina felt an early night coming on. She defrosted a spaghetti bolognaise which they ate in front of the early evening TV programmes. When he put the film on, Tina announced her intention to go and have a bath and an early night.

He did not look up and merely said, 'See you later.'

She had a long soak, washing her hair, paying particular attention to leg hairs and general appearance, before going to bed again in their spare room. She heard St John come up, ablute and then go to their room.

He came to her and asked, 'Why are you here?'

'Simply because I want to be.'

'If that's the way you want it,' he said without rancour and, unexpectedly, left her.

Tina wanted to be alone with her thoughts. Her hand drifted down and she started playing with herself, the familiar movements producing the desired sensation and, as she came, rubbing herself gently, she thought of Ralph and tomorrow.

Ralph, after the Fortescues had left, soon started to feel at a loose end. He was not able to concentrate on his case and decided he was wasting his time. He could come back to it later if he chose, or do the work as intended, on Sunday. He was missing Virginia and Tina simultaneously. He was not often alone, and rather disliked the emptiness of the house.

He decided to drive into a nearby town and selecting a suitably seedy looking newsagent, went inside. He found an extensive display of magazines and a very large top shelf selection. Casting about, he felt mortified at the thought of being seen by anyone, let alone recognised, he picked, by appearance rather than content, a few of these together with a motoring magazine which he took to the counter. The young girl behind grinned at him when she saw what he had chosen.

'Lonely night in then?'

'Pardon me?' said Ralph.

'Not going out then?' she giggled. Ralph was about to turn on his heel and leave them all on the counter when he became aware of an elderly woman behind him tutting loudly. This was awful he thought.

'Hurry up please,' he asked the girl who seemed to take a delight in slowly scrutinising each lurid cover, with its scantily dressed woman, for the price. The elderly woman was joined by an elderly man.

'We've got a pervert in front of us,' he heard her say to the newcomer.

After the girl announced the total he handed over a £20 note, got surprisingly little change, and left the shop feeling like a dirty old man.

When he got home he went through the porn magazines quickly. He carefully tore the pages out that had photographs of women who resembled Tina. He then compared all of these, refining his selection picture by picture, until he decided which of the girls most resembled her. He then chose the image he liked the best. She was lying on a bed, in a come-hither kind of way, but it was the eyes that had it for him. They had exactly the same look of anticipatory pleasure that he had witnessed in Tina as his hand went down across her stomach. The rest of the magazines and torn out pages he put in an old carrier bag, knotted it up and took out to the dustbin, lifting a couple of bags and tucking the incriminating evidence towards the bottom and replacing the others on top.

Back in the house, he took the photograph to the main bedroom and left it on the bedside. As he did so the phone rang. It was Virginia. The news was not good. Her mother was in intensive care and, 'Daddy has gone to pieces. I'm going to stay until Monday at least. Is that all right?'

'Of course it is. I'm OK. I've done some of the Rose work and I'll do more tomorrow.'

'Right, I'll go now. Ralph I miss you. I wish you were here or I was with you. I'll be thinking of you tonight. Think of me won't you.'

'Yes, I miss you too. Love you.'

'Love you Ralph.'

He hung up morosely.

Later he went to the local pub and had a couple of beers with some people he only vaguely knew. He did not really want company but did not want to be by himself and alone with his thoughts. He went home and opened a bottle of Chablis which he drank quickly. He did not eat anything except a Brie sandwich. He had no hunger. He went to bed early and fell asleep instantly. Before he had put out the light, he had looked at the photograph for a long time, toyed with the idea of masturbating and then decided it would be undignified.

Once asleep he experienced something totally new to him. He had a wet dream. He woke up incredulous. At the age when his contemporaries were talking of their wet dreams and masturbating and the rest. Ralph, although never showing his derision, would not join in their conversations. He was already having real sex with a real girl about which, of course, he never spoke. He had something of a contempt for men ever after, presumably he thought, deriving primarily from that period. He found crude jokes, as well as innuendo, boring and demeaning. But his dream had been remarkable. Both Virginia and Tina had been in it. Both undressed. Both in black stockings like so many of the models in the magazines he had thrown away. Both had been on a bed on all fours with their bottoms in the air. Both, he stopped. He could not remember what had happened next. He presumed he had woken very shortly afterwards. He paused in his thoughts. What on earth is happening to me? Ruminating on this, he fell into a totally dreamless sleep.

When he woke the following morning, he felt refreshed and lighter. More confident. Still not sure how to resolve things but happier. Virginia was up in Yorkshire. He was down here. He had a case to prepare and win. He went down in his dressing gown and put the kettle on. Filling a cafetiere he thought of Tina yesterday and the way in which she had said that real coffee was a treat.

The doorbell rang. He looked at his watch. 9.00 am. He had overslept a bit but could not think who might be at the door. When he opened it, still in his dressing gown, he saw Tina. He was completely nonplussed.

'You're just in time for coffee.' He recovered. 'Would you like to come in?'

She nodded and came through the door. He shut it behind her and suddenly she was in his arms, kissing him familiarly and excitedly.

'Oh God, I've missed you.'

'Me too,' he managed to say. His hands ran down her back, across her bottom, he stopped and put one hand under her skirt and ran it back up her legs.

'You're wearing stockings,' he said, inconsequentially he later thought.

'I've dressed up for you.'

He felt her, sliding his hand and fingers down her stomach and into her.

'God, Ralph. I want you so much, I've never...'

He kissed her again, but her wetness and obvious physical desire overcame him and, rather than going upstairs, he pushed her gently into the sitting room where they had fast and excited sex. She came quickly. He too. Only afterwards did it occur to him that he had not undressed her, but had got on top, pulling her skirt up and her knickers to one side. He had found the encounter much more erotic than the day before and told her so. He stroked her hair and looked at her. She was lying on her side, clothing dishevelled and smiling broadly at him.

'Oh, oh, oh.' She giggled then laughed. 'Was that nice or was that nice?'

'Nice.' He laughed as well. 'What are you doing here?'

'I came to see you.'

'Well here I am. What next?'

'Let's recover and then do it again slowly.'

He looked at her. She was serious. OK, why not, he thought and nodded. He got up, drew his dressing gown together and helped her to stand. She stood, smoothing her skirt in a brisk, business-like way.

'Where's the coffee you promised?'

'Kitchen,' he said and disappeared, returning with the cafetiere, mugs and milk.

Watching her pour coffee, he suddenly had a most prosaic thought. Where? Not the marital bed. Spare room was still made up of course. Last time he had been in there it was to put St John to bed. He wondered if the same thought would occur to her. She looked at him again and seemed to have read his mind.

'In the room like yesterday. I want an action replay but without the anxiety.'

He thought she must be joking. Without the anxiety? Anxiety was the least of his worries, but he replied, 'This time slowly and without anxiety.' She nodded and kissed him again.

After they had drunk the coffee, saying little but laughing and smiling a lot, they went upstairs and to the same room. He unbuttoned her shirt, kissing her neck, nibbling her ears, kissing her again, caressing her and unzipping her skirt, which fell to the floor, leaving her dressed only in the black stockings, briefs, suspender belt and bra.

'Do you like what you see?' she asked.

'You are simply, simply too lovely, and you've arrived

gift-wrapped' he murmured kissing her shoulders, upper breasts, undoing the bra strap, letting it fall away, kissing her nipples, trailing his lips across her stomach. Pulling her down to the mattress, he moved lower until he was tasting her. She smelt of nothing, no body odour, no perfume, but clean and sweet. She had stiffened for a moment as he started probing with his tongue then relaxed. Tina had abandoned herself completely and was now so aroused that she was as if without thought. She told him afterwards that she had felt she was swimming in a sea of molten liquid pleasure. She arched her back, crying out and he knew that he had succeeded in producing a first orgasm. He kept on licking as her fingernails dug deep into his shoulders, before licking and kissing all the way back up again. He was ready for another and putting himself inside her, she wondering again whether it was all in, no not quite, yes, that felt lovely, he stroked her until he felt her back stiffen, the gasps that he recognised as the prelude to her orgasm and, having held himself back until then, let himself go so they came together, he kissing her furiously at the same time. She held him tightly for what seemed to him an eternity. Neither said anything. He was not sure what he wanted to say, could find no words to express the enormity of the emotion. He felt himself go limp and kissed her again before taking his weight off her. She did not want to let him go and said, 'No, stay there.' He noticed she was biting her lip. He had seen her do this before. She opened her eyes and there were tears.

'Why are you crying?'

'It's never been like that before. Nobody has done that to me. I just feel so relaxed and happy.'

He wondered why it had never been like that for her, but

dismissed the thought quickly. It had been special for him too he acknowledged.

'Will we do this often?' she asked him, smiling through her hair.

'As often as you want,' he replied, kissing her and thinking of the practical difficulties which she obviously, otherwise she would not have asked the question, was prepared to find a way of resolving with him.

He had always felt uncomfortable with the terminology for genitalia and sex. He, in his way, was a bit of a prude. He generally, when going out with a girl, had contrived to find out what she preferred to call the man's bits, the woman's bits and the sex act and then he used those during the currency of the relationship. He pondered on what Tina might call them. Pussy and, he stopped. She did not strike him as crude. Pussy maybe, but he had no idea about the man's bits.

'If we're going to do this often,' he began, but she stopped him with a kiss. When she finished, he started again. He was annoyed to find himself somewhat self-conscious.

'Tina?'

'Yes'

'Do you have names for this?' He felt her there. 'There.' He touched her there. 'And this?' He glanced down at himself.

'Not really,' she said, thinking to herself that the words St John used were unacceptable in polite society. 'What do you call them?'

Ralph had never, but never, been asked this question before. He had gone out with girls who had called theirs a fanny, pussy, one very modest girl a front bottom, another relationship, which had not lasted, had been focused on her growler and his dong, he inwardly shuddered when he thought back to that one, and his had also been called a willy and the noodle. What did he call them?

'I don't know.'

'Don't be silly.'

'I'm not. I'm being deadly serious. Let me try and think.' He supposed he thought of his as 'it'. And the sex act, when he thought about the sex act, was 'doing it'. Why? And then it all came back to him.

Playing in a corn field which had just been cut. He was with, he had never thought of this, another girl also called Virginia and her brother Norman. They seemed a lot older than him then. They were, he guessed with hindsight, a bit simple, children of the farm worker who had done the baling. They had rearranged a stack of bales to form a small, covered enclosure about five feet high into which they crawled through a gap left between the bales. They were sitting there, in a half-gloom, on bales when Virginia said, 'Let's play mummies and daddies.'

'Yes, let's. Let's do that,' said Norman enthusiastically.

'How do you play it?' Ralph asked.

'We'll show you.' Virginia smiled at her younger brother. 'Who'll start?'

'You do,' he said.

Virginia lay back against the side of the bales, still sitting on one like an armchair and spread open her legs. She pulled her knickers to one side for a moment and Ralph caught sight of a small crack. Ralph was bemused and found himself stiffening for reasons that he was unable then to comprehend. He had never seen a girl behave like this before. She then put her legs together again, lifted her bottom, took off her knickers and spread her legs as wide as she seemed able. She then took off her shirt revealing a totally flat chest.

'Watch,' she said and put a finger into herself. She pulled it out and leaned forward to Ralph, 'Smell it,' she commanded. He did so. It was not a smell he had ever come across. He was not sure that he liked it.

'Watch,' she said again, and she pushed her finger in and out. She went a little red. Ralph was transfixed. He knew that what was going on was naughty and felt that he ought to be horrified. Virginia stopped and looked at him. He was looking at the pink slit. She put both her hands down there and parted the lips revealing a little pink hole.

'Should we let him put it in Norman?'

'Oh I think so,' Norman said.

Ralph was alarmed. Put what in? He presumed she meant 'it' was to go into the little pink hole.

'Oh come on Ralph. This,' Norman said and Ralph looked at him. Norman had undone his zip and had, in those days what Ralph called a willy out and it was stiff and upright. Norman was rubbing it enthusiastically.

'Come on Ralph. Have a go, like this,' and with that, he went over to his sister and pushed it into her. They remained locked together for a while and then Virginia said 'That's called doing it. That's what mummies and daddies do. Your turn to be daddy.' Norman withdrew and, turning towards Ralph, said, 'Get it out. Your turn now.'

Ralph was in a frenzy of indecision. It seemed incredibly rude but he wanted to try it. An intellectually curious little boy, he would try most things. He undid his zip and got his willy out. He rubbed it. It stiffened further.

'Come on, what are you waiting for,' Virginia grumbled. He went over, knelt in front of her and pushed it in easily. He thought the sensation was lovely and, without any conscious decision, rocked back and forth a few times before Virginia said, 'Right, that's enough.' He withdrew reluctantly. He had put 'it' in. He had done 'it'. Hence he thought of it as it and the act as doing it. He was eight, Norman ten and Virginia eleven. He supposed he had seen them subsequently, but they had never again played mummies and daddies.

He was aware of Tina waiting for an answer.

'What do I call them?' he repeated. 'I suppose I call it, it.'

'You can't'.

'Why not?'

'It must have a name. You must call it something.' She wanted to ask what Virginia called it but felt it was an inappropriate question so soon.

'Well, when I was little it was a willy. Later on,' he stopped, self-conscious, he did not want to give her the impression of a vast sexual past.

'Well, we'll call it willy. What about this.' She guided his hand to the top of her legs. She was hugely moist, he thought as he desperately tried to come up with something acceptable.

'Making love to you is like dipping it in a honey pot,' he said finally.

'There we are. Honey pot. Making love is a bit old fashioned isn't it though?'

'Yes, but it struck me while we were doing it,' the phrase again, 'that making love was not just the right phrase but actually accurate.'

'What do you mean?'

'I felt as though we were making love, not bonking or whatever. It all seemed much more real and significant than ever before.'

'Oh Ralph, what a lovely thing to say to me.' She felt very flattered and was genuinely touched. 'And that is exactly what we'll call it. I hate all the other words anyway.'

He had been outwitted and wrong-footed and believed it would show a prurient interest to pursue the question of what terminology she used.

She clung to him for a moment and he had the impression she was thinking of leaving.

'What would you like to do?' he asked.

'Stay with you in this room forever. Just us. As we are. No one else,' she sighed:

'But...'

'You don't have to go back yet do you?'

'Oh no,' she said. 'We've got plenty of time.' He felt the words had been underlined in some way.

'Then let's go out,' he suggested.

'Lovely idea. Where?' Again he had to think quickly. Locally was out of the question as undoubtedly they would hold hands; he wasn't going to be able to resist any tactile temptations and did not want to be seen. He looked at his watch again. Half past ten. Two hours' drive would take them practically anywhere. He was afraid of not being able to spend the entire day with her and wanted to find something to amuse them both.

'An art gallery,' he suggested, thinking of a city about an hour away.

'That would be lovely. And perhaps lunch?'

They got into her car, he thought to leave hers outside his

house all day might invite suspicion, and he drove, although she said she would have preferred to, but she stopped complaining when he rested his hand on her upper thigh. They had lunch in Chinatown, a large steamy restaurant full of Chinese people. They ordered dishes together and shared the food, the plates and the chopsticks. They sat close together and Ralph kept on thinking, simple-mindedly, that he had never felt as felt as happy or sexually contented. He watched her and thought again how lovely she was.

'What are you thinking about?'

'I'm happy,' he said.

'So am I. Very.'

After lunch he they went to the Art Gallery, where they spent a long time holding hands, looking at the Pre-Raphaelite collection.

'Most of us come to like art through these pictures.'

'How so?'

'Such popular images. Used everywhere for everything.' It had not occurred to her but he was right. She had been given a book about the Brotherhood when younger, had looked hard at the reproductions and very shortly afterwards bought a book on Monet and thus developed an interest in art generally. They had coffee in the rather unattractive museum cafe and then walked, hand in hand, to her car.

Ralph was aware that the afternoon was drawing to a close and that soon she would have to leave him. Could the day ever be repeated? Virginia was unlikely to go away again soon, although it was not clear how long she was going to be away, and it was Monday tomorrow and he and Tina would both be working. Oh Christ. He remembered the Rose case and that it needed several hours more preparation. In his total pleasure at seeing Tina, the sex, the lunch and her company he had forgotten what was, in truth, one of the most important cases he had ever taken to trial. It involved a novel, but important, point of law of general relevance and he had wanted to be the man who had established the ruling. He felt utterly torn.

'I suppose we should be getting back,' he said.

'Yes, let's go back to your house now,' she agreed.

This time she made no objection when he suggested he drive again and he negotiated the roads that made the city such an unpleasant place with, she commented, great facility. He pulled up outside his house. 'Would you like to come in?'

'Of course,' she smiled. They went into the sitting room.

'Music? Help yourself.' He had noticed the answer machine blinking in the hallway and then, deciding that it would probably be Virginia, was about to listen when it occurred to him that the very last voice either he or probably Tina would want to hear was that one. He could get back to her later after Tina had gone. He would claim that he had been working in his Chambers because he needed the library facilities there. Tina had gone over to his CD collection, housed in a low cupboard.

'You've got so many. And they're in alphabetical order. It's incredible.' She chose a Beethoven sonata and put the record on. Ralph watched her, she moved with a feminine grace that invited sexual attention. He, and this urge worried him, wanted her again, wanted her nakedness, warmth, stickiness, gasps, her eyes widening, and his orgasm inside her.

'Tina, when do you have to get back?'

She blinked, looking surprised. 'I don't have to get back. I've left him. Didn't I tell you earlier?'

Ralph knew she had not. It was as though someone had just physically hit him, very hard. 'What do you mean?' He almost gulped.

'I've left him. I'm not going back. I told him this morning. I've got a suitcase in the car. I'll sort other things out later. I've told him I want a divorce, a fast one. I never want to see him again. I've had enough.'

Ralph looked at her nervously. 'Did you say why you'd left him?'

'Yes. I told him.'

Ralph sat down and put his head in his hands, trying desperately to collect his thoughts. 'Where are you going to stay?'

She smiled at him. 'What about here tonight?'

His immediate reaction was one of sexual anticipation and he obeyed this first instinct. 'Yes, of course. How lovely.' Then he sat silently for a moment, gathering his thoughts. Virginia was not coming back till the morning at the earliest, Tina's car would be parked outside all night but it was not visible from the road and he was not expecting any callers or visitors that evening. She could slip off in the morning. 'What did he say?'

'He was shell shocked. Couldn't believe it. I left him sitting there like a goldfish, mouth opening and shutting. A bit sad really.'

A bit sad. He wondered if that was all she could find to say about the end of a marriage. Her marriage was presumably over. Or was she one of these women, hysterical and histrionic, who serially walked out, drama queens, only to go back days or even sometimes hours later?

'What are you thinking?' she asked looking anxious.

'Of course you can stay tonight,' and worried that he might

have over emphasised the last word, 'I'd love you to but,' a rising tide of panic, 'I've got some work to do for tomorrow.'

'There's something more interesting to do than work, isn't there?'

He considered this quickly; if they did it now, he could work later. If they did it later, he would not work now.

'Would you like a drink?'

'Oh yes please.'

'What would you like?'

'Should we celebrate?'

Celebrate what, he wondered with a kind of grim realisation but looked quizzical.

'Celebrate being together,' she added.

'What a lovely idea,' Ralph smiled in what he considered an appropriate way and went to the dining room and then into the cellar. He selected a bottle of champagne, one of the very last left from his wedding all those years earlier. Last time he and Virginia had had one, their previous wedding anniversary, it was still delicious although the taste had paled with the passage of time. He decided he could not face enquiries from Tina and picked instead a non-vintage throwing champagne, as he thought of it, and went back to the sitting room. Tina was lying on the sofa, curled like a cat, shortish skirt just revealing her stocking tops. He sat beside her and smiled.

'I got the glasses,' she said.

She had already, only the day before, memorised the kitchen layout and could move around the room as freely and efficiently as Virginia or Ralph. Tina was not sure at this point what was going to happen to her. She had told St John she was leaving and she did mean it. She had said it before to him, and meant it then as well, but had never seen it through. But never before had she had a Ralph to whom she could go and cling, for at least the beginning, and whose existence and what they had done together, also made it easier for her to confront a future without St John. He had been gobsmacked. Opening and shutting his mouth like a goldfish. She had wanted to hit him. To shake him out of his complacency. When she had first told him on Sunday morning that she was going, he ignored her. When she became insistent, he merely replied, 'I've heard it all before.' When she got annoyed at his refusal to believe that she meant it this time, she said, with a calculated fury, 'I've got another man.' That was when he sat down and started opening and shutting his mouth.

'Who? Who, in God's name?' She did not want to tell him and regretted actually having said anything.

'I'm not saying,' and walked into the hallway, picked up a suitcase and left. When she arrived at Ralph's house she felt nervous and diffident. Of course, she knew that Virginia was not there, but Tina felt that she could not guarantee that Ralph would take her in, even for at least the first night. She wanted to be held and feel protected, was sure she would be made welcome to the extent of some sex, and that she anticipated with pleasure, indeed had got wet while driving thinking of it. When he opened the door and his polite indifference changed to, she thought, a look of joy when he saw her, she could have cried with relief. The rest of the day had been, for her, wonderful. She had loved the restaurant, the fond holding of hands in the art gallery, the companionable way in which he talked, his extensive knowledge of art about which he was quite diffident, his breadth of interests and now, sitting drinking champagne with him, she felt, as far as she could, happy.

'Sante,' he said.

'To us,' she said. He had lit an already laid fire and they sat together, his arm round her, sipping their glasses, not talking, looking at one another and from time to time lightly kissing. The bottle nearly finished, Ralph had been careful to put more into Tina's glass than his own, he turned to her, kissed her and ran his hand up her leg. She moved her knees apart and he stroked her upper thigh and felt her through her knickers.

'Should we go up?' he whispered as he nibbled her ear.

'Yes, please,' and she stood, held out her hand and led the way to the spare room. As they went through the hall, Ralph noticed the answer machine again and said to Tina, 'I'll just get the bottle and follow you up.'

She nodded and continued upstairs. He went back to the sitting room and quickly dialled Virginia's parents' number. Virginia answered. 'I left a message for you.'

'I know,' he said. He did not, but had guessed correctly. However, he had no idea what the message contained and also wanted to get off the phone quickly. He searched for an anodyne remark that would be consistent with whatever the message said were her mother improved, deteriorating or dead, 'How's your father?' he asked, quite pleased with this on the spur of the moment. 'How's he coping?'

'Oh, he's all right, he's desperately worried about her though.' So she was still alive.

'She came out of the coma after I called you. She's going to be in hospital for another few days. I'm going to stay until she comes out. Probably Wednesday. Is that all right?'

Phew. He wanted to mop his brow. 'Of course. Give them

both my love. How are you?'

'Missing you dreadfully Ralph. If it weren't for that case you could be with me. How's the work gone?'

'Terrific,' he said thinking that he had never, in his professional career, put less work in on a case than this important one. 'I've got on well. I went to Chambers, the library.'

'Oh, that's why you weren't in when I called. I wondered. Are you all right otherwise?'

'Yes. I am. I've been a bit preoccupied with things today.'

'I understand. Call me tomorrow. Daddy wants me so I'd better go. Miss you Ralph. I miss you inside me. Love you.'

'Love you,' he replied mechanically, put the phone down, picked up the bottle and glasses and went upstairs.

Tina was lying on the bed, dressed only in the black stockings and underwear, provocative and alluring. The light from a bedside lamp accentuated her beauty and she, if photographed as she was, would have been among the best in, he thought, any of the porn magazines he had bought only yesterday. He lay down on the bed beside her. She lay there. She did not move. He thought she might want to undress him, or at least unzip him or at the very least unbutton his shirt but he accepted that he was going to have to take the initiative and so undressed fully.

Again, he felt as though his intellect was submerged into a sensuality and intimacy that existed beyond himself. He had always liked sex but in the past his mind would remain disengaged, often miles away, preoccupied with cases, books, people, things. He had never before drifted languidly, emptily and erotically across the landscape of total sexual arousal and involvement. He abandoned himself to this and finally, when he came, looked at her and said, 'Tina, I love you.'

'I know. And I love you,' she replied, kissing him again.

She did not want another glass afterwards and lay, smiling, under the sheets. He lay beside her just looking and sipping thoughtfully. He noticed that her breathing was soft and steady. She had fallen asleep. He stayed on his back, arm around her, encircling, even clutching, until he too fell into a completely dreamless sleep.

When he woke it was morning. He felt beside him for Virginia, an automatic reaction. The bed was empty and he remembered, with a jolt, the previous day and night. Where was Tina? It was only then that he remembered the trial that was to start today, and it was then that his insides felt as though they had turned to water. He looked at his watch. 7 am. Trial in the High Court listed for 10.30. Oh God. At that moment Tina walked in. She had a tray in her hands. She had found oranges, squeezed them, found croissants, warmed them, put out jam and butter and made a cafetiere of coffee.

'Morning,' she said. She had his dressing gown on which she undid, revealing that she was naked. 'I've had a quick bath. I hope you don't mind. Here's breakfast,' she added superfluously.

'Lovely.' She took the dressing gown off and got into bed with him, totally unselfconsciously he noticed, and they ate together.

'Mm, that was nice,' she said, licking some jam from her finger. 'Better get on - we've got work to do.' She was matter of fact and business like. He felt an immediate regret, a pang. His preference was to stay in bed with her. He pulled her towards him. Ten minutes was not going to make any difference to the inadequacy of the way he would argue his case.

She responded immediately and, despite his anxiety and dread of what the day had in store, he lost himself in his physical passion.

'Mmm. That was a nice start.' She kissed him, got out of bed and walked across the room to a suitcase.

'When did you get that in?' he asked, puzzled that he could

not remember.

'While the kettle was boiling.'

'What, in that?' He nodded at the dressing gown.

'Yes, why not?'

Why not, a number of reasons but, 'Oh nothing,' he said dismissing the thoughts. She was dressing now, a dark business suit, pulling tights on and adjusting her clothes, looking at herself in the mirror. He got up and went over to her and said, 'Do you want to stay tonight? She's not coming back till Wednesday.'

'Of course I do. Of course I will.' She was delighted. 'I was thinking I'd go to my parents. I haven't told them yet but I don't think it'll be a surprise to them. But a bit of a shock to have me back nevertheless. Probably.'

'What will you do after that?'

'Find a little flat somewhere. Possibly near to work. I'll be a bit hard up but it doesn't matter. I'll survive. I've really got to go now.'

'Wait.' She stopped. 'Would you like me to drive you in? It's not far out of my way.' He did not want to lose her. 'I could pick you up later. After work.'

'OK,' she said simply. 'Should we take your or my car?'

'Yours,' he said quickly. He could park in a different multi-storey and thus avoid seeing anyone he knew and complicated explanations. He dropped her outside the shop. They had not spoken much. He had held her hand whenever he could and when they arrived, parking a hundred yards away, he wanted to kiss her but she stopped him.

'No. People might see. I want to. I will later,' and got out and started walking away. As she turned the corner, she stopped and waved. A man came up to her. Tall and fair, he looked the kind who probably worked out in a gym. Very short hair. Muscular. Not the kind of person Ralph felt drawn to, but he saw Tina and the man exchange what looked like greetings and they walked together out of Ralph's sight. He wondered idly who it was, let in the clutch, drove to an anonymous car park and walked to his Chambers. He felt elated, exhausted, exhilarated and sensual on the one hand but on the other, abject, embarrassed and faintly disgusted with himself.

Sir Geoffrey was in the Clerk's room. 'Good morning Ralph. I thought I might totter down to Court and listen to your opening speech this morning. Feeling lucky?'

'Not particularly,' Ralph said.

Most men would have envied his weekend and, looking back on it, Ralph thought it had been one of the best in his life. He had got exactly what he wanted. Four times already and again tonight. However, he had to get through the day first. He went into his room and stared for a moment out of the window. He remembered that Rumpole had once, in a particularly difficult courtroom situation, faked a heart attack. He dismissed that option. He could hardly try and settle the case with the other side after the bullish opinions as to success he had given. There was nothing for it but to rely on his native wit, albeit he lacked confidence that it could be successful.

He went to the Court and entered the robing room which was empty, except for the barrister who represented the opposing party.

'Good morning, Tim,' said Ralph.

'Morning Ralph. How's things?'

'Terrific. How are your clients? Nervous or just terrified?'

'Haven't seen them yet,' Tim replied. His clients were an insurance company who would be represented by two or three faceless suits. 'How about yours?'

'I'm going to find them now.' No talk of settlement, no way out, no easy option, nothing for it. The other barrister left and Ralph looked at himself in the mirror, tipping the wig just enough to give a raffish touch to his appearance, before picking up his papers. He found his instructing solicitor with his client. Ralph gave no appearance of nerves or any hint of apprehension, but exuded a kind of measured confidence that clients always found reassuring. They discussed the case in general terms. Ralph suddenly felt the urge to go to the lavatory. Fear washed over and through him and he then realised he was frankly scared witless that he would look a complete fool. He had completely forgotten Tina and Virginia. The various people involved in the case waited around, in groups and huddles, for the usher to call out and announce that the judge had arrived and that they should assemble in Court. Ralph looked at his watch for the umpteenth time. The case was listed for 10.30 and it was now 10.45. He wondered why there was a delay and went into the Courtroom. The Clerk had just put down the telephone.

'Hello, Ralph,' he said. 'Bad news I'm afraid. My Lord has just been taken to hospital with suspected appendicitis. We can't go ahead today. We'd better have everybody in and tell them.'

Ralph wanted to scream with joy. Feeling lucky he had been asked. He was the luckiest man alive. Like a last-minute reprieve before a death sentence, his thanks were unbounded. He wanted to embrace the Clerk, lie on the Courtroom floor and laugh and roll around. His face however remained impassive.

'What a shame. I was really looking forward to this hearing.'

The usher had gathered everybody together and the clerk announced, in suitably bland tones, that the case would not be proceeding, no other High Court judge was available this week and therefore the case would go back into the lists to wait for another fixture which, he promised, would be within two months.

Not for the first time, Ralph considered the system one of complete lunacy. All these people, all this expense, all the wasted costs. All because the system was designed and still is administered for the convenience of judges. Today however, he was grateful for this. In an efficiently ordered legal system, there would have been another judge to stand in and he, Ralph, would have stood exposed and certainly looking utterly stupid and incompetent.

They left the Courtroom, the insurance clients muttering darkly. Ralph explained the situation to his clients and apologised for the law's delays.

Sir Geoffrey came up to him, clapped him on the shoulders and said, 'Great shame. Never mind.'

Ralph gave the impression of disappointment but thinking that perhaps there was a merciful God after all; but then why would a merciful God let such a sinner as himself off the hook so lightly?

Back in his Chambers, he went into his room and worked for the next six hours conscientiously, concentrating entirely on the Rose case, noting cases and citations and preparing in such a way and manner that, if the case were called tomorrow, next week or next month, he was ready. He did not stop for lunch, a junior clerk brought him sandwiches and a coffee, and finally at 5.00 pm he snapped the books shut, grinned and thought of Tina. He also thought of Virginia and decided it would be a good time to phone her. It would get the call out of the way and that way there need be no nervous anxiety if the telephone rang in the evening. He dialled and her father answered, almost barked. 'Hello.'

'Hello George, it's Ralph. I'm dreadfully sorry about Mary. How is she?'

'No change. Still in hospital.' The authoritative voice, continually used to obedience, seemed to crumple. Ralph had the impression of a man close to tears.

'Let me know if I can do anything.'

'Yes, yes. Have a word with Virginia. She's being wonderful.'

Virginia came on the line. 'Ralph, how are you? How did the case go? Are you ahead?'

He explained what had happened.

'Oh, what a shame,' she said comfortingly.

Ralph felt guilt. 'Well, it's not so bad. I still get paid. As will all the other lawyers. How's it going?'

'Nothing to report. I'm with Daddy. He's beside me in fact. I'll call you later when we can talk.'

That was not what Ralph wanted to hear. 'I said I'd go for a drink with the solicitors at six and then I thought I might have an early night.'

'You call me then. Call me later. Love you. Bye.'

Ralph hung up feeling a touch distracted and disconsolate. He was like a little boy whose toy has been taken away but, like a child, he brightened immediately at the thought of seeing (and having) Tina again. He had arranged to meet her at 6.00 pm around the corner from her shop, where he had left her that morning.

He was there, waiting, and saw her in the lamplight at the end of the street, talking to the same man he had noticed earlier. She waved a goodbye to him and turned towards her car, walking faster than before. She got in.

'Who was that?' asked Ralph as she leaned forward to kiss him.

'Mm,' she kissed him lengthily. 'Ian, my assistant manager. Nice man. Very helpful. How did your case go?'

He had suspected that she had not registered the fact of the Rose case at all. He had not mentioned it to her and could not recollect what had been said about it on, what was it, Saturday morning? Or had they talked about it over supper on Friday night or at the party? He could not remember but simply answered, 'It's been adjourned. Good thing too. You know I hadn't done any preparation to speak of.'

'I'm sure you'd have been just fine.' She settled back in her seat and asked, 'Home or what?'

'What would you like to do?'

'Have a drink, some supper, a bath and go to bed,' she promptly replied.

'Sounds very domestic.'

'It would be except I'm going to have a drink with you, eat with you, have a bath with you and then go to bed with you.'

He felt, yet once more, a twinge of sexual excitement and leaned over and kissed her again. 'That will be lovely. What would you like to eat? Indian, Chinese, fish and chips, steak? In or out? You choose.'

'We had Chinese yesterday,' she said. He had forgotten, it seemed already weeks ago to him. 'What about stopping at a Sainsbury's or Tescos and I'll nip in and see what I can find.'

'Right,' he said and soon, he having waited for her, she reappeared with a bag, the contents of which she displayed with some excitement. Poppadoms, bhajis, pakoras, tikka, bhuna, naans, it was all there. He laughed at her excitement.

'Well, it's a treat for me.'

'And for me too,' he said solemnly.

'I don't believe you,' she said with mock anger. She was right. Ralph and Virginia ate well, and a supermarket curry was not quite haute cuisine enough for them to want to eat one very often. They returned to the house where Ralph laid and lit a fire, opened another bottle of champagne, while Tina went into the kitchen. She came into the sitting room in his dressing gown.

'Are you coming for this bath then?' Ralph was taken aback. He had heard her say she was bathing with him but had not taken the suggestion literally.

'Now?'

'Yes, come on.'

Once more he followed her up. The guest bathroom was not particularly large, but she had already run the bathwater and was in before he had noticed she had removed her dressing gown. He was not sure of shared bath etiquette. It looked a bit small for both of them and certainly even Virginia had not suggested sharing or having sex in the bath. This was new to him. She was lying back and looking at him, smiling broadly.

'It's your first time isn't it?' she teased.

'Yes, I was just wondering if there is room for both of us.'

She sat up, 'Here, get in this end.' She squeezed herself in sideways. He got in and sat at the curved end.

'Cosy,' he said.

'Now I'm going to wash you' was the reply. 'Lean back,' which he did and she kneeling between his legs began to softly soap him, under the arms, across his neck and went downwards.

'It wants attention,' she said teasingly and touched it, seemingly tentatively. He suddenly wondered if she would suck him, thinking of Virginia and her enthusiastic appetite. If she did not, then perhaps she could learn. He murmured and made pleasured sounds, saying quietly, 'Go on then.'

'Go on what'.

'Lick it. I'd like that.'

She paused. She seemed to be thinking, her eyes were closed and she held it lightly between her fingers. She dropped her head and licked the tip. She then licked the length and the tip again, very slowly. Then, as though she had made a sudden decision, she put her mouth round it. He made noises to show how much he was enjoying it and said, 'Don't stop.'

She carried on for a minute, then looked up and, with it still in her mouth, mumbled, 'Enough?'

'God, it's so nice. Let's stop now.' He wanted to savour this in bed.

She looked relieved, saying, 'I thought I was going to get cramp. I've never done that before.'

At school, she had graduated to oral sex in the last term of the fifth form. The first time she had done it to a boy, he had come nearly immediately in her mouth, making her splutter and cough; she had not been expecting such a quick response. The boy had apologised and she had said, thoughtfully, 'No, it was nice. Don't worry.' She expected him to reciprocate but he had, when she started pushing his face down towards her stomach, merely rested his head on her breasts and played with her until she had her own orgasm. The turnover of relationships was not especially high but oral sex, for Tina, became routine. She had never, as two of her friends claimed to have done, practised on coke bottles trying to perfect a technique. She preferred simply to do what she felt was right, but she initially always withdrew when she felt the boy was ready, preferring to rub it with her hands and aiming the spurt back towards his face. Later however, having read that boys liked it being swallowed, she decided to keep it in her mouth and then, when the boy had finished, she would open her mouth just enough to let it all drop out, usually into the boy's navel. It never failed, the first time, to give him a shock, being so terribly unexpected. Of course, it got round that she did head, as it was called there so, once in the sixth form, she could have had a queue of boys at her study. She was able take her pick. Only later did she hear that her new nickname was Wondermouth. She shrugged that off; she was happy and secure enough for this not to bother her at all but she was still not ready for full blown sexual intercourse. She would get there in her own time, having decided that since it was to be the first, it would have to be with someone rather special and made a special occasion. The combination had not yet occurred. Had it, she thought, she would already have done it but there was time enough. Bringing herself back to the here and now, she was thinking ahead.

She had put the oven on and slipped a dressing gown on to go downstairs. Ralph went and got dried and dressed and when he came into the kitchen, she was laying the table, the food already in the oven.

'Why have you got dressed?'

'Someone might come to the door.'

'So what. You don't have to ask them in.'

'I suppose I think it a bit, sort of...' he searched for the word, 'immodest, really.'

'Don't be so silly. It's not as though you might be naked. I'm not dressing. I'm going to eat like this and then,' she looked upwards, 'we're going to have an early night.'

He enjoyed the curries. She evidently did as well, taking little mouthfuls, using the naan to transfer the sauce. As they were sitting at the table, the phone rang.

Oh God, it'll be Virginia, he thought. He was amazed at how few times he actually thought of her, and he picked it up. 'Hello.'

'Ralph, sorry to bother you. I'm phoning on the off chance. Is Tina with you? It's St John.'

He hesitated before answering, 'No, why?'

'I'm trying to find out where she is.'

'No. Sorry. Can't help you. No idea,' he replied, feeling uncomfortable.

'Thanks anyway. Goodbye.' The voice had been controlled but angry. As he put the phone down, Tina looked quizzically at him.

'Only someone trying to sell me double glazing,' he quickly explained. They finished their meal and went upstairs to the spare room. Is it a routine, he reflected? Lying in bed he said quietly, 'Why don't you carry on where you left off?' She was lying beside him and moved down to do as he suggested. He adored it but could not wait any longer, pulling her upwards, he turned her over and kissing her again, entered her, abandoning himself to the exquisite sensation, to him so unfamiliar, of submersion in something out of time and place. This time he paced himself carefully though and, when she started making the little mewing noises that were her prelude, he waited, making sure that they had a simultaneous orgasm.

'Oh God, lovely, lovely, lovely,' she murmured. She was kissing him frantically, still writhing beneath him when the phone rang again.

'I'll ignore it. Don't worry. The answer phone will deal with it.'

The phone rang several times that night but Ralph was not aware of this. He was in a dreamless sleep holding Tina closely to him. She tossed fitfully, lightly dozing, part waking when the phone rang but never quite enough to pick the receiver up.

They were woken by a banging at the front door. 'For God's sake, what's that noise?' Ralph groaned as he sat up in the bed, looking at his watch. 'It's 6.30 am.'

'Let me in. I want to speak to her,' in a shout.

'Christ, it's St John. What the hell is he doing here?' Tina muttered.

'St John? How would he know you are here?'

'I don't know. I haven't told anyone. Perhaps an inspired guess. I'd better go and see him.'

'Let me in,' and the banging on the door continued.

'No, I'll go. He's got a shotgun remember.'

'What the fuck does that mean?'

'He's got a temper, a bad temper and he owns a shotgun. That's all.'

'That's all? If that's all, you're not going either. I'll call the police.'

'No. I'll go and talk to him.' This conversation was conducted against a monotonous series of thumps on the door.

'No, Tina. I'll go.'

'Look, I know him, you don't.' She was firm.

Ralph paused. He did not, could not believe that Tina was serious. But she might be and in which event calling the police was the reasonable option. But the police would mean publicity and publicity was the last thing he wanted or needed.

'Tina, open the door with the chain. I'd rather go myself but...'

She was out of the bed, into a dressing gown and out of the door as he spoke and before he had finished the sentence. Ralph tried hard to listen. He heard angry words exchanged but it was difficult to make them out. Tina returned after five minutes or so.

'Well?'

'He's gone.'

'Did he have a shotgun?'

She shrugged. 'I didn't ask him.'

'What did he want?'

'To shout at me I guess. Get it out of his system. He was very angry. He's not angry with you, I don't think. Just me. Pride. I don't know. He called me a slut, a whore, a tart and others and worse. He recognises it's over.' She started to cry. Ralph put his arm around her and pulled her closer.

'Why are you crying?'

'I've no idea. Maybe it's the relief, maybe it's knowing I've finished with it, maybe... I don't know. Hold me Ralph.'

He did and experienced the familiar sense of arousal. He ran his hand down her back and towards more intimate areas but she pulled away.

'No, not now. I can't. I'm too upset.'

Ralph felt let down and was inclined to press, but she took his hand and kissed it.

'I'd just like to get away. I wish we could. Just you and I. It would be lovely.'

Ralph thought for a moment. 'Look, my case was scheduled for three days. It's collapsed. I've got nothing else on. Only paperwork which can wait. I could go away for tonight.' He was thinking of Virginia's return the following day but was attracted by the idea of somewhere comfortable and luxurious, a meal and sex in a big hotel bed. He had, he knew, started living dangerously. 'You could take the day off. It would have to be tomorrow as well.'

Tina said thoughtfully and being practical. 'I haven't used my holiday at all this year and I'm sure Ian could manage at short notice.'

'Why not simply phone and say you're ill?'

'It's a lie. I don't like lying.' She sounded as though she meant it, thought Ralph and decided against pressing that as well.

'I'll phone him at home quickly.' She disappeared out of the room again and Ralph wondered if she expected him to wait in bed for her or get up and dress. She returned before he had made up his mind. She seemed suddenly very cheerful. The tears had gone and she was smiling.

'Ian was very sweet about it. I said something had cropped up. No problem, he said. Get it sorted. I'll cope. So here I am. All yours for two days.' She knelt down in front of him and she put her arms round him and kissed him.

'Where do you want to take me?'

'I'd like to take you here, on this bed, now.'

'Let's save it for later. Let's go. Let's get dressed and go.'

Ralph thought for a moment and went to get a copy of a glossy magazine which had featured a particularly attractive hotel in its last issue. 'How would you like to go there?' he said pointing at a photograph of a beautifully proportioned Palladian house. 'Michelin starred restaurant - very good review.'

'It looks lovely. Where is it?'

'About two hours' drive. Be there in time for lunch. I'll phone and see if they've got rooms.'

He kissed her and went to the telephone. He saw the red light blinking and turned the volume down and listened to the message. Virginia: 'Where are you Ralph? What's wrong? Why haven't you phoned?' She sounded frightened. St John: 'Ralph. Is that slut of a wife with you? Christina, I mean. What's going on?' He sounded angry. Another one from Virginia: 'Ralph, where are you? Please phone.' St John: 'Look Ralph. I know she's with you. I've seen her car in your drive. I want a word with her. Tell her to fucking well phone me.' He sounded angrier than in the last message. Ralph dialled the hotel.

'Certainly sir, we have a deluxe suite or one of our ordinary rooms.'

The deluxe was 50% more in price and, on being reassured it was very comfortable Ralph decided that, even if it was enough to feed a family of four for a month, and far more that he had ever spent on a hotel room in the past, since it might be the only time he and Tina had the opportunity, he would go for the expensive option. He gave his credit card number and hung up. He thought about Virginia and wondered how her mother was. He was not at all sure what his feelings were for Virginia any longer. She was a good friend. In many ways his best friend. She was his lover. His confidante. Did he love her? Was what he felt for Tina love? These were two separate, discrete, totally different emotions. He liked going to bed with Virginia; he wanted, badly, to go to bed with Tina in a way, he reflected, that he had never wanted to with any other girl. He was used to Virginia. Tina was a totally unknown quantity. He felt guilty about both of them. Tina had left her husband after she had been unfaithful to him - the whole act of infidelity having taken less than ten minutes. Had those ten minutes shaped her life and destiny? She had said not. He walked into the bedroom. Tina was lying naked on the bed, legs apart, smiling.

'Take me,' she said.

So he did, and forgot Virginia immediately.

He thought of his wife again when they were en route to the hotel. He decided that he needed to talk about her message with Tina. He put his hand on her leg.

'Tina?'

'Mm?' She was looking happy and relaxed, and he reconsidered. 'What?'

'Oh, nothing,' he replied. 'I ought to stop and phone my Chambers. Should have done it this morning. Let's have a coffee and I'll call my Clerk.' At the next hotel, he pulled up and they went in.

'Two coffees please.'

'Certainly. In the drawing room there,' they were told and Tina went through. He went into the booth and called

Virginia's parent's number. Virginia answered and Ralph found, for what was about the first time in his life, that he did not know what he was going to say.

'It's Ralph. How's things?'

'Ralph, where have you been? I've been so worried. You said you were going to call me last night. What's wrong?'

He paused. What was wrong? Nothing was wrong as such. He had been with Tina.

'I was out drinking with those solicitors. Got back late. Sat down on the bed. Just about to phone you and fell asleep. Stress I guess.'

'Mummy's worse. Much worse. They think she's had a second, bigger stroke. I'm not coming back tomorrow. Can you come up here?'

'Oh no,' he started, 'what terrible news. Look, I'm on my way to Chambers. I'll see what's going on and call you later.'

'Promise?'

'Promise.'

'I love you, Ralph. This is all terrible. I feel ghastly. I miss you. Speak later,' and she hung up. Ralph called his Clerk and said that he was not going to be in today or tomorrow but would telephone the following evening.

Tina was sitting, drinking her coffee. 'Everything all right?' she asked.

'Yes, no problems.'

They talked little during the rest of the journey. Tina was quiet and looked lost in her thoughts. He concentrated on driving and, as they turned the last corner on the drive, she exclaimed, 'What a beautiful place.' It was a perfectly proportioned Georgian house with portico and columns, flights of stairs to the entrance and exquisite detailing. They went in.

'I've booked. Ralph Edwards,' and they were led to a room on the next floor.

'This is sumptuous,' Tina murmured as she looked around, sinking into a large armchair. 'I've never been anywhere so lovely. Thank you for bringing me Ralph.'

He took in the large bed, the window opposite it, the luxurious fabrics and furnishings and decided Tina was worth the expense. The porter was just about to leave when Ralph said, 'A bottle of champagne please.'

'Certainly sir, house or something special?'

Ralph knew that the something special would probably be three times the cost of the house champagne which in turn was going to be three times the cost of the same bottle from a shop. Would he seem a cheapskate if he said house? A way out presented itself. 'Two bottles of the house champagne for now, the wine list for later please.'

The porter returned within minutes with both bottles and list and Ralph gave him a tip, saying that there was no need to stay. Immediately he had left Ralph started taking the foil off and Tina prowled round the room.

She went into the bathroom and called out,' It's wonderful. Come and look.'

He followed her in with the tray. It was genuine luxury, Ralph thought. Real marble floor and tiling, down lighters, huge, at least double size Jacuzzi bath, masses of fluffy towels, soaps, unguents, bottles.

'We're going to enjoy this,' Tina laughed. 'Should we have a bath now or later?'

'Have some champagne while you decide,' he replied,

handing her a nearly full glass. He filled his and clinked it against hers.

'To us,' he said.

'To us.' They both drank, looking at one another as they stood reflected a hundred, a million times, in the mirrors that surrounded them.

'How many of us are there?' she said, apparently telepathic.

'Only the two of us here and now. But hundreds of other ones of us. It's like life. All reflections. All illusions. Only the here and now is of importance or substantial,' he replied quietly. 'And we are the here and now.' He put his glass down and took her hand.

'Tina. Come with me. It's later. We've saved it for later.'

She smiled and put her glass down beside his. She led the way to the bed.

'You surely can't manage it again so soon?'

'Oh yes, I can. It's you. The effect,' and he started unbuttoning her shirt. When he had finished, she sat on the edge of the bed, shirt undone, her eyes on him. She undid his trousers which fell to the floor. He felt her reach out and closed his eyes, once more abandoning himself to the sensation. Then, disengaging himself, he sank to his knees, pushing her backwards.

'Oh, oh, no, put it in, put it in,' she muttered, and he savoured the exquisite moment. She was moaning, her eyes partially closed, the pupils disappearing. He leaned forward to kiss her and, in doing so, came out. He was seized with a sudden, overwhelming desire to try it from behind. He made to turn her over.

'What are you doing? Why have you stopped?'

'I haven't. I'd like you to turn round.'

'What like this?' She knelt on the floor and leaned over the bed.

'Yes,' he said and guided himself in again. 'God, that's lovely.'

'It's hurting my knees. Come on. If you want to do it like that, let's get on the bed,' and she scrambled up and knelt, skirt round her waist, shirt undone, stockings still on and knickers pulled to one side. Ralph thought he had never seen, let alone experienced, such an erotic image and climbed onto the bed, taking his trousers off as he did so. She was facing the window, head lying on one side with her eyes closed. Ralph entered her again and rocked backwards and forwards. He was looking towards and out of the window very absently, enjoying the immediacy, warmth and wetness of Tina, when he noticed, above the trees, a modern looking rooftop and a large chimney, with light and occasional wisps of smoke. In an absent sort of way he wondered what it was. He then remembered seeing signs for a crematorium on the way and it struck him, with a peculiar horror, that their bedroom looked out on it. It was late morning so presumably they had fired up and he was witnessing, in the act of making love, the light industrial incineration of someone who had once lived, breathed and loved as he was doing. He shut his eyes but remained conscious of the image. Crematoria always reminded him of the Holocaust with all the utterly unimaginable ghastliness that entailed. Those millions who had perished, upon whim and caprice, because of a madman, those who too had lived and loved and done nothing to deserve their horrible fate. Ralph had always been conscious of his own mortality, had a vastly great sense of the shortness of life and faced the prospect of personal extinction, and indeed that of anyone close to him, with terror and dread.

It was then that the decision came to him. The eroticism of Tina, her appeal, her prettiness, her sense of humour. That was as much as he knew about her, but he felt it was enough. If there was such a thing as love at first sight, then this was it he decided. He thought of the building set in the woods and shrubberies and the fact that we all, he concluded, have an appointment there, or in the earth, very soon, even on the human and personal scale of measuring time. We have an obligation to ourselves, and I shall never feel that I could be as happy with Virginia as I might be with Tina, he reasoned. He had mechanically, but gently, been stimulating Tina as he had been thinking and she suddenly pulled away, rolled over and said with urgency, 'Ralph, on top, I'm coming. I want you on top.'

He acquiesced quickly and as he bent down over her, he looked once more. The chimney had seemingly stopped smoking and it was only by looking closely that one could discern only almost invisible wisps creeping, another cliché he knew, lazily into the sky. Appointment with destiny he thought as Tina cried out. 'Oh more, Ralph, more,' and he simultaneously came, closing his eyes and thinking only of her.

They then bathed together, wallowing in the bath and finishing the bottle. They talked little but Tina, catching sight of herself in the mirror and Ralph watching her, asked, 'What are you thinking about?'

'You,' he answered truthfully.

'What exactly?'

'Who are you?' He was aware that he had reached a decision but was completely unsure as to how to tell her or move anything forward.

'I'm me. Tina. The girl you've just ravished, satisfied and who is extremely, extremely happy. I've left my husband. I'm on the brink of a new life. I'm with you in a lovely hotel. I'm happy. That's who I am.'

Ralph had meant the question in a much broader sense. He wanted to know all about her. He was on the point of committing himself, throwing away an old life, including Virginia, and needed to know more. 'I really wanted to know more about you, your background, your likes, your dislikes, your fears, your happiness. Everything about you. I want to understand you.'

'All I've ever wanted is someone like you.'

'What do you mean?' Ralph felt flattered.

'Someone who wanted to bathe with me, who took the trouble to satisfy me sexually, who looks at me the way you do. Who strokes and touches me and says nice things. Who cares and wants me.' She smiled. 'Thank you.'

'Tina,' he started and found himself once again grasping for familiar words to explain an unfamiliar position.

'What?'

'I'm happy too. There's nowhere I'd rather be and there's nobody I'd rather be with than you. Are you hungry? It's past lunchtime. Should we get some sandwiches sent up?'

'What a lovely idea.' She paused, 'Have you seen a room service menu?'

'No, I'll just phone down. Any preference? Smoked salmon, egg, ham?'

'I love smoked salmon.'

He got out of the bath, kissing her as he did so, and stepped down, put on a dressing gown and went into the bedroom. She heard him order sandwiches and reserve a table in the restaurant at 8.00 pm. He came back and stood looking at her again as she lay full length in the bathtub.

'Do you know, I don't think I've ever met someone as unselfconscious as you are,' he said thoughtfully. 'It's, well maybe, immodest.'

'That's a funny thing to say. I'm with you. It's natural. It feels right.' She got out stretching, cat-like he thought, and put on a dressing gown as well. He had shut the curtains, deciding as he did so that they would remain shut until they left, to block out the image, and had switched on the side and table lamps. Tina started to arrange her clothes in the wardrobe and was happily choosing something to wear for the evening. There was a knock, a pause and the porter entered with their order, placing it on a side table, waited for a tip which Ralph duly paid and left. They ate slowly and talked lightly, of nothing in particular and perhaps nothing at all.

Neither was able to remember, later, how the afternoon had become evening and by 8.00 pm they were both quite tipsy, laughing at silly little jokes and inconsequential puns. They went downstairs holding hands and were taken to a table, where they sat side by side. The meal justified the Michelin stars and by the time Tina pushed away her main course, quite a lot uneaten, they had drunk another bottle, this time of Chablis, and Ralph was thinking of ordering a pudding wine. Their waiter appeared beside him and put down two glasses of port.

'With the compliments of the house to the newlyweds,' he murmured before apparently simply disappearing as unobtrusively as he had arrived.

'The newlyweds,' spluttered Ralph laughing. 'Is that the impression we give?'

'Well, I suppose we did disappear to our room and stay there all afternoon drinking champagne and then the porter came in... well... the bed was crumpled and there were towels everywhere, curtains shut although it was still daylight and...'

'No, no stop. It's nice. It's flattering.' He sipped from the glass. 'It's a very good port.' He knew enough to make that judgment but not enough to get the make or year.

'It's nicer being thought of as newlyweds than as another couple on a dirty weekend,' she said, looking suddenly dejected.

'It's not the weekend.'

'You know what I mean. They think we're married rather than on a dirty overnight.'

'It's not a dirty overnight stay.'

'How do I know that?'

'Because I'm not like that,' he said with a flash of temper that he managed to conceal. It had occurred to him she might be, but he dismissed the thought.

'Pudding, or cheese,' he asked instead of saying what he actually would have preferred.

'A little bit of cheese, but really I'm full. I can't finish the, what was it, *poulet de Bresse dans sa sauce jaune*.'

'You have a very nice French accent. Do you speak it?'

'Did it at A Level and went on an exchange when I was in the lower sixth. Don't use it much now though.'

'Cheese then?'

'A little bit.' He ordered cheese for one, which arrived already cut, nine unusual little segments which the waiter identified, and they shared together. Finishing the port, Ralph raised his eyebrows and looked upwards.

'Yes,' she yawned. 'I'm ready. I've had the nicest day of my life. Let's go up.' She got up, stumbled, recovered and he stood up, put his arm round her and they left, clinging to one another like survivors after a shipwreck. Upstairs, she let her clothes fall to the floor, came to him, put her arms round his neck and, kissing him, said,' Thank you. I shall always remember today.' Climbing into bed, she yawned and snuggled into the pillows, pulling the duvet up around her. Ralph noticed the bed had been remade in their absence. He washed, cleaned his teeth and then got into bed beside her.

'Tina?' he asked quietly. There was no answer. She lay on her side facing away from him. He lifted himself up and leaned over her. 'Tina.'

'Mm,' she responded.

'Thank you too,' and he put his arm around her, pulling her back towards him so that her bottom nestled against the top of his legs, and she was enfolded protectively into a near-foetal position. He, despite being drunk, took a long time to go to sleep. He was just drifting off when he remembered Virginia and he came back to consciousness with a horrible jolt. He knew that he should have telephoned. She would have left messages at home. He now also knew that he had decided to leave her. The fact of articulating the decision, which until then had been unformed and inarticulate, made him feel cold.

I have decided to leave Virginia? Why? She's done nothing to me, nothing at all. But I've decided to leave her. She'll survive. She'll be upset. Very upset. I can't rationalise this to myself. How on earth am I going to rationalise it to her? I can't tell her there's another woman. The affair, if it is an affair, has only been one of three days. That's hardly an affair. He thought back. Yes, it is an affair. And it is because of Tina I'm leaving.

If Tina had not been there, I would be in Yorkshire now with Virginia. Why am I leaving her? It means penury, not penury exactly but my earnings only.

It was after an hour of confused thinking that he then arrived at the perception that he would leave Virginia whether he lived with Tina or not. The act of betrayal had crystallised many doubts about his marriage and his life. He knew, with a certainty that would not have gone in the morning, that his marriage was over, that he had to tell Virginia, but whether he told her before or after he told Tina he did not yet feel sure, that he would ask Tina if she would live with him and that undoubtedly life was going to be so wholly different he could not, in his words, legislate for everything. With that thought, and the knowledge that all control was slowly but seamlessly slipping away from him, he fell asleep.

Tina woke the next morning still in his arms. She did not seem to have moved in the night. She felt Ralph entering her, very gently and let him, pretending not to have woken. Once inside her, he just lay there, holding her. He said nothing, did not move, just lay there. She liked the sensation of being filled up, comfortably, and found his physical desire for her, he must already have been aroused she thought, strangely reassuring. She wanted him but had not told him so. In fact, all she wanted was to live with him, anywhere, even a little flat would do.

She had enjoyed the previous day. She found it odd that Ralph was seemingly so untroubled by his mother-in-law's illness or the case and the ease with which he seemed to cast thoughts of Virginia to one side. Still, she reflected, she had not thought of St John once since he had turned on his heel outside Ralph's house yesterday morning, saying she was a dirty little slut and that anyone was welcome to her cunt because he had finished with it. She was tired of the crudity, the drunkenness and the arguments and reasoned that Ralph was not crude, was a bit drunk last night but was still pleasant and witty, and he seemed a rational easy-going person. She wondered if she could commit to him. She felt she could if he would. Could he leave Virginia? Would he leave Virginia? She had no idea and had no idea how to broach the subject that had been absorbing her since she and Ralph had first made love. She felt ready to let him know that she was awake and reached down between her legs and held him.

'Morning willy, how's things?'

'You're awake. I thought you were still asleep,' Ralph said.

'I am. I was.' She pulled away from him. 'Let's have some breakfast. I'm starving. Do you want to one, have yet another orgasm now and then go for breakfast or two. Ditto but order breakfast to be served here or three, have breakfast and then do it or, four as I'm getting to understand you, one now, breakfast and another later.' She smiled as she said it and Ralph was unsure how to respond. It all seemed put rather baldly and he was not sure he really quite liked the idea of sex on a menu.

'What would you like to do?' He smiled at her as he gave what seemed a safe response.

'I'd like to a) have a pee, b) order breakfast up here and c) do it once more in this lovely room in this lovely hotel but slowly and leisurely and without worrying about knocks on the door. How about that?'

'Good thinking Dr Watson. What do you want? Full English, small continental, mixture of each or something completely different?' Ralph reflected on her matter of factness. Virginia was matter of fact but in a more medical way. Neither woman was coy. What was the difference between them? Each was attractive, each was intelligent, one was more successful professionally, Ralph thought he was mature enough for that to be irrelevant, but he firmly, firmly believed that he wanted to cast one aside for the other.

'I'd like coffee, a bacon sandwich, one croissant and you in that order, thank you.'

'I'll organise it now.' As he picked up the telephone and ordered she got up, moved towards the window and was just about the open the curtains when he cried out,' No'. She, startled, looked at him. He was determined not to have what he considered the horrific image reinforced again.

'No, let's keep it lamplit. It's much more romantic,' he explained. He was not ready to tell her of the previous afternoon's sight and how it had suddenly pushed him into the decision.

'That's nice,' she said and sat on the bed for a few minutes kissing him and stroking his shoulder. She then went into the bathroom and leaving the door open as she ran a bath. There was a knock at the door and as Ralph said, 'Come in,' Tina began a noisy pee. The porter affected not to notice as he put down the tray on the same side table. The noise stopped as the porter left the room. Ralph felt unaccountably embarrassed, but Tina seemed so oblivious to any apparent indiscretion that Ralph said nothing. They ate their breakfast sitting in bed, rather than at the table.

'God, what a lot of crumbs croissants produce,' said Tina looking faintly appalled.

'Never mind. The room gets cleaned as thoroughly in a place

like this if it's dirty, filthy or clean,' he replied finishing his coffee.

'What was the last item on the menu?'

'You,' she said, reaching for him and pulling him on top of her.

They left the hotel hand in hand. Ralph had been completely taken aback at the size of the bill but had produced a credit card, with what he hoped had been a debonair grace, and signed the slip without showing his internal wincing and grimace. The most expensive night he had ever spent with a woman, but worth every penny was his considered judgment.

As they drove back towards his house, Ralph was contemplating his next step. Undoubtedly there would be messages from Virginia; he was altogether uncertain as to how to deal with those or indeed Virginia herself. He had made a decision, he suspected that he had made it earlier than in fact it came to him as a decision, but whenever, Ralph felt that the decision was final. However, Virginia was a rational woman and would demand an explanation and, Ralph believed, in fairness she was entitled to one. The major problem was that Ralph could find no explanation within himself that satisfied his logical and deductive approach and without that, he knew, there could be nothing that would satisfy Virginia. She was probably returning tomorrow he remembered, so whilst he could fob her off on the telephone, he had nearly a day to arrive at a view. He was sure, given his natural ability, that something would present itself.

'You're very quiet,' Tina said, reaching over and putting her hand on him.

'I was thinking about you.'

'In what way?'

'I like being with you.'

'I like being with you.'

'What are we going to do about it?'

'Which "it" do you mean?' Tina said with a shy smile.

'The "it" of liking being together.'

'Well, I've left St John.' Ralph was irritated to find himself annoyed by the sound of her husband's name. 'You're married to Virginia, it's you that causes the problem.' Tina felt bold enough to make this next move.

'I know,' he looked at her thoughtfully. 'But if I weren't married to Virginia, what then?'

'We couldn't have met. We wouldn't have met it I hadn't been married to St John either.'

'I take the point. But if I weren't married to Virginia now and we had met. What then? What would you want or do then?' He squeezed her hand.

'I think I'd like us to be together,' she whispered.

'I think I would too,' he replied, still not wanting to commit himself but feeling this was unfair on Tina. 'Look, what are you going to do about somewhere to live? You can stay with me tonight but what about after that? Where will you go?'

'I can always go to my parents, but I still think the flat idea is best.'

'Then instead of going home now, why don't we go and flat hunt for you?' Ralph had made another decision. He could help her find a flat, pay the first month's rent himself and this might be the way in which he could force everything forwards. Tina looked enthusiastic. She had been sitting anxiously wondering what next and her next, she decided must be whether he was going to drop her off, and then that was it, or was there something afterwards and what would that something be, if there was to be something. She was confused, exhilarated and rather frightened at the enormity of her decision.

'How shall we do it?'

'Decide whereabouts you want to live and we'll go to an agency in the city.'

Tina considered this for a moment and then named two or three districts in the vicinity of where she worked.

'Right,' said Ralph, looking for the motorway junction that best suited that course of action rather than the way home.

The agency had a choice. They were very helpful, and Ralph was able to talk the manager into allowing them to view the vacant flats unaccompanied. The first one they looked at was clean, modern, comfortable and totally anonymous.

'It couldn't be more different from your house,' Tina said. She was wondering if Ralph was going to spend more than just the occasional hour here. If he had been picking something he was going to live in, she reasoned, he would surely choose something with at least some character.

'No, it couldn't,' Ralph smiled, 'but on the other hand, it's convenient, clean and available today. The furniture is not too horrendous. I've looked in the oven, that's spotless. The bathroom smells pleasant. The view is awful but there are curtains which can close. What do you think?'

Tina thought, he's right. It will do. It's a start and gives me a base. 'Yes, I'll take it. Let's go back and see when I can move in.' She could move in today if she wanted to the manager told her. Ralph asked for a copy of the lease, read it through, pronounced it satisfactory and turned to Tina saying, 'Six-month tenancy in the first instance. One month's rent as a deposit and one month in advance. Rent perhaps a bit on the high side but otherwise the lease is unremarkable. Do you want it?' Tina felt she was on the point of losing an element of control in her life at a time when she had, she believed, asserted this but nodded.

'I haven't got enough in my account to cover it. I'll have to come back.'

'Not a problem,' Ralph said and asked the manager if he would accept payment by credit card.

'Certainly sir,' and Ralph again produced the same card with which he had paid that morning and handed it over with a prayer that the payment would be contained within his limit. The manager phoned for authorisation and Ralph had an agonising moment when he thought that he was about to be refused but everything was approved. Those formalities over, the manager completed the terms of the lease, inserting Tina's name her old address and then turned and said, 'I can give you the keys as soon as I have a reference. Can you fax me one?'

'What kind of reference?'

'Just from someone, bank manager, solicitor, accountant, vouching for your integrity and honesty.'

'Would a barrister do?' asked Tina smiling at Ralph.

'Certainly, on headed notepaper.'

Tina turned to leave the office, saying, 'I'll pick up the keys tomorrow lunchtime if I may. You'll have a reference tomorrow morning.' Ralph followed in her wake.

'Ralph, I'll pay you back. Don't worry. This month's salary went on the mortgage but I'm paid in a fortnight.'

'No, I don't want paying back.'

'Don't be ridiculous. I can't accept...'

'Look. Pay me back if you want to. If you need to. But only

when you can and it doesn't cause hardship. All right. I can live without it.'

Tina accepted, perhaps a little ungraciously, but acknowledging she had no option. She could borrow the money from her parents, but her preference was not to do this. On the other hand, she thought, whilst Ralph must be enormously wealthy, having paid the hotel bill without any discomposure and likewise two month's rent without hesitating, she wasn't prepared to have him make that kind of gift. She would feel bought and perhaps even cheapened were she to allow it.

'Is that all right?' she asked, looking at him. 'I'll pay you back later. It's very, very kind of you.' Tina was not aware of Ralph's earlier agenda and which he was now revisiting and filling up with options and anticipated outcomes.

'Of course. Do you want to eat anything? We seem to have missed lunch today altogether. It's getting on for teatime. Should we go home?'

'Where's home?' asked Tina.

'Well, my house today and then perhaps the flat as of tomorrow. How about that?'

Tina grinned. 'Yes, what about supper?'

Ralph was brought to reality by the comment. It was only three nights ago that they had had that first Indian warmed up instant thing. Perhaps it was only two nights ago? It seemed a lifetime away. As did Virginia, and that was a sudden urgent and unpleasant pressure. He had to get back and talk to her. He had failed to phone her last night or at all today. He wanted to phone her but also felt sick with anticipation and with, what actually felt visceral, fear.

His house looked undisturbed. Tina's car was where they had

left it. All the windows of the house were closed. His neurotic supernatural anxiety that St John and Virginia were sitting there waiting to confront them slipped away as he opened the door. The light on the answering machine was blinking. He decided to try and listen without Tina but she went to it and said, 'You'd better do this hadn't you?' and pressed the replay button.

Virginia's voice filled the hallway. 'Ralph.' She was sobbing. 'Mummy died half an hour ago. Ring at once. Soonest please. I'm too upset to talk.' He looked at the time of the message. It was late last night. He glanced at Tina. Her eyes were shut and she had gone pale. A couple of clicks then Virginia's voice again. She sounded upset and angry, 'Ralph where are you? I've tried your Chambers. They say they haven't seen you since Monday. What's going on? Ring me. Mummy's dead. I need you. I need you Ralph,' and she started sobbing before hanging up. He looked at the time again. Early this morning. There were no other messages.

'Christ, oh Christ, Oh God,' Ralph said. 'I could have done without this.'

Tina looked at him. 'So, I bet, could Virginia. What are you going to do?'

'I don't know. I just don't know. Do you know? I have no bloody idea.' He sat down in a seventeenth century wainscot chair and Tina went over to him. She stroked his hair. The moment was somehow pivotal, but she could not appreciate the reasons for this. Ralph was unutterably torn between phoning Virginia immediately, still not sure how to deal with her, he was nevertheless a humane person, or instead switching off to the horrible reality, closing the door literally and going to the bedroom where he had intended to spend the night with

Tina. He knew he should telephone but knew also that he was unable to face this. He looked up at her. 'What do you think I should do?'

'I think you should go up there. I want you here with me. I want you so much it's untrue. But you should go.'

'Why?'

'It's your mother-in-law.'

'It was my mother-in-law.'

'Don't be pedantic. You're married to her daughter.'

'But I'm not going to be for much longer.'

'What on earth do you mean?' Tina looked wide eyed at him.

'I think I'm going to leave her. A separation. I've been trying to decide how to tell her. I don't know how to. And now this.' He looked up at her again, he was abject, practically pleading.

'You can't not go up. You can't tell her now. It's not fair.'

'Then what on earth do I do?'

'You go up and then come back again. She either stays up there or comes back with you. Then you separate. Properly. Kindly.'

Tina's heart was beating quickly. She wanted to leap in the air with joy when he announced his intention to separate. She was more than ready to try and make a relationship with Ralph work. She felt herself in love and was enjoying the sensation. She knew she was adopting a high-risk strategy. If Ralph went up to Yorkshire and to Virginia, it was feasible, perhaps even probable, that he would stay with her and just write off this experience of her as a pleasant sexual conquest. If he did, Tina knew that she could cause trouble for Ralph with Virginia. After all, St John knew that she had left him for Ralph, and so St John's friends would know and that would in turn spread to Ralph and Virginia's circle. Even if Tina kept quiet, Virginia would hear about it. On the other hand, Ralph might confess his indiscretion, Tina knew the phrase was a cliche but could imagine Ralph using it, and Virginia might forgive him, absolve him even. God, they might even laugh about it together, Virginia asking, 'What was the little tart like in bed then?' and Ralph replying, 'Alright, bit quiet, not like you.' Tina had a horrible image of Ralph and Virginia having sex, could imagine Virginia on top, her large breasts swinging and long blonde hair brushing against Ralph's face, stroking it, teasingly down his body, down to his... Tina stopped. This was no way to think at the moment. She wanted to play to win him.

'When will you go?' she spoke and looked at him as though the matter was settled.

Ralph had a flash of irritation. 'I don't want to go. I told you.'

'Ralph. I love you. Go. Do the proper and right thing. Come back. I'll be here for you. Not here in this house I mean, in my flat.'

Ralph thought, her flat, my flat, my money, but was listening. Maybe he could square the circle. Maybe he could have all that he wanted. He was rather frightened of the idea of divorce and money anxieties, of which he already had many, but was especially frightened of telling Virginia that he wanted a divorce.

'I know,' he said with reluctance. 'You're probably right. I have to. If we'd separated, then it would be different. I can't just not turn up and write to her. I've been married to her too long. Do you mind if I phone her now?'

Tina shook her head and, with what Ralph realised was great consideration, went into the kitchen. He dialled. The telephone was answered, seemingly immediately, by Virginia.

'It's me, Ralph.'

'Where have you been? I've been frantic.'

'Look, I'll tell you when I see you,' Ralph was buying time. 'I'm on my way up. I'll be with you whenever the traffic allows. I'm so sorry. Truly, truly sorry.'

'Ralph?'

'Yes?'

'I love you.'

'Me too,' he answered thinking Tina might be listening and hung up quickly before Virginia started asking awkward questions. Tina had waited just inside the kitchen, wanting to listen but hoping Ralph would notice her discretion. She had heard him say that he was going up to Virginia immediately and decided to play what she thought of already as her trump card. She went to the sink, filled a kettle and put it on the Aga.

'Tea or coffee?' she asked him as he came through looking distracted.

'Coffee. I'm going up, as you said. I'll come back straight after the funeral.' Tina went up to him and kissed him.

'I know, Ralph.' She turned away, made the coffee and looking at him said, 'Let's take it to the bedroom.'

After they had made love, much more leisurely than Tina had expected this to be, she looked at him lying with his eyes closed and asked,' What are you thinking about?'

He had been thinking that Virginia would expect him to do the same to her, he supposed, even though her mother had died, perhaps especially since her mother died - they had more than once discussed the idea that lovemaking was a form of affirmation of life even if, in their case, it would never lead to procreation. He could have a shower or bath on arrival and that would rinse away any scent of Tina or smell of sex.

'Thinking about? Just you and me,' he answered with a reassuring smile. He kissed her and they finished the coffee unhurriedly. 'What are you going to do?'

'I'll stay here tonight if that's all right and I'll move my things in tomorrow. I'll go back and get whatever I need from my house - I shan't take much. Clothes, my jewellery, some ornaments. That kind of thing. Nothing large.'

Ralph had a moment's anxiety. 'Will he be there?'

'I doubt it but I don't care. When do you think you'll be back?'

'After the funeral. I guess that'll be on Friday or Saturday.'

'I've got my office party on Friday night,' Tina said as she remembered. 'I'll have to go to that. Why don't you give me a ring at work over the next couple of days?'

'What's the office party?' Ralph felt anxious again.

'Just a few drinks in the shop with the staff and then a meal at a local restaurant. Nothing fancy.'

'If I'm back, can I come?'

Tina looked at Ralph and thought he would be like a fish out of water. 'You'd hate it. It's not really for partners anyway. Duty calls and all of that. Lead from the front.'

Ralph did not feel reassured. He was already at that stage where any moment away from her was a moment regretted and the fact that it was a moment away from him, which she was sharing with others, produced a twinge of disquiet.

'You'll be there for me on Saturday though - or whenever?' he asked.

'Yes,' and she kissed him again.

He packed quickly and efficiently, taking out a dark suit and a black tie, and folding everything neatly into an expensive looking leather suitcase. When he had finished, he was not sure what to say and stood for a moment watching her. He really did not want to leave and really did not want to see Virginia, her father or dead mother ever again. It was only an old-fashioned sense of propriety that was making him do this and for once he regretted his rather strait-laced upbringing.

'I'm going, Tina. Kiss me. Wish me bon voyage. It's only au revoir.'

They clung to one another for a moment before Tina pushed him away and said, 'Go quickly. No looking back. Until I see you again. Take care, Ralph,' and kissed him on the nose. She stood at the door and watched him get into his car, start it up, drive away without a backward glance but only a wave of his hand through the open window. She turned and went in.

It took Ralph longer than he anticipated to reach the little village in the hills. He had stopped for a coffee on the way and had sprayed himself with aftershave and felt reasonably confident he did not smell of another woman. He stopped the car at the head of the village and looked down towards the green, the pub, the church and the manor house. The tranquil scene, seemingly unchanged for hundreds of years, still produced an effect in him of awe. It had impressed him the first time he had seen it; turning to Virginia he had exclaimed, 'How beautiful,' and she had acknowledged the compliment from her husband to be, who had been brought up in a dreary suburb in a dreary manufacturing town in the North Midlands, with a smile, 'Yes, it is.'

He sighed, reflecting on whether it really was to be the last time he saw the old grey buildings, drove down the street, turning into the carriage drive of her father's house and, pulling up, switched off the engine. Virginia was outside within seconds. She ran to him, put her arms round his neck and started sobbing uncontrollably. He put his arms round her waist and then stroked her back and her hair. At a loss for words he simply murmured, 'There, there.' He waited. The sobbing continued. She put her face up towards his and he kissed her lightly.

'Come on. Let's go in,' he suggested with what he hoped was a considerate squeeze of her shoulders.

'No, not yet. Daddy's in the library with the vicar and Brigadier Jones discussing the service. He'll expect you to join them. You'll be reading one of the lessons. Mummy's in the drawing room.'

'What do you mean Mummy's in the drawing room?' Ralph asked with a frisson of horror. His experience of the death of relatives was one where the body was discreetly kept in a Chapel of Rest, only to be seen by those who actually wanted to undergo what he thought was a grisly task, and then everything operated as a sanitised waste disposal, either into the earth or into the yaws of the curtained opening.

'Daddy thought Mummy would like to be at home until the funeral. I agreed with him. She would have, so we had her brought back.' Virginia said this as though only an imbecile would have asked her the question.

'Oh right. We'd better go in.'

'No, Ralph. Not yet. I want you to hold me.'

Christ, he thought, she can't want to do it outside in December with her mother lying cold and still a few yards away.

'I've missed you so Ralph. All I've wanted is to be beside you. Your warmth. Your laugh, except there hasn't been much to laugh at here over the last few days.' She remembered and looking at him said, 'Where have you been?'

'I'll tell you later,' he said, once more playing for time, and stopped her talking by kissing her with a passion that was both tender and distant. She responded with enthusiasm and started to clutch him, pushing her hips against his and, in a spirit of dispassionate scientific curiosity, he felt himself becoming aroused. He found this rather difficult to believe, but as he sensed it so did she and her breathing became more urgent.

'No, Virginia. Not now. Not here. Not in the car,' he said anticipating what he thought might be. 'Later. Someone might come out. I'm cold, so are you.'

Divert this, he thought. 'Where's the funeral?'

'Ralph. We're together again. I've missed you. Follow me. I know where we can go.'

No, no, no, he thought again. 'I can't,' he tried to say. She was leading the way to the swimming pool pavilion. The first time they had arrived together, when he was going to be introduced to her parents, she had warned him that they would be in separate bedrooms and that the only opportunity for any hanky panky would be in there. She opened the door, and by the moonlight he saw the same cloth covered chairs, towards one of which he was being firmly led. She was squirming out of her jeans, and had lowered them to her ankles, knelt on the chair and said, 'Quickly, quickly, Ralph.' With increasing arousal, he suddenly decided. What the hell. I'm not being unfaithful to Tina. We're not an item. I'm married to this woman after all. This is what she wants to do and she wants me to do it. So I shall.

It seemed only seconds later that she called out, very swiftly even for her he thought, 'Ralph, it's soon. Let's have one together.' He paused briefly and wondered whether he could but then, as though she had touched a button in him, felt himself exploding inside her as she cried out. She stopped, he withdrew, and she stood up and pulled her jeans up, doing up the buckle on the broad leather belt and kissed him, saying, 'Oh, Ralph,' and started crying again.

He put his arms round her. 'Let's go in.'

Her face was flushed and red. He thought his might be as well but a quick wash would sort that out. They went back to his car, holding hands, and then took out his suitcase before going into the house. Inside he was, as always, struck by the antiquity of the building and the beauty of the old oak furniture. There was a murmur of voices from behind one of the doors and Virginia, catching him looking towards the door, said, 'Go upstairs. We're in the Pink Room. Have a wash. I'll get you a drink. What would you like?'

'Extremely large gin I think. Very little tonic.'

She smiled wanly and went towards another door that led to the old servant's quarters. He went up, put his suitcase on a four-poster bed and ran the taps, plunging his hands and face into the water. He thought of having a shower, but decided any scent of his prior encounter would now have been dissipated by the latest, so decided not to bother. He looked at himself in the mirror, combed his hair, tried a bright smile, tried a sympathetic smile and then grimaced. As he did so, the door opened, and Virginia came in with a tray and two filled glasses. She gave him one.

'Cheers'

'Sante,' he replied. He was sure she had not seen him smiling.

'How are things, Virginia?'

'Daddy's beside himself. Doesn't know what to do or which way to turn. I've had to arrange everything.'

Ralph knew that Virginia was very capable at dealing with the aftermath of death; the relatives of patients who had died could attest to that. 'What have you arranged?'

'Funeral service the day after tomorrow followed by private cremation.'

'Why cremation? I thought she'd go in the family vault?'

'She will, or rather her ashes will. She left instructions that that was what she wanted.'

'I see.' Ralph felt an emptiness in the pit of his stomach

at the thought of the modern soulless building and suddenly remembered the view from the hotel window.

'Why are you smiling?'

'I'm not, it's a grimace really. You know how I feel about crematoria.'

'Yes, and it's stupid. It doesn't vaporise the soul.'

'Catholics used to think so.'

'Well, they don't any longer.' Virginia was a firm agnostic, maintaining that it was her business to look after the sick and the dying and if there was anything afterwards, then there was time enough to find out later.

He had finished his drink and felt ready to face his father-in-law and guests. 'Should we go down?'

'Have you eaten this evening, Ralph?'

'No not really.'

'Would you like anything?' She looked concerned and he was touched by this.

'A sandwich. I suppose you've had dinner.'

'No, only a snack. Neither of us has felt like cooking. We've lived on sandwiches the last few days.'

'Is there anything in the fridge? I'll cook,' he volunteered.

'No, it's OK. I'll get you something. Come on.'

Downstairs in the library the three elderly men sat with whiskies in their hands. They started to stand as Ralph and Virginia came through the door.

'No, stay, please. Don't get up,' Ralph said and went to his father-in-law and touched him on the shoulder. 'I'm very, very sorry.' He was thinking of Tina as he spoke rather than his mother-in-law.

'It was so sudden. There she was last week, full of life, doing everything as usual and pouf, a week later, dead.'

His father-in-law, Ralph mused, had seen very active service in the second world war, had indeed been decorated for gallantry, although this was never spoken of, so must have seen some harrowing deaths in his time. This one was different though. His father-in-law had paused. 'You know the vicar and Brigadier Jones.' Ralph had often worshipped with the family in the village church and had met the vicar and the Brigadier on many social occasions.

'Yes, of course. How are you both?' Each replied simultaneously then stopped.

'We were just talking of the service. You're down for the address.'

'Virginia said a lesson.' He felt alarm. He had never revealed, even to Virginia, what his personal opinion of her mother was, as it was anything but complimentary. To have to deliver a eulogy was an anathema.

'No, we changed our mind,' Virginia said. 'You always speak so well. I'll get you a sandwich. Would anyone else like one?'

'No, we're just going. We'll leave you good people,' the vicar said, getting to his feet.

'You know where I am if you need me.'

The three men left the room and the door had barely closed before his father-in-law returned saying, as Virginia went towards the kitchen, 'She's next door, Ralph. She looks at peace. Do you want to see her? Say a farewell?'

'I shall, but tomorrow.' Ralph had not had enough personal experience of death to feel entirely comfortable in the presence of a body. In fact, he had only seen a few in real life while at university, although many in photographs, in fatal accident cases particularly. It was odd, he thought, that someone who made a living out of morbidity and violent accidents should have had so little exposure to the real thing.

'OK then. I'm off to bed. I'll see you in the morning. God knows what we're going to do tomorrow. Everything's arranged for Friday.' He caught his breath and Ralph could see that the old man was on the verge of breaking down.

'Where are Jane and her husband?'

'They were over earlier but they've gone home. I expect you'll see them tomorrow.' Ralph had always been quite fond of his sister-in-law and her husband, who were both vets in a local practice only a fifteen minute drive up the valley from the village.

'Goodnight, my boy. Sleep well.' He shuffled towards the door, having aged ten years since Ralph had seen him last. Ralph was left alone and looked around the room. It spoke of an old family, old money, old possessions, serenity and certainty. He had felt altogether privileged to be admitted to this when he and Virginia had married but now, in mid-life, he felt that it was all nonsense. You made your own bed, literally and metaphorically, he thought. Virginia was suddenly beside him with a bottle of claret, two glasses and some sandwiches on a tray.

'Here, have something to eat.' They sat on a sofa and ate in a companionable silence, broken when Virginia asked again, 'Where have you been?' It was not said unpleasantly or suspiciously but in a simple matter of fact tone. He had prepared what he thought was a very hollow sounding explanation and had rehearsed this several times trying to make it sound convincing.

'I went walking. After the Rose case collapsed I wanted to get away. Put my thoughts in order. I felt really muddled. Perhaps the beginning of a mid-life crisis.'

'Where did you go?'

'Into Dartmoor and stayed overnight in a pub. Went walking again today.'

Virginia and he had done a fair amount of hill walking together and he was sure if she would buy into anything it might be this.

'What do you mean a mid-life crisis? What on earth have you got to feel a mid-life crisis about?'

'You've talked of male patients with them often enough. The feeling that all is for nothing. All ambition is petty. The fact that you'll never, I'll never, achieve all that I hoped for or believed I could.'

'Ralph, that's for losers. Not for people like you.' She had accepted his story, he realised, and he had to stifle what would have otherwise been an audible sigh of relief. 'Look at us. I'm doing all right. I like my job. I'm now an equal partner. The practice is growing. I'll earn more. You're successful, a successful and well-known barrister. Think of all the others who aren't. Like that one we met recently. Do you remember? St John Fortescue and his wife. He's struggling to make a name. Might never succeed. She's in a dead-end job of some kind and will probably never do anything other than have babies. We're all right. We've got a lovely house. I've got my Porsche. You've got your Bristol. We're going on holiday soon.' Her face crumpled, 'and I've lost my mother, and Daddy's lost his wife.' She looked as though she might start crying again.

Ralph was thinking of Tina and her husband. Her husband

had lost Tina now. Life was about losing people. Through one's own choice or their choice or fate or death, it mattered not. An endless series of voluntary and involuntary goodbyes.

'I know, Virginia. You've seen enough death though, so you understand something about it.'

'No matter how much you see, it doesn't take away the personal pain of losing life. Who was it, on his deathbed, said to his wife, "Life is magnificent? Or was he French and said "La vie, c'est magnifique"?'

'Not sure.'

'He was right. Life, on whatever terms, is for the most part always worth living. Do you want to see her?'

'Not really, Virginia, but if you feel I should.'

'Come on.'

She took his hand and they went into the drawing room. The curtains were closed and the coffin lay in the centre of the room, candles lit at each corner. There was a faintly unpleasant chemical smell. Ralph's nose wrinkled. Virginia noticed and said, 'Preservatives, nothing else.'

He stood for a moment before advancing and then, nerving himself, he looked at his mother-in-law's face eerily illuminated by a nearby reading lamp. Pale and waxy, she appeared in a considerably better humour than she normally displayed when he and she were in the same room. She seemed, surely it could not be the case he wondered, to be smiling.

'She looks at peace.'

'Whatever peace is,' Virginia said as she went over and stroked her mother's cheek.

'I hope she is. I wish I could believe in an afterlife. I wish I could believe she was here, with us, and could see me, reach out to me and just say she was happy. I can't though. If there is something afterwards. We can't know but I'm sure it's probably the end. Just non-existence. What an appalling thought.'

Ralph agreed. It was an appalling thought and one he preferred not to dwell on.

'Come on Virginia. Let's go to bed.' She stooped and kissed her mother on the forehead, blew out the candles and then holding her hand out again, the one that she had stroked her mother with, caught Ralph's arm and said, 'Nothing we can do about it though. We'll go to bed.'

Upstairs, they both washed and got into the old bed together. They were immediately above the drawing room and Ralph lay there, after Virginia had kissed him goodnight, thinking of the corpse below, the fact that the only certainty that mortals had was that they all would be corpses one day and that he had decided to leave Virginia. It seemed an unspeakably cruel thing to do but he was sure that he was making the right decision. He had no idea what the future held other than ultimate death and extinction but eventually he drifted into his own dreamless oblivion of sleep.

The next morning he woke to find the bed empty. He felt confused and remembered that he was in Yorkshire, a funeral tomorrow, an address to be prepared and Tina would be packing. Would she see her husband, he wondered. Would she go through with it? Suppose she decided not to? He had just committed a large amount of money into a flat. As he was turning this terrible possibility over in his mind, Virginia appeared with coffee. She seemed brighter and slightly more cheerful. He muttered something to this effect and she said, 'I'm with you again. I always feel better when we're together,' as she got back into bed. She had put the coffee on a chest of drawers and leaned towards him, putting her arm round him and pulling him towards her.

'Virginia, I can't do it with your mother downstairs.' The idea was horrible.

'No, I don't want to here. I want you and me to go for a walk this afternoon. We'll go onto the moors in the Bristol.' She looked at him, was it even beseechingly, with anticipation.

'Yes. We'll do that,' he agreed, wondering if he could contrive matters so that this did not happen. She kissed him and reached for her cup.

'Here, coffee first. Breakfast next. Jane's already telephoned. They're coming over later for dinner. We'll have to get something.'

'I can do that. I'll pop out and then cook it as well.'

'That's nice of you. I was hoping you'd say that.' She finished her coffee, kissed him on the cheek and dressed quickly leaving Ralph luxuriating in the old bed.

He wondered what Tina was doing now. He would phone her later if he could - he would try her at work first and then at her home, or more properly, or hopefully rather he thought, her ex-matrimonial home. He could go shopping in the local market town and would have an opportunity then.

Tina had woken early that morning, and had immediately missed Ralph. She felt cold apprehension at the thought of his being with Virginia in what were awfully sad circumstances. It was a risk that she was prepared to take, a risk she had decided she had to take. She repeated to herself that she was playing for high stakes and wanted to win. Her plan was to phone her shop, say she was coming in late and then go back to her house, St John would be out, collect her things, not many she thought, and then drop them into the new flat, a thrill of anticipation thinking of the flat, then change and go to work for the rest of the day. She wondered if Ralph would telephone as she picked up the receiver. Ian answered and she explained that she would be late. 'Not a problem,' he had said, 'We'll cope without you, don't worry.' She had a quick shower, she wanted to get on with the day, and very shortly afterwards was drawing up outside what she still thought of as her house.

She was surprised to see St John's car there and considered, for a moment only, driving away again in case he was in the house. 'This is ridiculous,' she said to herself. 'It's my house. My things. And he probably isn't there anyway.' She got out, put the key in the door, opened it and listened. The house was quiet. She walked in, went into the sitting room and looked about trying to decide what, if anything, she wanted from the shelves. She was deep in thought and was startled when the door opened, turning in fright. St John was standing there, naked apart from a dressing gown that was undone and gaped open. It crossed her mind how deeply repulsive he had become to her physically; it seemed astonishing that she had ever found him attractive.

'What are you doing here?' His voice was cold, controlled and angry.

'I've just come back to collect some things. Don't worry. I'm not staying.'

'You meant it then.'

'Of course I meant it. I'd hardly spend nights with someone else if I didn't mean it. And anyway, even if I didn't mean it, it's over now. You'd hardly have me back after what I've done. I'm second-hand. Tarnished, tawdry goods now in your book.'

He did not answer; he just looked at her. She began to feel alarmed.

'Yes,' he finally said, 'you are. But you deceived me.'

She felt panic rising. 'No, I didn't. I have not deceived you. I have left you. I have gone because our marriage was not working. You were unhappy and so was I. There's no point in going into the reasons. I've tried to talk to you often enough but you've ignored me. Alright, I've taken the first step and it's me who has gone.' She was trying to pacify him, reason with him, as she feared his temper.

'All right,' he said, 'but you are going to have one last dicking from me that you can remember me by.'

'No St John. Don't be silly. You're frightening me. Stop it.'

'Do you want to make my dick big or should I?' He stared at her. 'Watch me rub my dick and think about it.' He was standing there, masturbating himself erect.

She was horrified. He appeared to mean it, she thought as she looked at his erection.

'Take your clothes off,' he said peremptorily, 'or I'll take them off.'

She was cornered. 'St John, it's rape. It's against the law. I'll complain to the police. It could ruin you. Don't be a fool. It's not worth it.'

'Then just take your clothes off.'

Oh God, she thought. Does it really matter? I've slept with him hundreds of times. What's one more? Let's get it over with. 'All right,' she said, 'where do you want to go?'

'Here and now.' She undid her jeans, stepped out of them and was just about to take off her knickers when he pushed her backwards onto the sofa, tore them off and entered her roughly. She bit her lip, felt tears coming to her eyes, closed them tightly and thought of Ralph.

When he had finished he stood up without a word and left the room. She waited, listening to the bathroom noises. She was still lying on the sofa when he came back in, she had not put her clothes back on.

'Christ,' he said, 'you look a real slut. But then you are. He's welcome to your cunt,' and left the room. She heard the front door close, his footsteps, the car door, the engine start and the noise recede. She got up, went to the lavatory, was sick violently and explosively, before going to the bathroom, running a bath and getting into it. 'I'm well out of it,' she kept repeating to herself. 'I'm well out of it.'

Later that morning Ralph drove to the local town. He had breakfasted well, had exchanged courtesies with his father-in-law and had started preparing the address for the funeral. He went round the various shops and bought all that he needed to prepare a good meal before going into a phone box. He thought he would try Tina at work first. A male voice answered.

'Is Tina there?'

'Is that Ralph? It's Ian. Hi Ralph. I'll get her for you.' She was there quickly.

'Ralph. How are you? I can't really talk at the moment. We've got lots of customers.' He thought she sounded upset.

'Did you get sorted?'

'Yes, I went back this morning. Got all the things I needed and wanted. Not much. I've moved in. When will I see you?' she whispered.

'Tomorrow. Is everything all right? Did you see him?' He couldn't bring himself to speak St John's name.

'No, I was lucky, I suppose. He wasn't there. Can you phone tomorrow?'

'Tina, I miss you. I'll phone again. Take care.'

'And you.' Click.

He felt it unsatisfactory, but the short conversation was better than nothing at all he reasoned. He supposed that he was anxious that she might reconsider.

He drove back trying to understand himself, asking over and over again whether it was indeed perhaps a mid-life crisis and why had Virginia been so accepting of what sounded a really implausible explanation for his absence? Maybe she saw something in him that he had not identified. He knew he was not truly happy. Like all ambitious people he was anxious to move on, climb higher up the slippery slope of success. He had recently applied to become a Queens Counsel. He had been encouraged to do so by many, Virginia included, and particularly his former Head of Chambers, Sir Geoffrey. He was young, too young he thought privately, to make application but having now done so he was desperately praying that it would be successful. It would involve a drop in earnings, the transition from junior barrister to Q.C. always did, but if he was to achieve his long-term ambition of at least High Court judge, it was a necessary step. He would, he reflected, find the drop in earnings unpleasant but it would only be for a couple of years at most, and might, if he worked at it, not even take that long to recover or even better his current financial position.

Yes, I would like to be a Q.C. Yes, I would like to be a judge. Yes, I would like Tina. But suppose I could stay with Virginia and have Tina as a mistress? Permanently. Is that the solution?

He dismissed this as quickly as he asked the question. Tina, he had already decided, was not going to be content with being a bit on the side. She seemed, to him, to have a steely kind of resolve and he had been impressed by the way in which she had made her decision, acted upon this and indeed put him in a position where he had to acquiesce. It was probably a straight choice between Tina and Virginia. He was saddened. His marriage had not failed. They had not even grown apart. Life with Virginia was pleasant, but she did not send, he was again aware of thinking in clichés, his pulse racing as Tina did. Life with Tina would be more fun.

But was fun, or the prospect of life being fun, a sufficient reason for giving up on Virginia? This was the question to which he returned. Would he rather be a Q.C. with Virginia or Tina? Why did it matter so much? He knew that the fact of his having had an affair would, inevitably, have to be addressed with Virginia. It was already partly public knowledge and however he jumped, at some stage, he would have to own up to her. She was sufficiently matter of fact, probably, if he pitched his explanation and apologies in the right way, to forgive him. She would be disappointed, distressed even, feel betrayed he was sure, but would probably forgive him. It might however, he thought, push her into an affair for retaliation and that was something he could not face. The prospect of her infidelity was more upsetting to him than his leaving her.

Again, trying to analyse the reason for this, he could find no rational reason for the view. He supposed the basis of trust would have been broken and without that basis of trust, a marriage cannot work. The 'open marriages' that some of his friends had boasted about, even flaunted, had all, without exception, ended in divorce. Perhaps that was the deciding factor, he mused. I've committed adultery. I've enjoyed committing adultery. There is no way that Virginia will not be made aware of my committing adultery. I can apologise. She may, but probably will not, trust me not to stray again. I can never be sure that she will not claim the same right. I will always be unsure of her. Every time she leaves the house I will wonder. Every time she comes back, I will be looking at her for tell-tale evidence. If she wants sex, I will think it is to reassure me. If she doesn't want sex, I shall be sure that it is because she has done it with someone else. What an awful prospect. I have to leave her.

He was relieved at having made these, to him, entirely logical propositions, and, having arrived back at the house, gathered the shopping and went into the kitchen.

Virginia was in there with her father, having yet more coffee, Ralph noticed.

'Like a cup? I've told Daddy that we're going for a walk. He doesn't want to come.'

He usually did, he and his late wife forcing the pace, always ahead of Virginia and Ralph to whom he would periodically turn and command them to catch up and not lag behind. 'What did you get for supper?'

'Simple stuff. Smoked trout for starter, fillet steak for main, some cheeses.'

'We've got plenty of that but never mind, one can never have enough cheese in the fridge. What time is Jane coming over, Daddy?'

'Sixish.'

'We'll be back before then. Come on Ralph. We'll take the Bristol.'

They drove up onto the moors, lonely, cold and lovely on a cloudless day. Virginia and Ralph did not speak much. She had her hand on his leg, stroking his thigh in an absent sort of fashion. They were approaching the summit of a hill.

'There's a lay-by at the top there. It's a wonderful view. Will you stop please?' He pulled in and she got out, turning to him, 'Are you getting out? Come on. I want to breathe in the air, the cleanness, the emptiness, the just being. Come on.' He joined her and she took his hand, then slipped an arm round him. 'Mid-life crisis? Ralph. What rubbish. We have each other. Would you like to make love?'

Not really, he thought but replied, 'Not here, Virginia. It's a bit public and besides it's not night-time.'

'So what. Night-time be damned. And you can see the road for miles. You'd see ramblers or walkers or shepherds and I've looked and there aren't any. Let's get back in the car.' She pulled him towards the passenger side, sat on the seat, pushed it back, reclined the backrest, lay down, pulled her tweed skirt up and said, 'Come on Ralph... Slowly, nicely, mutually.' He looked around. The road and moorland were deserted. They seemed the only living creatures apart from sheep and birds. He cast around for an excuse but could find none. Virginia was lying back, legs apart, eyes closed in anticipation.

'Hurry up, I'm ready,' she urged. He climbed awkwardly on top of her and then they slipped into the easy and natural rhythm of a long-married couple who knew exactly what the other wanted.

'An HMO.' She grinned at him as she said this. He lifted himself off her and she tidied herself up. Ralph had been surprised at how he had managed to lose himself, to the extent of not even listening out for cars. Indeed, had he been asked he could not have said whether any cars had passed them, so involved and intent he had been on the physical sensations. He kissed her gently and said, 'A hugely mutual orgasm,' before he went round and got back into the driver's seat.

'It's at times like this I sometimes wish I smoked.' Virginia announced.

'Why?'

'I just think it would be nice to puff and exhale and relax.'

Ralph had what amounted to a near phobic dislike of smoking in any form and Virginia, to whom health mattered, had never even tried a cigarette. Ralph had tried when young, been sick and never bothered again, and was contemptuous of those who, allowed themselves to become addicted, and even more contemptuous of those who once addicted, were unable to give up or kick the habit.

'Funny thing to say, Virginia. God. It's cold. Should I start the engine or should we go?'

'There's nowhere to go on to really. Let's just sit here with the heater on.'

He turned the key, the engine rumbled into life, and he was just about to turn the radio on when she said. 'No. Let's just talk.'

'What about?'

'The future. What we're going to do.'

They often spoke of their next property, both knowing that whilst their current house was, by any standards, special they really longed for a formal 17th century Queen Anne house, even though it would be too big for them.

'We've got to get through the next day or two before there's a future though, Virginia.' The future, whilst a subject of intense preoccupation to him, was not a theme he wanted to explore with Virginia.

'Yes, I know. It's gruesome, isn't it? What do you think Daddy will do? Do you think he'll want to stay in Yorkshire alone?'

'I'm sure he will.' Surely she wasn't suggesting that he come and live with them? 'After all, he's got Jane nearby.'

'I was wondering if we should make an offer, you know, buy another larger house now and turn part into a flat.'

'No it's too soon for him to think about that. Give him some time first.'

'Yes, I know you're right, but it might give him reassurance if we just mention it.'

'Whatever you think Virginia,' Ralph replied, knowing that it was all academic anyway. He was suddenly curious.

'Virginia?'

'Yes.'

'Do you know that we know next to nothing about one another?'

'What do you mean? We've been married for yonks. What else is there to know?'

'You know. Before me. I've never asked you. Were there others?'

'You've actually never asked me. Is it important? I've never asked you because it doesn't matter. I know there were others before me. You couldn't know what to do if there hadn't been and you do it so well. I've always been happy with that and the certainty that whilst I wasn't the first, I was going to be the last one.'

Oh God, how sad, Ralph thought. 'And as for me. Well, I had a boyfriend or two before you but nothing serious.'

'Really not?'

'No. I was, as they say, unsullied. Surely you realised? You've been the only man in my life. You're the only one I've ever made love to, the only one I've wanted to make love to and the only one I shall ever have.' This was not quite what Ralph wanted to hear. 'What I couldn't stand is the thought of your being unfaithful,' she continued. 'I don't think I could cope with that. Once someone's done that, well, it's like betrayal, isn't it?' She looked at him. He felt shifty and wanted to change the subject, regretting having brought it up. 'Why do you ask now? After all these years.'

Ralph looked out of the window. Unfinished business he supposed. 'I don't know,' he said simply. 'I just wondered. It's not important.'

She looked puzzled, 'It must be important otherwise you wouldn't have mentioned it.'

He thought back to their first time. He had taken her out a couple of times; they had held hands, a chaste kiss the first date, a more prolonged kiss the second. His hands had wandered, and she had firmly removed them saying she was not that kind of girl. The third time they had gone out together he had been determined to prove that she was that kind of girl and he had taken her to a very well-known local restaurant, too expensive for him but it was part of the overall plan, and had bought champagne and got her slightly drunk. He suggested going back to his room; she had agreed, giggling, and looking flirtatious said, 'Are you going to ravish me?'

'I'd like to,' he had replied and when they arrived there, he had closed the door, locked it very obviously and said, 'You're mine, all mine.'

'I think I might be,' she had replied thoughtfully, looking at the locked door before giggling again. He had wondered if he was taking advantage of her but after she had undone her belt, unzipped her jeans and had stepped out of them, then dropped her knickers, she had, he decided, made it quite clear that she expected him to fulfil his threat.

Afterwards she had said, 'That was superb.' He had tried, very hard, to ensure, as he always did, that she had orgasmed and had been taken aback when she had one, then another and then apparently another one after that.

'Will you stay the night?' he asked.

'I'd like to, but only if you promise to wake me early enough.'

'I promise,' and they had fallen asleep, comfortably entwined on the narrow bed. He had woken before her and had been looking at her face when she woke, smiled and kissed him.

'I think I'm in love,' she said and pulled him towards her. 'What we did last night. Can we do it again?'

Later, when she had dressed, she asked, 'See you this evening?'

'Yes, where?'

'I'll meet you at the Cross at 6.00. Is that all right?'

'Certainly. I'll look forward to it,' he had replied and he had. They drifted into a comfortable and steady sexual relationship while all their contemporaries were pursuing fairly promiscuous sexual careers, more the norm at university then. He had been rather pleased that they had, it was their private joke, risen above the bunny rabbit activities of their friends. Whilst his eyes had wandered, his hands had not except, very nearly but not actually, shortly into their marriage on two occasions which, to him at this distance now, did not seem to count for much.

'Hell, Ralph, what are you thinking about? You look a million miles away.'

'Life and sex and death and other trivial subjects,' he replied, frowning at her. 'Is it important? Sex I mean. At the end of the day, it's only rubbing skin together. Mutual exchange of bodily fluids. That sort of thing. Why do we all get so excited by it?'

'It, as you put it, defines us. Differentiates us from the animals. We choose, or elect, how, when, where, who with. Animals just copulate.' Virginia said emphatically.

'So do a lot of human beings,' Ralph began mildly.

'Yes, and look at them. People without imagination, without dignity, usually without self-respect. Little more than animals, many of them. Human, OK and entitled to respect as humans but lose self-respect and what have you left? Very, very little.'

'Virginia, surely we are beyond all that sort of thing now. There's been a sexual revolution. Everyone's at it. Even women are allowed to these days. Women are liberated. Feminism has triumphed.'

'You say that, but many men still view women with more than one or two sexual partners as casually promiscuous, call them sluts if they have the same sexual appetite as men. But men still feel entitled to play the field. Chalk up the notches in the belt. It doesn't impress all women though. I think, in fact I'm sure I'd see you differently it I thought you had slept with, say, fifty females rather than, say, five.' She's got no idea, he thought to himself. 'And I'm sure the reverse would apply, if I said fifty men what would you think?'

He paused, 'I suppose I might wonder what I married and whether it could last if the taste for variety was such that it had to be gratified by fifty different partners. But where do you draw the line?'

'No idea. I don't have to. You've been my only one. It makes it far simpler. I sometimes feel old-fashioned, but I also feel comforted by it. It's very reassuring in a funny kind of way. I can die an old maid thinking of Ralph, my only sexual partner and confidante.' She stopped, eyes filling with tears.

Ralph was moved by her declaration but could find no words. There was a logic to what she said and it was, to him, inescapable. He had never seen his bedroom activities as conquests but knew they could be characterised like that. He also found the idea of promiscuity rather repugnant. However, and he had to face this, he had committed adultery and the sex was significant. His emotions and intellect, he decided, were in conflict. Intellectually, he should stay with Virginia, confess all (despite or perhaps because of what she had just said) plead for forgiveness and sue for peace. He preserved his marriage, his house, their income. Emotionally, he dreaded the argument, the anxiety over her potential affairs, although again in the light of what she had just said, perhaps that was less likely but, and it was a formidable but, he badly wanted Tina.

'Ralph, you've drifted off again. Where are you? What on earth are you thinking about?'

He looked at her, smiled again and said, 'Whether it is important, and if it is, how important is it?'

'Too bloody cryptic for me,' Virginia said. 'Let's go home.'

Ralph spent the later part of the afternoon in the library formulating his address. He had decided to speak without notes and was concentrating hard on what to say. He kept on drifting back to his conversation with Virginia in the car. Why had they never talked about sex before? He could not recall any occasion, any time whatsoever, when she had stated her beliefs so emphatically. It was not as though sex was a taboo subject or that Virginia froze over at the mention of it - after all she could tell blue jokes with the best of them. Rather, it must be because it was such a normal part of their life, a bodily function even for Virginia that, as with other bodily functions, was not talked about, unless they went wrong. Since, unlike the odd urinary tract infection from which Virginia suffered and about which she spoke, sex had never gone wrong as such, it had never been talked about. The theory seemed plausible but took him no nearer any understanding.

He paced the room, stopping to make a note now and then. What he wanted to say was that he personally would not miss his mother-in-law, who had always managed to make him feel six inches tall, although he recognised others would miss her and grieve. She had been a pillar of the village community, a bastion of local society, not wholly popular but widely acclaimed as a charitable woman who had endless patience for others and always willing to give up time and energy for good causes. She was not a bad woman, just deeply disappointed that her daughter had married him. It was a shame she would not see him as successful as he hoped to be; he felt that had he become a judge she might then become proud of him. However, that was not now going to happen, and he had to find appropriate words in which to express the family's and the wider community's sadness. After another half hour or so, he was satisfied.

He ran through his notes a few times, spoke the more difficult phrases and then, putting the papers down, stood with his eyes shut and mouthed his monologue. He was already word perfect and when he finished he looked at his watch. Four minutes, he noted with pleasure. Exactly the right length. He thought also he had struck the right note and, ever the barrister, was now anxious to secure his audience and deliver himself of the speech.

His father-in-law came in. 'Finished Ralph?'

'Yes, I think so.'

'Good. Virginia's asked if you'd help in the kitchen. I'm going to sit in the drawing room for a while. I'll join you soon.' He left with a glass of whisky, having poured one for

Ralph, gesturing that he should help himself to more as he went through the doorway. Ralph walked into the kitchen. It was brightly lit and there was an expectant pause as Jane, her husband and Virginia stopped talking.

'Hi both,' Ralph said and kissed Jane on both cheeks. He shook hands with John and, realising he ought to say some words of condolence, and that 'Hi' was not really suitable, said quickly, 'What a sad business.'

It was a sombre evening. Normally there would be a lively argument about an issue of the day. Virginia's parents were stalwarts of the Conservative Party and their two daughters had become a liberal socialist and a Green. The socialist had become a vet and Virginia a paid-up member of the Green Party. Jane had married a liberal and Ralph was firmly apolitical, taking a cynical and detached view of most political activity.

Tonight however, no one had the energy to talk and the meal progressed in conversational fits and starts. Everyone was thinking of the morning and when Ralph, who had cooked and had drunk too much, announced that he was going upstairs to finish writing not even his wife tried to discourage him.

'A nice meal, thank you,' said Jane. 'We'll see you tomorrow.'

He went to the bedroom, undressed and got into bed, lying there with his arms behind his head, on his back, thinking again. He had decided to leave the following afternoon and was casting about for a good reason. He heard voices underneath him in the drawing room. They were obviously saying their last goodbyes. Ralph found this all rather morbid but respected Virginia's feelings enough not to tell her so. He was dozing when she came in. She had clearly been crying again and got undressed and into bed without a word, put her arm round him and lay against him. She fell asleep before him, her steady breathing forming an agonising counterpoint to the silence of the body beneath them.

They seemed to wake simultaneously. She kissed him and muttered, 'Hell of a day today. Got to get through it though. Onward and upward.' She was grim faced and clearly nerving herself for an ordeal. Ralph just wanted to get the whole thing over with, preferably as quickly as possible.

After breakfast, the family waited for the undertakers who arrived just before ten. Virginia said, with a surprising ferocity, 'I'm not going to listen to the lid being put on. I'm going for a walk.'

Jane and Ralph and John all took their cue and the four of them walked up the village high street. At the top Ralph remembered there was a phone box and suggested they return and that he would catch them up after calling his Chambers. None of them seemed surprised or questioned him save for Jane who commented wryly, 'One day Ralph might like to get into the same century as the rest of us and buy a mobile phone.' Ralph, who hated the devices, intrusive and unnecessary status symbols for mainly sad people who generally had nothing of any value or consequence to say to anyone at all was his opinion, did not reply and the other two were preoccupied with their own thoughts. He waited until they were well down the street again before going in and telephoning Tina at work. She answered.

'It's Ralph.'

'Ralph, I'm missing you. When are you coming back?'

'I hope today. Although it might be difficult.'

Tina was torn. 'I've got to go to this Christmas thing tonight but I could leave early.'

Ralph thought for a moment. It would look bad if he left today but good God, his name was going to be reviled in Yorkshire within the next few days anyway. Did it make any difference?

'No, I'll try and get back. I'll phone you again later. Got to go.'

'Oh Ralph, let me know though please. One way or the other.' She seemed anxious, he thought, but then why shouldn't she want to know? If he went back she'd leave her party early.

'I'll phone you. Bye.'

'Bye Ralph.'

He made his way back towards the house, noticing that mourners had started to arrive at the church. He went into the hallway and found the family ready, with the head undertaker looking ostentatiously at his watch.

'Sorry,' he said and ran upstairs, changed into a dark suit and was down again as the coffin was being wheeled out into the drive. He followed behind as the family party, now joined by other relations, filed into church. It was completely full; the village and the County had turned out in force. He ran through his oration, only paying half attention to the order of service. Virginia knew him well enough to understand that, as ever before performing, as he put it, he became very tense and preoccupied.

At a nod from the vicar Ralph went to the lectern and looked about him. A sea of faces gazed expectantly, and he felt suddenly stricken with guilt, horror and a fear of being damned for all eternity.

For richer, for poorer, for better or worse, he had been joined in the eyes of God in Holy Matrimony in this very church.

He concentrated, dismissed the thoughts and launched into his speech. He was sure, in the preparation, that he was going to strike the right note and, once he had started, the words and phrases came fluently.

People had often complimented him on his mellifluous voice, and he knew how to deliver significant lines to best effect. In the four minutes he produced two bursts of laughter and by the end, as he finished speaking of the loss to the community and to the family, he noticed with satisfaction, that handkerchiefs were being dabbed to eyes and his father-in-law was openly crying. He stopped, bowed his head for a moment standing still, hands outspread on the lectern, and then walked back to his place. It had been a masterpiece of showmanship and stagecraft. As he passed his father-in-law, he caught a murmured, 'Thank you Ralph. That was magnificent. Thank you so much.' Virginia gripped his arm and squeezed it.

The rest of the service was a blur, and it was only when he was sitting in the car that was to take them to the municipal cemetery and crematorium that he realised that he had sweated so much that his shirt felt uncomfortable. Once there, and in the chapel, he switched off completely, trying to force out of his mind the knowledge he had as to the temperatures of the furnaces, the other unseen and largely unknown machinery, that reduced a once living breathing human being to a small pile of finely ground ash, delivered back to the family in a plastic urn, to be cast to the winds, scattered on a football pitch, poured into a river, or simply deposited at a beauty spot.

He looked up though as the coffin slid jerkily away, to a room behind the ludicrous puppet theatre curtains, to be delivered to the ministrations of a couple of council employees. He was glad to be able to leave the hall but, as ever, he could not resist a glance at the chimney, where there were very faint drifts of smoke curling skywards and, as he did so, he was transported again back to the hotel only a few days ago and the lovemaking with Tina. He felt a wave of desire for her that pushed aside all thoughts of morbidity and he started planning his leave-taking.

They were silent in the car and on their return to the house, Ralph, noticing cars in the driveway and on the street, turned to Virginia and said, 'Do you know, no one's told me what next. What did you organise?'

'Outside caterers for a buffet lunch, immediate family, some distant family and some of my old friends, a few of our friends, a bit of the County and some of the village.' She ticked these off on her fingers. 'About sixty people.'

Ralph groaned inwardly. It meant that he would have to stay longer than he had intended but, on the other hand he reasoned, it might make getting away that bit easier. As he went in the front door, he was conscious of what seemed an enormous number of people all over the house. He was handed a glass of wine as he passed a uniformed butler and he sipped it thoughtfully looking around him. He knew many of the faces. They had spent most Christmases during their marriage with her parents and there was always a heavy social diary component. He recognised the wine amidst a growing sense of deja vu and pondered this uneasily.

It was the same wine as his father-in-law had served at their wedding fourteen years earlier, a generic white Burgundy which he quite liked. His deja vu was nothing less than the sense of revisiting his wedding; many of the people now present had been present then. That too, had been a church service followed by a buffet in Yorkshire. This time he had already made his speech. The last time, he had been so nervous that he had not had a single drink until he had delivered what was then intended to be one of his most polished and accomplished speeches to date which, mercifully, had been a success. He had complimented his mother-in-law then as well, had in fact been trying to woo her and win her over, wanting her to tell her friends that her daughter had found an excellent husband and wasn't her daughter lucky and so on and so forth. She had, of course, done nothing of the kind.

He drifted round groups of people, participating in the idle chat and even savouring the increasingly party like atmosphere as alcohol loosened tongues, and he became both more relaxed and stimulated. People were, by now, piling their plates from an elaborate array of different canapés, petit fours and sandwiches, and were clearly enjoying themselves. His father-in-law was among a group of people who were laughing uproariously at something he had just said. He cast about for Virginia and, as he did so, felt someone touch his sleeve. He turned to find Jane.

'You surpassed yourself Ralph. The speech I mean. You have a way with words. But then you know that. Even I, and I wasn't as fond of Mummy as I should have been...' Ralph remembered some of her vitriolic attacks on Jane regarding her socialist leanings, 'even I started crying. How are things Ralph?' she asked in a friendly and apparently uncomplicated way.

'Fine, I suppose,' he replied thinking of his incredibly complicated last few days and the rollercoaster of emotions as well as the decision he thought he had taken. 'More of the same really.'

'Virginia's been telling us that you're having a mid-life crisis. Did you really go walking in Dartmoor for two days?' She had a direct manner and could usually see through nonsense very quickly. 'It's not like you. You're so in control and so organised. What's the matter?'

'I'll soon be forty. I can no longer describe myself as young. I'll be young middle-aged. Middle age is the bit before the autumn of your years. I feel somewhat melancholy about everything. I thought I'd just take myself off and think.'

'And did you, you know, think?'

'Yes. A lot.'

'To any effect?'

'Not really. It's not the kind of thing you can make decisions about just like that.'

'There's not another woman is there Ralph?'

Ralph, with a nasty sinking sensation in the pit of his stomach, mentally gritted his teeth and responded easily. 'Of course not. Why on earth do you ask?'

'It's a common enough phenomenon. Late thirties. Men start eyeing up younger women. Some men of course do it all their lives. But I don't see you like that. Neither does Virginia.' So they had discussed this as a possibility. 'It would devastate her you know. If there is, and I'm not saying I think there is, if there is, well, my advice would be to keep it casual. Don't get involved. What you have with Virginia is something special. It's not vouchsafed to many you know.'

'I do know,' he answered firmly, and wondered if he could phone Tina from the house or whether it might be more sensible to slip out into the village.

'Virginia's been talking about the trip you've got planned. It sounds wonderful. When are you going?'

I'm not, he thought. 'Later this year,' he replied. 'I'm not sure that I want to go any longer though. It's an awful lot of money.'

'Come off it, Ralph. You two have got enough. You don't have to worry.' Jane and her husband, though both vets and having each got Distinctions at university, highly intelligent, motivated and able, scraped along on, Ralph estimated, about a third of his and Virginia's joint earnings.

'Yes, I suppose so. But we spend it.'

'You could stop buying expensive cars and pictures and furniture.'

I'll probably have to, thought Ralph, if it's Tina and me. 'Yes, we could. But Virginia loves her Porsche and I'm rather fond of the Bristol, and we both like old furniture and I like pictures.

'Yes. I'm just jealous. Virginia has everything really, doesn't she? Job. House. Money. Possessions. Security. Husband.' She paused. 'One thing she hasn't got, though. Has she told you our news?'

Ralph guessed immediately. 'That's terrific. When are you due?'

'How did you know?'

'Deduction. Job, house, money, possessions, security, husband. What's missing other than children?'

She looked crestfallen. 'I gave it away.'

'Just a lot. But when are you due?'

'I'm ten weeks down the line.'

'I'll bet you're both pleased.'

It was common knowledge in the family that they had been trying for some time to conceive, and there had been running jokes about the subject, at most of which his mother-in-law would sniff and then glare at the perpetrator.

'Yes. It's a shame Mummy won't see him or her. Are you still set on not having children? Still of the same view? Virginia seems to be.'

'Yes. I mustn't let you think that I'm criticising you, or anyone else for that matter who has children, but I'm still sure it's an act of monumental vanity and egotism. Even if it isn't that, it's the emotional responsibility.' He heard himself repeating very nearly phrases he had used recently and tried to remember with whom he had been talking at the time. It had been with Tina of course.

'I know. Mr Morbid. You give them life only to have them face death. It's the nature of life though. I'd prefer the option of actually being alive with a death to follow than not having ever been,' and with this she smiled companionably and took him by the hand saying, 'Come on into the drawing room. There are some old friends there.'

Ralph went with her, and found Virginia with friends of theirs from university they had not seen for a number of years. He joined them as Virginia was laughing about male mid-life crises. He had not expected his excuse to be turned into a subject for public discussion and certainly he did not believe he was having any sort of crisis. The others evidently thought it a bit of a joke.

'Ah. It's the mid-life crisis man.'

'Thank you Alan,' Ralph said. 'You should know about them by now. You've had crisis after crisis ever since you left university.' Ralph knew that this was a bit below the belt but Alan, who had never settled in any job, always claiming that it was the boss from hell and looking longingly at greener grass elsewhere, had still failed to find his niche in life.

'Come on,' his wife said. 'It's not given to all of us to be Ralph, the wunderkind.' She said it without malice.

'What on earth have you got to have a mid-life crisis about?'

'Same as everyone else. Age competing with ambition.'

'You're not yet forty. Everything lies ahead of you. You've put in the groundwork. Climbed up the first mountain face. You've only got Everest ahead.' They all laughed.

'Yes, Ralph,' Virginia took it up. 'Everest next. Not a problem. You put yourself in the horrid hot house competitive world of the Bar. You chose the slipperiest pole apart from politics.'

'But what else was I to do? All that I was ever good at was talking. Law was the natural choice.'

The group of friends was a microcosm of the professional middle classes, the chattering, able, intelligent, bright, university graduates to whom the world, they felt, owed more than a decent living. All were prosperous, self-assured and opinionated. Ralph was struck by how the last week appeared to have changed his views.

This was his world but he now felt distinctly not part of it. They had friends who had had affairs - some had led to divorce, others to patched up but even messier marriages but he wanted to step outside it all, physically, intellectually and emotionally, and run to Tina. She embodied other qualities he thought, more real and significant. He murmured, 'Excuse me for a moment' and left the group, reminiscing cheerfully about their golden youth.

He decided to risk phoning Tina from the house and, looking at his watch, noticed with horror that it was late afternoon. It was only then that he also thought about his alcohol consumption. He had eaten nothing but had drunk steadily and he estimated that he must have had at least a bottle of wine, maybe even more. There was an extension in the bedroom. He went and dialled the shop. She answered.

'Hello Tina.'

'Ralph, where are you?'

'Still in Yorkshire. I've not been able to get away. I'm going to come down tomorrow morning. Where will you be?'

'Oh Ralph, I was so looking forward to seeing you again. I'll be in the flat. Tidying and arranging.' She sounded disappointed.

'I'll see you there. Do you miss me?'

'Yes, Ralph. Do you miss me?'

'Yes. See you there,' and put the phone down quickly.

He only then remembered that she was going out that evening anyway. He wondered idly what she would wear and what she would do. Drinks at the shop followed by a meal she had said. She would have left the party early had he been going back. He then started wondering what Virginia's plans were. These had not been discussed at all. As he stood, lost in thought, Virginia came in. He was still holding the receiver in his hand and she asked, 'What are you doing?'

'I was just about to phone my clerk and see what was lined up for next week. I can do it later though. What are you doing up here?'

'Came to find you. Everyone seems very happy downstairs. Quite a party. Even Daddy's enjoying himself. It's a shame Mummy isn't here really. She'd have loved it.' She smiled sadly.

'What are your plans Virginia?' He sounded rather stiff and

formal. 'What I mean is, how long are you staying? When are you going home?' He noticed he had used the word going instead of coming but she did not appear to attach any significance to his lapse in concentration.

'I've talked to Daddy. He'd like me to stay a bit longer. I've squared it with my partners. They're happy. I've got to take it as leave though because of the locum cover. Do you mind? It might mean I've not got enough left to do the holiday.'

With an overwhelming sense of relief and knowing that all that had happened was that he had bought a little more time, Ralph looked at her and said, 'Whatever you think best or right. I'll have to go back tomorrow, I'm fairly sure I've got a hearing on Monday and ought to go into Chambers and pick the papers up.'

'Couldn't you do it all on Sunday?'

'No, I had better go tomorrow.'

Virginia, who was used to his decision making decided not to try and change his mind and coquettishly asked, 'Ralph, any chance of a quickie?'

'Not now, Virginia, you've just cremated your mother. The funeral party is still on downstairs. Are you out of your mind?'

'No, I mean it. Just a very, very, very quick one. I can lock the door. I just want you inside me. Now. Even if only for a moment.'

The urgency in her voice, her obvious sexual excitement, the frisson that he knew she would get from doing it in a crowded house at a funeral wake, all acted together upon him and Ralph, even though he knew that he did not want to, indeed found the idea morally dubious, became aroused. Virginia recognised this and came over to him, put her hand down his trousers, 'Come on Ralph, but quickly.' She was panting, her eyes gleamed and she sat on the edge of the bed as she pulled her long skirt up. Suppressing what he hoped was revulsion, Ralph did as he was asked until she cried out under her breath, 'Now, now, now' and he found himself once more, but as unwillingly as the day before, having another orgasm of extraordinary intensity.

'Tidy yourself up,' he said gently as he zipped and buttoned his trousers. She looked up at him.

'Kiss me Ralph.' He hesitated but she stood, put her arms around him whispering, 'Thank you for everything. You've made the day much more bearable. I knew it was going to be horrid, but it hasn't been quite as horrid as it might have been,' and kissed him unhurriedly. She then straightened her skirt, smoothing it back over her stomach and adjusting her jacket.

'We'd better go down again.' She unlocked the door, put her head out, listened and said, 'The coast is clear. See you downstairs,' and then blew him a kiss before stepping out, closing the door behind her.

Ralph was not sure whether he was disgusted with himself or Virginia. She was utterly incorrigible, her need for sex once a day still a mystery to him. A mystery that was compounded by her admission yesterday that he was her only sexual partner. She may have been lying but the circumstantial evidence, he having reviewed this, was in favour of her having told the truth. Perhaps it was a physical demonstration of her love for him rather than a need that required fulfilment. Again, he had never asked, merely accepted the fact of that being the way she was. He checked himself in the mirror, wondered what Tina was doing, and left the room.

Downstairs, people were just starting to leave. There was

debris everywhere but the caterers were tidying, unobtrusively and efficiently. He stood in the hall, with other members of the family, and scrupulously observed the social protocol of kissing cheeks, shaking hands, murmuring responses to expressions of sympathy and generally behaving as a well-mannered, civilised member of the middle classes. Virginia, he noticed, was doing the same, well-practised, smiles, frowns, solicitous, wonderful bedside manner, he thought. What do we know of anyone? What would all these polite, well-behaved people, friends and relatives, say, if they knew that only five minutes earlier she had been suppressing squeals of orgasmic pleasure? The atmosphere seemed laden with guilt, he supposed it was him transferring his own burden, but then people here had enjoyed themselves, knew that they had enjoyed themselves and knew also that they had been attending a wake. Perhaps it was not surprising that there might be some residual embarrassment.

Ralph had another glass of wine pressed into his hand and was taken aback to find himself rather drunk. This was unusual for him, and he decided to have some coffee as soon as possible. The last guests having departed, only the immediate family was left. They looked at one another uneasily, wondering how to fill the gap between then and bedtime. Ralph, who felt hungry as well as drunk, suggested they go and sit in the kitchen where he could pick at what was left over. All agreed that this seemed a good idea, so the early evening found them all around the table, subdued and melancholy, eating the remnants, drinking coffee in Ralph's case and more wine for Virginia, her father, sister and husband.

When Virginia suggested, more out of desperation to find something to concentrate on than because she actually wanted to play, Monopoly there was genuine enthusiasm. Jane went and got the old set, which she remarked had belonged to her mother when her mother was a child, and they settled down to serious play. It avoided all need for conversation and for that reason was diverting and therapeutic.

Finally his father-in-law, who had been drinking whisky all evening, in large measures and very purposefully, announced that he was tired and that it had been a long day, nobody was inclined to disagree. They counted up, established that Ralph was the winner, 'What's new?' Jane said and went to their separate bedrooms. Ralph changed and got into bed where Virginia joined him, kissed him tenderly, said, 'Good night. I love you Ralph. Thank you again,' and promptly fell asleep. Ralph fell asleep very quickly still thinking of Tina.

Tina had been disappointed when Ralph had said he was not coming back that evening and speculated anxiously about what he had been doing. There had been a funeral, hardly a time when Virginia might be able to exert any sexual control, but nevertheless she was afraid that his resolve, she identified it as resolve, might weaken.

He had said that he would leave Virginia but how many women, in her position she thought bitterly, had heard that sentiment only to have hopes dashed and plans ruined. She was under no illusions about what she was trying to do, tried to dismiss what might be sombre realities, and concentrated on getting through the day in the shop. There was an air of excitement however which she found infectious.

The staff was not large, just Tina, Ian, five other girls and a boy who worked in the storeroom. The girls were all looking forward to the evening party and, when the time came to close, were discussing anxiously what they were going to wear. Ian made a laconic remark about Tina being above such mundane considerations and Tina decided that she would show him otherwise.

She went back to her flat, it was her flat already, rather than the flat for which the deposit and the first month's rent had been paid by Ralph, and looked through her wardrobe. She had collected all her clothes but few other belongings. She decided she too would enjoy herself. It was a long time since she had been out on her own, thinking back on it, probably the last occasion had been the previous Christmas, and she intended to make the most of a freedom from St John's disapproval and she wanted to let herself go a bit.

She chose to dress all in black, a colour that suited her complexion and that she liked anyway. The fact that it was the colour of mourning and Ralph had been wearing black that day did not occur to her.

She put on black stockings, underwear, a short skirt and a fitted shirt. She looked at herself and thought she looked rather good, if a bit vampish. She decided to tone down the make up a bit. When she was ready, she checked her handbag, her keys, money, credit card - she only had the one, unlike Ralph who appeared to have dozens, gave an approving glance around the flat, she had subtly rearranged furniture and it already seemed more homely, and left to walk to the shop.

The others were already there and there were cries of, 'Tina you look fantastic.' They were used to her only in smart office suits. Ian was opening a bottle as she came in and he stared at her, in a peculiarly challenging way she thought before pronouncing, very deliberately, 'What a stunna.'

'Don't be offensive Ian,' she replied briskly.

'No, seriously, you look great.'

The girls were giggly and silly and Tina suddenly longed for Ralph, who was serious without being earnest and amusing without being superficial. She put him out of her mind and had a sip of her drink.

Rather nasty wine but never mind she thought, before joining in the general conversation. A table had been booked at a nearby Chinese restaurant and after they had drunk three bottles of wine in the shop, they went there together on foot, a happy, harmless group of people out enjoying themselves.

As the meal progressed, the atmosphere got even sillier, the girls flirting with Ian and Gary, Ian responding suggestively, which got them going even more. The bill paid, on Ian's credit card, with promises to settle up variously on the following day, week or pay-day, Sharon suggested they went back to the shop. Tina was a bit reluctant because she thought the atmosphere was now more than just disinhibited, and there might be damage which she would have to explain.

When she hesitated, Ian said, 'Come on, Tina. There are another couple of bottles of wine I left there. Let's just finish those,' and she, against her better judgment, allowed herself to be persuaded.

In the shop they put only the emergency lighting on, and Tina noticed Sharon and Gary, the stockroom boy, in a passionate embrace. Tina was not sure that Sharon's hand wasn't in Gary's trousers and was just about to intercede when Ian caught her by the shoulder and said, 'Don't, they're not doing any harm. It's they who will be embarrassed in the morning.'

'I suppose so. But I'm not sure I want anything more to happen.' There were sudden shrieks of laughter from the back office. Sharon heard these and was sufficiently interested to break off from Gary.

'What's that then?' she asked. Another shriek of laughter echoed out. Sharon went off to see and called back, 'They've got the photocopier on. Come on Gary.' Gary followed her and Ian looked at Tina with raised eyebrows.

'What are they doing?' asked Tina.

'I can give a guess,' he sighed and went through. Tina followed to find Sharon, sitting on the photocopier, skirt round her waist.

'Oh God,' sighed Tina looking at the others waving the

photographs about that they had already taken.

Sharon was giggling, 'Come on Gary, your turn.'

'But I haven't got any underpants on,' he moaned.

Tina thought this quite funny and giggled to herself at the thought of Gary who, if she allowed this to happen, would perhaps certainly be forced, now he had made the confession, to be made to sit, trouserless and underwearless, on the photocopier.

'Come on Gary,' they were chanting. Tina decided not to interfere and Gary, very shamefaced, ended up sitting on the plate, the girls watching the photocopy come out.

'Oh, oh, look at this,' the girls parroted as he got down pulling up his trousers. 'Who knew, Gary?'

'Sharon did, didn't you Sharon,' said one of them.

'Come on Ian, your turn.'

Ian, completely without embarrassment, pulled down his trousers, revealing Pierre Cardin boxer shorts, sat on the machine, laughed and said, 'No, I'm not going to get my kit off.'

They all looked expectantly at Tina, who not wanting to be a party pooper, was struggling between her dignity and the fact that she was wearing saucier underwear than any of the girls. Very calmly she lifted up her skirt.

'Christ, it's Mrs Sexpot,' Sharon blurted out wide-eyed. Just as calmly Tina sat down, allowed a photograph to be taken and smiled demurely as she climbed off and pulled her skirt down again. The others had been silent although Ian seemed to be looking at her with rather more interest. Tina glanced at her watch. The others, noticing the gesture, started talking of going home and tidying up. They were still giggly but the moment had passed. Tina was standing, waiting to lock up when Ian came up to her.

'How are you getting home? Taxi?'

'No I'm walking.'

'What do you mean? You live twenty miles away.'

'No, I live about five minutes away now.'

'How come?'

'I've separated from my husband.'

'As of when?'

'Recently.'

'I'll walk you home then.'

Tina decided to accept the offer. It was late, Friday night, the drunks would be out, and she had not been looking forward to the walk back. As they went along the dirty streets, strewn with human debris and litter, gangs of youths shouting and gesticulating, she was rather pleased that she had Ian for company. He was well-built and gave the impression of being able to look after himself. When they got to the door to the block of flats Tina turned and asked, 'A coffee?'

'I'd like that very much.'

Once inside, with curtains drawn, the real-flame gas fire lit, side lamps turned on, sitting opposite one another, coffee mugs in hand, Ian said,' You took them all by surprise. Me included.'

Tina nodded. 'Yes, I know. But what else could I do? Stand on dignity?'

'No, you impressed them I think. Certainly impressed me.'

'What do you mean?'

'I've always seen you as the married boss. To find that you're not really married, well separated anyway, and dressed like that. Well.'

Tina was amused. 'Well, what?' she goaded him.

'Well, I'd always rather fancied you. But tonight I really got the hotties.'

Tina was amused and found his expression of sexual interest rather arousing. She had always rather fancied him, wondering what he would be like between the sheets. She and her friends had often delivered themselves of the, well-worn, opinion that a woman could never truly know what a man was like until she had been to bed with him.

She idly wondered if he was making a pass at her and what would she do if he were. She felt herself unmarried and free. St John was consigned to the past, Ralph was part of the present but not yet fully of it and there were not that many opportunities to enrich her sexual experience, although, she reflected, she had enriched it pretty substantially with Ralph recently.

Ian moved to sit beside her. She did not discourage him. He put his arm round her and kissed her experimentally. She responded, despite her misgivings and felt his hand on her knee. She made no effort to remove it and, as he inched his way up her thigh, a combination of lust and sensuality overcame any inhibition or resistance that she had felt earlier. She wanted him very badly, acknowledging to herself that it had been the case the first time she had met him.

'Haven't you got a girlfriend, Ian?' she whispered.

'Not at the moment. Between them.' He was breathing very heavily. His fingers were working at her knickers, trying to roll them down over her bottom and she lifted herself slightly to make it easier.

What the hell, she thought to herself. I don't belong to anyone. It's my life. My body. My self-respect. And I want to do this. She groaned as his finger, then fingers, entered her and when he finally had his trousers off, and she was lying back on the sofa, he kneeling between her legs, guiding himself expertly in, she had an immediate, but small, orgasm.

He must have noticed because he then started to stimulate her, she crying out in little rustles of ecstasy until she had a shattering orgasm that left her drained and dizzy. He had clearly held back and then he too shuddered and, with what sounded like an animal growl, not a very nice noise she half thought, was jerking inside her.

'Oh God.' He was smiling. 'That was lovely.' He looked at her thoughtfully. 'Would you like me to stay the night? We can do that again but more slowly.'

Tina brought herself back to the real world and, with sudden decision, said, 'No, Ian. It was a one-off. Not to be repeated or mentioned ever again.'

He looked crestfallen. 'Why not?'

'Because that's the way it is,' she said very firmly, standing up. She, with a studied elegance, then picked up her knickers and put them on again, asking, 'More coffee?'

'You're amazing. I mean, we just do that and then you tell me it's a one-off and would I like some more coffee.'

'Would you?'

'What?'

'Like some more coffee?'

'No not really. I'd like you again though.'

'No. I mean it. Great sex but we're not for each other.'

Ian seemed to accept this with good grace and got up off the floor, doing himself up ostentatiously. 'Are you sure?' he asked one final time. 'I've got a lot of staying power.'

'I'm sure you have but I am sure. Thanks all the same. It's very flattering.'

'I'd better be going then. I'm in the shop tomorrow.'

Tina remembered that it was her Saturday off and agreed with him cheerfully. 'No hard feelings Ian.'

'Plenty of hard feelings.' He grinned. 'No regrets though.'

She went to him and kissed him decorously. 'We're both adults Ian. No regrets,' and led him to the front door. He left with a carefree smile.

As she shut the door Tina leaned against the wall and reflected on the fact of three men in such rapid succession. The one before, the one in the middle and the one afterwards. Whew. The one afterwards was supposed to be coming back tomorrow she remembered and, having tidied up and after a bath, she got into bed and fell asleep.

She was woken at 10.00 am by her telephone ringing. Ralph had arranged a connection the same day as he had taken the flat and she had been impressed by his efficiency. She picked it up, no one knew her number here, so she was not altogether surprised to hear his voice.

'Morning Tina. How's things? I'm on my way to you. I'm already on the motorway so should be with you by approximately midday. OK.'

She was pleased. 'Yes, look forward to seeing you. Everything all right?' By this she meant had he told Virginia, had they slept in separate beds, had he had nothing to do with her, was he coming to live in the flat, had he left Virginia for good, a multitude of questions, the answers to all of which were extremely important to her.

Ralph failed to catch any of these nuances and merely replied,' Everything's OK. See you soon. Just wanted to make sure you were there. Bye.'

Where else should I be, Tina asked herself as she replaced the receiver. Perhaps he thought I might be at the former matrimonial home, or at the shop I suppose, and started to dress for the day.

Ralph had woken early that morning, intent on leaving as soon as politely possible. Virginia raised no objections and they had breakfasted together before the others came down.

'Say goodbyes for me, please. Apologise. I don't mean to be rude.'

Virginia nodded. 'OK Ralph. I'll be back towards the end of the week. My place is here for the moment.'

'Yes. You're right.'

'But you could have stayed until tomorrow evening.'

'Virginia, you know that I've never liked staying here more than two nights.' This was true. It was about as long as Ralph could bear without losing his temper with his mother-in-law and long ago he and Virginia had decided it was the optimum length of visit.

'But she's dead.'

'I know but old habits etcetera.'

'All right then. But you will phone won't you Ralph? No more of this sliding off on mid-life crisis nonsense.'

Ralph was not sure he was going to phone. He was working up to writing a letter. He had in fact been mentally drafting this over breakfast.

'Take care of yourself Virginia. I mean it. Do take care.'

She looked perplexed and frowned. 'That sounds like farewell not au revoir.'

'No, take care, Virginia.'

It is farewell he thought as he kissed her, got in the car, listened to the starter engaging, the engine coming to life, selecting Drive in the automatic gearbox, lowering the electric window and putting an arm out to wave as he left the driveway. His spirits immediately lifted but he stopped, at the top of the hill, and turned round in his seat. He could see the house, could make out Virginia standing at the door, still waving. He waved once more, drove forward and out of sight.

He concentrated on practicalities as he drove southwards. House, large mortgage, small equity, contents, multitude of credit cards in both their names, more in his though, no savings to speak of; in truth, he and Virginia had always lived beyond their means. Divided up, half and half, with all debts paid, there should be enough for a decent deposit on somewhere else for each of them. Virginia would certainly want to stay in the area, he was inclined to think he may move away. He was not sure he could face coming across her at social events and if he moved, say only forty miles, he would be no further from his Chambers, but it would be a world apart from the present locality. He supposed he ought to close the joint account but that would have to wait until next week. He would go to Tina's flat, he thought of it as hers despite having paid the deposit, today. Eat in or go out tonight? See how it goes. Tomorrow he would go over to the house and collect some of his belongings, not sure at this stage what, but certainly clothes and one or two of the pictures, maybe a piece of furniture, he could not say.

When ought he to write to Virginia? If he did it and posted it today, she would receive the letter on Monday. He thought that he might prefer to write without Tina being present and decided to leave it until Monday, when he was in the quiet of his own room in Chambers. As a matter of courtesy, he ought to tell Sir Geoffrey as well as his clerk. No one else needed to know at this stage. They would find out soon enough and he felt weary at the prospect of trying to explain what many would undoubtedly consider an insane decision.

He stopped for coffee and to phone Tina. After he had spoken to her he called his clerk at home, 'Sorry to trouble you so early on a Saturday.'

'Not at all Ralph,' his clerk replied smoothly. 'I was waiting to hear from you.'

'Anything much happened?'

'Lots of paperwork. No court work next week actually

booked but there is a criminal matter that Mr Franks can't do, listed for two days in the Crown Court on Tuesday, if you'd like it. Legal aid rates of course but not a bad earner.' His clerk was one of the few people who knew that Ralph needed every penny he could get.

'It's not, you know, junior stuff is it?' By this Ralph meant a trivial matter which should have been dealt with in the Magistrates Court but where the defendant, advised by his solicitor that he stood more chance of an acquittal by a jury, who were often sceptical of the evidence of police officers as opposed to case hardened magistrates, had elected to have the matter dealt with in the Crown Court.

'No, not really. A nasty GBH. Husband and wife. Probably quite high profile.'

'Grievous Bodily Harm? High profile, newspapers?'

'Yes.'

'I'll do it Ken. See you Monday. Thanks.'

He went back to his car cheered up by the two conversations and thought of his letter to Virginia. He knew he owed her more than a scrappy, however long or elegantly phrased it could only be, by definition, a scrappy letter. He knew he should sit down with her and talk about matters, try as a mature adult to convey the changes he had experienced and the feelings with which he was struggling. He also knew, however, that if they sat together, he might lose his nerve and not be able to finalise the separation, an innate sympathy for a soul in distress and fondness for Virginia might act together to prevent this.

He drove straight to the flat and rang the bell. Tina appeared, and immediately put her arms round him, kissed him and dragged him inside.

'Look what I've done,' she said excitedly. He cast about and saw that there had been a rearrangement and yes, the flat had been improved by this. Congratulating her, he went into the kitchen where he saw two coffee cups on the draining board.

'Been entertaining?' he asked.

'Only Frances. She came over this morning to see me.'

'What had she got to say?'

'She's nice. She's supportive. She approves of you. I feel a need for a friend at the moment. It's all a bit scary.'

'Yes, I suppose it is. But I'm back.'

'I know. What's it been like?'

What had it been like? He was not sure. 'Gruesome,' he replied.

Tina very badly wanted him to say more, to reply in detail, but decided not to press things at this stage.

'Have you been back to your house yet?'

'No, I came straight here. I thought I might go there tomorrow. We could go together. I need to get some things if I'm moving out.'

Suppressing triumph, Tina said quietly, 'You're moving out then?'

'Of course I am. I said I was, didn't I? Didn't you believe me?'

'I just couldn't believe it. It's what I've been hoping and hoping for.' She put her arms round him and kissed him again.

'What would you like to do now?'

He said nothing but started pushing her gently towards the bedroom.

Afterwards, when he was still lying on top of her and in her, she murmured something he did not quite hear.

'What? I'm sorry, missed it.'

'That was lovely. Was it nice for you?'

'Tina, it's like coming home. For the first time in my life,' and as he said this he knew it to be true. There had been no sexual relationship that he had ever experienced that seemed as meaningful or as intense as this one. He moved to lie beside her.

'No, stay there for a little longer, just like that.' She held him tightly, with her legs clamped over his as though to lock him in place. 'It's the same for me,' she said, simply and diffidently. 'I've never really liked sex. But with you it's totally different. It feels natural and lovely and I could spend the rest of my life here, now, in bed with you and never want anything more.'

'You'd get hungry and thirsty,' he said with a smile.

'Yes, so would you. But imagine being able to stay here like this. Just us and together.'

He noticed a tear in her eye again. 'What's wrong?'

'Ralph, I'm happy and I don't deserve to be.' Ralph could not know of her encounter the previous night.

'Why on earth not?'

'I've walked out on a marriage, so have you. They'll be hurt, upset,' she paused, 'Miserable. Maybe he won't, but she will. It seems wrong.'

'No, we are together. This is right, not wrong.' He did not want to argue the point, only too aware that Virginia was going to be hurt beyond measure and preferred not to think about it. Tina was wriggling provocatively beneath him.

'Ralph?'

'Mm?'

'Again? Can you do it again?'

He needed little encouragement. He rolled onto his back and soon he found himself, without realising, having a simultaneous orgasm with her that he had not had to engineer, or contrive, in any way. This was a revelation; he had always been the one who had taken charge, worked, held back, judged and then let go.

'Wow,' he sighed, as he lay back inert. 'That was a bonus. You must have worked up an appetite for lunch.'

'My only appetite at the moment is for you.' Still sitting on him, she leaned forward and kissed him. 'We can come back later. You sound as though you're hungry.'

Ralph was more than hungry. He had only eaten a light breakfast and that seemed a long time ago. 'Have you anything in mind, Tina?'

'Not really. Got some basics in the fridge. Bacon, eggs, sausages, that kind of thing. What would you like?'

'A cup of coffee. Then we'll go out. We'll lunch somewhere and then buy some champagne and come back here.' He laughed and rolled her over, so that he was on top. 'It can't be early enough for me.'

'Or me,' she sighed, digging her fingers into his back. 'Or me,' she repeated.

They got dressed and went to his car. Ralph decided on the same restaurant as before. They ate again, with chopsticks and no ceremony, dishes selected by him with a view to Tina's enjoyment. She was appreciative and ready to try anything, cheerfully admitting that it was only the second time she had been to a first-rate Chinese restaurant, let alone one which was crowded seemingly wall to wall with Chinese people. Their conversation was light-hearted, to all purposes non-existent, each just revelling at being in the other's company. They touched often, he passed her choicer pieces from his chopsticks which she took, eyes glowing, smiling and laughing. When they finished he paid the bill, tipped lavishly Tina thought, and left.

They walked, arms round one another as though, Ralph used the cliché, in a separate cocooned world of their own reality. They passed an off-licence on the way back. Ralph went in and came out with a bag which he put in the back of the car, saying, 'Should see us through.' Back at the flat, she pulled the curtains, lit the fire and they had a glass of the too-warm champagne, sitting together on the sofa. She desperately wanted to ask him about Virginia, the urge was such that it felt irresistible, but she held back, stroking his face and watching him, eyes half closed in a reverie.

'I'm in danger of going to sleep,' he said.

'That would never do,' she replied and stood up. 'Shall I wake you up?'

He nodded and she knelt down, undid him and made a start. He stood and she giggled as his trousers fell down.

'Come on,' she said, 'take me to bed,' and held out her hand. They spent the rest of the evening once more exploring each other, slowly, then passionately and with urgency until they fell asleep, Ralph, in the moments before losing consciousness, thinking that he had reached an erotic nirvana.

When he woke she was lying on her elbow, gazing at him. He felt happy. So did she, reaching out for him and burying her face in his neck, kissing and nibbling him there. Sunday morning drifted past in a mixture of sex and pillow talk, mostly nonsense but infinitely enjoyable to them both.

'You've reduced me to a quivering and exhausted wreck of eroticism,' he jokingly complained as they lay there, 'but I've got things I must do.'

'Like what?'

'Like go to the house and get stuff. Write a letter to Virginia, no, I'll probably do that tomorrow.'

Tina felt a twinge of disappointment. She would have liked to have seen what he wrote but thought he might tell her anyway.

'The letter.' She emphasised the definite article.

'Yes, the letter,' he repeated with the same emphasis. 'Do you want to come with me to my house?'

'Of course I shall. I don't really want to, in the sense of needing to. I'm not sure it's entirely nice, is it, taking your...' she hesitated, looking for a word, 'girlfriend, mistress, lover or whatever back to the matrimonial home.'

'Oh come on, after what we've done there what difference can a visit make? How can that impinge on finer feelings?'

'Well, if I decide not to go upstairs or into your bedroom or whatever, you will understand, won't you?'

'Yes,' he said, acknowledging the fact that she did actually have some finer feelings. So far, whilst they had spoken of many things already that suggested a sensitive temperament, it would be hard for a dispassionate observer, he thought, to have said she had displayed any feelings other than lust for him and a wish for sexual gratification at the expense of two marriages.

He was quiet as they drove to the village, and passing through, he supposed he would see it again but perhaps not for a long time. He was mulling over the intended break with the area and his friends. He had not discussed this with Tina, only so far indicating that he was moving into the flat and out of his house. This appeared rather forlorn, he thought, as they approached the front door, opened it and stepped inside. Nothing had changed. He was surprised by this, just as though he had expected at the very least a burglary, some interference with the physical order of his existence that paralleled or reflected the earthquake that had taken place emotionally. He wandered from room to room, appraising the contents carefully, like an auctioneer who had come to organise a house clearance.

But that of course was what he was now, there simply to dismantle a carefully put together, jointly fabricated, environment that reflected his and Virginia's joint tastes, some of hers alone and likewise some of his, as well as those items that were the result of compromise or argument.

He felt suddenly weary. He needed none of it, not the furniture, not the books, CDs, not the pictures. No, he wanted one or two of those and wondered which were the most important to him. Tina had been silent, following him around but had made some coffee. There was no fresh milk of course, that in the fridge having gone off. She had tidied the kitchen up, putting the half empty containers of milk and other perishables into a black bag. He had gone upstairs and returned with two black bags filled to overflowing with his clothes. He had taken all of these. He had no intention of returning for anything. He then disappeared with a screwdriver and came back with a tall slim steel cupboard which Tina recognised as a gun cabinet.

'I thought you told St John you didn't shoot. What are you doing with a gun cabinet?'

'I prefer not to tell people. I bought a shotgun, not a double barrel, a Purdey or anything special, when we moved here to shoot the rooks and crows. It was so bad to begin with that every time you went in the garden you got filthy.' Tina stifled a giggle at the thought of Virginia and Ralph, the oh so capable

Virginia and the urbane Ralph, with guano in their hair. 'Why are you laughing?'

'Just the idea of the two of you covered in, you know, bird poo.'

'Trouble was, I'm not a good shot. I scared them away rather than killing any. But I can't leave it here. Shotgun licence and all the rest.' He paused. 'I'd like to take a couple of pictures though. Any ideas?'

'It's none of my business, Ralph. You have to decide. I don't know which you bought, she bought, you chose together. I'd prefer it, I guess, if you took a couple that you chose, that you liked or you paid for.'

'Very honest of you. More finer feelings.' He went and removed the Peake drawing and another, larger oil painting. He then got out his toolbox, went through it quickly, removing only duplicate hammers and screwdrivers.'

'Why don't you take the lot?' she asked.

'Don't need them at the moment,' he lied. He had nearly decided to let Virginia have absolutely everything. It would not mitigate the enormity of what he had done but it might just lessen some of the inevitable criticism from others. He could say, 'She had the lot. I had two pictures, a screwdriver, a hammer and an adjustable spanner.'

Tina helped him load everything into the boot of the Bristol. This swallowed the two bags and cabinet.

Tina said, 'You could fit much more in if you wanted.'

'What's the point,' he replied quietly, perhaps even sadly. 'I'm starting again.'

Tina was not to appreciate the significance of that comment until some months later, when it hit her, in a flash of recollection, that annoyed her so much she wanted to scream, 'Why didn't I do something about it then?' But that was the future and today they went round the house together, tidying up, removing all traces of their occupation.

Tina had decided that, after all, she did want to see the bedroom that he had shared with Virginia, had followed him in, standing just inside the doorway, looking at the old brass bed, the evidently expensive oak chests on each side, had gone into the bathroom and when asked by Ralph what she was thinking about had replied, 'I suppose I feel sad for you.'

'You shouldn't feel sad. It's because of you I'm doing it.'

'I'm not sure I'm worth it though. You might be making a horrible mistake. How can you be sure?'

He gathered her in his arms, kissed the top of her head and said, very slowly, 'I know I'm not. You are worth it. It's what I want.' With that he went out of the door. He waited for Tina who, when she came out, was wiping tears away.

'Why are you crying?' he asked not brusquely but concerned.

'It's so, so sad. But I feel so happy. I'm sorry,' and she recovered her natural gaiety. 'Let's go. Let's get on. It's the rest of our lives.'

He cooked that evening, wondering as he did so if he should have listened to the answer machine at the house. The indicator had said there were seventeen messages and he had deleted them all without bothering to play back. If any were important, he felt that the callers would get him in Chambers. Otherwise they would just be from Virginia and these he dismissed, with a now near casual cruelty that he knew had to characterise his dealings with her from now on.

Tina had hung his two pictures in the sitting room and

had distributed his clothes in the wardrobes. She had done this efficiently and neatly, in an orderly way that Ralph liked, contrasting this with the domestic chaos that had been such a bugbear for so many years.

She produced candles, 'I got some yesterday,' she had said when he commented, and they settled down to a candle-lit supper of eggs, bacon and sausages, washed down by champagne.

Ralph asked her at one point, 'What was Friday night like?'

She looked up at him and said, 'You weren't there. I'd have preferred it if you had been.'

'What did you do?'

'Had a drink in the shop. A curry down the road as planned.'

'Was it fun?'

'Not really. But I had to go. Lead from the front.'

'Who was there?'

'All of them.'

Ralph wanted to ask about Ian but thought better of this. It might make him sound small-minded or worse, so he left the question unasked.

In bed later, tracing little patterns on her lower stomach with his fingers, he looked into her eyes, marvelled at their luminosity and said, 'I love you Tina.'

'Ralph, I love you,' she replied sleepily before turning onto her side, nestling back towards him, moving his arm so that it encircled her and his hand was resting against her breasts, and falling asleep. His last thoughts that night were of deep contentment and a complete certainty that he was making the right decision.

He woke the next day feeling cheerful. He knew where he

was and remembered exactly why he was there. Tina was not beside him. He could hear her in the bathroom and he called out for her. She came back already dressed for work.

'You're up.'

'Oh yes, it's Monday. You and I both have to work.'

He was disappointed, having anticipated perhaps that there might be time for some love-making.

His disappointment must have been manifest for Tina, looking concerned, asked, 'What's wrong?'

'I just wanted to say good morning, you know,' and he held open his arms.

Tina, looking at her watch, made a decision, said, 'I thought I'd let you sleep to the last minute,' and took off her dress, 'but it'll have to be quick.'

Ralph needed no encouragement but when he tried to stroke her she said firmly, 'No, only you. Not me. I feel pretty wrecked as it is,' and as he came, she closed his mouth with hers, kissing him languidly before getting off, disappearing into the bathroom and returning looking as spruce as before, as though the act had never taken place at all. He had been taken aback at the apparent clinical efficiency but, still glowing erotically, made no comment.

'Are you getting up then?' she asked, once more smiling.

'Yes,' he replied, 'I am,' swinging his legs over the side of the bed.

She leaned forward, pulled him up, kissed him and said, 'We've got all evening. Would you like any breakfast? I usually only have coffee on week days.'

'That suits me,' he said but decided to get a bacon sandwich from the shop near Chambers.

She was distracted, clearly anxious to get on and Ralph dressed and washed quickly. She had made coffee, real coffee he noticed, and they drank this standing in the small kitchen.

'I've got to go now,' she said and Ralph, getting his coat and briefcase, went down the stairs with her, through the door and then, at his car, asked if she wanted a lift.

'Yes please. I wonder what they'll think if they see me arriving in this?' She gestured at the Bristol, a huge, deep blue and obviously expensive, if unusual, car. 'It's lovely, isn't it?'

It was the first time she had mentioned the car which hitherto had been one of Ralph's most treasured possessions. One of the few left now, he thought.

'Why don't you want me to drop you round the corner like last week?'

'Oh, no. Things have changed now, haven't they?'

Yes, indeed, he thought, things had changed. He stopped near to, but not outside the shop. He noticed two girls stop and stare; she saw him looking.

'Sharon and Mary. They'll have something to talk about now,' she laughed and kissed him, not demurely, but a hungry, cheerfully sexual kiss that made him shut his eyes as he responded.

'Bye,' she said. 'Have a good day. See you later,' and was gone, joining Sharon and Mary and walking briskly away. He sat and watched as they went into the doorway and then he drove towards his orderly world of Chambers, his Clerk, colleagues, briefs, books and papers.

True to his intention, he bought a bacon sandwich, which he put carefully into a handkerchief and then, and only then, into his briefcase. Entering Chambers he saw Ken.

'Morning Ralph. Everything all right? I've got the brief for tomorrow here.' He handed him a thickish wad of paperwork.

'Everything's just fine, Ken. Just absolutely fine,' and he took the bundle before going into his own room. He was now sufficiently senior not to have to share this with anyone and he delighted in the deliberate austerity of the surroundings. He had pared furnishings down to a large desk, four chairs and some carefully chosen prints. It reflected, he had self-consciously decided, the personality of a hard-working, focussed, not to be distracted, lawyer concentrating on the issues that were important, either people or papers. If he needed a book, he would get it from the library and then return it. He kept his desk as bare as possible. The telephone rang; he answered. 'It's your wife,' the girl said, 'Can she have a word?'

'Could you apologise to her and tell her I'm in conference and I'll get back.' He felt cheap as he said it but had resolved to write and did not want to be distracted from a task he faced with no relish at all, by trying to have what could only be a meaningless conversation with her. He took out a piece of paper and wrote 'Dear Virginia', changed it to 'My dear Virginia', crossed out the 'My'. 'This is not easy' he wrote 'and there is no easy way of telling you this.' God, where were his powers of expression, he wondered. He finally decided upon simplicity.

He was not happy with his final draft but, reflecting on the fact that people wrote complete novels round letters of this kind, and acknowledging that he was a lawyer not a novelist, decided it would have to do. He hesitated before signing, 'Ever, Ralph'. He put the letter in an envelope, addressed it and leaning out of his door called for the office junior.

'Could you stamp this, first class, and make sure it hits the eleven o'clock post please?'

The junior took it from Ralph's hand and nodding, went back towards the Clerk's room. Ralph went back to his desk, dismissed it all from his mind, undid the pink ribbon, spread the papers out, checked the numbered enclosures against the list and started reading.

The instructing solicitors had set out the facts succinctly. The defendant, a respectable accountant who had doted on his very good-looking wife, had come home unexpectedly one afternoon to find her in bed with a male neighbour. He had taken a cricket bat to them both and fractured her skull and broken the man's leg in three places before the screaming had attracted the notice of neighbours, several of whom had finally managed to pull him away and hold him until the police arrived.

The supposition was that he would have killed them but the prosecuting authorities, having decided that there was insufficient evidence for a charge of attempted murder had, instead, fixed on G.B.H., or grievous bodily harm. The defendant was adamant that he was not guilty as he had been provoked, that the attack was justified and could be excused.

In vain, his solicitors had tried to persuade him that English law did not know of such a defence in circumstances such as these, stating in terms that, even if you come home and find your faithless wife stark naked in your bed and being enthusiastically penetrated by another man, the English stiff upper lip should prevail and that trying to beat the pair of them to a pulp was not to be excused or encouraged. It would have been different, they had explained to him, had he been drunk, drugged, in a state of automatism or insane.

He had declared, adamantly, that he was perfectly sober, knew what he was doing, would do it again, felt no regret and indeed felt entitled to have done what he had. He seemed, the solicitors said in the brief, to be genuinely mystified that English law frowned upon this self-help and that he was likely to go to jail.

He had been examined by two psychiatrists who had both pronounced him sane, aware of his actions and totally lacking in remorse. He had been advised by his solicitors to plead guilty and make as much as possible of the situation and his, 'loss of temper' was the phrase that they suggested, but he was resolute and not to be deterred. He was not guilty and that was how he intended to plead. The brief concluded, in the time-honoured way, 'Counsel will please represent the Defendant'.

Ralph looked through the enclosures, the witness statements, the psychiatrists' reports and concluded that the solicitors were right in their view. He was amused by the irony of representing this man, who he supposed could so easily have been St John and wondered whether, in all decency, he should not refuse the instructions. However, he liked a legal challenge and the solicitors had already fixed a conference with the client and themselves at his Chambers that afternoon. Ralph thought he could probably talk the client into pleading guilty, and he would then mitigate and hope for, at the very best, he thought, a light jail sentence. Ralph read the brief again as well as all the enclosures; his training was such that all the facts were now fixed in his short-term memory and he was as conversant with these now as a professional actor who has learnt his lines and is word perfect. When the time came for the conference, he put the pile of papers neatly on his otherwise empty desk and answered the telephone as it rang.

'Show them in please,' he said and went to the door where

he greeted the solicitor and Mr Deacon. Mr Deacon, the Defendant, was the kind of man who would pass unremarked in any Rotary Club or church service. Middle-aged, middle height, he had nothing to distinguish him from millions of other Caucasians, except for this burst of violence. His solicitor looked a solicitor.

Why do so many solicitors have shiny suits and shirts that don't do up properly, thought Ralph not for the first time, they always look so grubby and seedy. Ralph was fastidiously neat.

Having exchanged opening pleasantries Mr Deacon, 'Call me Jim,' he had said immediately, was looking edgy and nervous. The solicitor was running through the advice he had given him and Ralph motioned to him to stop, saying, 'It was a very well drafted brief.'

The solicitor flushed with pleasure and Ralph thought that here was yet another poor sod who was used to the high and mighty barristers lording it over him - Ralph had always tried to be approachable and most solicitors liked him for this, 'and the advice you gave Jim was impeccable. Down the line. I have to agree with it.' He turned to Jim.

'I can't go to prison for what I did,' he unexpectedly burst out. 'They deserved it. The bitch. After all I'd done for her.'

'What had you done for her Jim?' Ralph asked conversationally.

It turned out, sadly and inevitably, that Jim had done little more for his wife than most men. He had married her. He had not required her to go to work but had required her to cook for him, have his children, look after them, him, the house, do the school runs, supervise the homework, the shopping, the domestic economy and all this in return for providing a roof over her head, sex measurable by the clock, if not the day of the week, and a housekeeping allowance that to Ralph seemed pitifully inadequate.

Jim got a photograph out of his wallet and said, 'Do you want to see her Mr Edwards?' passing it over to him.

Ralph looked and saw a stunningly attractive woman, doe eyed, sexuality almost dripping from her, and wondered what on earth she had seen in Jim. Security? Love? Tenderness? He asked how Jim had met her. She had been his secretary and he had seduced her within two weeks.

You can make a wife your secretary, but you should never make your secretary your wife thought Ralph, appalled at the clichéd banality of the sentiment, but recognising its force in the present circumstances. He carried on listening, however, and gradually a picture built up in his mind. The man had been passionately in love with her, had been unable to willingly let her out alone, had isolated her within the house at times, but had worshipped her. It had not been enough though and, like Madam Bovary, his wife had taken a lover. Jim had no idea when it had started but the shock was profound, the distress real and when Jim started crying, great racking sobs, Ralph understood the depth of the anguish, hurt, betrayal and bewilderment. Ralph produced a clean white tissue from his drawer, where he kept a box for such occasions, and allowed the man to compose himself.

'Jim,' he said kindly, 'you have two options. You do not, and I do not expect you to, have to make up your mind now. I consider what you have told me is substantial mitigation. The judge tomorrow,' he had checked, 'is known for his compassion. He is not a hanging judge.' Jim gave him a frightened glance. 'He is usually lenient, sometimes over-lenient. There is an outside chance that you could get off with a suspended sentence if you pleaded guilty. This would be my advice to you. However,' and he paused and looked at Jim thoughtfully, 'if you really want to persist in a plea of not guilty then, if you are found guilty, I consider the likelihood is that you will receive an immediate prison sentence. You will have taken up what is called 'valuable court time' with an unsuccessful plea and that would have to be reflected in the sentence. Nevertheless, if you want to plead not guilty then I undertake to represent you as best as I can and do what I can to get you acquitted. But the chances are very remote.'

Jim looked anxiously at his solicitor, 'What do you think?'

'You heard Mr Edwards. He puts it very clearly and you know my views.'

'Look Jim, sleep on it and tell me at ten o'clock tomorrow.' Ralph stood up and Jim and the solicitor did likewise, each shaking hands with Ralph. Jim was out of the door before the solicitor, who turned to Ralph and asked, 'Why didn't you lean on him a bit more, get him to plead guilty?'

'It's not really fair to do that though is it? Not tonight. Maybe in the morning. Let's see what he decides?'

The solicitor nodded with, Ralph thought, something approaching understanding and left. Ralph made two cups of coffee and went into the Clerk's room where Ken, the senior clerk, was sitting at a desk with a computer screen, his several minions likewise circumscribed, around him.

'Ken, may I have a word?' Ralph asked and Ken, realising this was to be a private conversation, followed him into his own room. 'Thought you might appreciate a coffee.'

Ralph had always got on with Ken, long ago having understood that a clerk could make or break a barrister's career, but that reality had not inhibited a relationship approaching a real friendship between the two men. Ken had taken to Ralph from the start, had seen him as something of his own protégée and had talked solicitors into instructing him with bigger cases than perhaps they should have done, with the result that Ralph had spent most of his years in Chambers punching above his weight. Ralph was grateful for this and had always made known his gratitude.

'What's up Ralph?' Ken observed the protocol of formal address when in professional company but used first names privately or in the pub. 'You look anxious. That's not like you. Is it the Deacon case? Franks was rather relieved not to be able to take it on, I must say. Wasn't looking forward to it at all.'

'No, it's not that. I can see why though. I suspect Deacon will be in the slammer tomorrow night but no, it's something else.' Ralph felt that Ken ought to know the change in domestic circumstances sooner rather than later and certainly wanted Ken to hear it from him, rather than by way of second-hand and possibly, salacious, gossip.

'It's just that,' and paused, looking for the words, 'what I'm going to say will be a surprise, but I owe it to you to tell you personally.' Ken was looking bemused. 'I've left Virginia.'

Ken was non-plussed. 'You haven't. You're joking Ralph. Surely?'

'No. No joke. For real.'

'Why? Why on earth? You're seen as the perfect couple. You know that.'

'You've also seen enough divorce papers Ken to know that

these things happen. There's someone else. I've moved in with her.'

'It's serious then?'

'Oh Christ yes. It's serious. I just wanted to tell you first.'

Ken was busy calculating the effect that this change in circumstances might mean professionally. He had socialised with Ralph and Virginia, knew their circle and which solicitors might stop using Ralph as a result.

'You know, don't you, that Virginia is very friendly with a number of the solicitors who instruct you on a regular basis?'

'I know, Ken. I know.'

'They might stop using you.'

'They might. But I'm prepared for it.'

'It's a bit of a bombshell. Totally unexpected. What's she like?' Ken was a male through and through, and as such, felt no need to make any apology for his question.

'Very different from Virginia. Not a doctor or a lawyer.' Ralph had forgotten Tina's law degree. 'Quite serious, very attractive.'

'Virginia is bloody attractive. I've always thought so,' Ken murmured. 'She must be a bit special. The new one, I mean.'

'She is Ken. But please. Can you get your lot to block any calls from Virginia? It's early days. I don't want to talk to her at the moment. Not until everything has settled down anyway.'

'Yes, of course. Not a problem. What did Virginia say?'

Virginia of course had not yet said anything, because Virginia did not yet know, but Ralph decided that revealing this might be somewhat embarrassing, so answered equivocally, 'She's not impressed. But you ought to know my new address and phone number.' He pushed over a piece of paper.

Ken glanced at it saying, 'A bit of a come down after the other house, isn't it?' but smiled.

'Let's hope it's only temporary,' Ralph said smiling back at him as they finished their coffee. 'We'll see what's left after the divorce.'

It was the first time he had used the word out loud or in the open. He had not mentioned divorce even to Tina, who he knew had most right to know what his intentions were. Perhaps, until that moment with Ken, Ralph had considered that there could be a going back, a retrieval of his earlier life, and that by simply saying the word 'divorce' to Ken, he had actually set in motion the events about which hitherto he had only been thinking.

'It'll be expensive. The divorce I mean. They always are. Who will you get to represent you?'

'I'm not sure. We'll see. Maybe I won't need anyone.'

'You always need a good divorce lawyer when you get divorced. Virginia will probably go to Pinders. I'll bet.'

'Why? I'm not even sure that I know the firm.'

'Well you wouldn't. You don't do divorce anymore. But they are the up-and-coming fashionable outfit. Two women partners. Specialise in expensive family cases. Very good as well. Pound to a penny she goes to them.'

Ralph sighed. 'Whoever she goes to it'll be the same though. Like taking all your clothes off isn't it. Stripping yourself financially naked.' Ralph did not relish the idea of Virginia discovering that they had been living beyond their means for some time now but that was for another day. 'Got to get through it. I'll manage.'

'Do you know Ralph, I don't doubt it. You're a survivor.

I've seen that many times. Back against the corner in a seemingly impossible case and then suddenly 'pow'. Like Bulldog Drummond, or was it Sapper, with one bound he was bloody well free. I just hope she's worth it.'

'She,' said Ralph 'is called Tina. And she is.'

'I'll do my best to help you through it,' said Ken, suddenly standing. 'Do you want me to tell anyone? Quietly?'

'No, keep it to yourself for the moment. I'll give you the nod when I'm ready, if that's all right?' Ralph stood beside Ken, touched him lightly on the shoulder and said, 'I've always been extraordinarily grateful for your help and advice Ken. I owe you a lot.'

'Ralph, it's kind of you, but I'm not even going to try and give you any advice this time. I just hope you know what you're doing.'

As Ken started to leave the room Ralph found himself thinking, so do I, but asked, 'Is Geoffrey in?'

'Former Head of Chambers or the other Geoffrey?'

'Former Head of Chambers'

'Yes. He's in his room. Why?'

'I want to tell him next.' Ralph knew that Ken would be flattered that he had been first to hear, even before Sir Geoffrey, but then Ralph had decided to tell them in that order to achieve just that result. He wanted them on board and was acutely aware that Ken's support was professionally more important to him than anyone else's could possibly be over the next few months, probably longer. After Ken had gone Ralph picked up the phone, dialled the extension and heard Sir Geoffrey's voice, neither welcoming nor otherwise.

'It's Ralph, Geoffrey. Can you spare me a few minutes?' It

was a question that Ralph had asked in the same way many times and had always been a prelude to a conversation, which they both enjoyed, when Ralph would try out a line of argument or reasoning on him and seek a view.

'Of course, come down.'

It always amused Ralph that Sir Geoffrey's room was as unlike his own as any could possibly be, with its profusion of pictures, legal cartoons, photographs of the Oxford College and the old school, legal reports, books and more books, arm chairs, tables; it was more like a gentleman's club than a study.

'Sit down Ralph,' motioning towards an armchair, Sir Geoffrey advanced towards him. 'Would you like a drink? It's gone six.'

'Do you know I hadn't realised. Yes, I would. Small whisky if I may.' There was a pleasing splash, and a glass was put into his hand as the older man sat down opposite him, holding his own glass to his eyes and saying, 'Wonderful malt. A present. Sixty-degree proof. You can see the islands when you taste it.'

Ralph had remembered that he had promised to meet Tina and was preparing an apology as he answered abstractedly. 'Lovely. I can see exactly what you mean.'

'You haven't tasted it yet,' the older man said with a laugh. 'Taste it first.'

Ralph sipped, 'No truly, it's lovely.'

'What can I do for you? The Deacon case?' As former Head of Chambers, and a very effective and popular one, he still kept his ear to the ground and knew, generally always, what all the various barristers, who numbered about twenty, were doing.

Ralph was therefore not at all taken aback by the question and said, 'No, not really. A personal matter,' but his curiosity was such that he was unable to resist asking, 'What do you know of it?'

'I read the brief last week. Hopeless. Has to plead guilty and try and get away with mitigation.'

'He wants to plead not guilty.'

'He might want to, but he shouldn't. What are you going to do?'

'Let him if he still wants to tomorrow morning.'

'Do you think that is wise?'

'Maybe not wise but he's the client. I'm just the trained mouth remember.' This was Ralph's stock response at dinner parties when he was asked, as he often was in the days when he had a large criminal practice, 'How on earth can you represent someone you know is guilty?' Rather than going into the technical issues, that it was for the state to prove guilt, that the evidence had to be assessed and found to be sufficient beyond reasonable doubt, that people were entitled to be assumed innocent until proven guilty and the other remarks that were always dismissed as lawyer's self-serving crap if the questioner was uncouth, or elegant rubbish if more educated, he would say, 'I'm just the mouthpiece. I say what the client would say if he had my knowledge and training and was able to express himself adequately and confidently in an intimidating and frightening situation. I am merely a mouth.' It usually ended what Ralph had increasingly come to feel was layman's nonsense.

'Yes,' Sir Geoffrey said, 'a mouth. But a mouth attached to a mind and I've met few people who are as fast in terms of mind to mouth as you are.' It was a compliment and Ralph recognised it as such. 'You should talk him into pleading guilty.'

'I've left it to the morning. We'll see then. No, that's not why I wanted to see you Geoffrey. It's another matter. More personal,' and deciding to launch into this without any preamble said, 'I've left Virginia.'

Geoffrey, who had never married, spluttered into his glass. Ralph had not expected such a reaction. 'You've left Virginia. Don't be ridiculous. You can't leave Virginia. She's an admirable woman. Exactly what you need. You must be insane.'

'No, Geoffrey. Not mad. I find myself thinking in clichés but I'm not mad. There's someone else.'

'There always is someone else. Men don't leave wives like Virginia unless there is someone else. Do I know her?' He seemed to shout the last question and Ralph, who had thought he had nothing to fear from this conversation, now found himself uncomfortable and tongue-tied.

'Well, you've met her.'

'Where, when?' He looked at Ralph grimly as though he was challenging him to produce an intellectual rabbit from an intellectual hat that would somehow justify what he evidently considered not just a perverse but wholly irrational decision.

'At our house, our drinks party just over a week ago.' He still did not want to reveal Tina's name.

The older man was confused, shook his head and said, 'I've no idea. Who?'

'She's called Christina. I introduced her to you.'

'Christina. I remember a Christina. Attractive girl. The Pre-Raphaelite hair. Mid-twenties probably. Pretty. Bit of a flirt.'

Ralph agreed with all the sentiments except the last which had not crossed his mind.

'Yes. Tina,' he said but the old man looked thoughtful,

mulling over the news as a dog might chew an old bone.

'I would never have believed it, if you hadn't told me. I think, and forgive an old man and an old friend of yours speaking like this Ralph, that you must be fuckstruck.'

The vulgarity seemed a touch obscene coming from this cultured and civilised old lawyer sitting in the dignified surroundings of his room and Ralph was appalled. He had never heard the expression before, found it extremely distasteful, and was not sure how to reply.

'Yes, completely and utterly fuckstruck,' he repeated. 'That's the only explanation. You'll get over it. Get it out of your system. Screw her but go back to Virginia. That's my last word on it,' and he glared at Ralph. 'I hope you come to your senses before it's too late. You're the last person I thought would be led by that particular organ.'

'Why, gee thanks,' Ralph wanted to reply but he smiled, as easily as though he had just been paid another compliment and said, 'Geoffrey, none of us know very much about anything let alone understand it. Marriages are always the biggest mystery, followed by human attraction. There's no explaining the chemistry. Others call it love.'

'Love be damned.'

Ralph wondered whether the old celibate could appreciate just what a caricature he sounded, perhaps he was only a caricature, a two dimensional old man who had never loved or felt those flames - of lust Geoffrey would have answered scornfully - and had never felt passionately about anyone. 'You shouldn't jeopardise your marriage.'

'It's too late. I've left her and I wanted to tell you personally.'

It was going to be the stock phrase from now on if he was

telling anyone, Ralph thought, and was content with the blandness of the words. 'I'm sorry that I've upset you. I had no idea that you would feel quite so strongly,' and, he wanted to say, be so fucking rude and outspoken.

'Well, I do. I like Virginia. Always have done. From the moment I met her. Few women are a patch on her and you should know that,' and he gazed into his glass.

'Have another?' he asked in a more emollient tone. 'I'm sorry too if you think I've spoken out of turn or exceeded my brief. I'll get used to the idea I suppose.'

'Thank you Geoffrey but not now. Another night perhaps. I must get on.' The words were spoken lightly but Ralph was thinking of Tina waiting for him.

'Ha. Back to bed. Back to the red-hot tart,' he grunted. 'No, I'm sorry Ralph. Joke in very poor taste. Forgive me.'

'Of course Geoffrey,' said Ralph, seething and biting back some very strong sentiments. 'Thanks for listening,' he said, knowing that he would need Geoffrey's continued support as well and taken aback, but completely taken aback, at the strength of the old man's reaction. He left, closing the door and went back to his own room. He picked up the brief, put it in his bag and walked briskly towards the car park.

At their flat, Tina had been waiting for him for over two hours, a fact which she was quick to point out, quite good naturedly. Ralph apologized but all she said was, 'I actually waited in the shop for half an hour but didn't waste my time. Ian and I went through the monthly figures. When we finished, he dropped me round here and I've been cooking ever since.' She did not say that Ian had asked if he could come in and she had politely but firmly refused. 'I've made a stew.'

Ralph's heart sank. Still, she could not be expected to know that he had a contempt for standard English cooking that bordered on the inexplicable and he smiled saying, 'I'm sure it'll be lovely.'

'Ready in about forty minutes,' she said, looking at her watch. 'How shall we occupy ourselves? I've started running a bath. Should we have one together?'

They sat in the over-bright bathroom, white-tiled and antiseptic, so unlike the one at the hotel and he kissed and stroked her until she, saying 'Ralph, I want you now,' stood up and started towelling herself dry. He looked at her, thought once again how beautiful she was and how sexually exciting he found her and stood up and held her closely to him.

'I love you Tina.'

'And I love you Ralph.'

'How do you know?'

'I just do. Come to bed.'

Then later, as they were lying together, his arm under her neck and his head resting protectively on her breast, gently stroking the nipple, he asked, 'Have you had many lovers Tina?'

She narrowed her eyes like a navigator at sea looking at the horizon, closed them momentarily and it was a moment before she spoke. 'How odd. I never thought that kind of thing would bother you. It's not a question I would ever have expected you to have asked,' and sitting up, kissed him, long and hard. 'I've just got to check the food,' and so saying, she stood up, putting on a dressing gown and disappeared towards the kitchen.

Ralph was bemused, it was as though he had trespassed on some private area. Perhaps it was not a question that he should have asked at all but the lack of an answer intrigued him. He decided to ask the question again, but on another occasion, and filed his decision in the extensive list of things to do that he held in his memory.

She returned and said, 'It's ready. I've set the table too. We don't have to get dressed.'

She had lit candles, poured some red wine, and the stew in a casserole on a serving board smelt rather good, he conceded.

He tasted it and complimented her. 'It's nice.'

'Good. I splashed out on some decent beef. Normally, I use a cheaper cut. What have you been doing today?'

He told her of the man he had seen and would be representing tomorrow, the events and his reaction. She was appalled. 'He shouldn't have done it. He might have killed them.'

'It was a crime passionel. The French would definitely excuse it. It was a spur of the moment thing.'

'Did he keep a cricket bat in the bedroom then?' she asked. It was a very pertinent question and Ralph, mentally running through the documents he had read, was taken aback, having to concede that neither he nor anyone else had thought of asking this. She continued, 'I suppose if he kept it in the bedroom and on impulse just grabbed it, that might be one thing. If, on the other hand, he came into the house, heard noises, suspected and took it up with him, wouldn't that be another?'

'Only surely in part. His reaction to the event itself would still have been quantitatively the same.'

'I suppose so but. Do you really think it was justified?' She stressed the personal pronoun.

'I don't know,' he replied thoughtfully. So far he had only considered the case on its legal merits, and had not assessed his own feelings or the moralities involved. 'I can imagine his horror, his sense of betrayal. I can't personally imagine, if you loved the woman, wanting to kill her although I can imagine wanting to beat the man to a pulp.'

'Why?'

'Well they say that any woman can be seduced by any man if he talks to her long enough, uses the right words, persuades her. That, in a sense, makes the man the guiltier party but it also implies that women are incorrigibly unable to resist. Which is a bit damning.'

'Men fall in love with their eyes, women their ears. I fell in love with you first because of your voice and what you talked about.'

'Not then because you found me attractive?'

'Oh yes, that as well. That was a bonus.'

'Did you make a habit of seductions in the kitchen?' He asked this as lightly as he could. The fact that he might have been one of many bothered him.

'God, no. I just wanted you so badly and I think I was already in love with you.'

'When did you fall in love with me then?'

She looked at him. 'I think that first night we met. I thought of nothing but you afterwards. I kept on thinking of you. I was so pleased when you asked us to your house. I so wanted you.'

'What do you mean?'

'Wanted you physically. And it was so nice, that first time.'

He remembered their first time as rushed, hasty, a guilty but erotic coupling that had lasted only minutes. He did not speak.

She continued, 'Perhaps you talked me into it in a sense but then I wanted to. If I hadn't I wouldn't have. It's as simple as that. And I love you.' She looked at him rather earnestly, 'and that makes a difference.'

'I don't think I talked you into it but if I did I'm pleased that it worked,' he replied trying to catch what he thought was her mood. He felt reassured. 'I hate the idea that you could be talked into it by anyone else.'

'I couldn't be. I've got you now.'

He wondered which of the last three words in that last sentence was the most significant to her - got in the sense of possessing him (and he felt both possessed and possessory and liked the sensation) - you perhaps meaning he was the most important thing to her (and he wanted to feel that he was) or now - meaning that this relationship, like that with St John and all of his predecessors, could be transient. He did not pursue the analysis, either mentally or aloud but asked, seeking he supposed, more reassurance, 'Do you think you will always love me?'

'Yes.'

'How can you know?'

'I can't know. I just believe I will. You're everything I ever wanted.' Like all men Ralph was susceptible to a woman's flattery.

'How?'

'I like your body. Your brain. The way you speak. The things you talk about. You're interesting and intelligent. Funny. Successful. I like your occasional legal pedantry. I like the way your hair falls over your eyes. And the way you push it back. And we've got the rest of tonight, and the week and the month and the year and so on to talk, make love and be happy. It's as simple as that.' The words had tumbled out. For no reason that he could think of, Ralph recalled Sir Geoffrey and his dismissal of Tina, his explanation for all Ralph's actions being that he, Ralph, was 'fuckstruck'. He decided not to talk about this with her tonight but was interested in her view or reaction as to the sentiment and filed this question away as well.

'What's going to happen tomorrow then?' she asked with what seemed real interest.

'The indictment first...'

'What is an indictment in that sense?' She was curious.

'The formal statement of the charge against him. Then the opening speeches, prosecution evidence, wife and lover. Doctors' reports on the injuries. Might get to the defence case.'

'What is the defence case?'

'There isn't one. There's no defence whatsoever.'

'What are you going to say, then?'

'I'm not sure. I've got an idea, but I suspect he'll plead guilty.'

'And if he does?'

'Prison. Could just be suspended. If he is lucky.'

'And if not?'

'Three maybe four years. Society doesn't approve of people who do things like that.'

'Have you sorted out what you're going to say?'

'Not entirely. I've got lunchtime for that.'

She looked at him. 'Seriously? Lunchtime? Don't you think you should be doing it now?'

'No. I want to hear how the evidence comes out if he pleads not guilty.'

'God,' she said apparently impressed. 'You must be able to think quickly.'

'I usually can and so I shouldn't be too late to bed.'

'No. Let's go now. I want you to hold me. Leave the things.

I'll do them tomorrow.' She piled the dirty dishes neatly on the draining board, went to the bathroom, cleaned her teeth and got into bed. He stood for a moment at the window, having drawn the curtains back, looked out the at the urban sprawl and tried to think about the future. He found himself unable to see beyond the night to come and the day to follow.

Living for the moment, he told himself and followed her to bed. She was already asleep. He kissed her, she moaned quietly, and he too then fell asleep full of thoughts of love, jealousy and possession.

The following morning she was again up before him, but not yet fully dressed, clothed only in a dressing gown which fell open, revealing pubic hair and the sides of her breasts, a sight that prompted Ralph to say, 'You look ravishing'.

'I've only put some make-up on.'

'Come here.'

She laughed. 'Before or after a cup of tea?'

'Now,' he said.

The sensation, as he entered her, was he thought, indescribably lovely. He tried to differentiate between love and fuckstruck. Fuckstruck was rubbish. How could he be? Virginia, and so many other girls, had all been sexually available to him. This was different. This, after all these years, was the real thing, the closest he had ever come to a physical and mental rapprochement, engagement or melding, with another person.

'That was a lovely start to the day. Now you can drink your tea.' She pushed him, 'You've got to get on.'

'I am on.'

'No. Not on me, on with the day.'

Regretfully he agreed and rolled from her, kissing her as he did so, reluctant to withdraw.

'There's always tonight,' she said.

'I'm already looking forward to it.'

Breakfast of coffee and toast over, they both dressed, in dark suits each, and left the flat together holding hands.

'Do you want a lift?'

'Mm. Please. I love the car.' Getting in, she noticed a piece of white material behind the passenger seat which she bent to pick up. He looked and realized, with a sinking stomach, that she was going to pick up a pair of knickers that Virginia must have discarded the day before the funeral, when they had driven on the moors.

'What's this?' Tina asked.

He decided on a partial truth rather than an evasion. 'Looks like her knickers. She was always so bloody careless and untidy with her things.'

'In your car?'

'Will have fallen out of an overnight bag or her handbag. God knows when, leave them.'

Tina looked at them distastefully. 'Well I don't think I'd let my knickers get left around like that or,' she paused, 'did she take them off for you? Here, in the car.'

'Of course not, Tina. Come off it. Don't be ridiculous.' He felt like a small boy caught out in a simple lie. 'You can't imagine that, surely.'

'No, but I wouldn't mind, you know, here in this car, with you. You'll get rid of them, won't you?'

'Yes, of course,' but the thought of Tina, in the car, on the big leather seats was a pleasant one. 'I've never done it in a car. It would be rather nice.'

'Yes,' she replied dreamily, 'I never have either. We'll try it but,' with sudden resolve, 'not now. Another time. I'm going to be late.'

He reflected, as they kissed and she got out and walked towards the shop, of how, and he searched for a word, mature? sensible? practical? her reaction had been. Matter of fact acceptance. A simple enquiry that had been satisfied by a simple answer. Then the day and the trial pushed these thoughts out of his mind.

He arrived at the Courts early but found his client and solicitor already there. They went to a conference room and sat down.

'Well,' Ralph asked, 'what thoughts?'

'I want to plead not guilty.'

'So be it. I'll do my best.' Ralph had a strategy, and decided not to lean on the client, even though his plan was high-risk, he knew.

The courtroom's public gallery was nearly empty, but Ralph noticed the press box had more than the usual number of reporters in it. Ken had been right, there was media interest. The jury was sworn and Ralph, who had made no objection to any, looked at them. His client's fate depended on their response to Jim - if they disliked him they would convict. If not? Well, maybe. Prosecuting counsel, a man Ralph knew well, leaned across to him. 'Going to change his plea to guilty I trust,' a formal plea having been taken some weeks earlier.

'Good God, no,' Ralph replied. 'Why on earth should he?'

'Because there's no defence.'

'Let's see,' and Ralph smiled at him.

Everyone in the court rose to their feet when the judge

entered and then they all sat down, apart from Jim who was told to remain standing. The clerk put the charge to Jim in the dock, looking sad and forlorn, Ralph noticed cheerfully, but who said firmly, 'Not guilty.'

The prosecuting barrister opened his case, referred to the horrific injuries, reviewed the law, stated that he believed there could be no defence and that the jury, after hearing the evidence, would agree with him and convict the defendant.

The first witness was the wife, in real life every bit as attractive as the photograph had apparently indicated. The prosecuting barrister sat down after he had taken her through the evidence of, yes she had been having an affair with another man, yes she had been in bed with him when her husband had arrived back and yes, he had attacked them with a cricket bat. Yes, she had suffered a fractured skull and still had headaches. No, the marriage was over. Yes, she believed her husband intended to kill them both. It had taken three neighbours to hold him down while the police were coming. Yes, her lover had been screaming in agony and yes, both had pleaded with him to stop the murderous assault. Ralph got to his feet and smiled benignly.

'Mrs Deacon. It came as something of a surprise to your husband that you were having an affair, didn't it?'

'Yes,' she said suspiciously.

'In fact, a complete surprise?'

'Yes.'

'He knew nothing of it?'

'No.'

'He had no reason to suspect had he?'

'No.'

'Why not?'

'I'd kept it quiet.'

'For how long?'

She was silent.

'For how long?' he repeated.

Prosecuting Counsel, sensing danger, stood up. 'Your Honour, surely this is not relevant?'

'We'll see, Mr Prentice. I'll stop Mr Edwards soon enough if I consider any question irrelevant.'

Ralph continued. 'For how long?'

The actual reply did not concern him. A long time or a short time, he could make something of either.

'For about six months'

'You'd been deceiving him for six months?'

'Yes.'

'And he had no idea?' Ralph glanced at his client who, when he heard six months, had audibly let out breath.

'He had no idea that your lover was Derek Barrens had he?

'No,' sullenly.

'He had been your mutual friend had he not?'

'What do you mean?'

'Had your husband lent him money, when his business failed? Put another business plan together for him? Hadn't charged?'

'Yes, he'd done that.'

'And then he found you both in bed together?'

'Yes.'

'How did he find you?'

'What do you mean?'

'It's a simple question. How did he find you?'

'In our bedroom.'

'In the marital bedroom?'

'Yes.'

'What would he have seen as he came in?'

'I object, Your Honour.'

'No, I'd like to see where Mr Edwards is going.'

Ralph repeated the question. 'What would he have seen as he came in?'

'Us, I suppose.'

'Doing what?'

'Having sex.'

'Were you both naked?' Deacon was looking more and more uncomfortable.

'Yes.'

'And I think you were on top, weren't you? Was this your first affair?' She looked shifty, trying to decide which of the two questions she had to answer.

'Mr Edwards,' the judge interrupted, 'I consider this becoming too salacious. I'm not sure this is relevant.'

It is, thought Ralph, it's all that is relevant, but said 'I shan't press it further Your Honour.'

The judge looked at the clock. 12.40. Just right, thought Ralph, please lunch adjournment, let the jury be left to discuss the image he had created for them of the naked woman on top, bouncing away, possibly having had other affairs, contrasted with the huddled, miserable and pitiful husband in the dock, and he was delighted when the judge announced, 'We'll break for lunch. Resume at two.'

They all stood again as the judge left. The jury filed out and the other barrister turned to Ralph and said, 'Where are you going? You can't plead provocation. What are you up to?'

'Setting the scene, just setting the scene,' Ralph replied. He had decided not to cross examine the wife any further and, knowing that he was only going to ask the lover a few questions, thought that the case might finish today. He perhaps would not have to spin it out until tomorrow for his plan to have any chance of success.

At 2.00 pm the proceedings started again. Ralph had spent the interval preparing a final speech in readiness if he had to deliver it later that afternoon. The lover was next. Rather arrogant, Ralph thought, and unlikely to make a good impression on the jury. One or two of the men looked at the man, contemptuously Ralph hoped was an accurate description, but he could not be sure. Juries were always inscrutable and unpredictable. He caught the eyes of two women jurors, both of whom smiled at him, not perhaps obviously noticeable, but nevertheless smiles.

The lover's evidence was largely the same as Mrs Deacon's, save as to the injuries. No, he was unable to walk properly, and the Doctors had said he was always going to have a pronounced limp. Ralph stood again.

'My client had been good to you, hadn't he?'

'I suppose so.'

'Helped you when you were down?'

'Yes,' grudgingly.

'And this is how you repay him. Let him walk in on you both, naked, fornicating in his bed, in his bedroom, in his house, with his wife. Fornicating.'

'Objection,' but Ralph had sat down. He hoped the jury would hold his last words, the only ones he wanted them to remember and discuss that too. Medical reports were distributed. These had been agreed by the defence in advance. Police evidence was likewise agreed, and this was simply read out. Ralph was busy calculating, looking at his watch. If he kept his client's evidence very short there was just time for prosecuting counsel to begin and perhaps finish his closing speech.

Sitting in the dock, Jim cut a proverbially pathetic figure. Ralph made a sudden decision and when the barrister had sat down again after saying, 'That concludes the case for the Prosecution,' stood up saying,' I offer no evidence.'

The other barrister looked worried and alarmed. He had not prepared his closing speech and had to fumble his way through the facts and the law, sitting down again very quickly and looking bewildered.

Then Ralph stood up and, assuming a casual, conversational pose, talked of love, and life, the unfairnesses, the injustices, fidelity, chastity, sexual immorality, immediately caught and held the jury's attention. He badly wanted the judge to interrupt him, to interrupt him several times, to give the impression that the judge was against his client. He was successful.

'Mr Edwards, this is not a defence. You know perfectly well provocation is irrelevant on the issue of guilt in all crimes other than murder.' It was a quote from Archbold, the definitive tome on criminal law.

'Your Honour, I'm not pleading provocation as a defence. Although of course the jury can acquit if they believe the case has not made out.'

'Please keep to the point Mr Edwards.'

'Your Honour is well aware that juries are only required to answer to their own consciences and that a verdict of acquittal that is contrary to Your Honour's direction must nevertheless be accepted by the Court. It's simply that juries are never told this but...'

He was interrupted again by the judge who was losing his temper.

'Mr Edwards. You are totally out of order.'

'Your Honour, I apologise if I seem so, but the jury are entitled to know the true position' and he held up a book by a very eminent former Lord of Appeal. Several lawyers in the courtroom drew in their breath. 'I can read out the relevant passage should you so wish.'

'Get on with your speech,' growled the red-faced old man.

Ralph returned to his carefully rehearsed and planned speech, so bound up with his thoughts and emotions over the last week, or was it two, that it came over with passionate sincerity, interrupted a couple more times by the judge and after the fourth such interruption, turned to the jury and said, 'If he had killed them he could have pleaded provocation. English law doesn't allow him to.' He pointed at Jim, head in his hands and staring at the floor. 'Law or justice. It's up to you,' and sat down.

The judge was angry and made it apparent. 'Mr Edwards' words are a farrago of nonsense. It is for me to direct you on the law and for you to decide the facts.'

Ralph noticed with satisfaction that a number of the jury looked appalled at this, to them, obviously contemptuous, dismissal of the defence case, except that it was not a case, for the judge was right, but so indeed was Ralph in what he had said about their right to acquit should they so wish. However, juries dislike antipathetic judges and this judge had contrived, unwittingly but so carefully orchestrated by Ralph, to demonstrate what Ralph hoped they might see as a prejudice against both Jim and them.

In all other respects the summing up was unremarkable and fair except that the judge, perhaps unwisely, concluded by saying, 'You have to disregard all that Mr Edwards said,' before they were told to go and reach a verdict.

The minutes or hours between the jury retiring to consider their verdict and their returning, are among the longest in a criminal barrister's life. Success or failure. The fate of the client hangs in the balance. Ralph's habit, in days before or already as a newly qualified barrister, was to spend the time reading or doing the crossword. Today however, having very quickly spoken to his client, who still looked bemused, he went into the robing room where he found the prosecuting barrister.

'Bloody hell, Ralph. If that goes wrong your client is for the high jump.'

'I know, but he wanted me to do it.'

'Well, I don't think old Horseface was very impressed.'

'No, I know, but there it is,' and so saying Ralph went to the window. He thought of Tina and then Virginia. What would Virginia's reaction have been had she found him and Tina in flagrante? Incomprehension? Cold fury? It was during these preoccupations that an usher told him that the jury had returned a verdict.

Looking at his watch, Ralph thought that, as only forty minutes had gone by, there was no way of guessing what the verdict might be. It could go either way and, going back to the courtroom, he ran over the prepared speech in mitigation.

Ralph knew that what he had done was wrong, in that he had ignored the textbooks and procedures, but had been so caught up in the man's plight, knowing that he must have felt about his wife exactly the same as he felt about Tina, sympathy and empathy, that he was prepared to risk professional obloquy for Jim's sake. He caught the eye of one of the women jurors who had smiled earlier and, as she smiled again, Ralph's hopes rose.

He stood as the judge entered, sat down again and, when the foreman announced that they had reached a verdict and, on being asked, replied,' Not guilty,' actually felt tears come to his eyes.

He had not appreciated the extent to which he had become emotionally involved and sat for a moment blindly listening to the noises of the courtroom, hearing the usher say, 'The court will resume at 10.30 tomorrow,' standing mechanically as the judge left, and looking at the jury, who were smiling and talking amongst themselves.

His solicitor tugged his gown from behind him, 'Mr Edwards, that was a bit irregular but fantastic.'

'What?' he said absentmindedly. 'We'll need to talk to the client,' then recollecting himself and gathering his papers, listlessly, soaked in sweat, feeling completely drained, turned round.

His solicitor looked excited. 'You've just assured yourself of a continual stream of work from my firm. Thank you very much.'

Ralph glanced again at the name of the solicitors on the brief; a well-known large criminal practice with a dubious reputation even, it was alleged in the city, not above concocting evidence and arranging alibis. It was the kind of firm with which Ralph would never have wanted to become professionally involved. He sighed and said, 'Thank you.'

He nodded to the client, still sitting in the dock apparently unable to move and then, as he was about to pick up his papers, the usher was beside him saying, 'The judge would like to see you in his room. Immediately.'

He went in thinking, I suppose I should feel like a naughty schoolboy going before the headmaster but I don't, and was confronted by His Honour, now an ordinary little man without his purple robes and horsehair wig, sitting puffed up and belligerent behind his desk.

'What on earth do you think you were playing at?' He did not greet Ralph, proffer a hand or ask him to sit down.

Ralph, suddenly weary of all the nonsense, paused and looked at the judge, meeting his eyes until the judge looked away, at which point Ralph asked, 'Is this to be a long conversation or a short one?'

'What do you mean?'

'Are you going to ask me to sit down or not? Are you observing the civilities?'

The judge said, 'A short one.'

Beginning to feel cross himself, Ralph sat down, deliberately and ostentatiously and snarled at him, 'Then do carry on, please.'

The judge, taken aback, spluttered, 'Don't be so bloody rude.'

'I don't apologise for stating the obvious, but it's you who's being rude. Not me.' Had anyone spoken to him like this in years, Ralph wondered, as judges, especially judges who try the lesser cases, are a breed whose self-importance is legendary.

'I'm going to make sure that this episode is known about, Edwards. It was a complete dereliction of your duty to the court, to your profession.'

Ralph leant forwards, 'No it bloody well wasn't. Get real. You've been on the bench too long. Your emotions have atrophied. That man had suffered more, much more than his wife or her lover. His pain will last as long and be much more devastating.' Ralph paused again and then said, conversationally and contemptuously, 'The law sucks. Is there anything else? Your Honour,' investing the last two words with an antipathy that was so offensive the judge coloured.

'I'll see that you pay for this,' he exploded angrily. 'You've got to appear before me again you know.'

'And if I do, and you behave otherwise than properly, I will draw it to the attention of the authorities. What I did was not wrong in any moral sense of the word. What I did was simply to represent my client. To the best of my abilities. And the jury sympathised with him. They acquitted him. Not me. Is there anything else?'

The judge shook his head, not meeting Ralph's eyes.

'Good day Your Honour,' Ralph said affably as he left.

Oh fuck, he thought as he went to the robing room. What have I done? In there he found his opponent, in the act of knotting his tie.

'Ralph, what madness impelled you to take that course of action? I know you got your result, but did you see old Horseface? He was livid. It won't go down well with the judiciary.'

'I know his kind. We've just had a chat. He tried to tell me off. I think I might have told him to fuck off. Not quite in those words though. But much the same sentiment.'

'Bloody hell, Ralph. Why?'

'Didn't you think it unfair that the man might get sent to

prison for what he did?'

'Oh yes, I can see the point you made but... the law's the law and we are lawyers.'

'Then perhaps I don't want to be a lawyer anymore. Cheers. See you around.'

He left. He wanted to go home but was not sure where home was. Where was home? Tina, he thought, and went to her there, where he waited until she too came home and he took her wordlessly into the bedroom and made love to her, she asking no questions, making no demands, accepting with joy his need for her, physical and emotional and where she held him, for what was a long time, after he fell asleep.

He woke up at about 9.00 pm, opened his eyes and found Tina looking at him.

'I'm sorry,' he mumbled, 'I fell asleep.'

'I did notice.'

'What time is it?' She told him. 'How long have I been asleep?'

'Only a couple of hours.'

'What have you been doing?'

'Holding you and thinking.'

'About what?'

'You and me. What will become of us? Are you all right?'

'Yes, I think so. That bloody case.'

'Did you win?' She had asked nothing of him, having seen his need and understanding that she could fulfil this, had wanted to ask, but had seen the haunted look in his eyes, the haggardness, the exhaustion, had noticed the shirt, soaked in sweat and had enjoyed the sex, driven, it seemed to her, by an animal passion that Ralph had never shown before.

'Win. Not win. He was acquitted though.'

'Good God. How?' He told her, playing down his role, but otherwise honestly.

'Have you really damaged your career?'

'Probably, in one sense at least. In another maybe not. It will be in the media I guess. Any publicity like that is good publicity for me I suppose. I could have a lot of work on the back of it maybe which I don't want - criminal work.'

'Why not go for criminal law?'

'I lost sympathy with most of that years ago.'

'Will it be on the local news do you think?'

'You can switch on later if you want. Are you hungry?'

'A bit. I got an M&S instant. I'll put that in and get you a glass of wine. Stay there.'

Ralph lay, did as he was told, in bed and waited, not regretting his tactics in the trial nor the conversation afterwards, and wondered whether he really wanted to carry on with law. Perhaps he could get a job in the local university, something where he didn't arrive back home or Chambers, shaking and sweating, the plaudits and approbation forgotten. No, it would mean far too much loss of earnings. He had no intention of ending up in a three-bedroom semi driving a Ford. Tina brought two glasses and the bottle and poured some wine for them both. She asked no more questions and sat quietly on the edge of the bed as Ralph lay there, leaning on one elbow, his chin resting on his hand, eyes closed, sipping his wine periodically. She poured him some more when his glass was empty and went to check the supper.

'Are you ready to eat yet?'

'Yes. I'll get up. I don't remember undressing. When did I

do that?'

'As you came through the doorway,' Tina smiled. 'Come on, let's eat. It's soon time for the local news.' She switched the television on, laughing and saying, 'It seems ages since I watched T.V. We don't really need one, do we?'

She turned first to the national news and then the local news. The acquittal of Jim Deacon was the second item and there was a clip of him and his solicitor coming out of the courtroom, then Jim being interviewed.

'It was all due to my barrister, Ralph Edwards. He was magnificent,' the solicitor nodding his agreement.

Tina turned to Ralph, who was leaning back, a faintly surprised expression, perhaps embarrassed she thought, and said, 'Was it?'

'I suppose so.'

'You're so modest. You must have been marvellous. God, I love you.'

The news items having finished, the T.V. was turned off and it was only after Tina said, 'Let's have an early night,' and he replied, 'It's not exactly early,' but got up and was in bed and asleep before she came in, that she understood at all just how the day, or perhaps she thought the last week or so, had affected him.

The next few days passed in a honeymoon atmosphere of intimacy, Ralph thinking from time to time of Virginia, her father, Virginia's reaction, the money realities, but forgetting those the moment he was back in their flat, making love, talking non-stop but always inconsequentially, making love again, lost in a deep and fathomless passion that Ralph no longer bothered to try and analyse. It was enough that it was and Tina seemed to accept it likewise.

The letter, for Virginia did not telephone, was short and to the point.

'Dear Ralph. I have your letter of Monday. I am not sure I believe it but having telephoned around learn that you are living with that tart Christina.' How people already knew, Ralph had no idea but there it was. They did, so now she did as well. 'I know you well enough to realize that you would not have written to me unless your mind is made up. I am not going to try and change it. But that said, I cannot recognise the Ralph I fell in love with, in your recent behaviour. It is too machine-like, too callous, and too ill-considered. There will never be anyone else and I'm not sure I can contemplate life without you. To lose a mother and a husband in the same week is unbearable. I do not know, nor will I ever probably understand, why you should choose to walk away from fourteen years together for someone, (presumably it is for her?) you have only known a few weeks and who, unless you have been having a daytime affair (a thought I cannot dwell on) must be a complete unknown quantity. But there it is. I shall be seeing lawyers next week and let them sort matters out. In the meantime, I see that you have taken your clothes and the Peake drawing and the oil by Goodwin. If you want anything else, it can be sorted in the divorce proceedings. Presumably you will admit to adultery. Goodbye Ralph. Thank you for the happiest years I have had. I would not have missed them even though they have ended like this. With love, Virginia.'

He sat and stared at the letter for a long time. This was not quite what he had expected. He had anticipated a telephone call, a plea for a meeting, crying, remonstration, sexual persuasion. This was so extraordinarily matter of fact and accepting. Although she had not said she would have him back. Did that get-out still exist, he wondered?

He thought of a married couple, mutual friends, to all intents and purposes happy together, until she, deciding she had missed out on sexual experience due to a repressed and repressive mother, embarked, fifteen years after seeing him last, on an affair with her former geography teacher, a man twenty years her senior who, she said, she had always desired when a fifteen-year-old virgin.

The affair over, or the point proved, she then told her husband all about it. Devastated, to the point of intellectual incoherence, he had tried to understand, to talk himself and themselves through it, to see the whole episode as something that could, with a bit of fancy psychological footwork, enhance their marriage. It did no such thing. The couple did not separate but Stuart would often reflect, in his cups late at night, to Ralph, that he would have swapped all his professional success (of which he had much, in terms of fame and money) for a more successful relationship with his wife.

By this, of course, he meant that he should have been alert to the signs and acted on them. Ralph, who had heard her side of the story, tried to convince him the failure lay less in his shortcomings but deep down, the seeds having been planted before he and Nancy had ever met. She had done it because she was the person she had already become when they married. Even if he had known more about her then, it would probably have made no difference. But had he known more about her, Stuart claimed, he might have been able to factor something in that would have addressed the deficit and inhibited or even prevented the episode altogether.

Was their marriage, the failure - if an affair of the kind that Nancy had, can make a marriage a failure, for she had come back with a revived interest in Stuart, viewing the whole episode with a detached scientific curiosity, in short a settling of unfinished business and completely unable to understand his continuing distress - an argument for much greater honesty about each other at the outset?

But what kind of honesty would Nancy have had to display to make it apparent, or even alert Stuart to the possibility that many years later, she would deliberately seek out her old teacher, approach him, seduce him, sleep with him only a few times and then return, invigorated, to her husband and expect him, if not to approve, at least to understand and accept the need that she had satisfied?

Should she, when they met, have said, 'Look Stuart, I don't feel particularly sexually experienced. Four years ago, when I was fifteen, I had a geography teacher I always fancied, but I didn't sleep with him.' No, Ralph thought, you'd have to be a clairvoyant - there was perhaps nothing that could have averted it, save for Nancy's self-control. But even that was unfair. She had consciously exercised choice, indeed exhibited a great deal of determination in tracking the man down.

It was not the same (was it perhaps more or less reprehensible for that?) as getting completely drunk and waking up in a stranger's bed when away on a business trip. Could Stuart have coped with that more easily Ralph had asked? Stuart thought he probably could but was not sure. He felt sexually betrayed. He put it rather crudely. Nancy was like having an ensuite bathroom, private, to himself. Only he used it. Now someone else had invaded his privacy, had performed a bodily function in his en suite and it was no longer the same. No amount of cleaning, rubbing or scraping could alter the fact, this was said when he was very drunk, that someone had knocked on the door of his en suite, found it open, gone in, lifted the lavatory seat, and dumped his load in it. Ralph found the metaphor an ugly one but was sympathetic to Stuart's unhappiness. He and Nancy were still together, however. Was that how it would be if he and Virginia resumed their life together? Even if she had the capacity to forgive, and more importantly to forget, how would he feel about Tina with whom he felt more alive than at any time before?

He felt as though he had taken a drug that heightened reality. Colours seemed more meaningful, sounds were different, the very sense of being was enhanced. He was convinced; it was as though his life had been lived in black and white until then. It was a sensation that he was not just reluctant to, but knew he could not, forego.

He would show the letter to Tina later, but he wanted to reply to it immediately.

'My dear Virginia. Thank you for writing so quickly. I am sorry but, you are correct, my mind is made up. You can have the house and everything in it. Ask your lawyers to write to me direct. I shall sign anything that they require and shall try to make everything as straightforward as possible. Yours ever, Ralph.'

Tina had told him that she did not care if he came to her with nothing. He would come to her with nothing and start again.

That evening, having made love, they had a bath and then during supper, he handed the letter to Tina without comment.

She read it, also without comment, handed it back to him and raised her eyebrows, quizzically and expectantly.

'It's not quite what I expected,' he said rather lamely.

'What did you expect?'

'A bit more emotion. Not acceptance. Not just like that.'

'Perhaps she's too proud and dignified. God I'd fight for you. I'd do anything to stop you going. I'd be round here.'

Was Tina saying this to try and draw the contrast; she, Tina, loved him more than Virginia did or could? If Virginia really loved him, she should do more.

'No, I suppose it's not Virginia's style. But at least it's going to be straightforward.'

'What do you mean straightforward?'

He hesitated. Should he say that he had just disposed of the house, the furnishings, paintings, the kitchen equipment, the lawnmower, the washing machine, the dishwasher, toolbox, his cellar of wine, in short everything that he had worked for because he was so relieved that it was to be straightforward and because he felt guilty. Probably not the time he decided.

'She'll divorce me. That's all. And that's all I want.'

This was true, it was all he wanted. He was determinedly taking short views. In retrospect he should have taken longer ones, but at that time he simply wanted to be free of the past, the past of his marriage, his friends, his possessions. He simply wanted a new life with Tina and nothing carried over from his previous existence.

'Have you replied?'

'No, not yet. What do you think I should say?' Would she

ask him to defend her, to repudiate the description of her as a tart?

'I'd simply say thank you. And not to contact you otherwise than through a solicitor.' Tina was also alive to the possibility of his being persuaded back if he met Virginia in person.

'Are you going to a solicitor Ralph?'

He did not need to. There was to be no argument as Virginia was to have everything.

'I will if I need to. What about you? What's he,' Ralph could not bring himself to even say St John's name out loud, 'going to do, do you think?'

'He told me I'd hear from his solicitors. I expect they'll write to me care of my parents. I'll let him make the running. There's no hurry after all, is there? It's not as though we had much. Largish mortgage, smallish equity. Not like you Ralph.'

Was Tina expecting him to bring a lot to their relationship - Ralph suddenly hoped not. He would remind her of her sentiment when they were further down the divorce trail. He was tired.

'Let's go to bed Tina. I want to hold you.'

The following morning, when he awoke, he found himself already aroused. Tina was lying facing away from him, he lying against her. He did not want to wake her, but just to enjoy the sensation of being within her, the total intimacy. He did not move but lay quietly, right arm around her waiting for Tina to stir.

'Mm,' she felt down between his legs and grasped him there. 'Make love to me. Ralph. Make love to me.'

'That was lovely,' and she buried her face in his hair, nuzzling him and licking the inside of his ear. 'God, sex with you is so nice, Ralph. It must be because I love you,' and then, springing out of bed, stretched like a cat, naked and beautiful, Ralph thought. 'I wish we didn't have to go to work Ralph. Wouldn't it be nice to do something together?'

'I could or I can,' he replied, 'I'm only doing paperwork today.'

'I've got to go though. I'm not like you. I've got a proper job.'

'I've got a proper job too.'

"But you can structure your job the way you want to. I can't. I'm a wage-slave. Anyway, I've got to do the monthly returns with Ian.' So saying, she got dressed and went to the kitchen.

He followed her, vaguely conscious of an intense dislike of Ian with whom she was to spend her day, and thought of trying to persuade her to a more congenial activity with him, rather than the monthly returns with the tall, muscular, rather common young man that he considered Ian to be. 'I can't persuade you to come with me to,' he hesitated, 'a special lunch.'

'I'll meet you for lunch, but it won't be special. Not in this area anyway.'

'If you took the afternoon off...'

'I can't Ralph. I've got to go,' and with that she kissed him, grabbed a coat from over a chair, threw it on and ran out of the door, leaving him with a palpable sense of loss. All he wanted, and intellectually he knew that it could probably not last with the same intensity, was to be with her, preferably in bed, holding her tightly to him. She had, however, said that she would meet him for lunch. He would telephone her later and see if she meant it or whether that had been merely a throw-away remark. He washed, dressed and went to his chambers;

unable to concentrate there he decided to walk around the shops instead, he wanted to buy her a present. Something extravagant, he thought, but gave up.

He still had little idea of her as a personality, her likes and dislikes or preferences, let alone her aspirations or ambitions. These had never been talked about, their conversation always resting on the here and now.

All that he knew was that Tina had told him that she had been unhappy in her marriage, that she had always wanted someone like Ralph to love her and to hold her and that sex with him was lovely. It was not much when all was said and done, and he determined to ask her more, ask for some Further and Better Particulars as the more detailed pleadings in a case used to be called. He went back to his room and dialled her shop. A girl answered brightly.

'Is Tina there?' he asked.

'She's busy at the moment. Can I ask who's calling and she'll get back to you.'

'Could you tell her it's Ralph?

'I don't really want to interrupt them.'

'Is she with Ian?'

'Yes.'

'Just tell her if you would.' He waited and Tina spoke.

'Hi Ralph?'

He was relieved and knew that he would have been unreasonably cross if she had not taken his call.

'Is lunch on then?'

'I can't really. I've got to finish this work today but listen.' She was excited. 'Mummy telephoned me. There's a letter with a solicitor's post mark on it at home. I didn't ask her to open it. I thought I might drive up this evening and get it. Do you want to come?'

He knew nothing of her parents either. It would be interesting to meet them. 'Yes, OK. See you at home after five.'

'I'll call then and invite us for supper. See you later.'

He put the phone down and, in doing so, wondered where they were actually going for supper. He did not even know where her parents lived let alone what they did, their circumstances or background. Perhaps he did not want to know, but he was sure that his life was now to be inevitably bound up with hers and speculated on what he would discover about Tina that evening.

He was waiting for her when she returned.

'Why so excited?' he asked.

'Oh, it's progress. It's decisions and action. Moving things on. Like you've started already.'

He put his arms out and she came to him. Resting her head on his shoulder she licked his cheek, like a cat he again thought, and started undoing his shirt.

'We've got time, haven't we?' she asked.

'I've no idea. Where are we going?'

'To my parents.'

'I know that. Where do they live?'

'Haven't I told you? Good Heavens. About ten minutes' drive from where I used to live, so yes, we've plenty of time,' and pulled him towards the bedroom.

In his car, a little later, driving out on the motorway, in the dark, her face illuminated by the glow of various dials, like an aircraft she had said the first time they had got in the car together, he looked at her profile. He felt he at least knew this well, and said, 'I know nothing about you. But I love you. Is that inconsistent or simply stupid?'

'You don't need to know everything about anyone to love them. You can love them for what they are,' she smiled.

Or for what they seem, he thought with a lawyer's realism. 'Should I know anything about your parents before I meet them?'

'Not really. They're like me or I'm like them. Uncomplicated. A bit disappointed in me. They made sacrifices to send me to school and I don't think I've repaid them. They'd hoped that I'd be more successful. I used to want that as well but it seems less important now that I've met you.'

What had she told them about him? He asked her.

She did not answer immediately then said slowly and carefully. 'I've told them that you are the most important thing in my life. That I think that I have found real happiness,' smiled at him, that smile which he so liked. 'That's all.'

They arrived in a neat suburban street, mid-war semi-detached, mainly well-tended gardens, spruce paintwork, flowering cherry trees now bare of all leaves, orange lamplight reflecting on the rain drenched road and pavement.

'Here,' she said, 'number eighteen. You can park in the drive. Daddy always puts his car away.'

He eased the Bristol through the gateposts, just managing to avoid scraping either side and drew to a stop. The car filled the driveway and he, for the first time ever, thought that maybe his car was rather large and ostentatious. He struggled to get out from between the car and fence and squeezed along the edge getting his clothes damp in the process. Tina had stepped out into the flower bed and cursed when a rose bush had snagged her dress. The porch light had gone on and the door was opened by a perfectly ordinary looking middle-aged couple.

'Hello Mummy, hello Daddy. I've brought Ralph.' They looked at him as he advanced, right hand outstretched.

'How do you do?' and then shaking hands, stopping, not knowing their surname.

'I'm Bill and this is Betty, my wife,' her father said. The latter introduction did not need the qualification Ralph decided, but shook hands with each.' Come on in.'

The front door led to a small hall off which there were three doors and a straight staircase rising to the first floor. Her mother opened the first which gave into a small sitting room. Ralph could not suppress a smile. The reality of Tina's background was so different from what one might have expected. If he had been asked, and he had not been, he supposed he would have put her parents as upper middle class; after all it was usually the upper middle classes who struggled to pay school fees. The truth was both more interesting and more prosaic. Upper working or lower middle class, her parents both had strong regional accents and their evident pride in their daughter was quite touching.

'Would you like a drink lad?' asked Bill.

'A cup of coffee would be welcome,' Ralph replied.

'No, I mean a proper drink. A beer or something stronger?'

'No thanks very much, I'm driving.'

'I noticed the car. Big isn't it? What make is it?' Bill asked with interest.

'A Bristol.'

'Aren't they aeroplanes?'

'Same company but they've made a few cars each year since

the late forties.'

'Expensive are they?'

'Well, yes, when they're new but mine's nearly five years old.'

'Doesn't look it.'

'A previous owner cared for it rather well.' Tina was meanwhile talking to her mother and Ralph heard a whispered comment to the effect of how sensible he was not to have a drink. 'Not like the last one,' her mother added before she went out with her daughter.

Ralph was left with Bill. He was not sure what to say and Bill was evidently uncomfortable too. It was a situation neither had encountered before. Ralph guessed that her parents must have been pleased when she married St John. 'Going up in the world,' might have been a comment they uttered, 'hope she doesn't get too grand for us.'

Now Tina had swapped a young barrister, struggling at the outset of his career to make a name and reputation for himself, for an older model, already successful and well known. This older version had taken Tina away from the marriage, which had no doubt been celebrated, Ralph wondered where and at what cost and whether it had been another financial struggle for them, in an atmosphere of excitement and happiness. Only a few years later, the relationship was finished, the wedding presents due to be divided; all that money and hope were wasted. Why? Tina said because she wanted him, Ralph. Why marry when she did then? He knew why he had married Virginia. She represented stability, warmth and affection at the time. He did not believe, then, that such a thing as 'romantic love' existed for him after Lucy. His love for her was based on companionability, affection and friendship. It was a different kind of love; not as intoxicating as the emotion Ralph had felt both previously with Lucy, and again now once more with Tina, and identified as love and which he felt fervently for Tina.

Their wedding had taken place in the old church beside Virginia's house, had been followed by a rather grand party. He could remember details as though it had only happened a week or two earlier; the line-up, the speeches, the one he had taken such care with, had prepared as thoroughly as any brief in a difficult case. What had Tina's wedding been like? Had her parents gone upmarket for the reception or had they opted for something more straightforward and low key? He would ask Tina. Whatever it had been however, the reality of the marriage had been disappointment.

'What are your plans then Ralph?' said Bill conversationally but after a lot of thought.

'Plans, I'm not sure at the moment.'

Does he mean plans for myself, Tina, us or what, he considered and replied further, 'I think we'll have to wait and see how things shake down, really.'

'How do you mean lad?'

'I'm not sure what I'm going to be left with after I'm divorced,' he replied knowing in truth he was going to be left with little or nothing.

'I suppose that's sensible,' grunted Bill as Tina and her mother came in with a cup of coffee for Ralph, a beer for Bill and, Ralph noticed to his horror, sherry for Tina and her mother.

'Here, look at this Ralph,' and Tina handed him a letter. 'What do you think?'

It was written in the usual identical terms all such first letters are phrased in divorce proceedings.

'Dear Madam, We are instructed by your husband in connection with proposed divorce proceedings, based upon your adultery with Ralph Edwards. We enclose a statement as to this which we invite you to sign and return to us so that the proceedings may be issued without delay. Our client invites proposals as to the division of house and contents. We suggest that you consult your own solicitors and look forward to receiving a reply.'

'It's standard stuff,' Ralph said as he handed the letter back. 'Do you want to see solicitors?'

'Do you think she ought to?' asked Betty anxiously.

'It depends. Something of a waste of money if it can all be agreed. Will there be an argument about anything?'

'I don't really want much, a couple of bits of furniture, some books, a share of the house, it's not worth much though after the mortgage is taken into account. He can have the rest. There aren't any savings or anything like that to speak of.'

'Probably no need then. I can help you with the letters. God knows I've seen enough of them in practice.'

'Well that's all right then,' Betty said, relieved. Just then the door opened, and a younger version of Tina came in.

'Hi everyone.'

'Hello Squirt,' said Tina. 'How are you? Here, this is Ralph. Ralph, my sister, Sylvia.'

Automatically getting to his feet and extending a hand to shake Sylvia's, Ralph was momentarily non plussed. Tina had never mentioned a sister but then he, Ralph, had never, so far as he could remember talked of his family, mother, father or brother. He supposed he had left them behind a bit; he made a duty visit every ten weeks or so to his parents' house, he remembered that he was about due for one soon, and his brother, who had become a teacher, geography and PE, the two subjects Ralph had despised the most at school, lived a very different life from Ralph.

Tina's was clearly an affectionate and happy family, he had noticed how warmly they had all greeted one another, and he envied them this rather; his family was cold and, he believed, somewhat emotionally repressed.

In due course, they went through to a rather chilly dining room, the table laid with elaborate care. Ralph, if asked later, would have been unable to tell anyone what they actually ate. He contributed little to the conversation which revolved largely round other family members, friends and local events of extreme unimportance.

Sylvia, sitting opposite Ralph, suddenly asked, 'What do you do then?' It was so blunt it verged on rude.

'I'm a lawyer,' he said simply.

'What kind of lawyer?'

'A barrister kind of lawyer,' he smiled.

'Like the last one then?'

'Yes, like the last one, but different kind of law.'

She looked at him with interest. 'St John always regarded his kind of law as the most interesting, most intellectually challenging he used to say.'

'I wouldn't agree with him. I rather enjoy my kind of law. I'd actually hate to do his. What do you do?'

'I'm training to be a solicitor.'

Ralph was startled. 'Where do you practise?'

'Locally. A small firm. I quite like the partners though.'

'How far have you got? Do you enjoy it?'

'Yes, I do and I'm in my second year now. All things being equal I'll qualify next June.'

Tina joined the conversation. 'Sylvia's actually very clever. She got a first in PPE at Oxford.'

'Why didn't you go to one of the smart firms then?' Ralph was interested.

'I like the idea of smaller practice. Who, in their right mind, would want to be part of a huge machine, a law factory, teams, managers, targets, corporatism? The very idea makes me feel ill.' She spoke with real passion. 'I think you have to be a particular kind of idiot. Most of my friends who did law seemed to be attracted to that kind of thing. A very superficial glamour I always thought. You know, we act for Megalopolis Plc and Darth Vader. Big deal. Someone's got to act for them and the nature or identity of the client doesn't change what the law is.'

'Couldn't agree with you more,' said Ralph. 'I became a barrister because I liked law but wanted to be my own master.'

'And you are, aren't you,' added Tina.

'Yes, but only to an extent. There are still constraints - you still have to take cases you don't like or don't want to, still have to go to work etc.'

'Yes, but much nicer than my job,' smiled Tina.

Although they were evidently sisters, Ralph noticed that whilst all traces of background accent had vanished from Tina's voice, her sister retained some roughening in her speech that gave away her origins, indeed the locality of those origins, as she spoke. There was an interesting contradiction; the one who had gone to a metropolitan university and not become a lawyer had changed, whilst the other, Oxford and a lawyer, had not.

'Which college did you go to Sylvia?'

'I always think that a snotty question. No, I don't mean to be rude but I always wonder about the motives of the person asking it. What difference does it make?'

'I guess none really. The only reason I ask,' the only reason he was in fact asking was to establish whether she had gone to one that was regarded as generally better, 'is because the only reason I would have liked to have gone to Oxford, and it wasn't a good enough reason to go, was for some of the lovely architecture. I'd have liked to have spent a few years surrounded by beautiful buildings.'

'I went to Balliol.'

'Lovely surroundings then,' smiled Ralph thinking that Sylvia must be pretty bright. 'Did you enjoy it?'

'Yes, but I was pleased to leave. Hot house stuff and all of that.'

Tina was pouring coffee. 'And now she lives at home again.'

'Do you really?'

'Oh yes. We don't get paid much in the small provincial firms; not like the big smart ones. But then I wouldn't be doing it at all if I just wanted money.'

'How much do trainee solicitors get then?' asked Ralph who was aware that the Law Society imposed a minimum figure. This turned out to be approximately one tenth of what Ralph had earned the previous year and he sympathized. 'It can only get better.'

Tina got up, saying, 'Come on Sylve, let's do the washing up before I go.' Ralph stood up too but was waved back.

'Sister talk probably,' Betty said.

'They look alike, don't they,' said Ralph, feeling as he made the remark, the obvious stupidity of it.

'Yes, they're very close. We're very proud of them. It's a pity Tina didn't carry on with her law though, but so long as she's happy,' Betty seemed to realise the incongruity of this comment, and Bill said, 'Let's hope she will be,' and looked meaningfully at Ralph, who still did not know what Bill did, or had done for a living. He was a strongly built man. Ralph estimated him at about fifty, twelve years or so older than him, who in turn was ten years older than Tina, a funny idea being midway between them. He wanted to ask and decided to anyway, 'Did you like Tina's husband?' He wanted to know, although there was no guarantee that either would be honest in their answers.

'No, not really,' said Bill with what Ralph considered either surprising honesty or tact.

'If Tina hadn't married him she'd be a lawyer now as well. I said at the time that she was making a mistake. But she wouldn't listen.'

'Ssh, it's a long time ago now, Bill.'

'Well, it might be a long time ago, but we went without a lot to send those two girls away.'

'Yes, but Tina made her own choice, and she's done well.'

'Oh aye. Done well. She could have done what she's doing without ever having gone anywhere. She could have started at sixteen and worked her way up.'

'Water under the bridge, dear. Don't embarrass Ralph.'

Ralph was far from embarrassed. He was actually very interested, and some of his suppositions or assumptions were already proved correct. The parents had made a sacrifice, they did want both their daughters to do well, that was clearly the reason for the sacrifice and father was unhappy at Tina's decision. Mum was clearly the peacemaker. Ralph speculated on how far Tina's father had tried to persuade her not to marry but to carry on with her career and thought he might ask Dad rather than Tina on another occasion.

The two sisters returned and Tina held out her hand, 'Come on Ralph. We ought to go. Thanks Mum, thanks Dad,' kissing them both. 'Bye Sylve,' kissing her too. Ralph wondered what the right etiquette was for him, handshakes he decided. A bit stiff and formal, he thought but probably appropriate, as he stepped forward. However, he was caught up in a warm embrace by Sylvia, who kissed him on both cheeks whispering, 'Take care of my big sister, won't you,' words nastily reminiscent to Ralph of what his sister-in-law had said to him not long ago, 'who tells me this is the real thing not an immature infatuation like the last one.'

Betty took her cue from Sylvia and pecked at Ralph, on one side only, and Bill stood up and shook hands, a firm and strong grip. Once in the car Tina turned to him and asked, 'What did you think then?'

Ralph sat and considered, 'You're obviously a close family,' seemed a nice neutral comment. He was not actually quite sure yet what he thought. Everything had been something of a surprise. The house, not what he had expected, the parents likewise and a sister.

'Yes, we always have been. Did you like Sylvia?'

Was this a loaded question? Did she mean that had he met Sylvia before her then he would have chosen Sylvia in preference? To answer 'yes' might appear to suggest this and to answer 'no' was clearly wrong.

'She's obviously a bright girl. As you said. You both went to the same school then.'

'Yes, she was two years behind me.' Ralph wanted to ask if she was going out with anyone, engaged perhaps but was sure he would find out in due course. Tina's hand was resting on his leg, and he closed his hand over hers, squeezing it. 'It was a pleasant evening. They're nice people. What does your father do? I assume he still works. He's not very old.'

'He used to be steel erector but now, because it's a young man's game, he says, he's become a foreman in a building firm. He can put his hand to anything round the house. If you gave him a piece of land he could put up a house single-handed, you know, dig the foundations, do the brickwork, the plastering, joinery, electrics, the lot.'

'A useful man to have around then.'

'Yes, if anything needed doing in...' she paused and did not continue.

'Your last house,' Ralph finished for her.

'Yes, my last house, he would do it. The other one wouldn't.'

The other one. Is that what he was now to be called, Ralph mused? Better perhaps than 'my husband' as he technically and legally was but still a nasty reminder that someone had been there before. 'Steel erectors, I am told, earn a lot of money, in a building boom, relative to everyone else.'

'Yes. But most of it went on our school fees. Mummy works as well.'

'What does she do then?'

'She's a school cook. She loves it. Works in the local primary. The hours suit her she says.'

It was incredible, a steel erector and a school cook sending their two daughters to one of the most expensive and exclusive public schools in the country, Ralph pondered and said, 'Were they hard up then?'

'In a sense, no holidays or real luxuries. Still in the same house that they bought before I was born. No mortgage though. They had a party a few years ago to celebrate paying it off.'

Ralph had never met anyone who had managed to pay off a mortgage and was impressed. 'Lucky them. I've always seen mortgages as stretching into infinity.' Any new one certainly will be, he reflected, but never mind.

'Do you want to reply to the letter?' he suddenly asked.

Tina stirred, and sat up in her seat. 'Of course, what should I say?'

'Let's write it at home and I can post it tomorrow.'

'I'll have to handwrite it.'

They composed this together later that evening. A short letter saying that she agreed to a divorce, enclosing a statement admitting adultery and suggesting a division of all assets equally save for certain specified items, a list of which would follow.

'That's enough to get the thing moving,' Ralph had said and she, not knowing anything about the mechanics of divorce, was reassured. They did not discuss her list that night, he saying to her that it was probably best reflected on as it was, in his experience, difficult to add anything after it had been sent to the other side, much easier to concede items. Tina fell asleep trying to remember any items of importance or significance.

The following morning, he woke to find the bed empty. Tina was at the table writing and he got up and went to her.

'I've finished my list,' she said triumphantly.

'May I see it?'

'Of course.' It contained only a few named objects.

'The small lowboy. Aunt Louise's tea service. The second-best cutlery. The Le Creuset pans. The Whybrow year books. The yellow towels. Is that all?' he asked.

'Yes, I really don't want anything else. I was thinking about it last night and again when I woke up. He can have all the rest. I just want to get it out of the way. You know, over and done with.'

Ralph was doubtful. 'I've come across an awful lot of people who had awfully big regrets later. That they didn't ask for more at the outset, I mean.'

'No. It's fine. I'm going to send it as it is today.'

'It's up to you. It's just that I wouldn't want...'

'No, honestly, Ralph, I've got you now and that's all that's important.'

But we'll have so much to buy ourselves, he thought, remembering that he had not yet told Tina about his decision to let Virginia have everything.

'You look doubtful, Ralph, what are you thinking?'

'Only that it doesn't seem much.'

'It's enough. Come on, there's just time enough to,' and she rolled her eyes, 'make love before we go.' He did not need to be persuaded.

Lying on his back, her head cradled in his shoulder, he felt again a deep sense of contentment and ease. He watched her as she dressed, and knew that he would never tire of her.

She noticed him and asked, 'What are you staring at?'

'You. You're lovely.'

'You'll get bored with me one day. It frightens me.' She said this as she was stretching behind her back to fasten her bra, pushing her breasts out and slightly bending.

'No, I bloody well won't,' he said and jumped out of bed, grabbing her back and pulling her towards him onto the bed.

'No, not again. There isn't time.' She was laughing, 'I love the idea that I have that effect on you. You're stiff again. You're incorrigible. A Sex Machine. I bet you've always been like that.'

'No I haven't. It's you.'

This was true he thought. Except perhaps at the start of his sexual career. He remembered Trudie. He was technically not a virgin, for he supposed, that at eight he had had that sexual experience with the first Virginia, and he could still feel the sense of bitter disappointment when she had told him to stop. He still wished he had not but no doubt she would have pushed him away. Trudie was different; they were both fifteen and Trudie had made it clear to him that if their relationship continued that she would sleep with him. 'I want to know that you care for me before I do,' she had said. 'I do care. I do care, Trudie,' he had promised. She had pulled his face up to hers, he was lying on top of her, his tip very near her wetness and he had said, 'Truly, truly,' and she had opened her legs wide and said, 'but gently.' Oh God, the sensation he thought. And very soon he had an orgasm. He had read somewhere that teenage sex, the first few times anyway, usually lasted less than five minutes. He did not go limp, but carried on, until she had an orgasm and he had another. And then to his astonishment he was able to have another one. He had collapsed beside her, reduced he said, to a deliquescent heap. She had laughed and said if that was what sex was about she was all for it. The following day, when he telephoned, anxious to arrange another meeting and another steamy session he hoped, her mother had said,

'She's told me to tell you she'll call you back.' She did not; not that night, nor the next. He saw her in town at the weekend, holding hands with another boy, nuzzling up to him. She had not noticed Ralph who had experienced, for the first time, the flat, the all-embracing deadness of sexual rejection. Trudie had gone on to find great pleasure in sex, he had subsequently heard, becoming utterly promiscuous, both at school and later at university where all he knew was that she had contracted meningitis towards the end of her first year. He had not heard of her after that.

'You seem very far away Ralph. What's troubling you? You've just made love to me twice and now you're a million miles away.'

'I'm sorry. I was thinking of us,' he lied, rather than tell her the truth.

'Come on; let's get on with the day.'

Further days passed; for Ralph, divided between the sexual delirium of his love and the mechanical unimportance of work in Chambers. Then, when Ralph picked her up from work one evening and as they drove home, Tina decided to tell him.

'I've got to go to London for a training meeting tomorrow.' She was not sure why she had dreaded telling him, but anticipated he would object.

His first reaction was just to say, 'Why?'

Her response was immediate, 'Because my employers have told me to and the money is useful and I work for them.'

'OK,' he said, 'early train or what?'

'No,' and this was the part that she was not at all keen on telling him, as she had known about the commitment for some weeks, 'midday train, afternoon session, night at hotel, full day after that, another night and morning session, back on Thursday.' He did not say anything. 'What's wrong Ralph?'

'Do you have to go?'

'I've just said I do.'

He wanted to go with her. 'I could come as well. We could spend the evenings together.'

'No,' she replied firmly. 'I've got to go. It's the way it is. Come on, I'll be back and it's only a couple of nights.'

'It might as well be a lifetime,' he muttered. They drove on in silence. At the flat Ralph was uncharacteristically quiet and Tina suddenly decided that she had to do something, anything to try and restore his normal good humour. She slipped quietly from the room. He was sitting at the table, looking at the Times crossword, when she came back in. He turned and his mouth dropped open.

'What on earth,' he started but she, dressed as she was, began to wiggle her hips and stroke her breasts in a very convincing imitation of a traditional striptease routine. He sat, as she drew off a pair of gloves, bent down, up again, walked tantalisingly around him, and finally undid her bra, dropping it onto his knees. He leant forward but she said, 'No touching' and backed away. She started peeling off her knickers, rolling them down, then up again until she finally stepped out of them leaving her dressed only in a skimpy black suspender belt and stockings.

He had completely forgotten his morose and maudlin reaction and was only conscious of her power to arouse him. This hackneyed routine, parody even, of the traditional stripper, had certainly achieved this and he was conscious that his trousers would reveal the fact. As the thought occurred to him, it seemed to occur to her and she bent down in front of him. He turned the chair slightly. She undid his zip, felt inside and bent down over him massaging and teasing him with both her mouth and fingers.

After a few moments of this she stopped, stood up and kissed him, saying mock-demurely, 'I hope that was to your satisfaction, sir. That was your hors d'oeuvres,' and smiled again. He looked down at himself, and she noticing, reached down and deftly reinserted him, and did up his zip.

'It was an enormous...'

'More later, if you want it.'

She was totally without embarrassment, or he supposed modesty but, my god, how he desired her. She walked back towards the bedroom, and he noticed the swing of her bottom, the way the lines moved and redefined themselves, the darkness at the top of her legs.

'Is that all? After that? You walk away?'

'No, I'm waiting for you in the bedroom.'

'What do you mean?'

'Like I said. That was the hors d'oeuvres. Main course later.'

He thought for a moment when she was out of the room. Main course? He waited then went towards the door. He was about to open it when she said, 'No, wait a moment. I'll call you.' He paused. He could hear sounds of clothes being moved in the wardrobe. 'Now,' she called.

She was lying on the bed, on her side in a classically seductive pose. Same stockings, but a very short skirt, grey one, and a conventional white shirt with one of his striped ties.

'I'm your little schoolgirl,' she said demurely. 'Come round to see you.'

Ralph had never played sex games, had never thought of doing so and Virginia would have looked at him as though he had gone mad if he had ever suggested that she should dress up for the purposes of sexual arousal.

'Look,' Tina said, pulling her skirt up. 'I'm wearing naughty ones.'

Ralph wanted to groan at the sight of the crotchless knickers.

'I'm feeling naughty Ralph.'

He dropped his trousers, kicking off his shoes and was on top of her, lost in an eroticism he had never experienced, ceasing to think, surrendering himself instead to impulse and reaction.

Emotionally and sexually exhausted, he lay on the bed, still in his shirt and tie. She was partially undressed, shirt open, bra loose, skirt round her waist, the crotchless knickers still on.

'Was it good?' she asked impishly. 'No, but seriously. I was surprised by how turned on you got. Was it the costume? Didn't think you were the type Ralph.'

'No,' he replied slowly, 'nor did I. I'm not sure I am. I think it was more the thought of you getting turned on and excited by dressing up and then that affecting me. You know, because you did it, put on the clothes I mean, you wanted to do it and that made me want to do it more. I think. Does it matter? I love you,' and he kissed her.

She lay there as he stroked her and then, Ralph asked, because he could not contain his morbid curiosity, and he had been thinking about this and it was bothering him, 'Tina, you don't mind if I ask what you're doing with crotchless knickers in your wardrobe. I mean, you don't make a habit of wearing them do you?' This was a barely coded way of ascertaining whether she made a habit of wearing them during her marriage. 'Where did you get them?'

'I was given them by Sylvia.'

'Funny sort of present to give a sister.'

'No, it was a joke. I was complaining, if you want to know, about my sex life with him. The fact that he was no good and I didn't like doing it with him anyway. She gave me them and said I should try and see if they worked.'

In spite of himself Ralph could not help asking, 'And did they?'

'I never tried them.'

She was not being entirely truthful. He had bought them for her, together with a rubber bra with nipple holes, a very large vibrator and fishnet stockings. He had proposed a fun filled Friday evening, the fun was going to be Tina, 'strutting her stuff' was his phrase. He was going to watch, to be an audience, as his wife performed a strip and then, he suggested, used the vibrator while she lay on the coffee table, and he sat in an armchair. Tina had not known what to say when she opened the parcel. Her eyes had widened, and St John had looked brazenly triumphant. 'I bought you a present. You can try them out tonight.' He had then made his suggestion. Tina was reluctant but he, they were still getting on reasonably well at that time early in their marriage, had persuaded her and after they had drunk a bottle of wine together, she left the room and returned dressed as he wished. She put on music and then did what she thought a real lap dancer would do, thrusting her breasts in his face and grinding down on his dick which, she could feel through his trousers, was hard. Finally, she lay down on the coffee table, opened her legs and took the vibrator and started to play with herself. She was lying with her head on a pillow facing him so that he was looking straight at the vibrator. She teased it in and out, and then noticed that St John had taken himself out and was rubbing harder, a look of excited concentration on his face, and saying, 'Go on, go on, further, further.' She took it to mean that he wanted to see the thing right inside her and she pushed. It was uncomfortable but not unpleasant she thought and then abandoned herself completely. 'What the hell, why shouldn't I have an orgasm,' and started to concentrate on her own pleasure forgetting about him completely. Gasping and shuddering as she came, she was suddenly aware of him standing over her, masturbating furiously until he too had one, spattering over her breasts and her face. She lifted her head and sucked the end clean. 'That was what they call the money shot in the porn business,' he had said with a grin.

'Really, you never tried?' Ralph asked. He was relieved.

'No, I've told you. I know I was his first. Funny, thinking back on it. It seemed important to him that he was my first as well, so I let him think he was.'

'Wasn't he?'

'No. But it seemed to please him to think so. I had no serious sex life with him at all. Only the occasional Friday night shag. That was his delicate term which I always loathed. As I did the sex. I think he did it only because you were supposed to when you're married. He was almost asexual, looking back.'

Ralph found this a complete puzzle. The thought that anyone could fail to be completely knocked sensually sideways by Tina was beyond him. He knew that he would cheerfully spend all day and all night beside her, beneath her, on top of her, in any position she cared for in short, and he could not understand that 'he' hadn't. Human beings were a mystery, he concluded as he said, 'But the schoolgirl thing. What made you think of that?'

'Oh, I don't know. You looked so depressed. I just wanted to cheer you up. Besides I should have liked to have met you earlier, known you when you were younger.'

'Why?'

'Because then I'd have known you longer, we'd have been together longer, wouldn't we? It's simple. I just thought why not pretend I'm a schoolgirl and you're my boyfriend.'

'You must have been an extremely provocative schoolgirl,' and Ralph found himself unaccountably jealous of whoever was her boyfriend then, 'if that's how you dressed and behaved.'

'Oh God, no. I was boringly conventional. Really. That's

why I would have liked to have known you sooner. I might have done more.'

'What on earth do you mean?'

'I'm not sure. Got better A Levels. Gone to a better university. Done more after that.'

'I'd have been twenty-six when you were sixteen, twenty-seven when seventeen, twenty-eight when eighteen. You wouldn't have looked at me. I was an old man. I know I'd have looked at you though.'

'I bet you haven't changed a bit. I'd have fancied you as much at sixteen, I'll bet as I do at twenty-eight.' She kissed him.

'But why the dance first?'

'I told you, you looked depressed and needed cheering up. I've seen the effect stockings have on you.'

'What do you mean?'

'You like them.'

He had never considered these in any meaningful way. Of course, he knew that they were part of a woman's sexual armoury, advertisers' likewise, but none of his girlfriends had ever worn them, preferring tights or nothing on their legs at all. In fact, the only woman he could remember ever wearing stockings was his mother, a thought that troubled him for a moment but no more.

'You look thoughtful Ralph. Have I touched a nerve?'

'No. I didn't think that I'd shown any special reaction to stockings, that's all.'

'All men do. That's why there are all those adverts with long legged dollies with black ones on.'

'I know. Part of the iconography of sex. I understand all that.' He was a bit impatient, 'I'm trying to work me out, or more properly, my reaction out.'

'I love your seriousness. What's the problem?'

'Only that I'm not sure that I want you thinking that I'm just another man who gets excited by a woman wearing stockings. It's much more complex. As I tried to tell you a few minutes ago.'

'Oh come on, Ralph. You fell on me. You were totally carried away. Rampant. It was lovely. To provoke that reaction in a seriously successful and successfully serious intelligent barrister. It was great. I love sex with you. It's just right. Comfortable. It feels right.' She looked serious. 'It is right, isn't it? For you as well, I mean, better?'

She was looking for reassurance. She was jealous of Virginia; jealous of their past sexual history together, not sure if she had displaced his wife, sexually as well as physically.

'Oh Christ, Tina, yes, yes and yes. Like I've said. I feel as though I've come home when I'm doing it with you.'

'Good,' she nuzzled against him 'do you want some pudding?'

'What about after we've eaten?'

'What, Ralph, the Sex Machine, can't manage it again,' she giggled. 'Should I help? I can do it again.'

She started stroking him, but he was still thinking, intellectually rather than sexually aroused, but sexually curious about her.

'What did you mean when you said it felt right - comfortable, you said?'

'Oh nothing, except that it feels right with you. It's comfortable inside me. I just enjoy it with you and didn't before. That's all.'

'Why didn't you enjoy it before,' he asked, again not really wanting to put the question but desperately wanting an answer.

'Oh, if you want to be biological about it, he had a big one. He was proud of it. It was never comfortable. Yours is just the right size. It's lovely.'

This was not at all what Ralph wanted to hear. In fact, had he been slightly more sensitive, he supposed he could have worked her answer out for her without her actually spelling it out to him. He was not at all sure how to reply, she had been so matter of fact, and, in a sense complimentary, but the fact remained that she had made comparisons, again he supposed that all women do, but it was he who now felt diminished. He had never thought about his size before, taking it for granted that it was, so to speak, the right size. It had always worked, and no girl had ever made any comment in the past. What did she mean, 'He was proud of it'? Did that mean she had to look at it, admire it, kiss it from end to end, measure it, make plaster casts of it, swing on it, draw it, photograph it, enter it into huge willy competitions? He decided not to think about this further but could not resist saying, and he did then feel a surge of triumph that big dick had lost out to him, 'I thought size didn't matter?'

'It doesn't. It's what you do with it that does. And what you do is right.' She smiled again, totally oblivious to his darker thoughts. 'And I'd like you to do it to me again. If you can,' she added, taking the lead and initiative until against the odds, all the odds Ralph thought, they had another orgasm again simultaneously.

'I feel totally drained. Lifeless. Anaesthetised below the waist,' he said after a moment or two.

'So do I. It's like a wonderful warm glow all around my lower tummy. I've never had three in a row.'

'Maybe not with me?'

'I've told you. I wish you'd believe me. I never had an orgasm through sex before until you and I did it. And I had one the very first time. That's as much as anything how I knew it must be right. You and me. It's different for men. They can always have orgasms. I bet you're used to three in a row. A regular occurrence.' She was having dark thoughts about Virginia again, he guessed. She looked at him intently.

'You did, didn't you?'

'No,' he said quietly. 'It was a bit of a routine thing.'

'So you've never had three orgasms in a row.' She was anxious.

'No.'

'Then I'm the first. That's lovely. That's really cheered me up.' She looked happy.

'We may not have been the first for each other, but we've had a first together. Let's go and eat.'

They got up, went to the kitchen, looked in the fridge and at each other. 'I'll go and get a takeaway,' Ralph said, determined to bring a bit of order in the future to their housekeeping arrangements, 'and some milk, bread and something for the morning.'

After they had eaten and drunk a bottle of wine they went to bed. Her trip the following day had not been mentioned but Ralph fell asleep, with Tina nestling in his arms, anxiously still contemplating her absence. She was so fixed in his imagination and part of what he considered his sexual psyche, that the prospect of being without her, if only for two nights, filled him with a kind of hollow dread. He woke the following morning to find Tina sitting on top of him again, rocking very gently backwards and forwards. She bent forward and kissed him.

'I thought I'm not going to waste this and started without you. I couldn't resist it.'

The sensation was lovely, the sense of being sexually so desired and he did as she wanted.

Then, having once again achieved a sexual bliss, he remained motionless for what seemed like minutes but can only have been moments, before she moved, and came and lay beside him again.

'If you can time yourself to do that every morning at seven,' Ralph whispered, 'I won't bother with an alarm clock any longer.'

'If you want an alarm call down there every morning, I'll be happy to oblige. But I've got to get on now,' and with that she was out and off to the bathroom. He remembered then that she was going away and got up and followed her in.

'Do you really have to go?' he asked miserably.

'Yes. Don't look so morose. I'll be back the day after tomorrow. I'll phone you tonight.' He accepted then that he was not going to be able to persuade her and went to dress. During breakfast he suggested that he take her to the station.

'The train goes at 10.05 if you'd like to. I'd like you to,' she added as he looked disappointed.

'Right, I'll go and get some papers now for you to read it you want.' He couldn't think of any other way of filling a mournful interval.

She was brisk. 'OK. A Telegraph and Mail for me please. Do you want any money?'

'Of course not.' He was affronted.

'No, I didn't mean like that. I meant do you have money on you, or would you like some?'

'I've got enough for some papers.'

She did not seem to notice, simply said, 'I'm going to pack,' and pecked him on the cheek.

When he returned, having walked slowly to a further newsagent than their local one, and having glanced at the top shelf magazines, recalling the afternoon he had bought several and trying to find an image reminiscent of Tina, he thought again of last night and how she had managed so successfully, to become the living embodiment of his fantasy that afternoon. He had gazed at the carefully cut out selected image and now he was living the reality. It was most peculiar, he thought as he paid for the papers and walked back. Opening the flat door, he found Tina ready to leave.

'I was just getting anxious.'

'There's plenty of time,' he said, picking up her bag. He turned and she said, 'Not so fast, one last big kiss. I don't like kissing in public.' She held out her arms and he dropped the bag, enfolding her, clutching at her like a drowning man and kissing, longingly and tenderly. She broke away, rubbed the front of his trousers, said, 'Till Thursday then,' and opened the door.

He followed her down the stairs; once outside they held hands walking to his car. In the car he held her knee and they said little, he running his hand up her thigh, she moving, allowing it to settle at the top of her legs.

'Good job it's an automatic,' she giggled. He smiled but said nothing. At the station, he stopped and went round to her door to open it. She was already out, bag in hand, and kissed him very lightly saying, 'Take care. I'll phone tonight,' and was walking briskly away before he had time to say anything.

It was only then, when she was out of calling distance, that he saw Ian, in a smart Burberry, with an overnight bag and briefcase, waiting near the ticket booths. He saw Tina walk up to him, exchange greetings and the two then went towards the platform area together. She had not looked back. He felt cold and sick. Tina had not mentioned going with Ian. That must have been deliberate. She had deliberately misled him and was now, presumably going to spend two nights and the best part of three days in his company. What was he to do? Run after them, drag Tina back claiming her as his? Follow them down to London in his car? Arrive at the hotel and watch her, keep an eye on her? He was confused and angry, at once acknowledging that he was being irrational in his reaction, over-reaction he thought more soberly, but also frightened and insecure. He hovered beside the passenger door of his car, looked at his watch, looked again at the place where he had last seen them, sighed and then, shutting the door, went round, got into the driver's seat and drove to the car park near his Chambers.

He walked in, grunted in reply to the cheery greeting of Ken and the junior clerks, looked in his pigeonhole, picked up his correspondence and other papers, and went to his room. He sat down and spread his hands out on the desk, staring at them intently, thinking of Tina and then Ian.

He was in an agony of despair that he found not just uncomfortable but insufferable. His sexual possession of Tina had been so complete and so entire, he was utterly absorbed by her sensuality, but he was unable to rid himself of intrusive imagery of Tina having sexual relations, copulating, fornicating with others. He thought with misery of her cries of love during the sex act and then her squeals of pleasure. He thought of her husband and the fact that she had, must have had, at some time at least, a fulfilling sexual relationship with him. He thought of St John's predecessors and wondered about them and how long they had lasted and how often Tina had done it with them. He finally, and did not want even to countenance this, let alone dwell on the thought, had a horrible mental picture of Tina with Ian both naked and coupling, being screwed was actually the phrase that sprang immediately to his mind, furiously and athletically.

The pictures crowded in on him and he groaned and curled his hands into tight fists. He beat the desk and then rubbed his eyes. He was intelligent enough to understand that what he was going through was both rational and irrational. He could deal with the rational aspect. Of course, it was natural to be aware, even to be rueful and slightly jealous of the past. The irrational aspect was more difficult. He could not rid himself of the thoughts.

He decided to try and concentrate on the paperwork in front of him and he flipped through the envelopes and bundles tied with pink string. He came to one letter marked Private and confidential and looked at the postmark. A firm of solicitors whose name was only vaguely familiar and then he associated the name with Virginia. He opened it and took out a letter and some other papers. He unfolded these. 'Divorce Petition based on Adultery'. He put that to one side and read the letter quickly.

'We enclose by way of service divorce petition, acknowledgement and draft court order dealing with financial matters. You will note that our client does not claim any costs and we invite you to return the acknowledgement of service to the court. If you are content that the financial matters should be resolved in the way that you have suggested already, then please sign the consent application and return it to us. If you have any queries or doubts we urge you to consult your own solicitors.'

The divorce petition simply stated that he had committed adultery at divers addresses and on divers occasions with Christina Fortescue. He had no problem with that but considered whether Virginia had guessed at the divers addresses or whether the phrase had simply been a creation of her solicitors. He hoped that she would never find out about the first time but then there was no reason to expect her to. Adultery. He pondered on this. It was an ugly word with connotations of guilt. He did not feel guilty but acknowledged he had broken vows made in the presence of a God many people believed in and moreover, in the sight of the congregation gathered together to join him in holy matrimony.

Had he just left it at a casual fuck, a one-night stand, with Tina and then gone back to Virginia it would, in the eyes of the law as much as perhaps those of God, been technically adultery as if he had enjoyed a surreptitious affair with her for years or, as he had done, seemingly immediately decided that his marriage was over but, while still married although separated, carried on making love with Tina. There were no degrees of adultery known to English law. If you stuck it in or, as a woman, allowed another man to stick it into you, then that was enough to fuck the marriage legally.

He would have been devastated, but not surprised, had Virginia committed adultery. He agreed that it was a betrayal but only because they had promised each other not to do it with other people. He had done it with someone else and had so enjoyed it - although the experience in essence was no different from that he had enjoyed with others - that he was prepared to give up everything he had worked and striven for with Virginia.

He looked through the consent application which merely recited the fact that the house was to be transferred into her name, she was to assume responsibility for the mortgage, she was to have all the contents save for the two identified pictures, at least I keep those he thought, and that this was to be a clean break between them, neither having any claim in the future against each other or on their respective estates after death. There it is then, he thought, as simple as that. She gets the lot. He turned to the next page which asked for details of his income and assets. Her section had already been completed. He had no idea that her earnings were so high. She had said that she was now on an equal share with the other partners, but general practice was obviously prospering. Had he remained, or were he to remain with Virginia, they would be considered a really rather well-off couple.

He did a quick calculation and, taking the equity in the house with what they could jointly have raised on mortgage, knew that the Queen Anne manor house each had hankered after would have been in their grasp that year. He decided against revealing the full extent of his credit card indebtedness and merely entered his earnings, wrote a nought beside his assets, crossed it out and put the value of his two pictures in and, sighing, signed in the two places indicated. He wrote a short reply saying that he was not consulting lawyers, was returning the form to the court and enclosed the documents duly signed as requested. He put the letter in an envelope, addressed it, put the court form in another, addressed that and rang the clerks' office.

When a junior clerk appeared, he asked her to ensure that both letters went out with the morning post and leaned back contemplatively in his chair, his arms behind his head. What was Tina doing, he wondered.

He turned to the other papers. He had always had, and was ready to acknowledge this, a pathological hatred of leaving work to pile up and tried to turn all his around as quickly as possible. It was this speed and efficiency that made him much in demand among solicitors. Many barristers let requests for pleadings and opinions on liability, evidence or other matters, pile up behind them, sometimes literally as well as metaphorically. Some believed that a room filled with paperwork, waiting to be done, gave them an aura of magnificent busy activity. Others of course, it is part of human nature to defer the difficult and tedious, let them pile up against the day that they would get round to the less straightforward.

Ralph enjoyed his reputation and had worked hard to establish this. He went through the pile methodically. Nothing too demanding was his reaction and, pushing all except the top bundle to the side of his desk, took out a pad and, reading through the documents, made notes. He went out, for a moment only, to get a law book to check a fact. After half an hour or so he wrote out, in longhand, an opinion which would be typed and sent out that afternoon. He repeated the process, going through the stack, until he had finished. It was past six and he had worked through lunch without even pausing to consider whether or not he was hungry. He had periodically taken papers through for typing, and now took the last set into the clerks' room.

Ken was there, finalising arrangements for courtroom appearances the following day. He looked agitated, as he always did by that time of the day, having had to juggle the demands of the listing officers, calling cases at short notice, which had long ago been given to barristers who might now be part-heard in other matters in other courts across the country and whose cases would then have to be assigned to other barristers who, by definition, had not been wanted by the solicitor client. It was a ridiculous system, and could so easily be improved by the listing of cases for the convenience of the users, rather than the benefit of the judges, Ralph mused for the umpteenth time.

'You look shattered Ken,' Ralph said. 'Finished yet?'

'Couple more calls and then I should be. Fancy a drink?'

'Yes, I do. Should I wait?'

'I'll only be a moment.'

Ralph went and got his briefcase and coat and watched as Ken, perspiring lightly, swore, 'Bloody Tom. High and mighty so and so. He's not doing anything tomorrow and there's a case in a bloody Magistrates Court forty miles away that was marked for Rhona. She's finishing off something in town that started today so can't go. Tom says that any case for Rhona is a bit too lightweight for him and he doesn't want to do it. Lord High and Mighty. Who does he think he is?'

Ralph knew that Ken would never have spoken like this had anyone else been present but their friendship was such that each of them trusted the other enough to be honest. Tom was the Honourable Thomas, son of an hereditary Baron whose family had long provided judges to the legal system. He was considerably junior to Ralph but senior to Rhona who had only been called to the Bar for a couple of years.

'What kind of case is it?' asked Ralph with genuine interest.

'Only a totter. There's not much of a fee marked on the brief and that's why I gave it to her.'

'Totters can be interesting, though. Is there anything in it?'

'I haven't looked to be honest.'

'If it helps you out Ken, I'll go over and do it.'

'Seriously, Ralph. It's a bit beneath you.'

'Ken, I'm still the same as when we first met. Hungry for work. I'm not down for anything, am I? It just puts paperwork back by a few hours.'

'A few hours is hardly here or there is it? Think of Tom. He's got stuff going back months which I'm being chased about by bloody solicitors.'

'No, give it to me. Presumably listed for ten?'

'Yes.'

An hour's drive, could be hanging around for an hour or two, start case and then an hour back. He'd still be back for lunch. 'Give it to me then,' and taking it, he put the brief in his case. He would read it later.

'Thanks Ralph. I appreciate it, honestly. I'd only had young Philip to phone.'

'Well perhaps young Philip would like the case. If so, perhaps he ought to have it. He needs the money. His wife hasn't had her baby yet has she?'

'That's the point. He's off to the hospital with her tomorrow and crossed himself out.'

'Hardly fair to try and make him miss that.'

'No. And I hadn't thought of using you to be honest. I was going to pass it to another set of Chambers if Phil wouldn't do it.'

'Can't have that. Come on. Let's go for this drink.'

They went to a bar that was popular with both solicitors and barristers and several people nodded at them when they came in. Ralph was not really feeling like company, said so, and they went to a corner table.

Ken watched Ralph take a long draught of beer. 'We haven't been here for ages. In fact, you've been going home rather early for you. What's up? I've been meaning to ask.'

'Well you know that I'm living with Tina?'

'Of course I do. You gave me the telephone number when you moved in.'

'Of course I did. I've been going home to her.'

Ken made a crude gesture with his arm.

Ralph simply said, 'I like being with her.'

'Well why aren't you with her tonight?'

'She's in London, on a course.' It brought her back to mind, as well as the egregious Ian. 'She's back the day after tomorrow,' he said, wishing the intrusive thoughts away.

'So you're out with me instead? No nookie, see old Ken.'

'No. A chance to catch up on what's new and happening. Any gossip?'

'I haven't heard anything about your Q.C. application if that's what you mean.'

'No,' said Ralph, thinking Ken had hit the nail. 'But if you do, I'd like to know.' Barristers' senior clerks were often privy to all sorts of bits of knowledge that even more senior barristers would not hear about.

'I'll tell you if and when I learn anything. No nothing much. Pete's drinking too much and his work is suffering.

I've mentioned it to Geoffrey who's promised to have a word. Tom's getting seriously above himself, but you know about that. Geoffrey's gout is rather bad. I can't think of anything else. How about you? What's happened to Virginia?'

'We're getting divorced. I'm giving her the house and everything in it.'

'Phew.' Ken let out a whistle. 'Is that wise?'

'It may be neither wise nor sensible but that's the decision.'

'You sure you won't regret it Ralph?' He was concerned. 'You've struggled hard. You came here without anything, remember? No connections, no reputation, no solicitor clients. You've got one of the best practices in Chambers now. Couldn't you have got third or even a half?'

'I could have done I suppose but it seems unfair.'

'Why?'

'Oh God. If I've got one of the best practices, I'll carry on earning and can effectively start again.'

'But so can she. She's a GP. They earn good money.'

'Yes. But it assuages the guilt.'

'Expensive guilt. Expensive young woman, your Tina. Does she know what she's costing you?'

'She's got no idea. I haven't told her yet.'

'Don't you think you should have discussed it with her?' Ken had obviously assumed that Ralph had longer term plans for Tina.

'Do you know, Ken, we haven't even discussed ourselves. What we're going to do. Whether we'll get married or anything. I'm just living with her from day to day.'

'It's not like you. You've usually got everything mapped out.' He paused, 'Will you marry do you think?'

'It seems to be the last thing on her mind. She's not mentioned it. I think we're both happy with things as they are.' He pondered for a moment, realising this was wrong. He wanted to spend the rest of his life, eternity even, with Tina, and could not imagine an existence without her. 'I guess I should talk about it with her though.'

'Well, unless she's a ship in the night, and you'd hardly have left Virginia or moved in with Tina had she been that, perhaps you ought. I must get going Ralph.'

'Sure you won't have another? It's my turn.'

'No, another night. Are you coming?'

'Yes.'

They parted outside, each going in an opposite direction, Ralph back to the carpark and Ken to the station to catch a train back to his modest house and wife in suburbia. Ken, as the Senior Clerk to a prestigious set of Chambers, earned nearly as much as the highest earning barristers he managed. He had three children, all at expensive private schools, and a string of tenanted properties, but still led a very prosaic and ordinary existence and Ralph was simply unable to understand this.

He considered the question of supper. He would have to buy something and stopped at a superstore on the way home. He was thinking of Tina again, and what she might be doing, as he passed the newsagent he had visited earlier that day.

On impulse he stopped and went in. The woman behind the counter glanced at him incuriously as he surveyed the top shelf magazines. He scoured the titles, wanting to take these down and look through them before buying any. He decided on three which looked as though they may contain more than blurred softcore photographs, paid for them and put them in his briefcase. The shopkeeper accepted his money mechanically, just another commercial transaction for her, without any sense or indication that she was aware of the purpose to which he was, he thought probably, going to put them. At the flat, checking the time, he decided to phone Tina. He got the hotel reception and asked for her. He was put through.

'It's Ralph. How are you?'

'I'm fine.' She sounded excited. 'It's been pretty dull day but we're all meeting for a drink in a moment before supper. I'm going to have an early night. You just caught me changing.'

'What into?' He could not resist asking.

'Oh nothing special. Just out of office clothes. What are you doing?'

'Missing you.'

'I'm missing you too.'

'Not as much as I'm missing you. You're with others. All set for a fun time. I'm by myself.'

'Oh, poor Ralph. What are you going to do?'

He could hardly tell her that he was going to look at hard core pornography after supper. 'Like you, early night. I've got a case on tomorrow.'

'I'm missing you too Ralph. Really, truly.'

He was not sure how to reply. What he wanted to ask was whether she had been sitting beside Ian, was she, she was bound to be, seeing him tonight? Did he flirt with her? Ralph imagined him as the kind of man who would flirt with anything with two legs and a fanny at the top of them. He did not ask any of these questions, just saying, 'Have a nice evening. I love you.'

'I love you Ralph. I'll phone tomorrow. Bye.'

A click. An emptiness.

She was off to her evening, and he was sitting by himself in what was, he thought, a really rather cheerless flat. He put an instant meal of chicken in the oven, sat down and sifted through the papers. She had not asked him about his day or his case, he reflected but, on the other hand, no more had he about hers. He had not asked, he suspected, because he did not want to be told.

An old girlfriend, or at least what he had taken to be a girlfriend at the time, came to mind. Why, Ralph asked himself, why should I be thinking of her now? She was French, had worked as a stripper in Paris before ending up at the same university as Ralph. She had allowed him to pick her up in the Students Union; she loved his English accent she said and the way he spoke. They had ended up in bed together, hot and furious sex. She had expressed a dislike of sleeping close to anyone so left later that night to go back to her own room. She had sought him out the following day and they had had more steamy sex. When he asked if she wanted to go somewhere the following day she had replied that she was seeing a French assistant from the languages faculty and asked him to join them. He had gone to her room in the Halls of Residence and found her sitting on her bed beside a slim, handsome young man, each with a glass in hand and a half-empty bottle of Muscadet on the desk. She had patted the bed beside her, he had sat down, having taken the offered drink, and wondered whether he was *de trop*. He had said as much.

'*Mais non. Nous allons nous amuser,*' Angelique had said, '*N'est ce pas Pierre?*'

'*Ah, bien sur. Mais est il large d'esprit?*'

'*Je le crois,*' she had replied.

Ralph, whose French was just adequate enough to understand this, asked, in English, "What do you mean, *large d'esprit?* How are we going to amuse ourselves?"

Angelique had not replied but instead turned to him, kissed him, long, unhurried, tongue exploring, and started to undo his zip.

Ralph then pulled away from her and said, 'No, seriously, how are we going to amuse ourselves?'

Angelique, smiling again, said, in her breathy French accented English that many find sexually arousing, 'I am going to suck you while Pierre fucks me and then you are going to fuck me while I suck him, *et nous allons commencer maintenant,*' and had put her hand into his trousers.

In speaking about this episode in later years, it was the only sexual exploit that he would ever talk about, Ralph would say, 'Reader, I made my excuses and left.'

The next time Ralph saw her he had asked about Pierre, to be told that it had been the best day ever and she had 'so enjoyed herself.' Ralph wished he had never asked at all. Something of this disappointment must have seeped into his subconscious. Why risk the answer, why ask the question at all? He and she had remained friends but never had sex together again. Maybe she would have, maybe she would not, but Ralph never asked or made any move to try and persuade her. He was not going to risk rejection or comparison with Pierre.

He concentrated on the papers in front of him. The defendant, a prominent local businessman had ten points on his license, had been stopped for speeding and the policeman, having seen his license and knowing that the imposition of further penalty points rendered him liable to disqualification from driving under the totting up procedure, had referred the matter for prosecution in the Magistrates Court. It was an area of law with which Ralph was perfectly familiar, the kind of case young barristers cut their teeth on every day all over the country.

He looked for the fee marked on the brief. It was not derisory but about one third of what his clerk would have charged for Ralph's appearance. Still, it's all money, Ralph thought and ran through the facts, committing them to his short term memory and preparing the mitigation.

He finished and tidied the papers up, before having a bath and getting into bed. He opened one of the magazines and studied the photographs intently. He opened another, leafing through it. He picked up the last and threw it aside with a cry of exasperation. He did not find any of the photographs faintly erotic let alone arousing. He had experienced, it must be the case he decided, too much of the real thing, the living, warm, sensual, sticky, responsive, real thing, to be excited by photographs of tarts having sex with what the magazines, without any trace of irony, called studs. The only interesting question was who was exploiting who he thought sleepily. Traditionally pornography has been seen as the exploitation of women. But if a woman is having it done to her by a man, and the man is pictured with his penis either in or out of her, why is the man not being exploited as much as the woman? Ralph fell asleep puzzling over this conundrum.

The next day he was woken by the telephone and picked it up immediately.

'Morning Ralph. I'm missing you.'

'Hi. Me too,' he replied as he sat up.

'What are you doing?'

'I was still asleep. What about you?'

'Just got up. Off to breakfast and more dreary presentations. But, I'll be back tomorrow. Can you meet me off the train? 3.40.'

'Yes, of course.' Did he dare ask, and decided he would, 'Did you have a nice evening?'

'Not really. They all got a bit drunk and I slipped away early and went to bed.' Well, that was all right then. 'What are you doing today?'

'Going to a Magistrates Court. Just to fill my time.'

'Anything interesting?'

'Not really. But it'll pay for a decent meal out.'

'Phone me tonight again will you?'

'Yes. I love you. So much.'

'Love you.' Click. Again the sense of loss and a wave of fear struck him. Shaking his head, he got on with the day.

Walking into the barristers' robing room at the Magistrates Court he found it empty. He was standing with his back to the door when a vaguely familiar voice said, 'Well, well. It's Ralph Edwards, the wife snatcher.' An affable and agreeable voice. He was momentarily unable to put a name to it at all. He turned and was totally taken aback to be confronted with St John, who was smiling broadly.

'You look like a fish that's just been pulled out of the water. What's wrong?'

'I didn't expect it to be you.'

'Why not?'

Ralph did not want to say, Because if I ran across you, I expected you to hit me, or to be offensive or at the very least perhaps to ignore me, but replied, 'In the Magistrates Court.'

'I'm covering for someone else. I need the money now that I'm single again.'

'So am I. And I've always needed the money.'

They both laughed and Ralph felt his tension fade.

'What's it like with a second-hand woman?' St John was still smiling broadly.

Ralph was just going to say, as a joke, "Alright once you get past the used bits", when he remembered what Tina had said a propos St John and said instead, 'Most women are second-hand fairly early on I think.'

'Tina wasn't. I was the first. Not the last though, obviously.' He was extraordinarily matter of fact about it. 'I was a bit upset to begin with but, to be honest Ralph, you're welcome to her. We should have split a long time ago. Though what you see in her over Virginia I can't begin to bloody imagine. Care for a drink afterwards?'

Why not, Ralph thought.

'I'd be delighted to if our cases get through quickly. Mine should be short.'

'Mine too,' St John said as he left the room. 'See you later.'

Ralph was puzzled but also intrigued. How on earth could St John be so calm, so clearly unaffected? In the same situation Ralph suspected that, had he seen St John, he would have quietly backed away.

Ralph found his solicitor and the client and went into a conference room. The client was pleading guilty and hoped that Ralph could persuade the Bench not to disqualify him at all. Ralph pointed out that it would probably be more advantageous to go for a shorter disqualification which would wipe all the points off his license. Thus he could start with a clean sheet again, rather than having them hanging over him with a certain disqualification if he infringed road traffic law again. They could see the logic in this and Ralph was instructed on this basis.

When the case was called first, as a relatively senior barrister the Clerk extended this courtesy to him, Ralph stood up and addressed the Magistrates. He put the argument ingeniously but left the Magistrates, he hoped, feeling that an appropriate punishment would be to inflict a short period of disqualification on his client. He was superficially, at least, arguing for no disqualification at all. When they retired, he went to the client, who was looking nervous rather than relaxed and who said, 'I could follow your line but then I knew what you were doing. Bloody clever bit of speaking.'

They came back in, the Court stood, the client was told to remain standing. 'We've listened very carefully to what your barrister has to say for you but I'm afraid that we have decided to disqualify you for one month and fine you £400 together with £50 costs.'

A victory. Ralph was gleeful. One month instead of six and a clean license. He stood, asked for a formal fourteen days to make payment, bowed and left. The client was delighted. 'Perfect result. I suppose I could have hoped for a day or a week but a bit unrealistic. Here's my card. If ever you need help.'

'Financial adviser,' Ralph read, and putting it in his top pocket, said, 'Thanks. You've no idea how much I may need your help soon.'

'Anytime,' and the solicitor and client went off together.

Ralph decided to try and find St John and looked in the other courtrooms. Opening a door, he saw him sitting at the front in the middle of the solicitors' row; evidently his case was to be called imminently. Ralph elected to wait and slipped quietly into the area reserved for the public, full as usual of poor looking people, some anxious, others dirty, the single parents, the down and outs, a complete contrast to the mostly well-dressed, high earning, professionals who were representing them before a bench comprised of usually other well-dressed, albeit not all professional or high earning, Magistrates. The system was full of ironies and Ralph, although he had experienced a sense of elation at having achieved the desired outcome, thought, not for the first time, how pleased he was to have been able to give up practice in the Magistrates Courts.

Another defendant was called, and a young girl went to the dock. When the charge of shoplifting was put to her, she pleaded guilty and was told to sit down. The prosecuting solicitor outlined the facts and St John stood up and addressed the unsympathetic looking Magistrates with competence and authority. Ralph found himself impressed and was not altogether surprised when the girl was given a very light fine by way of punishment. The formalities dealt with, St John gathered his books together and came down the courtroom, Ralph getting up, going to the door and waiting for him.

'Fancy a drink then?' St John asked.

'Yes. But it's a bit early. What about a coffee somewhere?'

They walked out into the street, for all the world like two old friends, rather than a cuckold and an adulterer.

'This isn't bad,' said St John gesturing towards an Italian looking cafe. 'I've been in here before.'

Sitting down with their cappuccinos, Ralph wondered what St John, who had appeared to want to talk to him, was going to say.

'How's Christina?' The question surprised him.

'Fine. She's in London today,' he added.

'I'm divorcing her but then I suppose you know that.'

'Yes. I was aware of it,' Ralph answered dryly. 'Virginia's divorcing me too.'

'Funny old business. Christina and I were too young to get married really. We both should have had more experience.'

'What do you mean?'

'Well, it never does to marry your first does it? Look at Prince Charles and his Diana. She started playing about fairly quickly.' He noticed Ralph looking at him in bemusement.

'I'm not saying Christina played around. Although she might have done. She did with you, didn't she?'

'No,' said Ralph. 'She told me she'd left you. We didn't play around.'

'Oh. I'm relieved at that. I didn't like the idea of you two having an affair behind my back.'

'Look St John, forgive this question. But we're sitting here discussing your wife. How the hell can you be so clinical, so bloody matter of fact?'

'Because, quite honestly, it doesn't bother me. Like I said, we should perhaps never have got married. Just look after her.

She'll give you a run for your money, but I wouldn't like her to be badly treated you know. We had some good times together.' Again Ralph wanted to ask questions, but did not want to hear the answers, so he kept quiet. 'And she's always capable of surprises.'

'How so?' Ralph could not help himself.

'Well, I was taken aback when she said I could keep the house and she'd settle for the things on her list.'

Ralph spluttered. 'Pardon?' He hoped St John had not noticed his surprise.

'I didn't expect her to say I could keep the house. I anticipated she'd want at least half.'

'And she's told you?' Ralph wanted to keep the shock out of his voice.

'Oh yes. When I saw her the other day.'

'What?'

'When I saw her the other day. She told me you knew. She came round to go through the things, and we sorted them out. Didn't she mention it?' St John gave a wicked grin. 'Already hiding things is she? I told you she'd give you a run for your money. Anyway, I'm glad things are sorted out between Christina and me. I didn't feel half as bad about it all after that.'

Ralph felt a sick sensation at the pit of his stomach. When the bloody hell had Tina seen St John and why hadn't she mentioned it. What the fuck was she up to? The questions careered through his head, pell-mell and out of control, but he stayed calm, and collected himself before replying, 'I said she should do whatever she felt comfortable with.'

'Then I've got you to thank as well,' said St John. 'I was dreading selling up and looking for somewhere else. Thanks.'

He seemed sincere Ralph thought, and biting back everything he wanted to say, Ralph smiled and murmured, 'Don't mention it. I guess I ought to be going. Thanks for the coffee, St John.'

'My pleasure,' replied St John as they stood up and left together.

'My car's that way.'

'I left mine that way. See you around St John.'

'Good luck, Ralph,' St John laughed. 'You'll probably need it'

Ralph was in a furious mood. How dare Tina not consult him about this? How dare she see St John without mentioning it to him? How dare... and then he stopped. He did not own Tina. He had made no commitment to her. He had paid the deposit and first month's rent on a flat, that was all. But against that he had left Virginia, had moved in with Tina, had told her that he was giving Virginia everything.

No, wait a moment. I haven't told her that, have I? Oh God, did I or didn't I? I can't remember. Perhaps I did and she's acted on the same premise. But even if I have, shouldn't she have consulted me at least? I was relying on some of her money to buy another house. Driving back to his Chambers he was in an utter stew of indignation, inability to remember (and his memory had never let him down so comprehensively as just at this moment) and frustration.

He sat in his room that afternoon, unable to concentrate on the paperwork, mercifully there was very little he thought, and moodily paced the room, stopping to stare out of the window periodically. At five he tried her hotel. She was not there but he was told the delegates, 'delegates' what kind of word was that for a managers' training meeting he snarled to himself, were expected to have finished at six. He wandered into the clerks' room thinking he might chat again with Ken, but all was well and Ken had left already. He resolved to drive home. Home, that flat, but it was all he had so it had to be home he decided, and once there, opened a whisky bottle and poured a large drink. Some of the anger wore off as he sipped the alcohol, and a second drink took the edge off this further. At six he telephoned again and asked for her. He was put through again, very quickly.

'Hi Ralph. How are you?'

'Fine. You?'

'What's the matter?'

'Nothing, why?'

'You sound a bit odd.'

'No, I'm fine.'

'There's something wrong, isn't there? What is it?'

'I saw St John today.'

'Did you? Where?' She sounded interested.

'The Magistrates Court'

'What on earth was he doing there?'

'Same as I was, standing in for someone else.'

'You mean you spoke to him?'

'Yes, why not? I suppose we were bound to run into one another again sooner or later. We're both on the same circuit after all. I've seen him in other courts in the past. If it hadn't been today, it might have been next week, month or whenever.'

'What did you talk about?'

'You.'

'You sound angry, Ralph.' She sounded a bit cross herself.

'No, just puzzled. He told me that you're giving him the whole house.'

'Yes. I decided to. It seemed fair.'

'He also told me that you'd been to see him. You didn't mention that to me.'

'Didn't I?' she said thoughtfully, considered, 'I thought I had.'

'Oh Tina, you know perfectly well you didn't.'

'Well if I didn't, I didn't. I'm sorry. I just wanted to sort matters out quickly and without fuss and thought that doing it face to face would be easiest.'

'When did you go?'

'Lunch break, Wednesday afternoon.' He tried to remember what he'd been doing on Wednesday afternoon but would have to check his diary.

'And you got it sorted out?'

'Yes.'

'Well tell me about it tomorrow.'

'Ralph, you still sound cross.'

'Oh God, it's just that I like honesty and openness.'

'I was going to tell you. Don't be angry with me, please.'

'All right. I'll try not to be. I'll see you tomorrow?'

'Yes, off the train.'

'Bye Tina.'

'Bye bye Ralph,' and he put the phone down. Neither had said that they loved the other. No terms of endearment at all. He was seething.

Tina had decided on the spur of the moment to ring him and had got him at his Chambers.

'St John, it's me, Christina.'

'What do you want?'

'Only to talk. To sort things out.'

'Over the phone or in person?'

'Whichever you prefer.'

'What are you doing this afternoon?'

'Nothing. I can get away for a couple of hours. Should we meet at the house?'

'If you like.

'Two o'clock then.'

'OK.'

She had gone there with some trepidation and had waited, looking at the house for a good minute before getting out of the car and ringing the bell. She still had a key but was reluctant to let herself in. St John answered.

'Come on in. Let's sit down.' He was a bit grim faced but otherwise pleasant enough. They sat opposite one another, rather formally.

'What did you want to talk about?'

'Just the house and things.'

'Well.'

'I only want to take,' and she handed him the short list, 'you can have all the rest.'

He brightened, 'Seriously?'

'Yes, seriously.'

'Are you sure?'

'Yes,' she smiled at him, 'and I also wanted to say sorry. I didn't mean it to end like this. But it has. And I don't want any share in the house. Nothing. You can have the equity and take on the mortgage. I just want my name off the deeds.' It was her trump card and she leaned back to see his reaction. He looked as though he had been hit in the stomach.

'You can't mean it. Or do you?' He looked at her suspiciously but she felt genuinely sorry for him.

'No, St John, I mean it. I chose to go. You didn't make me.

I walked out. You deserve it.' She looked at him then sitting, with his head bowed and he lifted his face towards her. He was crying, trying to hold back tears.

'I'm sorry too. I know we've had bad times but we've had good ones as well. I know it's the right decision but, it's so sad.'

She stood up and went over to where he was sitting and stroked his hair. 'St John, you'll find someone else. You'll be happier with her than me. I'm sure of it.'

He stood up and folded her in his arms, kissing the top of her head. Tina promptly opened her mouth and suddenly he was kissing her with passion, holding her tightly. She could feel him becoming aroused and his hands were undoing her shirt, her skirt, starting to pull her tights down. She made no attempt to resist or assist him as he pushed her gently towards the door. She took his hand as they went up the stairs and led the way to the former marital bedroom where she lay, mutely, as he entered her and had his last ever orgasm inside her. Afterwards she had gone to the bathroom, cleaned herself up, and returned, fully clothed again after a few minutes. He was still lying there.

'I'm glad we're not parting on bad terms Christina. I'm glad we saw one another today.'

'I'm glad we're sorted out amicably. I've put together the things I want. Perhaps you can help me into the car with them.'

'Of course. Sure.' He got up, still in his shirt, and pulled on socks and trousers, looked for a pair of shoes and put them on. She watched the familiar ritual for what she knew was to be the last time. It already seemed faintly strange to her and would in due time cease, she hoped, even to be a recollection. The best dinner service had never been removed from its cardboard boxes and he put these in the boot of her car. The other, smaller, things she moved herself while he did the heavier work. Once finished, and still outside, she turned to him saying 'I'm not coming in again, nor am I coming back. Your solicitors can sort everything else out, can't they?'

'Yes. Take care, Christina.'

'And you St John.' They exchanged kisses, on the cheeks, like relative strangers, and she got in her car and drove off. For once she permitted herself a backward glance. He was watching her go and was waving. She did not wave back but drove away to her new existence.

Ralph stood, with the phone in his hand. No terms of endearment. He phoned the hotel again, asked for her and was put through immediately.

'Tina, it's Ralph. I just wanted to say I miss you.'

'Ralph, I miss you too. I love you.'

'I love you. I'll see you tomorrow. Bye.'

'Bye.' He was still angry and hurt but felt better at having phoned again. He had nothing on tomorrow, only what the post would bring and felt at a complete loose end. It was 6.30 pm. He picked up the phone and rang some local theatres.

Thus it was he found himself sitting in the grand circle watching a performance of 'Midsummer Night's Dream'. It was a play he knew well and a bad cast can ruin it. However, the director had taken an unusual angle, which had brought fresh insights and illuminations, and Ralph laughed out loud at many of the old jokes. Despite being by himself, he enjoyed the evening immensely and when he got home, having looked at his watch and decided it was too late to phone Tina, went to bed and fell asleep, untroubled by any black thoughts whatsoever.

Tina for her part, having put the phone down, felt cross. She was annoyed that Ralph had found out that she had been in touch with St John. She was going to tell him but at a time of her choosing. The meeting had short circuited a lot of correspondence and she had no regrets at all about having said he could have the house. She was annoyed too, that Ralph was annoyed. After all, he had shown no commitment to her. She was thinking in terms of marriage not cohabitation and he had not once mentioned this. No more of course, she thought, had she but nevertheless she was irritated.

She had arranged to meet some of the others for a drink in the bar before supper again. She had been bored last night with people she did not know, but Ian had said that he would join them, and he was always good for a laugh. She dressed casually and joined a group of people at the bar, where she was greeted warmly. Ian was already there.

'Can I get you a drink Tina?'

'Lemon and ice please.'

'Have something stronger.'

'I feel my arm being twisted. I'll have a gin and tonic.'

'Make it a double, please, barman,' Ian said.

Six of them sat together for the meal, Ian beside her. He paid her a lot of attention, flirting and complimenting her outrageously. The others, who were strangers to Ian and Tina, though not to each other, took little notice.

They had a mediocre meal, but a lot of wine was consumed, and Tina was conscious that she was a bit drunk by the time cheeses were brought. Ian offered her another glass.

'No thanks. I feel a bit squiffy.'

'Oh good.'

'Why on earth do you say that?'

Ian leaned forward and whispered to her 'Because I'm trying to get inside your knickers again.'

She giggled. 'Don't be ridiculous.'

'No, really, it was all a bit rushed last time. It could be nice and slow tonight.'

Tina felt herself get sticky. It could do no harm, she thought. No one need ever know. What the eye doesn't see, the heart wouldn't grieve over.

'You're considering it, aren't you Tina?' He reached under the table and put his hand on her leg.

She did not pull away. She was considering it. She was a modern girl and it was her body. She was entitled to decide how or what she would do. She put her hand over his, and said, 'I'm not sure, Ian.'

He moved his hand up her thigh slightly. 'No one need ever know. I'd like to and I think you'd like to. And it's not as though we haven't done it before.'

She felt sexually excited, there was no question of it. He moved his hand further. He was nearly within touching distance. And then he was touching her, down there. She felt hot and wondered if she had reddened. No one was paying them any attention at all. He was stroking her through her tights, her hand still on his.

She leaned forward, pushing his hand away, and whispered, 'My room in five minutes. Don't make it obvious,' and getting up, told the others that she was having an early night. They glanced at her, without a great deal of curiosity and Tina said goodnight.

She was not so drunk that she was unsteady on her feet but had to exercise some circumspection as she left the dining room. When she got to her room, after a slight problem with the electronic lock, she went to the bathroom and, after carefully trying to adjust her lipstick, sat on the bed and waited for the knock at the door. When she heard this, she got up, swayed but recovered herself, and went to open it.

Ian was there looking expectant. He came through, pushed the door to with his foot and, putting his arms round her, kissed her before starting to kiss her neck and ears.

'No, it might leave marks, don't do that.' She stood there, not really at all responsive, as he undressed her, slowly and carefully, pulling her tights down, she stepping out of them and then, kneeling in front of her, kissing her lower stomach. His hands ran up the inside of her legs and she moved position so that there was room for him to run his fingers all the way to the top. He was rubbing her gently.

'Bloody hell, Tina,' he whispered, 'you're so wet, a chap could drown down here.' She giggled and reaching down took off her knickers and let him lick her. Ian was a man who had long ago discovered the easiest way to get inside the front door was to pay attention to the door handle.

She started stepping backwards towards the bed, he following on his knees. When she got there, she sat down with her legs apart, his face disappearing between them. When he stood up, she noticed that he'd managed to undress himself without her realizing and then he was on top of her. Quite suddenly she did not want to carry on. He was just entering her, holding himself with one hand and nudging her open before easing himself in, when she cried out, 'No, Ian, we shouldn't be doing this.'

'Of course we should,' he groaned and pushed firmly but gently. She cried out again but then surrendered herself to sensation.

Ralph went to meet her off the train the following day. He was in a better mood generally, had been to Chambers and disposed of his paperwork with his usual dispatch. He was waiting near the ticket office, was early, and anticipating her arrival. He saw her first; she was smiling and alone. When she saw him she broke into a run, looking a little undignified, but she ran towards him, threw her arms around him and kissed him eagerly.

'Oh God, Ralph, I've missed you so much. I've been so looking forward to seeing you again. It's been weeks it seems since we lay next to one another.' She was still clinging to him. He held her tightly as well.

'Oh God, I've missed you. You've no idea how much I need you.'

'I'm never going to go away again. I'd rather lose my job. I want to be with you, Ralph. Always.'

'What do you want to do now? Do you have to go back to work?'

'No. Ian will be there. He can cover for me'

'Ian? Wasn't he on the train with you?' Ralph had forgotten about Ian.

'No. He went back early.'

Well, that's all right then, thought Ralph, with some relief. 'So, what would you like to do?'

'Whatever you'd like to do Ralph.' They were walking hand in hand towards his car and Ralph was feeling suddenly sexual.

'Should we go home and to bed?'

'Yes, let's.' She nodded enthusiastically. 'Yes, that's a lovely idea.'

Lying in their bed later, he turned to her and said 'I'm sorry I was cross last night. I just felt a bit let down, as though my feelings weren't of any importance in making the decision.'

'Oh Ralph, I was cross as well. I just wanted to sort things out. And you did say I should do whatever I thought was right. And we can start again.'

'Well so can they?'

'Why do you say they?'

Perhaps he had not told her about his offer to Virginia after all? 'I've made the same offer to Virginia.'

'You haven't?' Her eyes were wide with surprise. He was not sure of her reaction and anticipated annoyance.

'Do you mind?' he asked.

'Mind. No. It just means that you're a nicer person than I thought you were already. I'm relieved really. It means that we have nothing on our conscience and can start again.'

'What we won't have on our conscience is having taken our half shares. It's blood money isn't it? It doesn't alter the fact that we've run away with each other.'

'No, nothing can alter that. But it means no-one can say I've married you for your money.' She winced. She had not meant to bring up the subject of marriage. She had wanted him to do that. She was aware of his views regarding babies and children, but she was desperately anxious to have children herself. Ideally he was to have brought the subject up and she had intended then to say that she would only marry him if he could have children with her. It was not meant to be blackmail, nor was it going to have been a condition. It was, however, the way that she had thought it through and meant to approach the subject.

'Oops,' she said. 'I shouldn't have said that. A presumption too far.'

He was looking thoughtful. 'Marriage. We haven't talked about that at all. Neither of us. I wonder why not. I'm committed to you.'

'And I'm committed to you.' She licked his ear. 'What do you think?'

Ralph's initial reaction was to express pleasure, but he felt that undignified. 'I'd like that very much. Are you proposing formally?'

'Well yes, subject to both of us getting divorced. Do you know, I was going to wait for you to ask me? If you wanted to. I didn't want to push you. And then I'd have mentioned my wanting children...'

He stopped her. 'I expect I'll come round to the idea. You can probably persuade me to do anything. Anything at all,' and he kissed her again. 'What should we do tonight? More of the same?'

'Do you know? I feel I haven't been out anywhere for ages.'

'You were out last night weren't you?'

'Oh yes. I had a drink, then dinner and then an early night. The company was dull. There was better value in the Evening Standard in terms of entertainment. You probably had a much nicer time sitting at home than I did.'

'I went out. I couldn't stand my own company. I went to the theatre.'

'And what did you see?'

'A Midsummer Night's Dream.'

'Oh, Ralph, it's one of my favourite plays. I've only ever seen it once and not a terribly good production. What was it like?'

'Brilliant. I laughed out loud.'

'Oh, I wish I'd been with you. I feel quite cheated. Let down. Never mind. Perhaps I could go by myself.'

'Tina, if you would like to go, we'll go. I don't mind seeing it again. We'll go tonight if you want.'

'Are you sure?'

'Yes, of course I am.'

'God, you're so sweet. No wonder I fell in love with you.' Another long kiss.

'If we get going we could have a meal beforehand. That same restaurant we went to that first day.'

Tina screwed her eyes up. 'Which one was that?'

'Oh, surely you remember?'

'Yes, of course, the Chinese one. Sorry, I've got a rotten memory.'

Ralph did not enjoy the play as much as he had the previous evening but still laughed again. Tina thought the meal delicious, he had ordered some unusual dishes as he had been there sufficiently often to know his way round the intricacies of the menu, and the play wonderful.

Later that evening, lying in bed, Ralph turned to her and said, 'Have you thought about where you'd like to live? Us I mean. Any ideas?'

'No. It honestly doesn't matter to me. I'll be happy anywhere with you. A cardboard box on the motorway or Blenheim Palace. It doesn't matter. Wherever you'd like to go.'

'I've been thinking...'

'You've been thinking? So you had given it thought.'

'Well yes, of course I had. No, I was thinking that perhaps somewhere other than where I used to be. I actually don't want to live in that area any longer at all. I could go anywhere so long as I can get to Chambers relatively easily. In fact, I needn't go to Chambers that often. Mine is largely a paperwork practice. I could do much more at home.'

'That would be lovely. Except that I need to work.'

'Do you know, subconsciously I must be assuming that you'll have a baby and then you will give up. Good God. What has come over me?'

'I'm going to come over you,' murmured Tina as she crawled onto him and started gently licking him. He lay back and thought how lucky he was.

The days developed their own routine. In the morning she would usually wake him, she would be under the bedclothes, arousing him in the way that she had discovered he liked best. They would make love. They then had breakfast. He took her to work, went to his Chambers, passed the day there and picked her up again. They would stop to buy an evening meal together, go home, make love, eat and go to bed, holding one another.

Their respective divorces were in the hands of their spouses' solicitors and, as and when the few necessary documents came for signature in Tina's divorce, his papers already having been dealt with, these were signed and sent back the same day. Ralph had obtained confirmation that the mortgage lenders were prepared to release him and Tina from their mortgages. The Transfers had been prepared and sent to them both for signature. Ralph had waited with returning his until Tina's had arrived. He considered that there ought to be some kind of occasion, not exactly a celebration, but a recognition of the significance of the moment. The morning he saw the envelope on the mat with the solicitors' name in the franked postmark, he took it to Tina.

'Here you are.' He waited in silence as she opened it and took out the letter and its enclosure.

'It's the thing to give him the house.'

'I've got mine as well.' He retrieved this and put both the two side by side.

'Do you think its adding insult to injury if we witness each other's signatures?' he asked her.

'Well, at least they'll know that each of us knows that the other has given them their share.'

'Good point. Although I rather suspect that they might have put two and two together already. But if you think so.'

Thus each signed their own transfer and the other added a signature, together with name and address and occupation.

'Are you sure you're sure?' asked Tina.

'It's a bit late now. The court orders will be going through soon. Decree nisi in mine is the week after next. Yours will be soon afterwards and six weeks from nisi, she can apply for an absolute and that's it finished. Likewise yours.'

'Yes. And we'll be free.'

'To remarry,' he finished for her.

Tina, with the uncanny ability women possess to change the subject entirely without even noticing the non sequitur, glanced up and asked, 'Have you told your parents about it?'

'I spoke to them a few weeks ago, yes. Virginia had actually got there first with a letter. I had a bit of a row. They felt they ought to have been consulted for some reason. Or at least that I should have let them know sooner. I didn't see the point.'

'Why not?'

'I'd only have got a lecture about not taking things seriously enough.'

'But you seem to take most things pretty seriously.'

'I know. They don't see that though. I'm still a little boy who should be told what to do.'

'Am I going to meet them?'

'I really should visit at some stage. I'm not keen though.'

'I'd like to meet them though.'

'Maybe I'll give them a ring later today.'

After he had dropped her at work and gone to Chambers, Ralph sat thinking of his parents and childhood. It had not been an unhappy one. He had just grown apart from his family. His mother, particularly, was always disapproving and he had never had much of a relationship with his father. He picked up the telephone and dialled.

'Hello mother, it's Ralph.'

Her voice was rather cold. 'Hello, how are you? When are you going to visit us?'

'What are you doing at the weekend?'

'We're here as usual.'

'Could Tina and I come for lunch on Sunday?'

'Tina? The new one. I suppose so.'

Oh God, it's going to be wonderful isn't it, he thought but said, 'See you about one if that's OK?'

'Yes.'

'Goodbye mother.'

'Bye.'

He put the phone down and wondered why he bothered. He thought he might call Tina and just say that they were going on Sunday. When she answered and he had told her she asked something that made him wonder what they in fact talked about with each other. It certainly was not the past or their backgrounds.

'Where do they live, Ralph?'

'Haven't I told you?'

'No, never. And I never thought to ask.'

He named the depressing industrial town with reluctance. Even the sound of his hometown could lower his mood and the reality generally left him feeling only relieved when he drove away again.

'Isn't that where they've just opened the new Olympic size pool?'

'Yes, I believe so.'

'Would you like to try it out? It's years since I've been in a full size swimming pool.'

'I don't really like public pools. They're full of chlorinated snot.' She spluttered with laughter as he concluded, 'and the possibility of AIDS.'

'Don't be ridiculous. I'd like to. Go on let's. We could set off early and swim before lunch.'

'Well you wouldn't want to afterwards. It's pretty stodgy cooking. You'd sink.'

'We're agreed then.'

'Yes, we're agreed. Swimming first then lunch with the parents.' He didn't relish either prospect much but was curious as to why she was so keen. 'I'll pick you up as usual - love you.'

'To bits Ralph. See you later.'

When they met that evening she seemed excited.

'I've telephoned. There's a public session from ten to twelve which is just about right isn't it? I've been and bought a new costume and got you one as well as a present. Here.' She handed him a bag. He looked in it and drew out a pair of obviously expensive professional swimmers' trunks. He felt rather pleased. He had not told Tina that he had swum for his school with some success and decided not to mention this.

'Thank you. They're lovely. Look expensive.'

'Never mind. You're worth it.'

Over supper that night he suggested they went and looked at houses on Saturday.

'We can't stay here forever. It's a bit of a waste of money.'

'You know, Ralph, I quite like it. It's ours. Our first home.'

First home? The first home he and Virginia had owned had been a two up two down grim terraced property in a grim back street when he had been doing law pupillage and she was still training. That day they had moved in Virginia had said, a glint in her eye, 'I want to christen the house. I want it to be ours. We have to make love in every room.'

'Not surely every room today...' he had enquired, wondering where she thought he might get the stamina for this feat of sexual athleticism.

'No, but we can start now with the bedroom.'

So, in amongst the packing cases, boxes and suitcases, the bed without any sheets, the as yet uncurtained windows, the untouched by them spaces, she had made him have a 'quickie' before they got on with the serious business of moving in. Had Tina and St John been the same? Had they been overcome by a sense of private sexual territory that had affected them as it had Virginia? He had difficulty thinking of Tina in this context and was brought back to the conversation by Tina asking him what he was thinking about.

'Where to start looking. A needle in a haystack. What kind of house should we go for?' He had done calculations, having spoken to estate agents already, based on a cheaper area to the West. 'We can afford a four-bedroom executive detached on an estate or a two and a half bed cottage in the country. Or a smaller cottage or a smaller house on a larger estate,' he added for completeness. His preference was for a cottage. It would be something of a comedown after his last house, but he was prepared for this.

'Why don't we look at some of each?'

'Seems sensible.'

'I'll give some agents a ring in the morning.' He had already been sent a number of details that had arrived that morning at his Chambers, having asked to have these sent there to get an idea and feel before discussing it with Tina, but had forgotten to bring them home. He would do so tomorrow. Tina went into the bedroom. When she came out he did a doubletake. She had put on her new swimsuit.

'Do you like it Ralph?' He held back the comment he wanted to make, that it was rather revealing, and said instead, 'Can you swim in it?'

'Of course I can.'

She, he decided, was clearly not one of life's swimmers if that was how she proposed to dress. She looked pretty alluring though, very sexy indeed was his facile reaction, and when she said, 'Come on Ralph. Come and help me take it off,' and smiled suggestively, he needed no further encouragement.

The following evening they looked through the house agents details that he had brought home. He had brought only those that he felt they could afford based on multiplying his income by three and adding half of what he supposed her to be earning. The choice was limited but Tina seemed more attracted to the estate type houses. He did not know, but rather guessed that she was thinking in terms of babies, schools, school runs, coffee mornings with other young mothers and that kind of thing. His preference lay towards privacy, seclusion, isolation even, but he agreed to view some of those she picked out. She was happy to look at anything at all. There was something wonderfully settled and domestic, a quality that so far had been totally lacking in their relationship, about the whole business of looking at a place where they could live permanently.

'It's exciting isn't it?'

'It's more than exciting. It's wonderful. It's the start of our new life,' she said with enthusiasm. 'I'm so looking forward to it.'

The reality of looking at the various properties, he having telephoned first thing on Saturday morning to arrange some appointments, was more prosaic. The cottages were all, in his view, overpriced and looked variously onto flat fields of oilseed rape or rural petrol stations or council houses. They looked at two modern houses and Ralph, who had never lived in anything modern, as his three houses with Virginia had all been at least 150 years old, the last having been built in the sixteenth century, found himself rather liking the flatness of the walls and even the expanses of windows, which could be curtained, had their attractions. Nothing really though was suitable they decided as they drove home.

'Rome wasn't built in a day,' Tina said. 'There's always next weekend.'

He had agreed and said that he would contact more agents for more details the following week.

They went to bed that night happy, not disappointed but full of the excitement that a joint enterprise that interests both can produce. Ralph fell asleep thinking of manor houses in brick, quoined edges, hipped rooves, fanlights and butlers' pantries. Tina fell asleep, she told him she was going to, thinking of them together in their own house, furnished and decorated in the way that they chose.

'I'm so, so happy Ralph,' she whispered as she drifted off.

Tina woke Ralph up on Sunday morning with a cup of coffee, warm croissants and a selection of ham and cheeses. She was obviously elated at the prospect of the day. Ralph looked at his watch.

'For God's sake, Tina, it's only seven.'

'But it's over two hours' drive.'

'How long are you planning to swim for?'

'As long as you want.'

'I suppose I'm awake now anyway.'

They sat in bed to eat breakfast and then, putting the things to one side, Ralph leaned over to Tina and started running his hand up and down her back.

'There's plenty of time,' he said, 'Come here.'

'Let's do it later slowly.'

'Let's do it quickly now and again, but slowly, later.'

'That seems a sensible compromise,' smiled Tina, as she clambered on top of him.

In the car she was evidently considering something. She turned and said, 'Did you not get on with your parents? Is that why you don't see them much now?'

'It's not that I didn't get on with them, it's more that, rather than being Mother and Father, they were Smother and Further. By that I mean my mother's love was all-pervasive and suffocating, she just couldn't let go and I found it all a bit much and my father, or Further as I've always thought of him, never allowed himself to become involved. He was semi-detached from family life and, in retrospect I can see why. My mother never took his side in arguments and constantly undermined him.'

'How so?'

'Oh, only in that she would let my brother and me do things he'd forbidden or buy us things he wouldn't. I've always been surprised they're still together.'

'Why do you say that Ralph?'

'Because she was always threatening to leave us and him. She'd pack her bags and stand in the hallway saying she was going back to her parents. He'd ignore it but it upset me and my brother no end. We'd plead and implore her not to go. She never did of course, but we weren't to know she wouldn't. But they're still married.'

'Probably because you've both left home and there's nothing to argue about any longer.'

'Very probably you're right. But I don't look forward to the visits.'

'Smother and Further,' she smiled. 'Do you think it sums up parenthood?'

'For a lot of people. But then being a parent must be frightening. She went too far one way perhaps and he the other. Trying to find the right balance must be very difficult. I wouldn't much relish it myself.'

'But don't you feel guilty about not visiting them more often?'

'Up to a point. Sure, they gave me life, but they didn't promise it would be fun. They brought me into this world, not because I asked them to, but because they wanted a child. Genes may have played some part in establishing who, or what, I am and those come from them. In addition, if nurture did its bit as well as nature, then they are responsible for that also. In short I am me, now, as a direct result of their choice and choices, very few of them were mine. Latterly some, but from the moment of my creation until I was at least sixteen, I was theirs. I can't feel grateful to them at all, I'm afraid. You know my view. Having a child is usually an act of monumental egotistical selfishness.'

'It's a very clinical detached view. It needn't be like that. Look at my family. We get on.'

'Yes I know. Perhaps it's my failing.'

They were near the outskirts of his hometown and already the signs bore the legends for the new 'Olympic Swimming Pool'.

'All you have to do is follow the signs,' Tina said with no trace of irony.

'Really?' he said. 'I hadn't thought of that.'

Tina giggled, 'Sorry.'

Things had changed in the swimming world since he had last been to a public pool. Ralph mulled over the various amusements at the edge and the fact of a wave machine, other pool areas, the jungle flora and the apparent cleanliness. He was waiting at the poolside entrance to the women's changing rooms. He had not registered the figure that tapped him on the shoulder and, as he looked at the face, he exclaimed, 'Tina, sorry I didn't recognise you.' She was not wearing the swimming costume she had shown him but something very clingy, very professional looking, rather shiny, by Speedo together with a swimming hat and goggles on top, ready to be pulled down over her eyes.

'You look quite the business.'

'Oh I thought I'd dress properly,' she smiled. 'Are you getting in,' and held out her hand. He grasped it saying, 'Ready, steady, go,' and they jumped in together.

'Across to the other side and back,' he suggested.

'What stroke?'

'We're not racing are we?'

'No, let's just warm up, breaststroke perhaps.' This had always been his best stroke and they pushed off. He swam hard but did not exert himself. His was the old-fashioned stroke where the head remains parallel to the water. She did the new version, head bobbing down, far underwater and then up again, and a more complicated arm action. She was keeping up with him without difficulty. He started pulling a little harder and they turned. She kept up with him, he thought, effortlessly.

'Little bit faster,' she suggested. 'Let's do a length.' They swam to the end and set off together. Tina did not appear to be trying very hard, but Ralph was conscious that he was finding it difficult to keep up with her. He made a big effort, and they touched the far end together.

'You're not bad are you?' she said.

No, he didn't think he was bad, but he would show her that he could also dive. 'I might have a go on the diving board.'

'Go on, I'll watch from here,' Tina said supportively.

He took himself to the six metre and highest board and, having forgotten how far up one always seemed, hesitated for a moment. He recovered himself, stood on the edge and launched himself out. He did one whole somersault before straightening and entering the water. He was conscious it was not a perfect entry, his legs had been a bit too far back and had probably splashed but it was not bad. He swam to Tina.

'Pretty good,' she said. 'Should I have a go?'

'It's jolly high. Are you sure?'

'Well, if I get scared I can come down again can't I?' She handed him her goggles. He watched her as she climbed the ladders, noticing her muscles contracting and the curve of the swimsuit across her lower stomach and between her legs. She got to the top, looked about, checked for safety, turned to him, waved and then ran down the board, bounced and took off.

Time seemed to freeze, and Ralph watched in astonishment as she did two somersaults, languidly seemed to touch her toes and then straighten and enter the water perfectly cleanly without any apparent splash. When her head appeared above water again there was a ripple of applause from those who had watched the attractive young woman throw herself into the air. She acknowledged the clapping with a smile and came back to Ralph.

'Long time since I tried that before. Glad it worked,' she laughed.

'Where on earth did you learn to dive like that?'

'Come on, race you to the other end, any stroke.' He chose crawl, and set off powerfully. She was beside him and, at the three-quarter mark, she suddenly seemed to take off. He swam as fast as he could, but she was there before him.

'Back. Come on Ralph.'

'You're trying to humiliate me,' he groaned.

'No I'm not. I'm enjoying this with you. Come on. Breaststroke. Go.' And they went again but this time Ralph swam as hard as he could, pulling and pushing with ferocity just as he had when he had swum in the school team. He arrived at the other end a metre ahead of her.

'I couldn't keep up with you. You're good.'

'It was always my best stroke.'

'You're fast even with the old-fashioned style. You'd probably be a lot faster if I showed you how I did it. Look, like this.'

They spent a happy half hour with her teaching him the intricacies until Ralph said 'Can you do that dive again? I'd like to watch.'

'Sure.'

Again she climbed the ladders and some of the swimmers who had seen her earlier noticed her and stopped and pointed. She again paused before lightly running down the board, jumping, bouncing out but higher this time. Again he had the peculiar sensation of time freezing as he watched her describe a curve upwards and backwards, a complete back flip, and then a somersault and finally another clean entry. There was a respectful clapping when she appeared out of the water right beside Ralph.

'My God, you're good. Where did you learn?'

'At school. I was in the team.'

'So was I but I can't do that.'

'I was encouraged. I had quite serious ambitions at one stage.'

'How do you mean?'

'Well, I was swimming for the school and the County and hoped to do it for England. I just missed getting selected for the Olympic team when I was at university. I swam for them as well of course.'

'You're joking.' It was his turn to look at her wide eyed.

'No, why should I be?'

Ralph felt considerably chastened.

'I was bitterly disappointed. It wasn't as though it was my whole life, but I had tried really, really hard, training twice a day and when I wasn't picked, I sort of gave up.'

'How sad,' Ralph said affectionately and reached for her hand and squeezed it.

'But,' she said brightly, 'if I had not and had gone on, goodness knows where I'd had ended up and we would certainly never have met. That's more important. The present and the future. Not the past. That's a foreign country. Things are different there.'

'L P Hartley. Not my favourite writer.'

'No, I didn't care for him much either. Race you to the other end. Any stroke,' and off she powered. He did his best but simply could not keep up with her. She was laughing, relaxed and leaning against the wall when he got there.

'I think I might have to train seriously if we are to do this again.'

'I've always dreamt of having my own swimming pool. It needn't be large, but don't you think it would be nice?'

Ralph had often thought the same and simply said, 'That's easy then. We'll narrow the house hunting down to houses with swimming pools. In our price range that should limit the choice satisfactorily and make everything much easier.'

She laughed and then they swam together, leisurely and comfortably, backwards and forwards until the attendants started clearing the pool.

'See you in the foyer,' and off she went, confident and capable, having demonstrated unequivocally, that there was a lot about her he did not know, and that she possessed capabilities and capacities he had yet to discover.

On the journey towards his parents' house, Tina screwed up her mouth and muttered, 'Nearly as depressing as where I come from,' and on turning into the street that Ralph had said his parents lived in, burst out laughing.

'Why the hilarity?'

'Oh God, Ralph, I had no idea, I'd never have guessed.'

'What do you mean?'

'I've come home again; it's just like the street my parents live in.'

It was true. The same ordered suburban prissiness. Similar inter-war houses.

'Yes, I suppose it is. I just think of it, when I do think of it, which is not often, as the place I got away from.'

He parked the Bristol outside a house identical, except for the curtains, to those on each side, and they got out and went to the door. Ralph rang the bell and after a moment or two the door opened.

'Oh, it's you Ralph.'

Tina glanced at Ralph. His mother had sounded the L in his name. Tina had always known that his preference was that his name should rhyme with waif not Alf.

'Hello mother, hello father,' he nodded to the man who appeared behind. They stepped in. Tina hung back and when Ralph introduced her to them she said 'I've been looking forward to meeting Ralph's', (rhyming with waif), 'smother and further.' He flashed her a warning and mouthed the word, 'Please'.

'So you're the new one. Come on in.'

It was hardly a warm welcome and the conversation, such as it was, was one of longeurs and polite enquiry met with equally polite response. The meal, a traditional Sunday roast, seemed to last an unbearably long time, and it was only over coffee that anyone came to life. Tina had tried, deliberately and certainly, to make them like her. She had been charming, solicitous as to his mother's sciatica and his father's osteoporosis, even amusing about her job, but it was an uphill struggle. Coffee had been poured when his father asked, 'So you're divorcing?'

'Yes.'

'Why?'

It was a nasty bald question that had hung in the air. Ralph had paused before replying and finally said, 'Because I decided to.'

'That's not an answer and you know that perfectly well.'

'It's as much of an answer as I'm prepared to give.'

'Oh come on,' his mother said, 'after all your father and I have done for you.'

'Look mother, you didn't do anything special for me. I had a free education courtesy of the state. I had a means assisted grant at university which I didn't ask either of you to make up. I worked every holiday for the bit parents were supposed to give. I didn't come home much, as you know. You complained about it at the time. I was not, either then or now, any kind of a financial burden to either of you.' He was suppressing his anger.

'We gave you a good home.'

'Sure. You looked after me when I was little. You never once praised me though. If I got good marks it was always, why weren't they better? When I got a First, you, father, said Law was an easy subject. A memory test you called it. You diminished it. You even said that law was a soft career option. You never recognised the struggle I had to establish myself, let alone any kind of modest success I've achieved.' He spat this last comment out. His mother started crying.

'Now see what you've done,' his father said. 'The divorce has upset her and there's no need to be frankly abusive again.'

'I am not being frankly abusive. I just resent bitterly the way that you always, but always, seem to think that because I am your son, you have a right to pass judgment on me.'

'You are our son. We have an interest in you. Your welfare,' his father replied quite mildly. 'Your mother happens to disapprove of your divorce. She has a right to a view.'

'You have no right or business to be airing that view in front of Tina.' He got up. 'Tina we're going.' Tina looked appalled.

'Can't I help with the washing up Ralph?'

'We sound the L in his name Tina,' said his father.

'I don't,' snapped Ralph. 'And I haven't since I was fourteen. You couldn't even respect that could you? Twenty-four years later you still call me by a pronunciation I abominate.' Tina had gathered the plates together and taken them through. Neither Ralph nor his parents had noticed her doing this, rehearsing as they were, the worn-out repetition of a much played scene.

'Tina and I,' he looked round for her as she came back in saying, 'Sorry just tidying up.'

'Tina and I are getting married. We will be happy together. I don't expect approval. I can expect courtesy.'

'Not the way you talk to us,' his mother said with a stiff smile, 'can he Tina,' calling her into the battle.

Tina remained quiet for a moment and then said, 'I'm sorry Mr and Mrs Edwards. I know Ralph was looking forward to coming today. I know it's all a bit much but perhaps next time it'll be easier. Perhaps you might like to come and see us.'

Ralph held out her coat, helped her on with it and said, 'Thanks for the lunch. There's a small present for you both in the kitchen,' and bent to kiss his mother.

His mother, without warning, stood up and embraced Ralph. He found this, as ever, obscene; the intensity of the kisses and the way she clutched him repulsive. He disengaged himself without comment and shook his father's hand.

'Bye, I'll give you a ring,' he said and Tina, trying to say, 'Thank you again,' found herself ushered out into the dusk, into the car and away. Ralph was still angry, and said nothing.

Finally Tina enquired sympathetically, 'You don't really like them then?'

'It's less that than the fact that I thought they made it quite obvious that they didn't like you and preferred her.' 'Her' was, of course, Virginia.

'Oh that's not fair Ralph. It was a bit awkward I know, but they weren't hostile or anything.'

'Well they certainly weren't warm either.'

They were on the motorway now, heading back towards the conurbation, red lights, headlights, orange streetlights, the world was murky and miserable.

Tina leant over. 'You need cheering up,' she said and began undoing his zip. He nearly swerved violently.

'God, Tina, what are you doing?'

'Getting it out.'

'I'm doing 90 mph.'

'Well slow down then,' and she bent down.

'No, stop it.'

'I'm not going to stop unless you stop the car.'

'I can't. I'm on a motorway.'

'Well pull off then.'

'Promise to stop if I promise to pull off?'

'Yes.'

He didn't want to push her away; the sensation was too pleasant and no one had ever tried to do this to him at this speed. He saw an exit sign and indicated to leave, changed lane and she sat up.

'Where are we?'

'It's one of the quiet cross country A roads,' he said looking at her.

'You want to find a lay-by?'

'Only if you want to.'

She nodded and he drove a short way; it was a quiet road and there was very little traffic. He pulled into a deep lay-by and put on the hand brake.

'There, happy?'

She was down on him without a response.

'I thought it was to be a slow one later,' he gasped, reaching for her. 'Good God, where's your skirt and knickers?'

'I took them off when you weren't looking.'

He could just make out the whiteness of her flesh and the dark patch of hair.

It did not take long. He was, as ever with Tina, extremely aroused but he made sure that she had an orgasm too, before kissing her and moving back to his seat.

'That was lovely Ralph. Do you feel better?'

'A little more relaxed. It's a bit exposed though, isn't it?'

She was still sitting half clothed. He could not see her face.

'That was a first for me.'

'What was?'

'Doing it in a car. Was it a first for you?' Her tone was light, conversational.

'You don't think I make a habit of having sex in cars do you?' he answered equivocally.

'No, seriously, was it a first for you? I'd like to know.'

'Why?'

'I like the idea of having sexual firsts with you. Was it?'

'Yes. If you like the idea of sexual firsts then welcome to the chap who has never done it on a trapeze, in front of the paying public, under a restaurant table, in a public lavatory, at the opera...'

'Stop it.' She was laughing again. 'I only asked about the car.'

He suddenly wanted again to know more about her sexual history and development and longed to ask where the most unusual place was that she had "done it" but, again, decided that perhaps the answer would distress him.

'No, mine has been a fairly ordinary past,' he said instead.

'Perhaps we can change that.' She gave the impression of being so intensely sexually experienced and knowing, 'I'm putting my knickers on. It's dripping out and it's making the seat wet,' he heard her say, as well as immensely matter-of-fact, he reflected.

Perhaps a matter-of-fact approach was more sensible but, if totally matter-of-fact, then sex in itself became insignificant, just one more animal activity. It had to be more than that, he knew; sex with Tina proved that to him. They drove back home talking of houses, decorations, furniture and other non-contentious subjects. She did not mention his parents again that evening.

The day that Tina received her decree absolute and the final order relating to the financial matters, she came running into the bedroom.

'I'm free. I'm free. You're all mine.'

'No, I'm not. I'm conditionally all yours. Mine hasn't come yet remember.'

'Oh yes.' She looked crestfallen. 'When is it expected?'

'You're being disingenuous,' he smiled, 'you know perfectly well she can apply next Wednesday.'

'It's a long time to wait.'

'Do you know, it's only a couple of months or so since we moved in here? It's all gone incredibly quickly.'

'It's because we love one another. We're happy and we weren't before.'

'I know. Come back to bed. I want to cover you.'

'And I want to be covered,' she laughed as she slipped back between the sheets.

Afterwards she got up and came back bearing a handful of estate agents details and two cups of coffee.

'These came by the last post. Let's look at them together.'

They sat in the bed, he going through some, and she the others.

'No,' she exclaimed, 'it's got to be more than a coincidence. It's providence. It's meant to be,' and passed him a sheet. He glanced at the photograph with disdain, but started reading.

'Heated swimming pool,' sprang out at him.

'Look Ralph, look,' she pointed at the words. 'It's meant for us.'

'Don't be so dramatic.'

'No, it's like others we've looked at. It's on the edge of town. We can afford it and look...'

'It's got a heated swimming pool.'

'Can we go and look at it now? Immediately. Let's drive down and call the agents when we get down there. They won't be open yet.'

'Suppose the people are away? It would be a wasted journey.'

'We can go and look at it from the outside. Get a feel for the place. Poke our heads over the fence.'

'Look at the pool, you mean.'

'Yes, look at the pool.'

They in fact stopped en route, phoned the agents, held on while the agents called the owners, who were in, and fixed an appointment at ten thirty. Tina was beside herself, muttering, 'It's going to be the right one. I know it in my bones.'

He was non-committal. This was now only the second Saturday in a row that they had looked at houses and he was nearly sick of the sight of them. Tina remained uninhibitedly enthusiastic about the whole process, and refused to be chastened by another crop of dismal failures. Ralph had implicitly acknowledged that he was probably going to end up in a modern house, ruefully accepting that the cottages in their price range were altogether too much of a come down for him after his last house. Nevertheless, he still insisted they see older houses as well, and when they reached the town, he had spent fifteen minutes in a phone box arranging other views. He had thought Tina had set up a number of appointments, Saturday was already reserved by unspoken agreement for house hunting, but in fact she had only arranged two for later in the day.

When they pulled up at the end of the cul de sac he looked critically at what he saw. Four houses, quite large, each slightly different but only in detail, not in substance, standing in semi open plan front gardens, driveways with two smaller BMWs and a larger than usual Vauxhall. He was certain he could tell Tina the owners' social class and jobs without a great deal more evidence.

'We'd be living among middle management.'

'Oh, don't be so snotty. I like it. Let's go in.'

They left the car round the corner, Ralph saying the sight of it would ensure no reductions in the price, and walked to the door. Tina was exclaiming at the flower beds.

'Tina. They're only flower beds. You've seen them before.'

'Not true, I haven't seen these.'

They were greeted by a very young couple with a small, dirty-faced child lurking behind them.

'Forgive the mess. Children,' she sighed. 'They're so much work. The moment you tidy it's all untidy again.'

Ralph threw Tina a glance as if to say, 'See, just what I say,' but she had bent down and was talking to the little boy.

'Are you going to show us your nice house then?' The child started to cry and Tina stood up quickly. 'We're Ralph and Tina. Sorry to spring it on you...'

'No, it's quite all right. Come on in.'

They were led to what Ralph and Tina both called a sitting room, although it was described as a lounge in the agent's particulars and by the owners. It was a spacious room, off one end of which a door led to a dining room, another from that to the kitchen, then came a small utility room, a small family room and upstairs four bedrooms, a 'family bathroom' and a larger than expected en-suite to the main bedroom with a Jacuzzi corner bath.

Ralph thought it a perfectly ordinary house, but Tina kept exclaiming with delight as she was shown another fitted cupboard or washbasin. Outside there was a large garage, a larger than average garden but one that was dominated by a swimming pool.

'It's thirty by fifteen, a bit bigger than most. Three feet three going down to six feet.'

'It's lovely,' Tina said.

Ralph was nonplussed by this. As far as he was concerned, all one could see were paving stones and what must be some kind of winter cover.

'What colour is it?' Tina asked. The cover was pulled back. It was a standard swimming pool colour Ralph knew, but he heard Tina exclaim, 'It's a lovely colour.' He kept quiet and, when offered a cup of coffee, was inclined to refuse but Tina had already accepted. She was immersed in a conversation about the locality, what it was like to be a young mother on the estate, the shops, the neighbours, to the extent that Ralph felt a touch excluded.

'How do you keep the baby safe, from the swimming pool I mean?' Ralph asked. Tina turned to him and said, 'Didn't you notice? The pool was against two walls and there was a fence right down the side. We went through a gate.'

'Ah yes,' said Ralph, who had not noticed this at all. He went to the window and looked; Tina was of course right. He turned back and interrupted, 'Might I ask why you're moving? If it's not too personal.'

'No, there's no reason other than my mother died and left us enough money to buy a big house in the country. We've found one we like so much that we'd like a quick sale.'

'We're cash buyers,' Tina interjected. 'Would you accept less than the agent's figure?' The couple looked at one another.

'If it was quick we'd take ten thousand less.'

'What about fifteen?' Tina said.

'Twelve and a half,' was the response.

'We'll make an offer to the agent as we go home today, won't we Ralph?'

'Yes, if you say so,' and Ralph smiled grimly.

As they drove away he looked at her and asked, 'Why did you lead them on, saying we'd put an offer in? We haven't talked about it at all. We've got at least two more to look at today.'

'No, cancel the appointments. Come on Ralph. It's perfect. It's got everything we wanted.'

'Everything you wanted.'

'No, that's sour grapes. It's big enough. It's affordable. We've got twelve and a half thousand off. It's got a swimming pool. They're leaving the carpets.'

'They should take another two and a half off if they're leaving those.'

'No. It'll save us some money in the first place. We can always re-carpet later.'

Ralph thought of the carpets, flecked and patterned, so different from bare boards and the Persian rugs that Virginia now owned and sighed gloomily, 'If it makes you happy Tina.'

They went to the agents, made the agreed offer, Ralph nominating an old solicitor friend to do the conveyancing, and Ralph dutifully rang and cancelled the other appointments. They had lunch in a pub. As they ate Ralph noticed Tina watching him warily.

She had decided to tell him. She had spent frantic lonely hours at night, in the shop, with her thoughts in turmoil wondering whether she should, she thought Ralph would appreciate the joke if not the circumstances, 'dispose of the evidence'. What if the child looked like St John or, perhaps worse, Ian? She could not put a date to conception, in fact had no idea and knew she had been a fool but in the frantic sexual activity of those weeks she had not, and she disliked the phrase but how apt it was, taken proper precautions.

'Why are you looking like that?'

She was biting her lip. 'I think I might have some news.'

'What do you mean news? You're divorced as of yesterday. That's news. We appear to have bought a house you like. That's news. What other news can there be?'

She looked down before looking back up at him.

'I've always had erratic periods,' she began.

He dropped his glass. 'Sorry, there wasn't much in it.'

Tina dabbed at the liquid. 'You've guessed.'

Ralph had guessed and had been shocked to discover how disturbed he felt.

'Are you sure? How can you be? Sure I mean.'

'I'm really sure. And I didn't mean to be. It's an accident. But a nice one if I am, surely?'

Ralph's first thought was how could she know that he was the father? It was less than, he tried to count up, it seemed only a few weeks since she had still been living with St John. He was not quite sure how to put the question.

She seemed to have anticipated his doubts and said, 'When we met I wasn't taking the pill. It was a way of stopping having sex with St John. I told him it was making me ill. I hadn't, you know, slept with him for several months before you and I did it. No Ralph, I think you're going to be a daddy.'

Ralph's world seemed to have collapsed in on him. He was struck speechless and just sat there tapping his teeth with his fingers.

'Ralph, that's a very annoying habit. I saw your father doing it.'

'What?'

'Tapping his teeth.'

'Sorry, I'm trying to think.' How long had she known or suspected? Did this explain the hurry to get divorced? No, she can't have known already then. It would certainly explain the hurry for a house and also why she seemed desperate for this one.

'Have you done a test?'

'Yes. Yesterday. It was positive. They're never 100% but I've been feeling different for the last week or two.'

'Why didn't you say something sooner?'

'I wanted to be more sure.'

'Are you sure you want a baby already?'

'I wouldn't have an abortion if that's what you mean.'

'No, I wasn't thinking of that. Just that you'll have to give up work.' Oh Christ, he thought, and her income, 'and well, put it this way, we're not going to be exactly well off.'

'Come off it Ralph. You're a successful barrister. We'll have enough. Aren't you excited?'

Ralph did feel a certain grudging pleasure at the thought that he had perhaps successfully made a baby.

'Yes, of course I am. Are you going to the Doctor?'

'I thought maybe on Monday. Will you come with me?'

'Of course, Tina. It's just come as a bit of a shock.'

'But a nice one,' she pleaded.

'A nice shock.' His mind was racing. This was so totally unplanned. Or was it? He looked at her and wondered, shook his head and tried to dispel the idea that everything might have been planned. It was too grisly a prospect. He knew himself to be in love with Tina and he was sure that she was in love with him. But not to take one's contraceptive. He had been a fool not to check on it, but then, surely a twenty-eight-year-old woman would not have unprotected sex with a comparative stranger, as he was then. By the same token he had not thought of precautions, he had just assumed that all would be safe. But then why assume it was conceived the first time they did it. Because, he reasoned, wouldn't she have started taking the pill again when they started their physical relationship? Ah, but it took time to establish, weren't you supposed not to rely on the pill for the first fortnight or maybe even month? He could not remember what Virginia had told him; her preference had been an alternative method which was not, according to her, chemically harmful. But then Tina should have warned him. He had been a fool not to ask and do something about contraception himself. He had, subconsciously he expected, not wanted to consider condoms which he considered rather nasty and sordid. He had still been a fool.

While he was thus preoccupied Tina watched him anxiously.

'What are you thinking Ralph? Do please tell me?'

'There's a lot to sort out now isn't there? Suddenly everything's changed. It's all a bit sudden. I've got to get used to the idea.'

'Ralph. It'll be lovely. You, me and the baby.' She seized his hand and pressed it to her stomach.

'There's a little you in there.'

'I'm not sure I want a little me. One's enough,' Ralph tried to joke. 'It's just that I would have liked a little more time with just you and me.'

'If I am, it's ages away.'

'How do you know? They all take about nine months to cook don't they? Deduct how long... oh never mind.' His natural instinct was to make the best of things; there was no use railing against the inevitable. 'Let's enjoy everything as much as we can. Short views, remember?' Tina, he thought, looked relieved.

'Ralph, I've been so torn between excitement and dread. You know I've always wanted a baby. I didn't want one this quickly but if it's to be it's to be.'

'That's a bit fatalistic.'

'Well I am a fatalist. If it's happened, it's happened and you couldn't countenance an abortion.'

'No. I couldn't. I believe in a woman's right to choose though,' he said, thinking he might leave the door open just a little.

'I do as well. But only in extreme circumstances. Like rape or incest.'

'Aren't there enough unwanted babies in the world already? Not that ours is unwanted,' he added hastily.

'Yes, there are a lot. Of course there are a lot. But there are also a lot of people who would like children but can't have them.'

'Sounds too totalitarian for me. Here you are, childless couple, you can have this one from her over there and so on.'

'It's not quite what I meant.'

'I know. I'm exaggerating for effect.'

'No, I just can't accept a general principle of killing a foetus, which really is a baby, simply because of inconvenience.'

'So abortion is murder.'

'Yes, I think it's as much murder as cold-blooded killing. And in just the same way there are defences to murder, like, oh I can't think.'

'Insanity,' he answered for her.

'No, don't be silly. That's not what I mean at all as you know. Duress I think. Force, that kind of thing, there are defences, morally, to abortion.'

'Women's rights lobby wouldn't agree.'

'No, but they're not necessarily right.'

'Any more than you are. Come on. Let's pay and go home and think about this new house.'

They left the pub, Ralph's arm around Tina, and driving home she talked of nothing else but the new house. Ralph decided, had already decided because he knew it had been decided for him, not to put up any resistance but simply to accept what now appeared to be inevitable. As Tina chattered on, and he made appropriate answers, he was actually running sums through and calculating mortgage payments and the like.

'You're not listening Ralph.'

'I am. I promise.' He had no savings, his only assets were a couple of pictures and the Bristol which was by no means paid for. He, they, would need as big a mortgage as possible but it was likely that he would have to find a minimum of 5%, more probably, 10% of the purchase price. The house that Tina had chosen was not as expensive as they could have bought but, on the other hand, they would only have his income so perhaps it was just as well. The ghastly, to Ralph, prospect loomed of having to sell either both pictures or the Bristol or perhaps even all three.

'You're not listening Ralph. What have I just said?' Tina demanded suddenly.

'You've been incredibly sympathetic to my idea of selling the Bristol.'

'No I haven't.'

'I know you haven't. But that's what I'm going to have to do to buy that house. Or, in fairness, any other house.'

'Oh Ralph. Really? That's a shame.' Perhaps she was sympathetic he thought. 'Maybe you can buy another one later. When you're a Q.C.'

'Look, I'm realistic enough to know that if I sell it now, I'll never get another one. There'll always be other demands, children, Disneyworld...'

'No, you can buy another Bristol before we ever go on holiday.'

'That's fine then. We'll go down to your car and use that.'

'It makes a lot of sense though doesn't it?'

Yes, Ralph wanted to scream, it only makes a lot of sense if you don't mind driving an old knackerbox when you had been used to a Bristol and a Porsche but he said nothing.

'Perhaps we could sell mine and buy something a bit better, something we could all use.'

'A pushchair?' he suggested.

She laughed again, 'We'll need one of those anyway. No, I'll need to go to clinics, and the Doctor and Tumbletots.'

'And I can walk to Chambers.'

'No, you can walk to the station, or I can take you.'

She's ever practical he thought. 'Yes, it'll be good for me. I can jog to the station after an early morning swim, wash in the carriage lavatory, change and emerge at the other end fit, clean and tidy.'

She was not completely sure whether he was joking but then he laughed. 'Well, it's certainly all change isn't it?'

On Sunday Tina decided she'd like to look at 'their' house again. She announced this just at the moment she was about to lower herself onto him after their first cup of coffee. Ralph immediately said, 'Of course,' and then she, as expertly as ever, rocked backwards and forward until, squealing with pleasure while he rubbed her, she fell shuddering on his chest.

'It just gets better and better,' she said.

Ralph, feeling drained himself, agreed but silently thought of what was happening inside her. This was something to be taken further on Monday.

They drove to the estate. Tina wanted to visit the house again but Ralph was reluctant. 'They're not expecting us.'

'They want to sell it. It they're in, they'll surely let us see it again,' and getting out of the car, she walked down the cul de sac and knocked. The door was opened. Ralph saw her talking and then she turned and beckoned to him. He joined her and Tina said, 'We've been asked in for a cup of coffee.' In they went and sitting in the kitchen, Ralph listened while Tina chattered on again. She seemed happy he thought, but then was this house what she expected when she and he had started thinking more permanently? He supposed it could be and in the car he asked her the question.

She replied, quickly and with what seemed to him like sincerity, 'Oh yes, I'd have liked a house like the one you had before but if that's not to be, that's the way it is. What about you?'

It was exactly what he had wanted to take himself beyond, surely she could see that, but they would be together and it would be theirs, so he replied, 'As you say, it will do.'

On Friday, more promptly than he expected, when he collected the post he found a letter bearing the words 'Lord Chancellor's Department'. Opening it he stared at the first piece of paper that announced that he was no longer married to Virginia and then the other piece ordering him, by consent, to transfer the house to her and declaring that all items, save for his two pictures and personal belongings, now belonged to her.

Tina came up to him, as he stood in the hallway, and caught him by the waist.

'It's come then?' she said with glee.

'Yes. It's arrived. I'm a free man.' He felt unexpectedly gloomy.

'Then it's no longer adultery, is it?' she said looking at him and licking her lips provocatively.

'No, it's no longer adultery,' he said, trying to take the sadness out of his voice.

'Then come and do it to me,' and she turned, lifting her night-dress up to her waist, wiggling her bottom at him.

Tina squealed, panted and seemed to be more sexually abandoned than ever before. He dutifully went through the motions, but he could not help dwelling on the sense of loss, rather than what Tina announced was a 'brilliant bonk'. He resented the phrase; even Virginia, who was a fairly earthy person, had never used that particular colloquialism. He gritted his teeth and said nothing, taking her to work as usual and driving onto his Chambers.

He went through his paperwork, methodically but mechanically, and noticing that it was lunchtime, decided to go and buy a sandwich. He was on his way back when he saw a headline on the early evening newspaper hoardings that made him stop. He found himself immediately so cold that he shuddered.

'GP killed in road smash.'

For whatever reason, had he been asked he could not have given a rational explanation, he stood for a moment and knew.

He found it difficult to walk the few steps and hand over a few coins to the street seller, but did so and, with a dread and a certainty, read the headline on the front page. 'Popular GP killed at accident blackspot' There was a photograph. Ralph read on. 'Dr Virginia Edwards, a popular local GP, was killed this morning when her car left the road at Rowans Corner, a well-known accident blackspot. Firemen took an hour to free Dr Edwards, who was certified dead on arrival at hospital. No other car was involved and police are appealing for witnesses. Dr Edwards was a partner in the Church Street Medical Practice. Dr Johnson, another partner, when asked for a comment, stated, 'Dr Edwards was an immensely good doctor, very popular with her partners, staff and her patients. She will be a great loss to us all. Dr Edwards had recently separated from her husband.' That was all.

Ralph stood, unaware of the people behind him, oblivious to the city, anything, feeling a terrible anguish, a clutch at his viscera that made him physically nauseous, and started to cry. He rolled the newspaper up, pushed it into his pocket and walked. He must have, he reckoned later, spent two hours just walking through the city, quartering it, up and down, thoughtless, grief-stricken and so riddled with guilt, he was shivering. He finally found himself by a church, a small grubby urban one, unappealing on any aesthetic level, but a church. He stopped, pushed open the door and went in. It was fusty, a smell of wax and dirt mingled together. The interior was plain, unadorned and simple. He stared at the altar with the cross and sitting down on a pew, put his head between his hands and let out an animal cry of pain before sobbing uncontrollably.

She knew that road. She knew Rowans Corner. They had driven that road literally hundreds of times, she or he behind the steering wheel. If he was driving he would, in the Porsche, drop to third gear and gently accelerate out. If she were driving, she would approach the corner in fourth, do a very quick gear change and accelerate out, traffic permitting, choosing a racing driver's line, with an enthusiast's verve, grinning usually as she did so. There was no possibility of her making a mistake. Unless someone had been coming in the opposite direction and had been slightly too far over and she had to correct and then lost control. He pulled the paper out and looked at the photograph of the Porsche. He did not recognise the tree against which it had impacted. Was Virginia still in there when the photograph had been taken? He could not tell but retched as he stared at it. The more likely explanation, and the one he could hardly bear to contemplate or even formulate, was that she had deliberately accelerated as hard as she could and aimed for that particular tree and hit it, at God knows what speed, knowing absolutely and precisely what she was doing.

'God forgive me,' he kept repeating. 'God forgive me.'

He half hoped that a priest would turn up, as they do in fiction, and ask him what was the matter and, upon hearing, offer some words of comfort. However, there was no one else in the church and Ralph felt horribly alone and frightened.

Finally, pulling himself together, he got up, still trembling and, knowing that there was to be no divine intervention to pardon or appease him, started walking back to his Chambers. As he passed a litter bin he thrust the paper into it, deep down, and was filled with self-hatred.

In Chambers he went straight to the washroom and stared at himself in a mirror. He seemed the same as usual, he did not think he looked as though he had been crying, and he tried to smile but it came out as a grimace.

Still, I shall not need to talk to anyone he thought and, checking his watch, found that it had gone five o'clock. He went into the Clerks' room, there was only a very junior clerk sitting at her desk, and then checked his pigeonhole.

One letter, typed and marked Personal was there, which he picked up and opened. A single piece of paper, again typed, contained the words, 'You shit. Someone will see to you for this.' It was unsigned. The type size was nondescript, it could have been done on any word processor in Chambers or elsewhere.

His hand shook as he stood there and the junior clerk looked up and said, 'Anything the matter Mr Edwards?'

'No,' he said, 'who delivered this, do you know?'

'No idea, sir,' and the clerk bent her head again and concentrated on the papers on her desk.

Was the clerk looking furtive, Ralph wondered. Did she know? Perhaps they all knew? Ralph was feeling threatened and frightened. What on earth could, 'Someone will see to you for this' mean? Was it a joke in poor taste? He went back to his room and, remembering that he had promised to pick Tina up as usual, phoned the shop. She answered.

'It's me, Ralph.'

'Oh good. Are you on your way back?'

'Yes, I'm running a bit late though. Will you wait?'

'Oh no, it's all right. Ian can drop me off at home. I'll see you there.'

'OK then,' he replied dully. 'I'll see you later.' He was not sure he could face Tina just at the moment, not sure what he would or even could say.

'Bye then. Love you.' She was bright, cheerful, and put the phone down.

'Jesus Christ, what have I done?' he muttered, as he too put the phone down and sank his head onto his arms.

There was a bang at the door and, before he could say anything, Ken had come into the room. He caught a glimpse of Ralph, head on his arms, before Ralph had managed to straighten himself up and smile, 'Yes?'

'You know then?'

'Yes. I saw the newspapers.

'I just wanted to say how shocked I was at the news. I know you had separated but...' he spread his hands and shrugged his shoulders. 'It's pretty ghastly isn't it?'

'Ken, it's not just ghastly. It's so fucking awful I don't know what to say.'

Ken looked sympathetic but quizzical.

Ralph carried on, 'We weren't just separated. I had the decree absolute today. So must she.'

'You mean you think that it was...'

'Yes, deliberate. Fucking suicide. Oh God. What should I do?'

'Nothing you can do, is there?'

'I suppose not. Does Chambers know?'

'Yes, someone brought the paper in at lunchtime.'

'What's the general feeling?'

'Horror, really. Some sympathy for you. An awful lot of sadness. Everyone liked Virginia, you know.'

'Yes, I did know. Yes, everyone liked bloody Virginia. They're not going to like me very much though are they? I mean, when the news comes out that it was suicide on the day she received her bloody decree absolute.'

'You don't know it was suicide.'

'I do. She knew that road, that corner. She could take you round it as safely and quickly as a racing driver. It was deliberate. The inquest will prove that.'

Oh God, he thought, an inquest. It would be made public. The circumstances. He might have to give evidence. It could be in all the papers. Probably the National press as well. He took out the piece of paper and showed it to Ken.

'This was in my pigeonhole. Any idea who put it there or who it was from?'

Ken held it, read it, handed it back and then said, 'No, none at all. I'm sorry Ralph. I suppose it could be from any of the twenty-six people here, although I'd prefer to think not. Alternatively it could have been put in by any of the many people who pop in over the day. I just don't know. Not very nice.'

It could even have been you, thought Ralph, uncertain as to just who his friends might still be. Ken knew, but then so did others, that the decree absolute was imminent but no one could have known that the decree had actually arrived that morning.

'Would you like a drink Ralph?'

'Ken, I'm not going to be very good company. But if you don't mind, I'd rather not. If Chambers know, then other

Chambers will know, and I can't face going into a pub with people looking at me and pointing and whispering. There's Ralph Edwards, left his lovely wife and took up with some woman. Wife killed herself today, you know.'

'No one knows she killed herself. All that they, the world, know is that she was killed in a one car accident.'

'Oh no. They'll all guess. No, I'd better go home.'

'I don't think you're in a fit state to go home yet.'

'Why on earth not?'

'Because you're going to have to tell Tina and talk about it aren't you? Maybe you ought to compose yourself a bit. I've never seen you like this except before the Vincent trial.'

Ralph remembered that well. It was a huge case for him at the time and he felt then as though winning was critical to any future success. Ken had found him in the washroom, an hour before the case was due to begin, silently vomiting into a basin, had talked to him, talked him through it and had gone with him to court where he had watched, happily, as Ralph, gently but ruthlessly, had demolished the other side's arguments and had achieved a spectacular success.

'You're right Ken. I feel exactly the same. Physically sick. Perhaps a drink is a good idea but please, not at the usual.'

They went instead to another wine bar, not used by the legal world, where Ralph asked and heard about Ken's children. He suddenly remembered that he, too, was going to be a father and turning to Ken said, 'Don't, please, tell anyone, but Tina is pregnant. I went with her to the doctor this week. It was confirmed.'

'Do you know Ralph, I'd try and keep that quiet you know. It looks a bit unseemly.' He stopped. 'I'm sorry for saying that, but I think you'd lose quite a lot of sympathy if it were to come out.'

'Yes. I can see what you mean.' Ralph had told nobody, had kept the news to himself, although this had been difficult. He had been feeling like most men do in the same situation, as though he and he only was capable of the act of procreation and that, as a result, he was somehow rather special.

'You won't tell anyone, Ken, will you?'

'No. I shan't. I suppose you and Tina will be getting married?'

'Yes, we've talked about it. I was leaving it until after the decree absolute though before doing anything about it.'

'If Tina's having a baby she'll want to marry?'

'Oh yes. She's talking of nothing else. Babies, houses... Oh, I'm moving as well.'

'Christ, Ralph. House move, baby, wedding, divorce, death. It's all a bit much isn't it? Will you cope?'

'When have I ever not?' With that remark something of what already seemed to Ralph to be his old character reappeared. 'I'll cope.'

They parted and, as they did so, Ken clapped him on the shoulder.

'Good luck Ralph,' he said, before walking off towards what Ralph knew to be a very comfortable and orderly existence.

He drove home, silently and thoughtlessly, and upon arriving, let himself into the flat. He hung his coat up in the lobby and went into the sitting room. The lights were out and there were, it seemed, hundreds of candles flickering all around the room. The effect was beautiful, the very ordinary room had been transformed into a dark and magical chamber, with a cathedral like quality, a place of worship or celebration, and

Tina was sitting in an armchair looking pleased with herself.

'You're late but never mind. I had time to arrange a surprise,' motioning towards all the candles, 'and to get a meal ready.'

Ralph was speechless. He stood there gaping, his mind still reeling from the news earlier in the day. Tina stood up, stretched and he saw that she had dressed up for him again in a very short tight mini skirt, just showing, he knew they would be, stocking tops rather than tights, and a halter neck black top that revealed more than it covered.

'You look delicious,' he finally said, 'good enough to eat.'

'I'm glad you like it. It's to celebrate your being free.'

As she said this his stomach turned, but Ralph, considering it unfair to Tina who had gone he knew, to a lot of effort to please him, decided to say nothing of Virginia and resolved to enter, at least physically, if emotionally and mentally disengaged, into the spirit of Tina's game.

'If I look good enough to eat, then come and eat me.'

But he forgot the day, forgot himself, forgot everything once more as they made love, and only subsequently, Tina lying in his arms murmuring words of contentment, did he remember Virginia. The reflection brought an actual pain to his stomach and Tina must have sensed something was wrong.

'Is anything the matter?'

'No,' and he knew he could not tell her tonight but had to wait for a more appropriate opportunity. 'I just feel very happy. When should we get married?'

'Ralph,' she was excited, 'I've so wanted to hear you say those words. Finally, they have meaning because we can now, can't we?'

'Yes. We're both free. When then?'

'As soon as possible?'

They dressed, Tina choosing something less overtly sexual and as she put away the tiny skirt, he asked, 'When did you get that?'

'Years ago. I had it at school. I found it the other day. I was surprised it still fitted.' He groaned inwardly; if she had the skirt at school, then she must have worn it. She would not have grown taller in the intervening years so she must have worn it at the same, absurdly indecent height then. What on earth had she been like as a schoolgirl?

'Well, I don't suppose it will fit for much longer,' he said, patting her stomach. 'This is going to expand.'

'I know. But it's exciting. Look I went to M&S and got your favourites.'

He saw the coloured boxes of food. Were they his favourites? Had he ever said so? He was not sure, his preference was for freshly cooked ingredients, but he assented and she busied herself, placing the pre-packed meals in the oven. Over supper she talked, he listening and chipping in occasionally with a short comment, of their marriage, their house and their baby. This was the order in which she thought events ought to take place.

Ralph wondered whether he should first go to a funeral, and then might be compelled to be a witness at an inquest, but agreed with Tina that her suggestion was both practical and right.

'Where do you want to get married?' he asked her.

'Oh Ralph, I'd so have liked a big church wedding with you. And a proper reception. Like I had the first time.'

Despite the fact that Ralph had been married in the little

church beside his former parents-in-laws' house, and there had been a massive reception in a marquee on the lawn afterwards, he felt a pang of envy or even jealousy at the thought of Tina, no doubt in virginal white, standing with St John in front of the altar, making their vows, before going to a reception, kissing in front of the guests, speeches, going away and then the first night of their honeymoon. He remembered his wedding, his feeling of relief when they had driven away, he completely sober not having touched a drop of Champagne, Nuits St George or the Macon Villages, Virginia's expression of satisfaction as she held his knee until, driving across the moors, in the same place as only a few months ago, she had asked him to stop.

'Why?'

'I want to look at the view,' and on stopping, she had paused only momentarily, 'I've looked at the view. I really wanted you to make love to me quickly, now, here. I want our first married sex to be here.'

His car was not a Bristol then, but a small sports convertible and the act was uncomfortable and difficult. Nevertheless they had managed before he, seemingly disengaging himself simultaneously from the hand brake and gear lever, wanting to rub what he was sure was going to be an unpleasant bruise on his leg, had got back into the driver's seat.

'That was nice,' Virginia smiled and they set off for their honeymoon in Scotland.

'I suppose you had a church wedding and a reception though with her.'

Tina did not know of course 'her' lay dead, white, certainly massively disfigured, in pieces even.

'Yes, I did. I didn't enjoy it very much though. Did you

yours?'

'I suppose I have to answer, yes I did at the time. But I wish it had been with you rather than him. Where shall we get married then?'

They decided on the registry office in the town where the house was. This meant that they would have to have lived in the house for 3 weeks for the banns to be posted and that, in turn, according to Tina, made it imperative that they tried to move the house purchase on as quickly as possible. She did not want to be too obviously pregnant at the time. He promised to speak to the solicitor on Monday, having already made a mortgage application. He had contacted the grateful client earlier that week, who had, as promised, been able to deliver a 95% mortgage which in turn meant that Ralph had only to choose between the pictures or the car.

'Which should it be then?'

'What do you mean?' Tina had no idea what he was talking about.

'To find the deposit and moving expenses. The Bristol or the Goodwin and the Peake? It's all I have.'

'Where's your income going at the moment?' It was not said suspiciously or accusingly, merely curiously.

'Rent, the Bristol, credit cards, food, expenses of daily living. It covers it. What about yours?'

'I've saved every penny that I've been able to. For furniture and a cot,' her eyes glazed over as she thought about the baby, 'and all the other things we'll need. As I said before. Sell the Bristol and we'll buy something a bit more suitable. An estate car. We'll need the space.'

Ralph's heart sank. His Bristol was his biggest toy, his biggest luxury and he still remembered the moment he had bought it, committing himself to a frighteningly expensive H.P. agreement for an idiotically expensive motor car, which he had never ceased to cherish. He liked the old-fashioned image of the car and he liked the car itself.

'It'll be like losing a leg.'

'Don't be silly. Cars just go down in value. The pictures will go up. Let's keep those. After all, they are of sentimental as well as financial value aren't they?'

'Yes. I know. I'll sell the car.'

No suitable opportunity arose over the weekend to tell Tina of Virginia. Tina, never a very enthusiastic reader of the newspapers, did not learn of Virginia's death from those and, since Ralph and she never watched television, preferring more homespun amusements, did not catch the small mention in the local programme. Ralph finally, after much consideration, decided it was unfair to tell Tina at all, so happy and preoccupied was she with her plans and excitement. He knew that she would hear of Virginia's end one day, if not from him then perhaps Frances or someone else, but he himself was so disturbed, and guilt-ridden, that he thought that he might break down in front of Tina, and he could not contemplate such a loss of self-control.

The next Saturday was spent in going round shops looking at furniture. Tina had managed to save a larger amount than Ralph guessed, and she wanted to buy a dining table, chairs, a three piece suite and a bed.

'My parents will buy us a cot,' she said.

'My parents won't buy us anything,' he had answered, 'but can't we have a new bed, an old sofa or two and an older dining table and chairs? Antique. I'll pay for those.'

'No,' she was firm, 'I've saved the money, so I'll pay. There's no point in having anything nice. Not with a baby. And there'll be another after that won't there,' she looked at him imploringly. She had never mentioned babies in the plural and now seemed a chance. 'We can always get nicer things later on can't we?'

'Babies,' replied Ralph, gloomily thinking of the years of mess, filth and destruction that lay ahead. 'Yes, you're right of course.'

So they had not compromised, for Ralph felt he had no choice in the matter, but rather he had acquiesced in her choice of a pine table and chairs. He tried to put out of his mind the thought of his Regency ball and claw dining table and the elegant sabre legged chairs. Then she chose a suite that was covered in an inoffensive fabric that was guaranteed to withstand all stains, Ralph thinking now of his cream damask Knole sofas, and finally she pointed at a very luxurious bed, which he rather admired. She had insisted on lying down on it in the shop and had embarrassed him when she told him to try it out as well.

'Come on. All the magazines say that you should do this. Bounce up and down. Check it out properly.'

Passers-by had looked at them lying there, Ralph trying his best to look nonchalant and Tina giggling and whispering in his ear.

'Come on, we're going to spend a lot of time in this. We've got to get it right.' She had paid with a cheque and delivery was promised at any time after seven days to whatever address they nominated later. They went to the fabric department. Tina had measured for curtains on their last visit to the house. Ralph was apprehensive.

'Suppose we don't get this one? Something goes wrong?'

'We can always use the fabric somewhere else. And it won't. It's our house and we're going to have it.'

She was certain as ever, confident that things would work for her and them. She did not like Osborne & Little, his preferred choice, but went instead towards Colefax & Fowler and Jane Churchill and, again, he ended up agreeing to flower prints rather than the plainer patterns that he, and it had to be said Virginia, would have chosen.

'That's a good day's work,' she had announced. 'What else is there to do?'

Bury Virginia he thought, but answered, 'I'm not sure. You tell me.'

'Carpets can wait.'

'I thought we were having theirs?'

'Yes. Only to begin with. No, we can go home.'

That evening they decided on a reception in whatever hotel was most local and suitable to their new house and started trying to agree a guest list.

'We can't go overboard. It's all too expensive,' Tina had said. 'Let's restrict the numbers.'

He agreed, he was actually not sure who he wanted to invite. Tina's parents, her sister, Frances and Henry, another couple of Tina's friends he had not yet met and their spouses, one had children already who would be bridesmaids.

'Do you have bridesmaids at Registry Offices?' he asked.

'I'm going to.' So that was settled and, she insisted, his parents and his brother.

'I'll ask Ken and his family.'

'Who's Ken?'

'My Senior Clerk.' Had she not even registered that he wondered?

'Anyone else from Chambers?' He thought for a moment but was not sure.

'I don't know yet. We've plenty of time.'

'Have you no other friends? What about all the people who came to your party. There must have been at least sixty.' He thought of them. They were, had been of course now, Virginia's friends and acquaintances as well. He was conscious that most of them would not now just disapprove of him, but actually perhaps dislike him, some mildly, some perhaps with ferocity.

'I'll give it thought,' he answered.

That night he fell asleep, thinking of his own wedding, and had nightmares where Virginia kept running away from him, laughing, and as he caught up with her, fracturing into thousands of bloodied pieces, like an exploding porcelain doll, blood spurting from every fragment.

On Sunday they followed their usual ritual; a long slow coupling, less passionate than intimate, before having breakfast.

'What shall we do today?' she asked brightly.

'Why not drive down to the house again?' He meant it sarcastically but said it in a dead pan way which she took seriously.

'Yes, let's. What a good idea.'

'No, we can't bother them again.'

'Why not, it's a house we're buying. We're going to live there. We've only visited it twice. You'd test drive a car more before you bought it, wouldn't you?'

'Not if you'd already decided on a particular car and you've decided on that house, haven't you?'

Ralph still entertained a hope that she might change her mind and come round to his view that an old cottage would be better.

'No, you're right, I have. That's the house for us. But what we could do is check out the local hotels and places for a reception.'

'You don't think it's premature?'

'No, we can get at least that decision made and out of the way.'

The third hotel was the most suitable she said. It was certainly more pleasant than the other two, both inhospitable, cheerless places that typified English hotel-keeping and hospitality. 'The Swan' was properly old, beamed, warm, a friendly owner and wife who were more than happy to discuss a small reception in a private room rather than the larger one which they would normally use. They were given menus and a price list and, on being assured that any Saturday five to eight weeks ahead would be available, Tina and Ralph ate lunch. The food was good, not gourmet let alone Michelin standard, but more than passable.

'There's another decision made.' Tina was checking them off on a mental list. She wanted to drive past the house again and, as they neared the turning, she, glancing at him said, 'What's the matter, you look so sad?'

He had been thinking of when he and Virginia had chosen their house, their excitement and pleasure, the shared superstitious fear that they might not get it, that it would sell to a higher offer, the relief when contracts were exchanged.

'I've got to get rid of this.' They were in the Bristol.

'Never mind, you'll get over it. Look. There it is.'

Indeed, he thought, there it was. A perfectly ordinary house in a perfectly ordinary road on a perfectly ordinary estate on the edge of a nondescript English town. He could derive little pleasure from the view but, and then the question hit him, with a physical force that should have made him wince. What had happened, or would happen to his house? Virginia was dead. The ink on the divorce papers barely dry. Surely there were grounds to have the order set aside? Might he salvage the lot, or at least half? He could not remember case law on the subject and wanted desperately to get to his Chambers' library. Tina wanted to stop and knock on the door again.

'Do you mind if we don't. I'd like to go to Chambers. There's something I'd like to look up in a hurry.'

'What?'

'Just a point I may have missed in an opinion I wrote on Friday. It won't have gone out yet.'

He could have mentioned Virginia then, said something, but again thought it unfair to take away the all too obvious pleasure Tina was deriving from their planning.

'I've never seen where you work. Yes, let's.'

He had a key and Tina looked around with curiosity.

'This is the Clerks' room,' he explained and, going down the corridor, opened the door to his own. 'This is mine.'

Tina looked at the desk, the chairs, the few pictures. 'It's like a monk's cell,' she said finally. 'It needs a woman's touch. Is there anyone around at the moment?'

'I don't know. Why?'

'Oh, just a thought. Are you going to look this point up?'

'Yes, in the library.'

He went further down the corridor, around a corner and opened the door into the library. It was probably the best in the City and would rival those of many universities. Tina was obviously impressed.

'Here, you browse, while I check what I want.'

He went to Rayden first, the standard text on divorce law, checked the index and, opening a page, read down. He then got out an All England Law Report and read the headnotes to the decision, and a couple of sections. He was excited, it seemed to confirm that he did have grounds, but resolved not to say anything to Tina at the moment, but to have a word with a solicitor in the morning, in case he was wrong.

'I've finished.'

Tina was sitting looking at a legal magazine. 'Good,' she said. 'Happy?'

'Happier. Let's go.'

'It's quiet, isn't it,' she remarked as they went back towards his room.

'Yes, I don't think there's anyone about.'

'Good.' Tina went in and lay on his desk. 'Haven't you always had a fantasy about having me on your desk?' Ralph had not. It had never even occurred to him. She shut and locked the door and he watched her. 'Don't you want to? I'd like to. I've never been made love to on a barrister's desk.'

She had done so once, nearly, in St John's Chambers, but just as he had entered her, they had heard a noise and had stopped, he zipping himself up again quickly. The opportunity had never presented itself again.

'Come on. I'm ever so ready.' She sat up and took her jeans off, and lay back again, pulling her knickers to one side. Ralph advanced towards her; she was aware that the sight of her like this was enough to arouse him and she lifted her knees and put her feet on the desktop. He was terribly anxious that someone might knock on the door and catch them. Even if he dressed quickly, and she did, the delay in opening the door taken with the fact that it was the two of them, would lead to an inevitable conclusion being drawn and at best nasty little jokes, at worst a considerable feeling of contempt for Ralph Edwards, who was fucking his new tart while his ex-wife lay in pieces in the mortuary.

He was desperately relieved when she started shuddering and he too was able to stop holding back, let the pleasure flood through him, and withdrawing, pull his trousers up and zip himself up again.

'That was nice,' she said, still lying there.

'Here are your jeans.'

'You're in a hurry.'

'I wouldn't like anyone to find us here like this.'

'Point taken,' she laughed and quickly put them on. 'Let's go home.'

The following morning he telephoned the solicitor who was doing the conveyancing of the house.

'Can I pop in and see you and at the same time see your divorce partner?'

He hung on, and was then told that both would be available at eleven. It was only a short walk from Chambers to their offices and, arriving promptly, he was shown straight to Neil's room.

'It's nothing much. I just wanted to check when exchange of contracts was likely. Tina is suddenly in a tearing hurry and I've got to raise the deposit.'

'Not a problem Ralph. I'll phone now,' and so saying he picked up the phone and rang the vendors' solicitors. A brief conversation took place, and then Neil, putting the phone down, said, 'They can apparently exchange at any time from now on. Their vendors have been told that their house is empty now so there's no chain. As soon as you can get me the money. All the paperwork is ready for signature. Tina will have to sign the mortgage and transfer, but you can sign the contract for both of you. As you well know. Sorry, I forget that occasionally I have lawyer clients.'

Ralph signed the contract and then said, 'Who is your divorce partner? Do I know him?'

'Her. Jane. She's very good. Should I introduce you?'

'Please.'

He picked up the phone again. 'Jane, Neil. I've got Ralph Edwards here. You'll come down? OK.'

She came into the room only seconds later, about the same age or perhaps a year or two older than Ralph and Neil, she was one of those women who, whilst wearing an air of authority, do not have a bossy or schoolteacher quality.

'Do you want to talk here?' she asked.

'I wouldn't mind Neil's view as another, even though not a divorce, lawyer. Has Neil told you any of the facts?'

'Only that you are a barrister, separated from your wife and that you are buying a new house with, forgive me for the expression, your girlfriend.'

'There's not much more to it than that. I left my ex. I agreed to give her the house, contents and everything else apart from my clothes, two paintings and my car. Consent order drawn up and made last week, same date as decree absolute. My ex was killed in a car accident on Friday. Are there grounds to set the order aside?'

'What a terrible coincidence,' she said.

'Yes.' He kept his suspicions to himself.

'Who was her lawyer?'

'Why?'

'I just wondered about a will. You normally do another after divorce. I always advise it.'

'Is it relevant?'

'Setting aside of an order or a variation is discretionary and so everything is relevant.'

'Her lawyer was Ann Cuthill.'

'I deal with her a lot. Know her quite well. Do you mind if I phone her now?'

'No, not at all.' He listened while she dialled.

Yes, Ms Cuthill was free and he heard Jane say, 'I'm acting for

Ralph Edwards and understand you acted for his former wife. Yes, I know. He's told me. Last Friday. Decree Absolute and final order through already. Do you mind my asking if there was a will? Yes. A new one. Made when? Leaving it to whom? No, that's enough. No. Thank you. Goodbye.' She turned to him, 'Your ex made a new will last week, in contemplation of divorce. She's left everything to her sister.'

Perhaps that was not surprising, Ralph considered and asked, 'What do you think?'

'Yes, there are grounds. Reasonable ones. There's another side to this but I anticipate you've thought that through already.'

'What?' Ralph had thought no further than the fact that he might be able to get some of his money back.

'How it would look. It's not the kind of thing that would stay hushed up, is it? There's her sister. Her lawyers. If they opposed it which I would expect them to, there'd have to be a hearing and so forth.'

Ralph had not considered this at all. It was a valid point. He had always considered himself fair and reasonable. To be revealed as a money grabbing grave robber would be anathema.

'Fair enough. I can see that. I should have thought of that earlier. I didn't. I'm afraid that what with…'

'I know. It's a wretched business at the best of times and to lose your wife in an accident in the same week. I know I'd not be thinking straight. Do you want to take it further? You don't have to decide now but fairly quickly.'

Ralph nodded, considering his 'public' profile and knew that he wanted nothing more to do with the money. It was bad enough having a divorce that no one seemed able to understand. It would just make things worse.

'No, I shan't. I'll sell my Bristol as planned.'

'Sorry?'

'My car. I'm selling it for a deposit. Virginia's sister and husband will be able to use the money.'

He remembered their small farmhouse and wondered how the sudden inheritance would square with their Socialist ideals. Virginia had a sense of humour; she would have considered this and might have laughed, even as she contemplated suicide.

'If I can help at all, please let me know.' Jane was leaving.

Ralph stood up, shook hands, and murmured, 'Your account.'

'Oh no, no charge. Bread on the waters. Nice to have met you,' and she was gone, taking with him any hope he had of an easy solution.

'Would you like a coffee Ralph?' Neil asked.

'If you have time. Yes, please.'

They talked of mutual acquaintances and then Neil said, 'You're remarrying then?'

'Oh yes, it was decided some time ago.'

As Ralph said this he was no longer sure who had decided. Had it been him, Tina or both of them together?

'I wish you well.'

'Why so lugubrious Neil?'

'I suppose the statistics for second marriages aren't ever so clever, really. Don't two thirds fail within a couple of years?'

'This one won't,' said Ralph, as blithely as he could, and took his leave.

He went back to Chambers, telephoned Tina to say that the house was on course and decided to bite the bullet. He had taken the finance documents together with the registration form for the Bristol with him that morning and now telephoned the finance company for a settlement figure. It was large but not as large as he had calculated. He had forgotten that early redemption would make the total less. He wondered what was wrong with him that he had overlooked something so obvious and, telling his clerk that he would not be back, he left for his final drive in the Bristol.

He headed out of the city, towards another town where, mercifully he decided, he had another grateful client with a sports car garage. He had spoken with Graham who had assured him that, yes he would buy the Bristol and, yes he would pay the going and fair price. Ralph savoured that last drive, perhaps his last link with his former emotional life, and was feeling nostalgic when he arrived.

He parked and went into the garage. Graham's taste in cars was both catholic and eclectic, spanning pre-war to contemporary, and there seemed to be examples of practically every famous marque in the showroom. Ralph wandered about, in an agony of indecision. He had worked out that he could afford the house deposit plus a car, not a desperately expensive one, but some kind of sports car nonetheless, if Graham kept his promise and Tina kept her old one.

'Ralph, good to see you.' Graham approached him through the cars, shook his hand warmly and said, 'How are things?'

'Do you really want to know?'

'Yes.'

The men had found themselves drawn to one another during Graham's case, and Ralph had often dropped in for a coffee if he was passing.

'I'm divorced. I'm remarrying. I've got no money and have

to sell the Bristol. Then I'll have no wheels either.' He shrugged his shoulders and smiled. 'Aside from that, everything is great.' Graham laughed.

'Hope she's worth it. Why no money?'

'Gave the ex the lot.'

'You lawyers are all fools.'

'I know. But that's the way the cookie crumbled. How about you?'

'Business is good. I'm always surprised. I suspect I'll even be able to sell your gas guzzler. What do you want for it?'

'Enough to clear the finance, pay the deposit on a new house and perhaps another car. What's it worth?' Graham got out his motor trade price guides, showed the entries to Ralph, and said, 'Yours is low mileage and I know it's been looked after. I'll give you a bit more than top whack - OK?'

'More than fair.'

'And a reduction on any car you buy from me. How much do you need for a deposit and to clear the finance?' Ralph told him and Graham's eyes narrowed.

'Let's have a look about then. See if there's anything you like.'

'Actually Tina, that's my wife to be, wants me to have an estate car.'

'You don't need an estate car. Not after a Bristol. You want something small and lively.'

'An MG?'

'No, don't touch them. Poseurs' cars. Perhaps a Lotus?'

'No. Lots Of Trouble Usually Serious.'

'You're right. Anyway I don't have one. What do you fancy?'

'You don't actually happen to have any estate cars do you? Really.'

'I've got my old Mercedes. 150,000 miles. Still going strong.

Why don't you have that and another one, a sports car as well.'

'God, you're incorrigible.'

'No, practical. We set up finance on one and you buy the other.'

'I don't think Tina will be too impressed.'

'I'm not ever so impressed at you getting rid of the Bristol. I thought you loved that car.'

'Yes. Come on. What have you got then?'

They wandered about, Ralph happily talking cars, drifted out to Graham's Mercedes, elderly, and a nasty colour Ralph thought, but he could approach it on the basis that Tina had a Mercedes and he had something else, discussed MG's and 'hairdressers' cars', as Graham called small Japanese sports cars, and ended up looking at a Morgan.

'It's the right image for you Ralph. A bit old-fashioned, eccentric even, bloody good performance, totally impractical but won't be seen as a great come down after the Bristol. You can't end up in a fucking Ford for God's sake. What will people say? You're Ralph Edwards, the barrister, a success. If you can't afford a Bentley or a Porsche, maybe not a Porsche, too city wide-boy,' he saw Ralph wince but he did not know of Virginia, 'whoops. Forgot for a moment your ex had one. No, if not a Bentley or an Aston Martin, buy a Morgan.'

Ralph could see his logic and found it appealing.

'Look at it. Bright red. Cut a dash, what, tally ho,' this last said in a mock very upper-class voice.

'Yes, it's got to be right. Let's number crunch,' Graham grinned.

Ralph allowed himself to be led to Graham's inner sanctuary where he did sums on a calculator.

'Yep, can be done,' he finally announced and so Ralph found

himself with enough for a deposit, an elderly Mercedes estate car in what he called 'guano' but was a kind of metallic gold, and a bright red Morgan. He also had another finance agreement, which he had been hoping to avoid, but he need not tell Tina about that. The decision was which to take away today, and which to collect later. Graham completed all the documents, finance, transfers of ownership and gave Ralph a cheque for 5% of the purchase price of the house.

'You always cheer me up Graham.'

'No, it's a pleasure to see you. And nice to be able to repay you for what you did for me.'

'You've paid once already. At the time.'

'You were worth every penny. I'm just relieved you're not going away with a dreary Eurobox.'

Ralph drove away instead in the Mercedes. He would give it to Tina that evening but not tell her about the Morgan. They could sell her car to pay the Stamp Duty and conveyancing costs. It was not as though there was going to be a removal firm's expenses. Their worldly goods would fit in the back of the Mercedes. He was waiting for Tina when she came out of the shop; she was about to walk straight past the car when he leant out of the window and called for her. She did a double take then exclaimed, 'It's you. What on earth are you doing in that? What a nasty colour.'

'Come on, get in. It's a Mercedes. It's for you. You wanted an estate car.'

She got in and looked around. 'It's comfortable. How old is it?'

'Ten.'

'Hm, is it really yours?'

'No, it's yours. I got it for you.'

'Ralph, it's terribly sweet of you but don't you think we should have had a newer one. Maybe not a Mercedes. A Ford estate or something like that?'

'I'd rather die than be seen in a Ford estate.'

'What's wrong with them?'

'Nothing. That's the problem. No. This will do fine. Let's go home.'

Tina was quiet in the car until, when he was parking near their flat, she turned and kissed him and said, 'I'm sorry. It was very ungracious of me. It's a lovely thought and very kind of you. I do like the colour. But what are you going to do? Sell the Bristol?'

'You don't like the colour. But then neither do I. I'll use your car,' until I get the Morgan he thought, 'and I've sold the Bristol. I've enough for the deposit.'

'Ouch, that must have hurt, selling the car I mean. But it's terrific. You've been busy then.'

'Yes, I've been busy.' He then resolved not to tell her about the Morgan yet, nor probably ever about his short-lived attempt to set aside the Consent Order, and certainly not about Virginia.

'I've been to see the solicitors. They say the conveyancing will only take a couple of weeks. Solicitors can work quickly when they want to,' he said to Tina.

'Or when they've got an important client they want to impress,' she said.

'Probably unfair, Tina.'

'No, you're a well-known barrister. They're bound to pull out the stops for you.'

'You've got great confidence in me haven't you?'

'Yes, why not? I'd like to see you in court one day.'

The thought embarrassed him and he did not pursue the subject.

Ralph had spent the last few weeks dreading a telephone call from the Coroner's office. He bought the evening paper every day and then, to his relief, saw an item about the inquest on Virginia. A verdict of accidental death had been recorded. There was another photograph of the wrecked Porsche and a strangely flattering picture of Virginia, one he had never seen before, in which she seemed younger, was smiling shyly.

She looked as she had that first night and tears came to his eyes, which he brushed away before looking at the photograph again. It must have been provided by her family he reasoned who, no doubt anxious to secure that verdict rather than one of suicide, must have somehow kept the date of the decree absolute, the divorce even perhaps, quiet. He thought of the money involved and, not for the first time, felt a measure of respect for the county and upper classes, and the way in which they could manage events to their advantage when money was at stake.

He had transferred the insurance policies into Virginia's name as agreed and, had a verdict of suicide been recorded, the insurers could, quite legitimately, have refused payment. He did a quick mental calculation and whistled. Virginia's sister was, as of now, a rich woman, but he dismissed the thought without any jealousy or envy, feeling only sadness at Virginia's tragic end and, permitting himself a passing twinge, regretted, with some ruefulness, his ignoble and misguided wish to even contemplate trying to set aside the order.

The day before they were due to move, Tina insisted that Ralph accompanied her to her first ante-natal appointment. He was reluctant, protesting and making excuses.

'Look, I've seen it all so to speak. I've been present at postmortems. I've seen such gory photographs that I think...'

'When did you go to a postmortem?'

'The first was at University, part of the Criminology course.'

'Didn't you feel ill? Weren't you sick?'

'I didn't particularly like the bit when the brains were removed. And several people did leave the room. A few didn't even turn up.'

'It wasn't compulsory then?'

'Oh no.'

'Why did you go?'

'Interest. Death is as much part of life as birth is. And it was interesting.'

'Morbid more like.'

'No, not at all.'

She shuddered. 'Let's not talk about it. You're supposed to be a new man. You're supposed to come with me to my pre-birth things.'

'Look I promise I'll hold your hand and mop your brow and rain kisses on your cheeks while you give birth but please...'

'No, I want you to come.'

So Ralph, defeated, sat with her in the hospital waiting room, until they were ushered into a tiny changing room where she was told to take her clothes off and put on a dressing gown.

'Why?' Ralph asked.

'Doctor will want to examine her.'

'What for?' Ralph was curious - there was surely nothing to examine at this stage.

'Don't argue Ralph. It's easier just to do as I'm told.'

The nurse left and, a few minutes later, they found themselves, through a door opposite the entrance to the cubicle in the presence of 'Doctor'. There was no greeting or even acknowledgement of their presence, but the young man seemed disconcerted by Ralph and looked at him questioningly.

'I'm a New Man. That means I get to be present throughout.'

The doctor did not seem terribly happy, but Ralph leant in a corner, refusing a seat, making the doctor look most uncomfortable. Tina glared at him, but Ralph remained where he was, smiling benignly.

The doctor ran through some standard questions and then started to put on rubber gloves. He motioned to Tina to get onto a couch and, snapping the gloves round his wrists, undid her dressing gown and started to insert a finger.

'Is it usual to do an internal at twelve weeks?' asked Ralph who had not realised that the consultation would involve him having to watch another man put his fingers up his wife.

'Are you a doctor?'

The question was polite enough, but it carried sufficient undertones of patronising superiority for Ralph to feel cross.

'No, merely a fairly senior barrister who specialises in clinical negligence.'

The doctor's professional smile, self-satisfied smirk Ralph thought, disappeared and the doctor looked at him suspiciously.

'And I have conducted a number of cases against this health authority as well as successfully representing them. Including ones where childbirth had gone wrong,' he added.

The doctor hesitated again and withdrew his finger. Tina was sitting up looking angry.

'Ralph, he's only doing his job. Leave him alone.' She instinctively understood that the doctor had been and was now intimidated by Ralph and wanted to avoid a scene.

'No sir.' There was a touch of respect there that had been missing before, 'An internal is not a necessary standard routine at this stage.'

'Then why do you want to do one?' Ralph smiled, having maintained his composure as well as a smile, throughout the tense interchange.

'Because our guidelines and good practice suggest it.'

'Well you'd better get on with it then.'

'No, sir, I'll leave it for now.'

Tina was sitting up, naked, breasts and pubic hair highly prominent. 'Oh come on Ralph. Look Doctor, I don't know your name. If it's routine just do it,' and she lay back opening her legs even more widely than before.

'I'm Dr James. It's not necessary Mrs Fortescue. It really isn't. Do please sit up and pull your dressing gown together.' His words tumbled out and he was blushing, a deep crimson from the neck up.

'What's your status, Dr James? No-one bothered to tell us. I thought we were seeing a consultant today.' Tina had gone on and on about seeing her consultant, and Ralph was certain that, given the age he supposed Dr James to be, he could only be a Registrar at the most.

'I'm a Senior House Officer.'

'Have you finished otherwise?'

'Yes.'

'Right, come on Tina,' and he stood up and started towards the door.

Tina got up, looking embarrassed, saying, 'I'm sorry Dr James.'

'Dr James,' Ralph said and the doctor, who had gone to his desk and sat down again, met his eyes with reluctance. 'Can I suggest that you remember patients are people? Their spouses are people. And people merit being treated as people. Not lumps of meat on a conveyor belt there for the gratification and self-importance of the medical profession. Try and go on a course involving communication skills. Good day,' and left the room, Tina following.

As the door closed Tina burst out, 'God Ralph, why did you have to do that?'

'Shh, everyone will hear, and if I tell you, I'll tell you loudly enough for no one to want to go in to see the wretched man.'

She got dressed, still muttering angrily, and they walked down the corridor towards the reception desk. At the desk, Tina paused to make another appointment and Ralph, who had walked on, came back and said, 'Don't bother, you can go privately. At least then the bloody doctors are polite enough to know your name and say Hello.'

'Ralph, I don't want to go privately. It's the same doctors and same hospital.'

'No, you can go to the Priory or somewhere like that.'

'Ralph,' she was effectively pleading. 'I don't want to go to the Priory or somewhere like that. I just want to know there's a bed available in the hospital nearest to us.'

'We'll have moved by then. So we'll check you in there. Don't bother with this place again.'

Ralph was unsure as to why he was so annoyed and started to consider the question. He had always been abominated by the holier than thou attitude of the medical profession towards the general public and had been involved in sufficient cases, talked to enough claimants, to know that the whole profession had a miserable record in terms of explaining things to patients. Save for Virginia he thought. Save for Virginia.

He had been present once, with a friend's wife, as moral support when the junior doctor told her that her husband had cancer and was going to die. Except that was not the way the doctor put it. Ralph had understood what the man had been trying to say but, despite the fact that he was an Englishman and had no difficulty with the English language, the words were so confused and confusing that Susie, who had been listening desperately anxiously to what had been said about her husband, after they left the room, turned to Ralph and said, 'Does that mean he's going to get better?'

Ralph had actually had to tell her exactly what the doctor should have said, with rather more compassion and time than the doctor seemed to possess. Susie had then started to weep uncontrollably, and Ralph had still not forgiven the medical profession their failure.

He was fond of saying, teasingly across dinner tables when doctors were present, that if he died without an heir he would probably leave all his money to a medical charity. 'Which one?' they invariably replied, with interest, keen to debate the relative merits of cancer or motor neurone disease research.

'Doesn't exist yet,' Ralph would respond, 'crying need for it though. Most overlooked part of a doctor's training.' 'What is it then?' 'A centre to promote communication skills,'

This always got them going, the doctors denying vehemently and bitterly, and usually 'incoherently' Ralph would throw at them, their supposed inability and other guests generally always having some horror story about the dreadful rudeness with which they or a relative or friend had been treated. It never failed and, as Ralph explained all this to Tina, he knew also that his behaviour had been as much to do with the man's off-handedness with them both, as with the fact that he was, in Ralph's eyes at least, going to legally sexually assault Tina in front of him.

'Come on Tina, as soon as we move we'll see someone there. They'll have to start afresh anyway. They're bound to lose the notes. Such as they are at the moment.' Tina mollified, was subdued on the journey home but asked, 'Do you think it was fair of you to do that to Dr James?'

'Yes, totally. If it makes him think a little and if he only remembers to make eye contact with his patients as he comes in and say, 'Good morning, Mrs Smith', it will have served some purpose. Rude bugger he was.'

'I suppose you're right. I hadn't thought of it that way.'

'It's because you're used to them behaving like that. That's all.'

'You seem to know so much more than I do, seem to understand much more.'

'I've been around longer and thought about a lot of things quite a lot. Been quite well paid to do the thinking.'

She brightened, 'And that's why I love you.'

Tina was by now putting on weight. She was in her second trimester, was short of breath and often short of temper. Ralph had long ago decided to economise on removal men saying, 'After all, it's not as though we've got much. Two trips in the Mercedes should do it.'

'Should I ask my parents to help?'

'Only if you want to. I can manage by myself. And we won't have a spare bed for them.'

'Yes we will, one of the sofas converts.'

'Does it? You didn't tell me.'

'It just seemed sensible. So I shall, shall I?'

'By all means,' and on the day of completion her parents appeared, smiling and cheerful; her mother went with Tina to the kitchen 'to brew up' and Ralph and her father moved all the boxes into the cars.

They drove together, Tina chattering excitedly to Ralph about matters that seemed entirely trivial to him, but were, to her, of sufficient importance to merit discussion. He left Tina and her mother at the new house and drove back to the city with Bill, who, by himself, he found surprisingly easy to talk to, ranging over a variety of subjects of general and specific interest. Bill was non-judgmental, made no comment about Ralph and Tina, except to ask if the wedding day was set, expressed pleasure that it was, and made only one comment about St John.

'I was never sure that it would last.'

'Why not?' Ralph could not resist asking.

'Because I don't think she was truly in love with him. Not

like she is with you. She must have been infatuated.'

Wasn't that the word Sylvia had used, Ralph mused.

'But not in the way she is with you. Her mum and I both know that.'

Ralph was quietly pleased and, despite the fact that there were a lot more questions he would have liked to have asked, did not pursue the subject. Later on, the second loading having been slightly more fraught because Ralph was determined not to have to undertake a third, so he had crammed everything in, he suggested they stop and have a beer.

Leaning companionably at the bar, Bill had said, 'We were worried to begin with when Tina told us. We thought it might be another infatuation . But you seem a good sort. Tina tells us you're quite famous already.'

'I'm not famous at all. I'm reasonably well-known in a small circle of lawyers,' he protested.

'Tina thinks that you'll go on to great things. That one day you'll be really famous because of an appearance in court.'

'I hope I won't be famous because of one appearance. I'd rather it was many,' he laughed. 'It's my bread and butter. Our bread and butter.'

'Tina works though. She's not stopping. Not yet anyway.' He seemed perturbed. Ralph would have liked to have told him their news but they had agreed to tell her parents over supper, Ralph having bought champagne, albeit a cheap one, for what Tina had dubbed 'the occasion'.

'Come on, let's drink up and get back. The girls will be waiting for us.' Did he really think of Betty and Tina as both 'girls', Ralph wondered as he finished his beer.

'Good idea, Bill, Let's go.'

When they arrived back they found a large van parked outside the house. The driver and his mate were at the front door. Ralph walked up towards them and heard Tina laughing. She said something he could not catch, and the men laughed uproariously. Tina saw him and called, 'They've delivered the furniture. Everything where it should be and not a scratch or mark on the paintwork.' Ralph was in an extremely good mood, felt into his back pocket, got out a note and saying, 'Thanks very much,' gave it to the older one. 'Have a drink.' They thanked him as they left and Tina quizzically said, '£10? A bit generous?' Damn, he thought. He had wanted to give them £5 but replied, 'What were they laughing about?'

'They pointed out the box with the long screws in it saying we shouldn't get them mixed up with the short screws as it was such a nice bed, and so I replied, we tested it in the shop,' investing the last comment with an uncalled-for sexual innuendo, Ralph suspected, otherwise why would they have laughed as they did?

'Is it a nice bed? I don't really remember?'

Tina turned her face to be kissed and said, 'We've got on really well, Mummy and I. Come and have a look. Daddy can start getting the things in. You don't mind, do you Daddy?'

'Not at all,' Bill said, a pile of boxes in his arms.

More than I could carry in one go, Ralph thought and decided that Bill must be exceptionally strong. Tina led him round the house. There was more furniture than he recalled buying and, looking at a very handsome modern desk installed in what was to be his study, in fact the fourth bedroom, he turned to Tina, 'We didn't buy that?'

'No, it's my wedding present to you. I hope you like it.'

'It's lovely,' and he meant it. The desk was a more substantial and upmarket version of the one he had bought for himself in Chambers.

'But what about the dining table and chairs?'

'A wedding present from my parents. I went out with them one afternoon and we chose that together.'

Experiencing what he knew to be an irrational pang at being left out of the decision, Ralph could only reply, 'They're great. It's very generous of them.' He had been used to eating at an old Regency table and wondered how he would enjoy sitting and dining at a contemporary, was it Swedish perhaps, table with matching chairs. It was pleasant enough in its modern, clean, way but Ralph could not find it attractive. Polite however, he went to her parents, kissed Betty and thanked them in a manner that would appear both sincere and enthusiastic.

'Tina thought you wouldn't really want to sit at a pine table in the dining room,' Bill explained as he brought in another load of boxes.

'No, that's gone in the kitchen,' Tina added.

Ralph had to acknowledge that the house seemed now much more attractive than before. Removing the previous owners' furniture, even though they had left the carpets and curtains, erased much of their personality and, Ralph considered, with a judicious choice of colour, the place would not be too bad after all. He went to the back door and stood for a moment, listening to the distant hum of traffic and staring at the swimming pool.

That will be fun, he said to himself and went and finished getting the last boxes in, Bill having done most of the work already. Tina suggested a takeaway.

'Chinese or Indian?' Ralph enquired.

'Whatever you prefer.'

'No.' He was firm. 'Whatever you and your parents would like.'

'Chinese then,' and he went off, returning half an hour later to find all the unpacking done, Bill sitting with a beer, Tina a glass of white wine and her mother with a cup of tea.

'Pop it in the oven. I've just put it on, to keep everything warm.'

He went into the kitchen, doing as he was told, picking up the bottle of Champagne he had earlier put in the built-in fridge, four glasses and went back. They were talking animatedly but, turning as he came in, they all fell silent.

'We're celebrating,' he said as he poured and handed them the glasses.

'To your new house,' Bill said holding his glass up.

'To ourselves and our marriage next month.' Ralph added.

'You've set the date then?'

'Yes Mummy.'

'That's wonderful. To your marriage,' she responded.

Ralph looked quizzically at Tina.

'And to your first grandchild,' said Tina.

There was a moment's silence and then, as she absorbed the news, her mother shrieked with delight, nearly dropping her glass.

Bill beamed. 'Well you haven't wasted any time then. When's it due?'

'In about five months,' Tina said. Her father's face screwed up as he performed what was evidently some rather difficult mental arithmetic.

'You certainly didn't waste any time at all,' he finally said raising his eyebrows at his daughter.

He looked, Ralph thought, unreasonably pleased with himself as he raised his glass again.

'Girl or boy?'

'Doesn't matter so long as it's a good one,' Ralph said.

'I'd like a little girl,' said Tina.

'Don't you want a boy Ralph?' asked Betty.

Ralph, to whom the question seemed redundant, had not considered this aspect at all, having spent so many years actually not wanting a child, the gender was irrelevant.

'I'd like a girl first then a boy,' Tina answered for him.

The meal was spent at the new dining table in cheerful chatter and, when Tina suggested an early night, no one disagreed. She pulled out the sofa bed, made it up, drew the curtains, put out the PCF or politically correct fire as Ralph had christened it, reminded her parents where the bathroom was and kissed them both goodnight.

Ralph, for his part, had locked and bolted front and back doors and was just about to follow Tina upstairs when he felt a hand on his shoulder. It was Bill.

'Terrific news. Thank you for making our Tina so happy. Good night.'

'Good night Bill, Betty.' He smiled at them as they turned into the sitting room and closed the door.

Upstairs, Tina was already naked, cleaning her teeth in the bathroom, and Ralph went to her, pressing his hips against her bottom. She turned round and he looked at her heavier stomach. Even this he found sexually stimulating but she, glancing down, said, 'You can put that away.'

'Why?'

'I can't do it with my parents in the house. I've never been able to.'

'Don't be so silly. They're a floor down on the other side of the house.'

'No, I can't let myself go, relax. It's no good.'

'Come on.' He pulled her hand, she allowed herself to be led reluctantly to the bed. He pushed her down, she sat, and looking at her stomach ruefully, 'And soon my tummy's going to be in the way.'

'It won't be at the moment.'

'I think it is. And you might squash her.'

'Or him,' Ralph said.

'Or him if you want to be pedantic.'

Ralph was not listening. He had bent down and she, about to push him away, with a small sigh of abandon leant back and whispered, 'Go on, then. Do your worst.'

He carried on while she, squeezing her legs so tightly together that his ears hurt, came, biting her lips and holding back her cries of pleasure.

'Now, you kneel down on the bed and I'll take a turn.'

'I'll feel like a dog.'

'It's the only way of doing it without me lying on top of you or you on top of me.'

'What's wrong with me on top of you? You like it like that.'

It was true, he did, even though he had always imagined, he could not explain why, this was probably the preferred way for she and St John.

'No, for a change,' and she did as she was asked, he entering her from behind and then, gripping her hips lightly, he cried out, 'Lovely...'

'Shhh,' she muttered.

He withdrew after his orgasm and she turned over and asked, 'Better?'

'Yes, a bit formal but thank you.'

'Kiss me,' and he bent and kissed her longingly and lengthily.

'That's the house christened.'

'Did you do that with her then?'

'No. Did you with him?'

'No. He got drunk. He was too tired.' So she had wanted to. Had she been disappointed that he was too drunk and could not? Should he ask?

'Did you want to then?'

'No, but I thought it seemed as though we should.'

In fact she remembered she had been very keen to have sex with St John in their new house. She could hardly wait. It was true, he had been drinking and he had trouble getting an erection but, after some due diligence with her tongue and hands, she had decided that it was stiff enough and lying on the bed, she on top of him, she had bounced up and down, stroking herself at the same time, until she had an orgasm. It was only when she had achieved this that she looked down at St John and discovered that he was asleep. She was faintly disgusted by this, as well as herself but, mentally shrugging her shoulders, had climbed off him, covered him up and gone to have a drink downstairs.

'What are you thinking about, Tina?' Ralph asked softly.

'How much I love you. Good night.'

'Good night.' He was annoyed at himself having asked about Tina's 'first night in the new house sex'. He was annoyed that she had answered honestly. Most of all he was annoyed that she had wanted to do it with St John.

But, he reasoned, what else can I expect. It's stupid even to think about it. But at least we are honest with one another. He was incapable of rationalising it further. He loved Tina and wanted to believe that she was worthy of that love. He took this, like everything else, seriously and was incapable of seeing any humour in the situation. At last he fell asleep, only to dream of Tina, always running away, ever elusive, he never able to catch her.

He was woken - the Saturday - by Tina, who had brought him a cup of tea.

'You've slept a long time.'

'Why, what time is it?'

'Ten.'

'You're joking.'

'No, look at your watch.' She was right and he was irritated with himself for a moment at what he thought was his indolence, but then remembered his dreams.

'Come here,' He pulled her towards him. 'You're still here. Kiss me.'

'You stink of garlic from the takeaway.'

'So do you. I had horrible dreams. You left me, ran away.'

She bent down and kissed him. 'You're stupid. I'll never do that. I know how lucky I am,' and then added, 'Do you know what I'd like to do?'

'No, and I don't think I can guess.'

'I'd like to be really extravagant and silly.'

'How so?'

'I'd like to get the swimming pool going, just for a day.' Tina looked at him appealingly.

'But it's still winter.'

'I know, but don't you think it would be nice? They told me it takes 24 hours to heat up if you put the pool heater on full. If you did it now we could swim tomorrow. Go on. Just once and then we'll leave it until the warmer weather. And you know, if we ran it through now, if there are any faults, we'll know what they are and can fix them before the Spring.'

'You've persuaded me. Have you looked under the cover? Is it full of bleached hedgehogs and drowned cats?'

'No. They'd put the winter cover on. I've looked underneath and pulled it off. The water's clean and clear and there's chemicals and stuff in the garage. Any idea how to use them?'

'No, but there'll be instructions.' He got up and found Tina's father taking some boxes out of the front door.

'Hope you don't mind. We breakfasted already. Tina said you deserved some rest, so she didn't disturb you.

'You've nearly finished?'

'Oh yes. Nothing much to do now. Tina and her mother have washed everything and put it all away.'

'What on earth time did you start?'

'About seven. Betty and I are used to getting up early.'

'I'm ashamed of myself.'

'Don't be silly. Have some breakfast. You'll find them in the kitchen.'

He went in, 'Morning Betty.'

'Morning Ralph. I've got some bacon going for you.'

'That's kind,' and he waited for a moment until she handed him a bacon sandwich and another cup of tea. Taking these, he went outside and stood thoughtfully on the poolside. Tina was right, the water was clean and clear. He bent down and put his hand in it. 'Ouch,' he muttered. 'It is desperately cold.'

Going to the garage, the door was open and it was full of the empty boxes that Bill had put there, he went to the boiler that heated the pool. It seemed simple enough, a timer with an override switch and a thermostat. It seemed to present no difficulties. Presumably, he thought, it will be linked to the pump so when the heating goes on, the pump will work. Setting the thermostat to maximum, he flicked the override switch and, after a very short pause, there was the sound of the gas igniting and a pump.

He went out again and looked at the pool and saw that the skimmer flap was gently moving backwards and forwards. All's well, he thought, bending down and putting his hand down to one of the inlet pipes. There was definitely a warmer stream of water coming through. Then, finishing his sandwich and tea, he hunted for the gas meter and, committing the reading to memory, looked for the heat conserving summer cover, took it out and, with some difficulty, as it was bulky and unwieldy, spread it over the surface of the water.

Only then did he go back inside. Tina was there, barely able to contain her anticipation.

'Well, have you managed it?'

'Yes.'

'You're so clever. Is there anything you can't do?'

'Heaps of things,' he replied cheerfully. 'But I'm always ready to give it a go. Like Archie Rice.'

'You mean in The Entertainer.' He was surprised that she picked up the reference so quickly.

'Yes, you know - 'they can say what they like, but I gave it a go'. It's a good enough philosophy.'

'Mummy and Daddy are just going,' she said inconsequentially.

'Why? Don't they want to stay a bit longer? I mean, at least for the afternoon,' he added quickly in case he might be taken to be issuing an invitation to stay for another night.

'No, they don't want to be in our way. They feel a bit guilty already. You know, being here on our first night.'

'It's not as though it's our honeymoon. Some tribal societies have a parent in the bedroom on the first night.'

'They don't, surely.' She shuddered at the thought. 'No, they want to go shopping on the way home. Come and say goodbye.'

He went to his car first and came back with a bottle of whisky and a box of chocolates which he gave to Tina.

'Give them these as a present.'

'My goodness, you think of everything. No, you thought of it and bought them, you give them the present. They'll be very pleased.'

They were, Betty saying, 'My favourites. And such a big box too. There's no need.'

'And a very good malt too,' Bill added.

'No, you were a great help. It's only a small thank you but it's...'

'No, it's very kind of you,' Betty said. 'Come on Bill, let's be off.'

Tina and Ralph stood, holding hands and waving, until the car turned the corner, when Tina turned and said, 'Do you know, I feel at a bit of a loose end. What are we going to do with the rest of today? And tomorrow for that matter?'

'We're going to paint,' he said firmly. 'Come on, we'll go to a decorators now.'

'But we haven't even discussed colours or anything.'

'I've got a colour chart in my briefcase. I've marked a few I quite like. We can talk about it in the car.'

She leafed through the charts as they drove into the town.

'Which colour for which room?'

'Maybe the yellow for the sitting room.'

'It's a nice yellow. Pale lemon. Yes, I'll go with that. What's the pink for, it's not really pink is it? It's deeper and fuller.'

'I thought you might like that in our bedroom.'

'I'd prefer something softer. More like this.' She pointed and he glanced down.

'I can live with that. Mark the colour. The other one I thought of was the bathroom.'

'It's a lovely colour, peony it's called. If we put some mirrors up and rejig the lighting, it could be really nice.'

'We'll do that then,' he said. 'Let's see how much we can get here,' drawing up at a builder's merchants on the outskirts of the town.

On the way home, Tina reached over and touched his leg. 'It's fun isn't it. I quite like painting.'

'Do you?' he replied abstractedly, concentrating on avoiding a pedestrian who had stepped into the road.

'Yes, St John and I decorated...' she stopped. 'Whoops, sorry.'

'What do you mean?'

'The SJ word, I know you don't like it.'

'How do you know that?'

'Whenever I mention him, or even the past, you seem to wince, ever so slightly, just in the corners of your eyes. Nowhere else.'

'I thought I was inscrutable.'

'Pretty well, but there are tiny little give-aways.'

'You've been looking at me rather closely.'

'Yes, I have. Because I love you,' and she squeezed his leg again.

Ralph was slightly taken aback by her comments but accepted the truth of the observation about the SJ word. He had not realised, however, that he had let any of his emotions show and found this subconscious reflex, about which he knew he could do nothing, rather disconcerting. He had no idea how to address it, let alone conquer what he immediately regarded as, and knew was, an affliction.

'You're quiet Ralph.'

'Just thinking about painting. I'll do the ceilings if you start on the walls. Where first?'

'I don't know.'

'What about the bathroom? We could probably get that done today.'

'OK.'

Later that afternoon, after several hours of sustained and concentrated effort, they looked at one another, Ralph saying, 'There, told you we could finish it. I'll fix the mirrors and lighting, while you start on the sitting room if you want to. Don't come back until I've finished. I want it to be a surprise for you.'

He removed the old shaving socket and neon light and, measuring precisely, chased a channel from the existing electricity cable in two directions, fixed a new mirror in place, then placed a series of lights down each side, like make up lights in a dressing room, checking that they worked.

That done, still working methodically and meticulously, he turned his attention to the bath. He carefully removed the top three rows of tiles, all of which came off as easily as he anticipated given the shoddy build quality of the house, leaving only two rows above the edge. He had guessed at the length and width of the bath and was relieved to find that he had underestimated only an inch on each side.

He hung the three large mirrors so that the walls above the

bath were now largely covered, put little silver caps on the screws holding them in place, stepped back, was pleased at the effect and then finally put up another two mirrors opposite and went straight onto the ceiling light. He removed the old one and ran a strip of halogen spotlights in its place.

Drawing the heavy curtains, in which the peony colour figured and which had given him the idea for the room, he turned on all the lights. It was precisely the effect he had hoped to achieve and, feeling very pleased with himself, he went downstairs. Tina had nearly finished covering the second of the walls with yellow and the room seemed transformed.

'Brilliant colour, Ralph. It's lovely. Clean and fresh.'

'I've finished upstairs. Do you want to see?'

'You bet.'

He took her into the darkened bathroom and switched on the lights. She blinked and then grinned. 'It's wonderful. It's like a fairy grotto or a fairground. The way the light bounces round. And there seem to be five hundred of us in here the way the reflections work.'

She moved about and watched all the different Tina's on the walls. A thought came to her. 'Ralph, let's do it in here. Over the bath. I'd like to watch us.'

'You've got a really dirty mind.'

'No, it's our bathroom. Our playroom. Why shouldn't we?'

He was amused. 'Now or later?'

'Later with a bottle of champagne. I think there's still one in the fridge. Before supper. How about it?'

'Why not now?' he said.

'No, let's look forward to it. I'm getting wet thinking about it and...'

'I'm getting quite excited at the prospect.'

She turned and put her hand down his trousers. 'So you are. Perhaps we'd better do it now,' she grinned salaciously as she started to undo her paint smeared jeans.

'No, later. We'll paint for another couple of hours.'

At seven he put his brush down.

'I'm going to get the champagne. Do you want to run us a bath?'

She turned. 'I've been thinking of nothing else for the last twenty minutes,' and putting her brush in an old paint tin filled with water, left the room. They had all but finished the walls, there was just one patch left, as well as the edges along the skirting boards and ceiling. When he went into the bedroom, the champagne and glasses in his hand, he found Tina in bed, covers pulled up to her face.

'What are you doing?'

'Waiting for you,' she said mock-demurely.

'Why?'

'You'll see if you pull the covers down.'

He lifted the duvet up and looked. She was in black stockings, suspenders, knickers and bra.

'You haven't worn those for ages.'

'I thought you might like to see me in them again. It might be the last time before the baby is born.' She looked a bit glum then brightened. 'Let's drink to our new bathroom.'

He poured the wine as she got out of bed, and they went into the bathroom together. The water was running; she had put bubble bath in and switched the Jacuzzi on, so the bath was already filled with bubbles, and the room was heavily scented. He stood and wondered how she intended to, but his thoughts were interrupted by her getting onto and then kneeling on a bedroom chair that she must have put there for the purpose.

It had the effect of ensuring that her bottom was reflected in all the mirrors and he could see that the way she had positioned herself ensured that she would have a side and back view of herself.

'Turn the water off Ralph and come here, come inside me in fact.'

'No kisses, no foreplay?'

'No.' She was pulling her knickers to one side and Ralph, putting his glass down, undressed quickly. 'You don't need any foreplay then. I can see a million willies, all of them ready. Look,' and she put her hand between her legs.

Ralph moved forward, trying to forget that only a few inches or so further in there was a human life forming, a thought he found rather off-putting.

'Ever so slowly Ralph. I want to watch,'

He entered gently, little by little, until he had fully penetrated her and then he saw myriad images of Tina's face, eyes widening, as she cried out, 'God, that was quick, I've come already. Now, hard.' More urgently. 'Do it harder.'

He obeyed, and watched a hundred, a thousand, an infinite number of Tina's faces, eyes opening then screwing up, then opening again.

'Ralph, I'm having another,' she started moaning as he withdrew and let his semen spatter across her.

'Jesus,' she said as she, a little bit awkwardly, got out of her kneeling position and, sitting on the chair, picked up her glass, sipped it and resumed, 'You've come in my hair.'

'That was the most erotic experience of my life. Now I know

why people like mirrors. What was it like for you? The same...' he asked feeling self-conscious.

'If you'll excuse the expression, fucking fantastic,' she murmured. 'Or if you'll excuse the expression, fantastic fucking. Oops, the corner of your eyes again. You don't like that word do you?'

'No, to be honest. I don't really like using it, I don't like hearing it and I suppose I don't like your saying it.'

'You are funny. It's what a lot of people call 'making love"

'Yes. Ignorant insensitive people. You're not like that. You're not like the girl from Newcastle whose story was in the legal press.'

'What was that then?'

'Oh, a young single mother had been sent to see a solicitor to claim maintenance for her child and the solicitor asked the name and address of the father. She replied that she didn't know it. The solicitor was a bit suspicious and asked why not. He was told it had happened at a party. But can't you find out, ask someone who he was. No, she replied, I never saw him. I was leaning over a balcony being sick at the time.'

Tina looked appalled. 'That's really awful. Is it true?'

'I don't know. Newcastle, I suppose it could be. But the point is, that's fucking. It's what people do when they go to prostitutes. What I do is not, I hope, fucking. It's got to mean more than that to me. Otherwise, like Chesterfield wrote to his son, it's just an act where you look faintly ridiculous and behave in a slightly ridiculous fashion but one usually preceded by considerable expense.'

She laughed, 'You're such a romantic. To most people it's just something they do. Part of being a human animal.'

'Part of the problem of being a human is being an animal. But sex is the only part of the animal being I really like.'

She snorted, 'That's nonsense. You like music, art, beautiful things, good food and wine. Those are all part of hearing and seeing and eating, all things animals do.'

'Yes sure, but filtered through the human intellect. The only way of filtering the act of sex through the intellect is by elevating it a bit, giving it a special quality and meaning. In a sense it's what marriage is about. All human societies have had social mechanisms and vows about sex, proscription of it between certain degrees of kinship and the like. That's not... You're not listening. Stop it.'

'Your willy had gone all shrivelled. I thought I'd suck it a bit and see what happened,' she mumbled looking up at him with her mouth full.

'Have you always been like this?' he asked, suspecting that she must have been.

'No, it's you. The way you talk about it, and obviously think about it, makes me excited.' She stood up and took his hand, 'Feel me.' He did as asked. 'Can you manage it again?'

'Probably later.'

'That's a shame, not now?'

'Come on, let's have another glass and get into the bath. It's full now.'

Sitting together in the Jacuzzi, glasses in hand, admiring Tina, Ralph felt happy.

'You've just sighed.'

'Did I? I was just thinking. Are you happy? I certainly am. I wouldn't change places with anyone just now.'

'No, neither would I,' and she moved forward, reached under

the water, saying, 'Here's another first. You're going to make love to me in the bath tub.'

Ralph lay back, eyes closed, listening to the air jets very gently swirling the water around them, and letting the sensations literally wash over him.

He had only done it in the bath once ever, with Lucy, and they had been interrupted by her parents arriving back, who mercifully had stopped to speak to neighbours for a sufficient number of minutes to allow him and Lucy to get hurriedly dressed, if not dried properly.

Virginia's preference for 'healthy' showers over baths meant that they had never had a bathtub big enough to try it but that, in turn, had meant that quite often, whilst he might begin a shower alone, it would end with Virginia in with him, deliberately arousing him and either having sex standing against the shower wall or on the bathroom carpet.

He opened his eyes and found Tina staring at him intently.

'Was that nice?'

'It was lovely.'

'You seemed a long way away.'

'I'd abandoned myself to physical sensation.'

'What were you thinking about?'

'Physical sensation and you.'

'Huh,' she sounded vaguely disgusted. 'I bet it's not a first for you.'

'It is. And I hope there's a second and a third and more.'

'There will be,' and she kissed him.

They finished the bottle still sitting in the bath and then, only putting dressing gowns on, had a light supper, Ralph going out afterwards to check the temperature of the swimming pool and pronouncing it to be heating up satisfactorily. She had come outside with him.

'Does that mean we'll swim tomorrow?' She was hopeful.

'Well you couldn't at the moment. It's cold, not as bloody cold as it was, but I think probably.'

'What fun.' She knelt and tested the water herself. 'That's not too cold. I could swim in that now,' and went and started to roll back the cover.

'You're not serious?'

'I think I might be.'

The cover back, she looked at the water. It was a coolish but not cold night, and shadowed but moonlit, the water looked bottomless. She took her dressing gown off, he could see her naked body, pale in the dark blues of the evening, and did a graceful shallow dive into the water, flat, only skimming the surface, and striking a leisurely stroke to the other end.

'Come on in, it's fantastic.' She turned and swam back towards him and stood for a moment in the shallow end. He could see her nipples like bullets and goose pimples all over her.

'I can't stop. Must keep on swimming.'

'But you haven't a costume on.'

'You know that no one can see us here. We're not overlooked, someone would have to climb the walls here,' she called out behind her.

He hesitated. What the fuck, he thought and, taking his gown off, dived in after her.

'Christ, it's cold,' he called out as he did a leisurely breast-stroke but she did not hear him, she was now in racing mode, backwards and forwards the length of the pool, a fast and elegant crawl with tumble turns at each end. He waited until she was beside him and started the same stroke, trying to keep up with her and struggling to do so. After ten minutes or so she stopped and stood up in the middle of the pool. He did likewise.

'Aren't you cold?'

'I will be if we stand talking. I'm ready to get out.'

'So am I,' Ralph said with relief. Grabbing their dressing gowns, and draping them around them like towels, they ran into the house and stood, shivering in the kitchen.

'A hot shower?'

'Yes, quickly Ralph. We'll use the downstairs bathroom,' and they huddled together in the tiny shower cubicle until they were warm again, soaping one another as the water cascaded over them.

'That's better. I finally feel human again. I'm going to put clothes on and put the cover back over the pool, or should I turn the heating off? We've had our inaugural swim.'

'Let's leave it on overnight and see what it's like tomorrow. Would you like a drink, I'll open a bottle of red wine while you do the pool.'

'That would be nice.'

In the kitchen, drinking what he told Tina was a quarter way decent Burgundy, he pondered for a moment before saying 'Do you, I mean did you make a habit at school of...'

She seemed to have read his mind and ended for him, 'of skinny dipping?'

'Well, not the phrase I was going to use but yes, that's effectively what I was going to ask. How did you know?'

'I could sense your disapproval and guessed it might be bothering you. No, I didn't. It would hardly be allowed would it?

They were in loco parentis and the parents would certainly have disapproved.' No, she thought to herself, not at school, but only at parties when parents were out and where, inevitably, someone would push someone else in, or fall in, to be followed by someone else and then usually everyone would jump in. One person would take his or her clothes off, followed by others, some of the girls hovered, keeping knickers and bra on, and the boys, often more modest than the girls, probably worried at the size of their willies, retaining their boxer pants, Y fronts and the like. She remembered, with a smile, one particular party where they had tried to dance the conga in the water, the laughter and cheering and whoops of derision at the boys who had become sexually aroused; it actually seemed to her that most of them had that particular night.

'What are you thinking about Tina?' Ralph asked, crossly, she thought.

'The sight of you. Just before you jumped in the water. Sheer panic terror. I love you,' she added tenderly.

He laughed, 'I'd forgotten how private the garden is. It's funny isn't it? We're on an estate but no one can see into it. I hadn't really appreciated that when we looked at the house.'

'No, the brick walls are a bonus and it'll be a lovely sun trap.'

'How do you know?'

'The back is south facing.'

'Is it? Do you know Tina, I hadn't registered that.'

'And I thought you were the human computer. Let's go to bed.'

'I'll be up shortly.'

Ralph soon followed her up and found her in bed, already asleep, and feeling wide awake decided to finish the sitting room. He liked the mechanical mindlessness of the task, which left his own thoughts free to wander, as only part of his brain had to concentrate on getting the edges straight. He was number crunching tonight, working out budgets and the payment of bills. Things were going to be all right until Tina gave up work, but if he made Q.C. in the next announcements, then his income was probably going to lessen for a time and this worried him. Even if he did not get appointed, then he knew things would be tight. This worried him as well; he had been used to a high standard of living for a long time.

Shaking his head at his financial position, he finished the last piece of edging round a plug socket, decided it was not a bad job, really quite neat for a barrister he knew people would say, but then they did not know that he had spent one holiday as a painter and decorator's mate, not terribly well-paid but it was the only work he could find at the time. He gazed round the room with satisfaction and then, carefully rinsing all the brushes in readiness for Sunday, he finally went to bed.

He slept fitfully and again had nightmares, involving Tina with other men, laughing at him and leaving him; he was relieved to wake and find her warmth beside him.

It was early, he guessed about seven and checked. He was right and wondered whether Tina would thank him for waking her. He got out of bed, put his paint clothes back on and, quietly laying dust sheets in the bedroom, made a start on the bedroom walls. It was much later when Tina stirred, moved several times, before waking and, seeing what he was doing cried, 'Christ, Ralph. It's Sunday. How long have you been up?'

'Only a couple of hours. I thought I'd get on.'

'The amount you've covered I thought perhaps you hadn't

come to bed.'

'No I came up to bed and you were asleep. I did a little more, then got in with you, held you close and fell asleep, woke up and got on.'

'You're amazing, would you like some tea or coffee? I'll make it.'

'A cup of tea and a sandwich would be nice.'

Tina went to the bathroom and then disappeared downstairs. A few minutes passed.

She must have gone to look at the sitting room because he heard a shriek of excitement.

'Ralph, you've finished it. It looks great. Simply fabulous.' She came through the door with two cups of tea and a ham sandwich. 'This do you? I think the sitting room is just... well, a perfect colour. I don't believe you've been to bed at all.'

'I have. I just work quickly,' he said from the top of the step ladder. 'Here, I'm coming down. Have you been out to the pool?'

'No, I completely forgot. Have you?'

'I'll do it now.'

'Ralph, don't. Please come back to bed. Take your clothes off and hold me and then...'

She was sitting on the edge of their bed, shrugged off her dressing gown and lay, like a starfish Ralph thought incongruously, on the duvet. He felt himself stir and finishing his sandwich and tea, took off his clothes and was just about to get on top of her when she said, 'No, it's not really comfortable like that anymore. It feels as though you're squashing the baby. Here, like this,' and she made him lie behind and beside her, lifted one of her legs and guided him in.

'Is that nice?' she enquired anxiously.

'Yes, it is. But I can't kiss you from here. You're at the wrong angle.'

'Never mind. We'll kiss afterwards. The great thing about this position, I read it in my pregnancy handbook, is that you can do this very easily,' and she took his hand and placed it between her legs.

He found the sensation of stroking her there, and also being able to feel himself sliding in and out of her with the same hand, strangely erotic and afterwards, when they were both lying in each other's arms, Tina said, 'Mine was brilliant. That position will see us through pregnancy. You don't mind do you? I mean, it felt as though you had a big one. Orgasm I mean,' she added, he thought, hurriedly.

'It was lovely and it doesn't feel quite as intrusive in terms of the baby. I have this troubled idea of a foetus staring down a tunnel and seeing this thing approaching then withdrawing, then approaching again.'

'Ugh. Don't Ralph. It's not nice.'

'I know it's not nice but on the other hand, thoughts do intrude and there's nothing I can do about them.'

'Think of other things.'

'Like what?'

'Like the first time we did it. I do.'

'When?' He was interested.

'If I want to get aroused. It always makes me sticky thinking of that. Even in a shop or in the car.'

'I had no idea.' He was vaguely disconcerted and found the idea of Tina arousing herself, not exactly repellent but, at the least, not very pleasant.

'I often think about it when I'm having an orgasm,' she added brightly.

'Why can't you think about the fact that you are having an orgasm in the here and now, rather than what happened in the past?'

'I can, but I like to think about other times as well, like the car, you know. I've told you. I had a really dull sex life before I met you. You seem to have switched me on. You're smiling. I know it's a cliche but it's all so different. I feel as though I've discovered what sex is about, that it can be nice, pleasant, fun, satisfying. Not wifely duty stuff.' She kissed him. 'And I've got you to thank for that.'

'You've never talked about your previous sex life. I mean previous to St John. Presumably you had one.'

Her eyes took on, Ralph was watching her closely and intently having dared to broach the subject again, what he could only describe as a 'faraway expression'.

'Oh not much. Not really at all.' She shook her head firmly. 'Not like you, I'll bet.'

'What do you mean?'

'Well I bet you've always had girlfriends and done it with them. Lots.'

'How many do you think then?'

'I've no idea and I don't want to know.'

'Well what number would you find acceptable, that is to say more than what number would you find unacceptably high?'

She thought for a moment. 'Five or six I guess.'

It was his turn to feel uncomfortable and he decided to turn the subject back to what he wanted to know about.

'Well, what about you?'

'No, let's not talk about it Ralph.'

'If we don't talk about it, all I can do is imagine and fill in the gaps myself. Have you ever thought how little people actually communicate? I often feel that people think that in some way telepathy does it all for them. It doesn't. You can judge people by actions and what they do, that is to say objectively. But what you can't do is understand them, get inside their heads. For that you have to rely on what they say. We talk a lot but if you added up, for instance yesterday, all that we said to one another and laid it out end to end, it would probably not even amount to two hours of actual talking. I maybe talked to you, all in all for an hour, and you to me likewise. The rest of the time was silence, each of us locked into our own head with our own thoughts. All I can know of you, or you me, is what we say, what we say to each other.' He was uncharacteristically impassioned and, suddenly feeling foolish, stopped. 'Don't you see that?'

She was quiet, 'Yes I understand. We must always talk to one another. You're right. But I'm hungry.'

Ralph sadly recognised the moment, the opportunity, had passed, and she had once again eluded him. She was soon in her old, now paint spattered, clothes and downstairs. He dressed and followed her. She was grilling bacon and had just poured water into a cafetiere.

'Nice smells,' he said and looked outside for the first time that morning. 'Oh hell, it's raining.'

'It's not heavy, and it's not cold. I've been out. The water temperature is nice. We can have a swim, can't we?' Her tone suggested that there was probably no doubt whatsoever that they would swim that day.

'Yes, of course, later. When we've finished the bedroom.'

'God Ralph,' she smiled at him, 'you're a real slave driver.'

'Well the weather might clear, mightn't it?'

'That's true and sensible. But on the other hand it might get worse?' She laughed. 'No, we'll do it your way and get the work done first.'

They were both painting steadily when Tina stopped, put her brush down and said, 'Look, blue sky, well a little anyway. And the rain's stopped.'

She pulled off her jumper and stepped out of her jeans quickly before going to get a towel. Ralph, uncertain, as he badly wanted to finish the bedroom before the evening, hesitated. Tina, now in her costume, said impatiently, 'Come on. What are you waiting for? I'm off.'

So much for discussion Ralph mused, but he changed and followed her downstairs again. She had just finished rolling the cover up. He watched her as she straightened up, walked to the edge of the pool, her stomach now noticeably pregnant he realised, wondering why he should only just have noticed, and then, standing for a moment, a flat racing dive straight in, emerging and immediately into a leisurely crawl, before rolling over, and floating on her back and calling out, 'It's lovely, it's amazing, can we keep it on permanently?'

Ralph grinned at her enthusiasm and dived in himself. 'It's a lie,' he said as he came up out of the water beside her. 'It's still pretty chilly.'

'It's not bad, it's not bad Ralph. It's probably been switched off for a good few months or more and it had about twenty four hours. I'm going to swim for twenty minutes.'

She did just that, concentrated training he decided, and he

did the same until she, at the shallow end, said, 'What a treat. God. I'm looking forward to the summer.'

'You'll have a baby by then, God willing.'

'Oh don't say that Ralph.'

'Why not? I'm worried sick that something might go wrong.'

'Come on, let's get dressed and put the cover back on. I don't want even to think about it.'

'Two more lengths Tina. A race?'

'Diving or from the edge?'

He calculated. Tina's was a better dive than his. 'From the edge. Ready steady go,' and the two disappeared into a frenzy of splashing water, Ralph practically ahead on the turn, but behind afterwards and Tina winning by a comfortable foot or so.

He stood panting. 'I'm going to beat you in the summer.'

'You won't, you know. I'll want my figure back and I'm going to train seriously again.' She was lifting herself out.

'You'll have a baby to look after.'

'They sleep a lot. Didn't you know that?'

'No, I thought they cried a lot, puked a lot, pooed a lot, sucked their mothers dry and generally made life intolerable.'

'We'll see,' she smiled and went into the house.

Ralph floated in the water; there was no denying that a swimming pool was a wonderful thing to own, and he relished the idea of swimming every morning, but he wondered about heating costs. Getting out and, thinking that there was no point in putting the cover on again, it would need its winter cover, he went to the gas meter in the garage. He had no difficulty in remembering the earlier reading and, when he did the subtraction, wondered whether his memory might actually have let him down. Probably not, he thought, but were two chilly swims really worth the price of a decent meal for two in a good restaurant? Yes, he decided but he would have to consider heating strategy carefully. He switched the boiler off and went in. Back in the house, Tina was in the shower. He joined her again and they soaped one another.

'We can do that every day soon,' Tina said happily.

'Only if you're going to get up early. I've got a job to go to.'

'Well, when I get up early then, or in the evening.'

'I've still got energy. Should we finish the bedroom or call it a day?'

'Let's try and finish.'

He carried on, after she had gone downstairs to make supper, and only put his brush down with reluctance when she called him.

'Come on, it's ready.' He looked at the meal, lasagne.

Oh Christ, more student food, he was about to say but held back.

'What's wrong Ralph?' She seemed anxious.

'Nothing. I was just wondering if I might be able to finish tonight.'

'No, I'll finish tomorrow. You've done enough.'

'No, I don't want you up ladders. Not in your condition. Sorry for the cliché.'

'I won't, but no more tonight, hey?'

'What are you doing tomorrow?' he asked. 'I'm only going to Chambers to collect the post. You've got the week off. I wish I could take a holiday. Mark the difference between working for someone else and self-employment.'

'You'd hate working for anyone else. No, I'm going to go to

the GP and register.'

'Try and find one who doesn't want to stick his finger up you too often.'

She sniffed. 'Don't be vulgar Ralph. Doctors aren't like that.'

'The hell they aren't. I know one GP who said, across a dinner table, that the best bit of his job was when the woman went behind the screen and you could see her feet, underneath, and then the knickers coming off.'

'That's disgusting.'

'That's men. Even doctors, or perhaps especially doctors.'

'You've got a thing about men, Ralph, which is a bit odd considering you are one yourself.'

He shrugged, 'All men are the same. Totally penis orientated. Sex driven. Haven't you ever seen any pornography? Don't you know what turns them on? Tales of bored housewives, I'll use the word but I apologise, screwing the coalman, the milkman, the plumber, the electrician.' She looked sceptical and he continued, 'I know that it is aimed at that kind of person in a sense, and it's fantasy, but every man, given the chance, will leap at the opportunity for sex. And the photographs. You've never seen any have you?'

She shook her head. 'No, but all that stuff about plumbers and milkmen. Women don't do that sort of thing.'

'Of course they bloody do. Back in my early days, I'd just qualified I think, I represented a milkman in the magistrates' court. He'd separated from his wife and she was suing him for maintenance. As usual, my instructing solicitors had done a sorry job in preparing the papers. All I had was a backsheet with minimum details. I had to sit down with him and prepare the case from scratch. Anyway, each party had to give to the court what was called a confession statement, confessing whether or not they had committed adultery and, if so, with whom, as I recall it. I asked him if he'd ever committed adultery. Of course I have, he answered. I told him we'd have to tell the court and asked him how often. 'I don't know,' he said. 'What do you mean you don't know? You've got to tell me all their names.' 'Christ, all of them. I can't begin to remember.' I asked him to elaborate and he told me then about the willing housewives.'

'Ralph, it was probably just bravado, his own fantasy.'

'Well, his own fantasy was sufficiently well grounded to recall one street where he'd had no less than four, or it might have been five he said, pretty recently and produce names and addresses.'

Tina looked amused. 'What did you do about the confession statement then?'

'Put those in and said there were others.'

'Did the court accept that?'

'They didn't have to in the event. I carved it with my opponent and it went ahead on an agreed basis.'

'Carved it?'

'The lawyers sorted out a deal which the clients were happy about and the lawyers thought the court would rubber-stamp. It did.'

'I'm still not sure I believe you, about the milkman.'

'Well, I must say, I've never seen milkmen in quite the same way since.'

'Anyway, I'll register at the GP. Get a hospital referral. I think I might go by myself next time.'

'I think I might let you.'

'I thought I also might go to the Registry Office and get

dates and then book the hotel. What do you think?'

'A good idea. Why not do it as quickly as possible? Get the free dates from the hotel and then try those against the Registry and take the first. If t'were done, t'were better done quickly.'

'Sounds like Macbeth.'

'Or P G Wodehouse.'

'Anyway, that's the plan, and then I might paint a bit more.'

'Only if you don't go up the ladder.'

'I promise.'

Ralph left the following morning, on foot, to go to the station. He kissed Tina, regretful at leaving her behind, and now resenting the fact that he had to go into work. He knew he could have taken the week off but believed, and he knew this to be stupid and irrational, as the graveyard is full of people who considered themselves indispensable, he should try and put in a daily appearance. It was an article of faith, a superstition akin to his belief, when aged six or seven, that if he did not reach the next lamp post before a bus passed him, his mother would die. He turned at the corner to wave but Tina had shut the door. He walked past the neat trim gardens, all laid to lawn at the front and bare of fences, these being prohibited by covenants in the deeds. He passed a milk float and thought of his milkman story which had indeed been true. He had decided to collect the Morgan and the memory of this cheered him. He bought a ticket, waited on the platform, and became just one of many suited men and women who boarded a commuter train.

HUBRIS

Tina only closed the door as Ralph walked down the drive because she felt an aching loneliness. 'Why on earth couldn't he have taken a few days off? Bloody workaholic,' she said out loud and went to get dressed.

She felt angry at him, annoyed at their lack of money and viewed her expanding figure with disgust. Whilst her stomach was not so distended that she looked obviously pregnant, she thought it large enough to make her unattractive sexually, not perhaps to Ralph, but just generally to other men.

She toyed with the idea of a swim again, but was in a hurry to get the wedding booked. Once dressed she sat down, phoned the hotel, was put through to the manager who remembered her, and gave her a list of free dates which she noted down. As she hung up, the doorbell went; she opened the door and a milkman stood there.

'You're new aren't you? Would you like milk delivered?'

'Yes thanks, one pint of semi skimmed daily please.'

She did not register the milkman at all at first but then, as she shut the door, she became conscious that he had been and was still scrutinising her rather carefully.

'Thank you,' she said as she closed it firmly, wondering for a moment whether Ralph's views were well-founded. Perhaps Ralph was right?

She was back in the house by lunchtime, having managed to find a GP, a nice woman who, after the receptionist had told Tina to wait as Dr Phillips might see her very briefly, had spent five minutes with her between appointments, had telephoned the hospital and arranged an appointment at the Obstetric unit.

This had cheered Tina up considerably and then, when she had gone to see the Registrar, been told there had been a cancellation for a Saturday only four weeks away, which happened to be one which was free at the hotel, and which allowed her to post the banns immediately, she felt a sense of very considerable luck and achievement.

She made a sandwich and, on hearing the key in the door, experienced a moment of alarm until she heard Ralph call out 'Tina, I'm home.'

'Gosh, you're home early. I'm ever so pleased to see you. Listen,' and she told him of her successes.

He was thrilled. 'We're to be married in less than four weeks. Good God, well done Tina. That's marvellous.' He kissed her and danced her round the kitchen table. 'And an appointment at the hospital. Things are looking up.'

He looked less pleased when she told him about the milkman and the way she had caught him looking at her.

'I'll cancel the milk tomorrow.'

'Don't be silly Ralph. It's nice having it delivered. What you are you doing home now anyway?'

'Have a look outside.'

'Why?'

'I've got a car.'

'Why? You don't need one.'

'I might. I might have to get to court somewhere where trains don't connect.'

'You could get a taxi.'

'Yes, you and whose bank? Don't be silly. I need a car and so do you.'

'What kind is it?'

'Take a look. Come on.'

He was disappointed at her lack of enthusiasm. She came to the door and stood, impassively, in front of the red Morgan. 'Oh really, really practical Ralph. A vintage car with two seats. It'll break down on every journey and it's not big enough for the three of us.'

'It's not a vintage car. It's a Morgan. It won't break down any more than any other car. It's the same age as the Bristol and anyway, there are only two of us at the moment and only one of me when I need it.'

'It's quite pretty though Ralph. Was it expensive?'

He swallowed. 'No, not really.' He did not think he could tell her a direct lie but his assurance seemed enough for her. 'Should we go out in it? It's not raining.'

In truth, Ralph had been disconcerted to find how uncomfortable a Morgan was to drive. Harsh and unforgiving, the suspension was such that he felt as though his bottom had physically hit each pothole in the road, the steering was heavy compared to his Bristol and the seats, for practical purposes, unadjustable. He had, however, liked the view down the bonnet, the little flat windscreen, the cutaway doors and the ring of the exhaust. He knew he had made a mistake only now after he had driven the thirty miles or so from the garage, he should have bought a car rather than a toy, but was not going to admit this to Tina.

She was not enthusiastic at his suggestion. 'My hair will get messy.'

'You can put a headscarf on.'

'Wouldn't you rather swim again?'

'It'll be too cold.'

'It looks cold in that car.'

'Come on, let's go out to lunch in it.'

'But I've had a sandwich.'

'You can have a drink then.'

And so Tina was persuaded. They went to the little pub only a few miles away and, in the warmth Tina, with reluctance he thought, said, 'I rather enjoyed the drive. It was fun. I'm not sure I'd like it as an everyday car though.'

Ralph was aware of an extreme sense of relief, he had been dreading her disapproval and was loath to part-exchange his buy for something more usable. He had already decided that he could take the Mercedes and leave Tina with the Morgan, at least until the later stages of pregnancy. They had a drink, sitting by the fire, the only customers in the pub, left comfortably alone by the barman.

'This is what retirement must be like.'

'It's a happy thought,' he replied, sipping at a lemonade and lime. 'Would you like to drive back?'

'No, another time. Unless you'd like a beer. I've only had a half.'

'No, it's OK. Let's get back and finish the bedroom and then christen the new colour scheme.'

She brightened. 'Yes, let's.'

After they put the paintbrushes away, having agreed not to do any other room for the time being, they bathed in what Tina called their new bathroom, made love, again in the new position lying sideways, before eating, watching nonsense on the television and going to bed.

For the next few weeks they observed this, had it become a routine he wondered, in the evenings, happy with one another as Tina grew bigger. Mercifully, she said repeatedly, she was spared the horrors of morning sickness, and remained apparently bright, cheerful and unperturbed by her distending stomach. She was anxious, however, that she might look horribly pregnant on their wedding day, and she agreed to leave choosing and buying a wedding dress until the week before, and then only to choose one that concealed her girth.

Ralph's contentment was shattered, but not for more than a few hours, when he received a letter from the Lord Chancellor's Department saying that his application for Q.C. had been refused and, having a quiet word with Ken, he only then realised how much Tina had cost him.

'I don't know for certain, of course Ralph, but I rather think that Sir Geoffrey did it for you. I know he was asked for his view, and he's told me that he's never forgiven you for leaving and killing Virginia.'

'Ken, I didn't kill her.' Ralph was appalled. Surely people weren't saying that?

'No, I know you didn't, but Sir Geoffrey is a prejudiced old bigot and his dislikes are as strongly held as his likes. I'm sorry. There's always another time Ralph.'

'But his comments, whatever they were, will be on my file in the Lord Chancellor's Department for the rest of my career. I'm professionally buggered. Bloody marvellous.'

'Look, I'll make sure the work keeps coming to you if you keep on doing it well. You'll just have to try even harder and get there on obvious merit.'

'I'm not sure that I won't lose some of my enthusiasm.'

'Please Ralph, try not to. Your only option is to keep going. You don't want to end up like old Fergus do you?'

Fergus was an elderly barrister, still in Chambers, who came in every day in the hope that there might be a brief or papers waiting for him. There never were and he relied on double bookings, when, at the age of seventy-seven, he would go to obscure magistrates' courts to conduct cases more suitable for lawyers at the beginning of their careers, rather than those in their twilight years. Not at all a figure of fun, he served as a living reproach and a warning of the consequences of a failure to try hard enough.

'No, I don't want to end up like Fergus. But I've always been a driven man Ken, you know that better than anyone. What will drive me now?'

'The opportunity to put two fingers up at Sir Geoffrey when you do get appointed.'

'It won't happen, you know that Ken. You're just trying to cheer me up. I'll go home and think about it. Thanks for the comforting words though.'

In the train, he tried on, metaphorically, a variety of emotions. He could not get excited. Had he been subconsciously prepared for rejection? He had never been rejected by anyone for anything before, and found some difficulty in accepting that it had occurred.

He knew he was a bit on the young side for a Q.C. but would not have applied unless he was fairly certain he would be successful. Indeed, Sir Geoffrey had encouraged him and assured him of his support. Ralph felt uncertain as to what he actually, deep down made of the result. Was he disappointed really? He was unsure. He knew he was going to be severely embarrassed when telling Tina, who seemed to revere him and his abilities so highly. He would rather not tell her at all, and upon arriving at this conclusion, immediately further concluded that he would not tell her.

If she ever asked then maybe, just maybe, he might say something but not now or in the near future. He cast around further, trying to make sense of his lack of overwhelming disappointment, and then it made sense to him.

As a Q.C. he would be expected to take on higher profile cases over a much greater area than just his circuit. It might have meant, in fact certainly would have meant, nights away from Tina, and it was she who was most important to him.

It was only a little later, still in the train, that he also understood that his money anxieties had abated; he should, all things being equal at least, continue to earn much the same as at present. The combination of these two realisations, or were they solipsistic rationalisations to comfort him, he was not sure, was enough to put him in a good mood again, and it was to be many months before his then failure came to mind once more.

Well, I gave it a go, he smiled to himself as he opened the door late that afternoon and went back to Tina, and his 'domestic bliss' as Tina called their life together.

Somehow the N.H.S. had contrived to smile, rather than sucking them in, chewing, masticating brutally and then spitting them out. Tina was sufficiently far advanced for the gynaecologist to fit her in at short notice, as did the X ray department for a CT scan. Ralph said he would accompany her to the first appointment but wait outside.

He was interested though in the CT scan and, to Tina's evident pleasure, agreed to come in and see the results on screen. She went in first and it was only after a few minutes had elapsed, that he was permitted to join them. Tina had tears in her eyes, and was smiling, 'Look Ralph, there's the baby.'

He peered at the screen. He was used to reading X rays but found the image very difficult to discern.

The operator, who struck him as again young and inexperienced, said, 'Here's the head, and there's the shoulder,' moving the cursor to show them.

'There seems to be an awful lot there,' said Ralph puzzled. 'Can I have a go?'

'Certainly not.'

Another officious medic he thought but, not wishing to upset Tina, held his temper in check.

'Would you like a copy of the scan?'

'Yes please,' said Tina at once.

'That will be ten pounds.'

Ralph found it amusing that people, including Tina, were prepared to pay for what was at best an image of dubious aesthetic or scientific interest but recognising that it was meaningful to her, paid and was told it would be in the post.

As Tina dressed he mentioned it again. 'Don't expect to see the scan photograph.'

'Why not?'

'It's the NHS. A byword for inefficiency and complacency. It'll get 'lost in the post' or something. Incidentally did your notes turn up here?'

'Yes,' she said with a smirk.

'Oh good,' he had to reply.

The night before their wedding, Tina thought that they ought to go out.

'What you mean I have a stag night and you have a hen night?' He sounded horrified.

'No, just the opposite. You and me together. Somewhere romantic. Did you have a stag night first time round?'

'No, some friends wanted me to, any excuse for sustained group drinking, but I'd been on enough, well two, but those two were enough for me, not to want ever to again.'

He told her about the last one, when he had stayed sober because he was worried about Duncan, a hard drinking Scotsman who was abandoned in the pub toilets by his other friends. Ralph had gone to check and found him slumped, head literally in the lavatory bowl, covered in and just about to drown in his vomit, and deeply unconscious. Ralph had fished him out, sprayed him down, dragged him home and put him to bed, lain him, on his side, in approved recovery mode. Ralph had then sat there, awake, until the morning when he had nursed him through an appalling hangover, helped him dress properly and then delivered him to the church. Ralph took his duties, especially as best man, seriously.

'What about you? A hen night?'

'Oh, I went out with some girlfriends to a pub. Quiet really.'

Except for the strippagram who had arrived at Stella's house where they had gone when the pub closed, she remembered. They had all been quite drunk by the time he had rung the bell and, once in the room, having located Tina, the 'wedding girl', he gyrated in front of her, egged on by the cheers of the others, until he was naked and waving a long and flaccid penis around. A good looking and well-muscled boy of about twenty she had guessed, he looked a little self-conscious when he had finished but then Stella, leaning over, had flicked at it and said, 'Is that all you can do, loverboy?'

The others had then chorused, 'Come on, come on, come on.' Shutting his eyes, he had reached down and to their screams of delight, had started to stroke himself to full erection. When he had achieved this, he opened his eyes again as if to say, 'There look at that,' but said nothing.

Stella cried out, 'Don't stop now, make it work.' He looked at her and, very deliberately, started masturbating. When he realised that the six of them were not going to object, he went faster, until his hand was only a blur. Tina had been amused to see Stella rubbing herself through her knickers, her legs spread wide open, an expression of total lust on her face.

'Over the wedding girl, man,' she called, 'over Tina,' and Tina, not moving, sitting wordlessly, watched with interest as he stopped rubbing, and standing in front of her, just lightly holding his dick, it had throbbed once, then a second time, before semen had exploded from the end and landed, as though a fountain pen had been shaken, in a neat line of blobs right up to her neck.

'Thank you girls,' she had said sarcastically, as she mopped herself up with a handkerchief. 'That was quite a treat.' They were helpless with laughter. Tina saw the funny side of it then and started chuckling with them. The stripper, paid in advance and for whom it was all in a night's work presumably, put on some fashionable sportswear taken from a bag he had left in the hall, and left, saying 'Night ladies,' in a totally matter-of-fact way.

'Crikey,' Stella had mumbled. 'I had a fucking orgasm just watching him. What must he be like in the sack? How many times a night do you think he manages to perform?'

'Well maybe not all his engagements are quite so demanding,' Tina grinned. 'It was you who wanted him to do it.'

'Yes,' the others chorused, 'it was Stella,' and they ended chanting together, 'Stella and her fella went fuck, fuck, fuck,' until laughter overcame them.

'No.' Tina brought herself back to the present, 'I don't want a hen night. Just the two of us, please.' They went to a small bistro that they both liked the look of, with what that knew to be cliched curtains, lamps, prints and where the food was adequate, but with a personable owner, solicitous service and where they talked little, but held hands over the table.

On their wedding day Ralph woke up at dawn. He was excited, twitchy, anxious and happy simultaneously. He went downstairs, made some tea, came back up then sat on the edge of the bed looking at Tina and sipping at the cup thoughtfully said to himself, this is it. Finally another start to my new life.

Tina shifted in the bed, moved in her sleep and settled again lying on her back. Ralph pulled the covers back and exposed her totally. He looked at the soft curves, the gentle plateau of her stomach, the softness of her inner thighs, her lips lightly parted, eyes closed. Her lovely hair spread out over the pillow. Her lovely silken pubic hair not concealing the mound, the wonderful slippery entrance.

Was she subconsciously aware of his scrutiny? She stirred again, turning onto her side, pulling ineffectually at where she expected the covers to be and settled again. Her breasts now hung slightly to the right, and he could not resist touching her.

She was instantly awake, a startled look flashed across her face, then a smile which turned into a broad grin. 'You've got a dirty mind haven't you? You're not supposed to see me on my wedding day, let alone look at me in that lascivious way.'

'I can't help it. You're so lovely. I could spend the rest of eternity just looking.'

She stopped him by sitting up and kissing him before reaching down between his legs.

'God, you're insatiable. But then you make me feel like that too. What time is it?' She glanced at her watch. 'What do you want? A long slow one or an even longer slower one? We seem to have plenty of time.'

'I'll settle for a long slow one,' he grunted as he buried his face between her breasts.

Over a coffee, smiling at each other, they discussed the day. 12.00 at the Registry Office, Reception at one, lunch at two.

'There's no hurry for anything at the moment. Let's have a bath together,' and luxuriating in the foam, saying little except to stroke each other, murmuring endearments, they idled away forty-five minutes.

Ralph started to put on a new shirt that Tina had chosen for him and then she handed him a small package. 'A little present.'

He opened it. An Armani silk tie in colours that she knew he would like.

'It's beautiful, I'll wear it today,' and he put it on. 'I got you a present too but I'm going to give you it later.'

'Why not now?'

'Because.'

They went down for breakfast.

'I feel all of a dither, nervous, schoolgirly. I don't understand it. I just wanted today to happen, so much, for so long.'

'I feel the same. It's as though I'm about to go into a courtroom for an important case before a particularly unpleasant and unpopular judge. No rhyme or reason. I think it's probably the thought of seeing my family.'

'Don't be so silly. What's wrong with them?'

'You've only met my parents, not my brother. I shouldn't have invited him. We've nothing in common.'

'Oh come on, blood's thicker than water. It's a wedding. Our wedding. You can't leave family out. I'm rather looking forward to seeing mine. I haven't seen them for ages.'

'Yours are OK. Mine aren't. My father's a bad-tempered so and so, my mother complains all the time and my brother...'

'What's wrong with your brother?'

'You'll find out,' he interrupted her. 'Come on, I'm ready for a cup of coffee. I don't feel like any breakfast.'

He made coffee while Tina finished dressing. She came down in her new dress.

'You look wonderful. That colour really suits you. Will you have my children? Will you marry me?'

'Yes and yes,' she laughed.

'Morgan or Mercedes?'

'It might rain.'

'Morgan then.'

'Don't be silly, we'll take the big one.'

They were a few minutes early and waited outside in the sunshine; as a well turned-out couple outside a Registry Office, they attracted attention from passers-by. One old woman stopped and said, 'You look so happy, I wish you a long and successful marriage. Bless you both,' and walked on.

'How did she know?' asked Tina.

'It's obvious, look at the evidence. A couple. Well-dressed. Holding hands outside the Registry Office.'

'I suppose,' she started to say but then saw her parents and sister approaching down the pavement. She broke off and ran towards them, laughing excitedly, kissing and embracing each of them. They stood, the five of them, waiting for the other guests. Ken and his wife appeared and Ralph made the introductions, telling Tina's family that this was the man whom he owed more by way of career than anyone else. Ken looked pleased and flattered.

As they were talking, across the road, waiting for a lull in the traffic, Ralph saw his own parents and his brother with a girl holding his arm. Ralph sighed. His parents were looking respectable enough, but his brother was wearing what Ralph thought of as a 'yob suit', slightly too large, too broad across the shoulders, formless and shapeless. The top button of his shirt was undone, a lurid tie, carelessly knotted, not tightened properly, the shirt a horrid colour, Ralph stopped his analysis. He would look later but he guaranteed that Jeremy was wearing white socks as well. The girl looked his type. Slightly tarty, a skirt that was too short, white tights, a short fur coat. Ralph was cross. His invitation had not included a partner for Jeremy. He would have to get another place laid at the hotel. Another thing to remember. They crossed the road, as a group and seeing Ralph, came up to him.

'Wotcher mate, this is my big brother, Ralph. This is Shirley. Shirley say hello to my brother.'

'Hi big brother,' she said, in a rather ugly regional accent that Ralph could not immediately place.

Ralph, ever urbane, ever affable to the outside world, shook her hand, kissed his mother, clapped his father on the back and, introducing them to the others, finally turned to his brother and said, 'How are you then?'

'Fucking good mate. It's all right, isn't it? I like weddings. You do as well, don't you Shirl? Get pissed, have a good time, have a laugh. Fuck a bridesmaid.'

Shirley giggled, 'Not while I'm around Jezza.' Ralph had forgotten that this was his brother's preferred choice of name. Ralph thought it more appropriate for a well-educated, middle-class, left-wing academic criminologist, all of whom always seemed to adopt ugly forenames.

'Nah, just joking. I'll disappear under a table with you instead.'

Ralph groaned, it could have been audibly, and said, 'I'd better be going in.' He went back to Tina, took her hand and saying, 'We're on,' led the group into the waiting room.

It was a bit like a crematorium, he thought, one group waits in one room while the business is dispatched in the other and, when the business is over, they leave by another doorway and the next group files in. Conveyor belt rites of passage. He wished that they could have had a church wedding, but at least it was a formal recognition and civil legitimising of their relationship. Their turn came, Tina and Ralph sitting at the front with Tina's sister and Frances and the two little girls as de facto bridesmaids and Henry, the best man, behind them.

The other guests, not that there were many, occupied seats in a haphazard sort of way, Tina's parents sitting together with Ken and his wife, Ralph's parents near the front, his mother dabbing her eyes in an unconvincing and rather histrionic way, and his brother at the back, sniggering with Shirley. The few other friends were dotted about. The Registrar cleared her throat and started speaking. It was over before he had time to take it in and they were outside, in the garden it seemed only moments after they had entered.

'Come on, kiss the bride,' his brother shouted, 'we want some dirty photos.'

'Kiss the bride,' the others chorused and, feeling self-conscious Ralph bent, Tina turning her face and whispering, 'I love you, husband.'

Photos taken, Ralph first ascertaining that everyone knew

where the hotel was, he and Tina walked to where the car was parked.

'Who knew it took so little time?'

'It's enough that we're married,' she said. 'Did everyone turn up? I was too nervous to check. It was all a bit of a blur.'

'I think so, we'll see at the hotel.' Ralph had deliberately, with the invitations, directed people to parking places a little further away than where he had left his car. He felt it important to be at the hotel first with Tina, to receive their guests and all having gone to plan, they were installed inside the door to the room in good time.

Standing in front of a table they waited and, within a much shorter time than he had anticipated, Tina's family were with them.

'No, you've got to stand with us,' Tina said to her parents.

Christ, Ralph thought, I'll have to ask mine too, and, when they arrived, did just that. His father was inclined not to bother but his mother insisted. The six of them greeted their guests, Ralph and Tina accepting their good wishes, compliments and presents cheerfully, making formal introductions as necessary. Ralph cast around. Everyone seemed to be in the room except his brother, who then appeared, pint glass in hand, Shirley with a lager, and came up to Ralph.

'Good on yer,' transferring his drink from his right to left hand, made to punch him in the stomach, but shook Ralph's hand instead, before turning to Tina and saying, 'Kiss the bride, right?' and bending down, kissed her full on her mouth, before turning again to Ralph and saying, 'Nice one mate,' and wandering off into the room.

Ralph was sickened and when Tina said, 'A bit OTT isn't

he?' could only reply, 'Yes, that's one way of putting it. I can think of others.'

They mingled, Ralph not drinking, chatting and again, it seemed within minutes, they were into the formal lunch. Ralph had secured an extra place for Shirley, had been assured that there was more than enough food, and all was well. The meal was good, the wine likewise and Ralph's speech was well received.

The best man's speech was to the point and he, having been warned that dirty jokes would go amiss, was happily uncontentious. Tina's father's speech, by contrast, had been most moving in its simplicity.

Ralph started to relax, and he drank a couple of glasses of champagne quickly. He wanted the artificial heightening of mood alcohol can provide, wanted to let himself unwind a little. Everyone was more cheerful, slightly less inhibited, laughing and joking and Ralph, moving easily among their guests, was actually enjoying himself. He found himself beside Tina's sister. 'How's things?' he asked.

'Fine. I'm still enjoying law, if that's what you mean.'

'No boyfriend?'

'Oh yes, still the same.'

'Why isn't he here?'

'I didn't think he was invited.'

'Oh God, that's appalling. I'm so sorry.' Ralph felt mortified. 'Why on earth didn't you say something to Tina?'

'Oh, it's all right. Honestly. Don't worry about it.'

'On the contrary, I'm desperately embarrassed. Will you and he come over for dinner one night soon? I'll apologise to him personally then. I can't begin...'

'We'd love to. He didn't mind. Didn't take offence and certainly I haven't. Apologies, though not necessary, are accepted,' and she kissed him lightly on the cheek. 'Welcome to the family, Ralph. I've never seen Tina looking happier.'

'Tell me something, in confidence and quietly.'

'What?' Her eyes widened.

'Does she look happier today than when .. you know?'

'She married St Jean?' Sylvia finished for him. 'Yes, much. The night before her first marriage I sat with her for hours, she was so unconvinced that she was doing the right thing.'

'That cheers me up a lot,' smiled Ralph. 'Thanks.'

Joined just then by another couple, Ralph, noticing that his bladder was uncomfortably full, made an excuse and went to the lavatories. Finished and washing his hands, he became aware of his brother standing beside him grinning.

'Nice one you've got there,' he said.

'What do you mean?' Ralph said, coldly and suspiciously, his mood darkening.

'Your Tina. They say redheads shag like bunny rabbits. What's she like? Is she a good fuck then?' He was drunk and swaying slightly. Ralph, disgusted, looked at him, up and down, judging position, moved back slightly and, drawing his right leg back, suddenly kicked Jeremy in the testicles as hard as he was able.

Jeremy fell to the ground, soundlessly, clutching himself, curled up, moaning and whimpering, lying on the blue tiles, he opened his eyes and gasped, 'You bastard'.

'Maybe. An over-reaction on my part, but it's really not good form to talk about another man's wife in those terms,' Ralph said grimly.

Jeremy picked himself up, leaning against the washstand, still bent double and was noisily sick into the basin.

'I'm sorry. I shouldn't have done that. I just snapped. I lost control.' Ralph felt contrite now, bending to turn the taps on, saw his brother draw back a fist, just managed to sidestep a vicious blow, and kicking his brother's feet away from him, Jeremy was on the ground again.

'Look, I didn't want a fight, OK?' Ralph said warily.

'All right. No fight. It's your wedding day,' and picking himself up again, stood straighter.

'I won't be fucking Shirley tonight, that's for sure. Maybe not tomorrow either.' He was still holding himself.

'Come on. Worse things happen on the rugby field. I've said I'm sorry.' Ralph held out his hand. Jeremy, still leaning forward sank his teeth into it so hard that Ralph cried out, then released him and grinned and said, 'Rugby field,' stretched out his hand, took Ralph's and shook it. 'No hard feelings. I need a drink.'

'I'll buy you one,' and they left the room, Jeremy walking stiff-leggedly into the hallway where he dropped into a chair with a grimace. Shirley was beside them within moments.

'What's happened, loverboy? You don't look well.'

'Fell over in the lav. Too much drink,' he muttered.

'I'll get you another,' said Ralph.

'He doesn't need any more,' said Shirley.

'This one I need Shirl.'

Ralph went into the reception room, found two glasses, filling them with champagne, before going back to his brother and handing him one.

'Cheers Ralph,' and drank it down in one.

'That's no way to treat a vintage champagne,' Ralph smiled, thinking of his brother's swelling testicles, 'but I'll forgive you in the circumstances. Cheers. I'll see you later,' and Ralph left him, still sitting in the chair with Shirley perched on its arm. He found Tina.

'Where have you been? You've been gone ten minutes.'

'Just sorting my brother out.'

'What do you mean?'

'He's drunk. Needed attention. All over.'

'What's wrong with your hand?' Ralph was holding the one his brother had bitten in his other.

'Nothing. I'll tell you later. People expect us to leave now. I'll be back in a minute.'

Ralph went out and found, as he expected, the Mercedes festooned in balloons, shaving foam, lipstick and the rest of the paraphernalia that wedding guests feel obliged to inflict on the couple's going away car. He went back in, looked at his watch, 'All timed nicely,' he thought and collecting Tina, they circled the room quickly, saying that they were going. People drifted outside, the perpetrators of the car decoration laughing and pointing. Ralph and Tina, emerging into the late afternoon, holding hands, grinned.

'Oh God Ralph. Look what they've done to the car. We can't drive through town like that.'

Ralph looked at his watch, 5.00 pm, just as a black taxicab drew up. Opening the door, he said to her, 'After you.'

She laughed. 'You think of everything,' she whispered before turning to the guests and shouting, 'Bye everyone. See you after our honeymoon,' and got in. Ralph, smiling, waved and followed her closing the door and the taxi moved away, followed by the cries of the guests.

'That's that then Tina.'

'That's that then Ralph. We're married.'

'Wonderful.'

'What next. Are we going home now?'

'Yes,' and the taxi stopped outside their house.

'Wait here a moment,' he said to Tina.

'Why?' she asked.

'I'll be back in a moment.'

Tina waited, wondering what was going on. Ralph came out of the house with two small suitcases and got back in.

'I thought we'd have a couple of nights away. It's my present to you.'

'But I've nothing to wear.' The taxi had set off already and Tina looked around.

'Where are we going?'

'You'll see. Here.' He handed her the suitcase and, opening it and moving the contents around a little, she found he had packed her favourite shirt, jacket, jeans, jumper, shoes.

'How on earth did you know? It's so exactly what I'd have packed myself!'

'I listen, I watch, I consider. I hope it's all right. My present to you is at the bottom. Leave it until later though.'

'You're amazing. Kiss.' Ralph noticed the driver looking at them in the mirror; their eyes met and the driver looked away. They sat holding hands as the taxi drove through the dark.

'How far is it?'

'We'll be there soon.'

'I'm not sure where we are.'

'Settle back.' She lay against him, quiet and trusting. Finally, as the taxi turned, she looked up and saw the hotel sign.

'Oh God. Ralph. How wonderful.'

It was one of the most famous country house hotels in Britain. Michelin starred, celebrity chef, haunt of the rich and famous, endlessly talked about in the media, they had once or twice spoken of going there but Ralph had always been put off by the cost.

'I feel like royalty,' she said as they got out and took their luggage.

'Mr and Mrs Edwards,' he said at reception.

'Ah yes, welcome. Sign here and James will help you to your room.'

The building was an old one and the interior was such that Tina said, 'It must have been spray painted with money. It's exquisite, perfection.' Their room. 'Oh God, Ralph, it's gorgeous,' she said as the porter closed the door behind him and they were at last on their own.

'Have you paid the taxi, is he still waiting?' She looked anxious.

'All paid in advance. No problem,' he muttered, concentrating hard on opening one of the bottles of champagne that stood in an ice bucket. Tina was exploring the suite.

'Look,' she said excitedly and 'look,' again in excitement.

'Have a drink,' Ralph handed her a glass, clinked his against hers. 'To us, my sweet and lovely Tina.'

'To us my kind, thoughtful and generous Ralph.' They kissed lightly and Tina then, looking a bit crestfallen said, 'You know, I've always wanted to eat here but I'm not hungry. It's a terrible waste or shame.'

'Why aren't you going to eat here?'

'Well, breakfast I suppose. We could stay for lunch?' she enquired hopefully.

'Why don't we stay for dinner tomorrow night?'

'Ralph,' she squealed, 'we're not staying here for more than one night surely? It'll be ruinous.'

'I thought two nights would be about right. I've ordered a light supper for us in here tonight and we'll eat in the restaurant tomorrow.'

'Oh, how wonderful,' she clapped her hands in excitement. 'What a treat. Let's have a bath, it's the biggest one I've ever seen. What time is supper coming?'

'Nine.'

'We've time to have more than a bath Ralph. Do you want?' She raised her eyebrows.

Ralph did, so they did, Ralph carried away physically and mentally; Tina mewing and moaning, baby completely forgotten, rolling around together on the bed but Tina having first turned down the silk covers.

In the bath they soaped each other, drank champagne, giggled for each was a little drunk, and were utterly carefree.

Supper when it arrived, was exactly the elaborate but simple meal that Ralph had envisaged when he had made the booking, a beautifully presented lobster thermidor on one plate, oysters on ice on another, slivers of toast, different kinds of bread, two creme brulees, a bottle of Montrachet Grand Cru, this being the most expensive bottle of wine that he had ever ordered or drunk or ever intended to order again, wheeled in on a trolley and deposited on the circular Regency breakfast table, which the waiter laid with appropriate flourish. He poured the wine; Ralph gave it to Tina to taste.

'Ralph, it's lovely.' The waiter filled their glasses.

'Will that be all sir?'

'Yes thank you.'

Another bank note changed hands and the door closed on the outside world again.

When they had finished eating, Tina licking her fingers as she cleared the little porcelain pot that had contained the remnants of her creme brulee, suddenly burst out, 'This has been utterly, but utterly, the best day of my life. I've never been so happy. I just want to cry.'

'Don't. Let's just enjoy ourselves. Would you like some more of the Burgundy or should I open another bottle of champagne?'

'No, no more for me thanks. It'll be wasted. Anyway don't forget I'm pregnant. You finish the wine, you're more of a connoisseur. We'll save the champagne for tomorrow. I might have to go to bed soon or,' as she stood up, she swayed slightly. 'Even now,' she concluded. She walked over to the bed, they had not unpacked, and opened her case. She took out her clothes with care, laying them on the sofa. She drew out what looked to be an expensively wrapped package.

'What's this?'

'My present to you.'

She opened it and spread out an assortment of lingerie, knickers and bras. Ralph had gone into the shop to buy them and had simply said, 'My wife is 36 25 36, cup size C. I'd like some really luxurious underwear,' had been shown an assortment, bought them all, blanched at the price, and had asked for them to be gift wrapped but nicely.

'Ralph, you shouldn't have.' She had looked at the labels.

'They're beautiful. You're so silly. They're too nice to wear. I can't wear these, I've got a good idea of what they cost.'

'You're being silly. It's just a present.' She started sniffing and then she sobbed, as she stood beside the bed, holding a pair of knickers up and then, wiping her eyes with them, she gave a wan smile. 'I'm sorry.'

'What's wrong?'

'I'm crying with happiness and regret. I just wish I'd met you sooner. First. I'm crying for all the years we didn't have together. The years when we could have... Oh, I don't know. Done anything and everything.'

He walked over to her, cradled her in his arms, kissing the tears in her eyes and said, 'We've got each other now,' and undressing her, slowly and carefully, he helped her into bed, where she lay, curled up and eyes closed. He started tidying, then stopped, deciding that it could wait until tomorrow for a chambermaid, undressed and got into bed beside her.

The next morning they woke, once again simultaneously and reached out for one another.

'What would you like to do? We can breakfast in here or in the restaurant. We can stay in here all day or go to Oxford. I've booked dinner for eight. It's up to you.'

'I've got lots and lots of energy,' she exclaimed. 'I would like you to make love to me, then have breakfast, then go into Oxford. I don't know the town at all. Then back here, a bath and dinner. Sounds perfection.'

They did just that, gentle love making followed by a breakfast Tina described as superb, a taxi into Oxford where they walked among the colleges.

'Why didn't you come here to do law?' she enquired at one

point.

'Perhaps I should have done. My father and the school wanted me to. But,' his eyes clouded as he remembered Lucy, 'I actually wanted to go to the place that had the very best reputation for teaching law at the time. And that was not Oxford. But my university was nothing like this. No beauty. No ancient colleges, no architecture, grim modern buildings but inspiring lectures I thought that would make up for it.'

'Did they?'

'At the time, but wandering around today, I'm not so sure.'

'But if you'd gone to Oxford we might never have met.'

'There is that, but I expect I'd have ended up on the same circuit and we might still have met then.'

'Don't say that. You can't live your life with 20/20 hindsight. You can only do what seems to be right at the time.'

'Yes, probably,' but he was quiet for some time afterwards, as they continued their exploration. 'I have friends who went here,' he finally remarked. 'They all had, what at least a couple describe, as a brilliant time. What about you, why didn't you apply?'

'I didn't think I was clever enough.'

'You diminish yourself too much. You'd have got in, I'm sure.'

'If I'd gone here, I'd never have met St John and then, absolutely and certainly, we'd never have met.'

Sadly he agreed this was true. 'Life is so full of accidents. Accidents of history. Accidents of circumstance. It's unplannable. Do you believe in Fate? Were we fated to meet, do you think, or is it that we just met?'

'It'd be nice to believe that we were fated to meet but, no.

It's like death. If the bullet's got your name on it, bang.'

'Fatalistic.'

'You're confusing me.' She smiled. 'We met. That's enough.'

They had a late lunch in an old pub, a sandwich and a beer. Ralph had always wanted to see the pictures in the Ashmolean and they spent the afternoon there, each agreeing that Pretty Baa Lambs was one of the most idiotic pictures ever painted.

A taxi ride back to the hotel, a long, luxurious bath again and then dinner in the restaurant.

'I think that was the best meal I've ever, ever eaten in my life,' she said, as she dabbed at her lips with her napkin.

'I know it was the best meal I've ever eaten. And some of the finest wines. It must be nice to be rich enough to do this frequently.'

'The pleasure would go, Ralph. Doing anything too often, too frequently, devalues it.'

'Even sex with you,' he whispered into her ear.

'Probably. You'll get bored.'

'Don't say that.' He was genuinely alarmed. 'Please don't say that. It's going to be wonderful. Forever.'

'I'll try,' she promised.

'It will be?' He was anxious and wanted reassurance, feeling a sudden cold and ghastly dread.

'It will be,' she replied firmly.

The next day she was awake and up before him. He woke to find her, dressed in some of the underwear he had given her, stroking and licking him.

'You look beautiful,' he murmured appreciatively.

'I love you Ralph,' and they again made love, tenderly and slowly.

'They'll have to throw these sheets away,' she announced afterwards.

'Why?'

'They'll be so stiff, they'll crack when they lift them off the bed.'

'You have a somewhat crude sense of humour.'

'Yes, but life is a bit crude isn't it? Blood, sex, excreta. Isn't that what Dali said?'

'It can be more than that. Honour, love, bravery.'

'You're just an old-fashioned knight in shining armour, rescuing a damsel who was in distress but is now happy in the arms of her chevalier.'

'Where are the dragons?' he laughed. 'Let me at them.'

She laughed too. 'There aren't any. I don't believe in them anymore.'

In the taxi, on the way home she said, 'Thank you Ralph, for the two best days in my life.'

They arrived back at the house, and Tina, climbing out of the taxi, showering the driver with, 'Thank yous,' ran to the door. Ralph picked up their two bags, tipped the driver and followed her.

'Oh, it's so nice to be back,' she sighed shutting the front door behind her and leaning against the wall. 'Our house, the start of our life together. And so much to look forward to. Kiss me Ralph.'

He stooped, only slightly for she was nearly as tall as him, and she held him, tightly and passionately, for nearly a minute, eyes closed as they kissed.

'Is it an anti-climax, Ralph? Home?'

'Life with you, my sweet, is a series of climaxes,' he replied and Tina giggled, in the way that always made him want to smile, 'so there are bound to be a few, but this is not one of them. It's good to be back. I feel as though I've been away for weeks. The house feels nice.'

Tina had gone upstairs to unpack and, downstairs again, would only say, 'It's lovely to be home again with my husband.'

The days started to pass rapidly for both of them. Tina dutifully attended her ante-natal classes, bringing back anecdotes that sometimes had Ralph howling with laughter but, under no circumstances, could he be persuaded to go with her.

'I'm not a lentil eating, bearded sandal type. I don't need to go. I'll be at the birth, I promise.'

'But Ralph, there are some perfectly ordinary looking people there. Men I mean. There were today.'

'Men who get off on the sight of fat women doing pelvic floor exercises. It's obscene.' He paused. 'I'll come with you next time.'

Intellectual curiosity had got the better of his innate distaste at what seemed a rather repulsive group activity. He did go but he had to walk out after the midwife, a stern woman whose appearance was better suited to a concentration camp, had said, 'Now ladies,' and then looking at the men with definite scorn, 'and gentlemen. I want to reassure you all again, that giving birth is a natural and usually painless experience. Is there anyone here who has had a child before?'

Curiously there was only one, a good looking young black girl put up her hand. 'I have.'

'Now then Mrs ..'

'Lords.'

'Now then Mrs Lords. You tell us in your own words what it was like.'

'Well,' a pause for perhaps dramatic effect, 'it was like the bottom half of my body was being torn bit by bit from my top half.'

There had been a collective gasp, whether it was at the girl's honesty or just that they had been vividly reminded of what lay ahead of them he could not tell, but Ralph had chuckled, then snorted and then burst out laughing. He could not stop. He wanted to stuff a handkerchief into his mouth as, when he later told the story across a dinner table, 'Veritable tears of merriment streamed down my cheeks.' He had got up, waving rather than speaking his apologies, the outraged glares only made him find it funnier, and left the room where he had stood chuckling until Tina found him.

'Honestly Ralph. What was so funny?'

'Everything, just everything. What the girl said, the thought of some of these couples copulating. What their babies will be like. The nurse handing over a child, like in the Charles Adams cartoon, and saying 'you've had a BABY?' The fact that most of them believe that childbirth will be a nice quiet clean affair when in reality it's painful, dangerous and not particularly nice at all. No sweet cherubs dancing round your head, no sound of harps tinkling, the gentle compassionate midwife, a relaxed husband saying, 'There there dear, it'll be all right in a moment and a child emerging, 'pop',' he made the noise with his finger in his mouth, 'no, they'll be lucky to have a midwife, midwifery is chronically understaffed, they'll all want gas and air, some will start screaming for an epidural when it's too late to give them one and, for some, the labour will go on so long, they'll have to use forceps or even,' and he looked at Tina with his eyes wide open, a smile on his face, 'cut them open. Oh dear, oh dear,' and started laughing again.

Tina was not impressed, 'Don't be so gross. It won't be like that.'

'No, our child will be born to the sound of doves cooing and its father and mother totally relaxed, lying together sipping champagne as someone else does the beastly business. Come on Tina. It'll be all right on the night.'

'You won't be. You won't know how to do anything. You'll be as useful as, I don't know.'

He was suddenly serious again.

'Tina, just because I'm not coming to these dreary ante-natal classes does not mean that I will know nothing about it. I've read the books.'

'When?'

'When you've been asleep. I'll be all right, I promise.'

Tina, of course, had no idea of the date of conception. She was pretty certain that Ralph was the father, but given the events that had taken place, could only hope that the baby would bear a resemblance to him. She was also certain that, since her body had always been regular, she could usually set a clock by her periods, that she would go full term and give birth within a day or two on either side. She had therefore pencilled out a whole week in her diary, telling Ralph that the baby would be born then.

'I don't know how you can tell. But I'll believe you. I'll tell them that I won't be in that week and they should forward post to me.'

'Can't you, just for once, take a week off?' she almost wailed.

'Look, I can do my paperwork while you're in hospital and afterwards when you're asleep. You'll do a lot of sleeping. I know this, believe me.'

She ignored him. 'We'll see,' she replied.

As the week approached, Tina became more and more anxious. She did not want to let Ralph out of the house to go anywhere, let alone his Chambers.

'What happens if my waters break in town?'

'Don't go to town. Tell me what we need and I'll get it.'

Tina did not, however, so he did not do any shopping but did, in fact, only go to Chambers for the minimum amount of time necessary.

CATHARSIS

The Wednesday of the week before B Day, as Tina referred to it, was like many others. They made love in the morning, Ralph having overcome his fastidiousness about doing it, with a baby only inches from the end of his willy, a long time ago, had reconciled himself to the thought. They had got up, Ralph washing and putting a suit on, when suddenly Tina said, 'My waters have gone. I've got funny pains in my tummy.' She was standing in a puddle on the carpet. 'I've got to go to hospital. Now.'

'No, there's plenty of time. It will be hours yet. I'll take you when I get back.'

'You'll fucking well take me now Ralph. I think I've started contractions. In fact I'm sure I have.'

Ralph, slightly irritated, because he had spoken on the phone to solicitors about a particularly interesting case the day before and, having promised to send formal instructions immediately, if they had posted them, the papers would be in his pigeonhole today, sighed.

'Why the fuck are you sighing Ralph? Interfering with your day am I? I'm sorry but if your job is more important than your baby...'

'It's not that. It's just that if we go now, we might be sent home...'

'...or you might have to wait hours and hours,' she finished for him. 'So be it, you can take a book,' and went to get her hospital suitcase which had been packed already a month earlier.

'Come on then,' and Ralph went to get his hospital bag

which he too had already packed.

In the car Tina was silent, grimacing from time to time, and was out of the car, and walking towards the entrance before he had switched the engine off. Ralph trailed in afterwards to find her already being led to a side room. 'Would you please take off your clothes and put this gown on Mrs Edwards,' said a softly-spoken young midwife, who Ralph immediately liked and at whom he smiled encouragingly.

Tina did as she was asked and the midwife said, diffidently, even apologetically, 'I'm afraid I'm going to have to do an internal. Would you mind spreading your legs as wide as possible. There,' putting on rubber gloves, 'just relax while I,' inserting her fingers, Ralph watching with what he hoped was a detached and scientific expression, 'yes, I can feel it now. You're about four centimeters dilated already.' Pulling out her fingers, or was it her whole hand, Ralph was already not sure, she turned to Ralph and said, 'Just as well you got her here quickly. I suspect that its going to be a quick and easy labour.'

Tina stuck her tongue out at him and he shrugged his shoulders.

'Let's connect up the monitors,' the midwife said and then they could hear the sound of a heartbeat, which seemed arrhythmic to Ralph and caused the nurse to wrinkle her nose and say, 'I'll just get the on-call doctor,' and go from the room.

Tina looked frightened and called out, 'Don't leave me.'

'Don't worry. Your husband's here and I'm only just round the corner.'

She came back within a few minutes accompanied by an incredibly pretty blonde doctor, who unaccountably reminded Ralph of Virginia.

'Hi, I'm Dr Seymour. Call me Jennie please. You're?'

'Ralph and Tina,' he answered. 'Are you Australian?'

'Yes. Now, Tina, may I do an internal quickly?'

Rubber gloved hands went into Tina again, and the doctor smiled, 'Yes, dilating nicely.' She had been listening to the monitor, concentrating on the noises and then, asking Tina to roll first on one side, the other, palpated her stomach gently.

'When were you last seen by my boss, Mr Phillips?'

'I haven't actually seen him. I saw a junior doctor the last time.'

'I'll check your notes, but I'd like Mr Phillips just to check you over.'

'Why?' Tina's face had an air of panic and Ralph was becoming concerned.

'Jennie, what's wrong? Is there something amiss?'

'No, absolutely not. Your wife is a picture of health, there's certainly a healthy baby in there. It's just that I think it might be...'

'Yes what?' Ralph thinking of all the bad taste baby jokes he wished he had not told.

'I think Tina may be having twins.'

'Christ,' Tina muttered, 'no wonder I felt as though...'

'What? Acute indigestion and terrible runs,' finished Jennie. 'Let's see what Mr Phillips says. I'll be back soon,' leaving Ralph and Tina by themselves.

'I don't believe it,' muttered Ralph.

'I do. I've told you over and over again that there seemed an awful lot of activity in there. But I never thought it might be two.'

Ralph remembered the scan, he had been wrong as the image

had turned up in the post, and the difficulty he had had in reading it. This would certainly be an explanation.

Tina's face suddenly screwed up, 'God, that was a big one.'

'I think you're supposed to start counting between them about now,' Ralph muttered again, and looking at his watch groaned, 'Tina, we're not ready for twins.'

They had been superstitious, had agreed that they did not want to be as flies to wanton boys and killed by the Gods for sport, so had delayed and delayed buying any baby things, she capitulating on an agreement that immediately it was born, Ralph would go to the baby shop and buy a carrycot, a proper cot, a pram and baby clothes from a list that Tina had compiled in conjunction with the owner. Ralph was to decorate the child's room in the first week after the birth.

'You'll just have to buy two of everything,' Tina said with grim satisfaction.

'I should have taken out an insurance policy,' he replied.

'Too late, smart arse.'

'What's with the language? It's not like you.'

'I'm cross with you.'

'What on earth for?'

'Being so bloody complacent.'

'I'm not complacent.'

They were both annoyed, as though the news, but not yet news, had unsettled them and left them each feeling stupid at the expense of the other. Just then Mr Phillips came in with Jenny, smiling broadly.

'Mr and Mrs Edwards? How do you do?' He held out his hand to Ralph who shook it, surprised at the courtesy.

'I'm Ralph. This is Tina.'

'Ralph Edwards, do I know that name? I'm sure I've heard it.'
'There was a famous furniture historian in the twenties.'
'No, no, I've heard it in connection with someone else.' He stopped and thought. 'A barrister called Ralph Edwards successfully represented one of my colleagues a couple of years ago.'
'I'm a barrister. What was your colleague called?'
'Jim Sullivan.'
'I represented him in a medical negligence case about three years ago.'
'Did a bloody fine job for him. He was, we all were, very pleased. Good to meet you. I'd better take special care of Tina, hadn't I,' and chuckled. 'Internal time and more examinations, I'm afraid.' Just then Tina grimaced again.

'A contraction. Any idea how long between them?' he asked. Ralph looked at his watch. 'Six minutes, thirty-five seconds.'

'You're like a bloody computer,' Tina said admiringly. 'It seemed more like three minutes.' Mr Phillips had finished his examination.

'I can't be certain but I'm absolutely sure that there is more than one baby in there. Well done Jenny. I'm glad you called me. Let's ready ourselves for two should we? I'll be back later.'

They were left alone again.

'Ralph, I'm not enjoying this. I'm a bit scared. It hurts a lot. I didn't want to tell them.'

'Just have some gas and air.'

'I'm not sure I don't want an epidural.'

'Epidurals carry risks. They're not exactly good news.'

'Having babies is a risk.'

'Gas and air,' he replied, 'gas and air.'

The midwife came back periodically, and then when Tina was

six centimeters dilated, and the contractions were at three-minute intervals, started readying herself and the room, pulling out trays, swabs, getting a gas cylinder out of a cupboard, a trolley out of another.

'Christ Ralph, it's suddenly like an operating theatre in here,' she groaned, face white and wet with perspiration, biting her lips violently as another contraction convulsed her.

'It's got to be soon.'

'Come on, it's not long now,' the midwife was sympathetic, 'I'm going to stay with you until the baby or babies are born.' She smoothed Tina's brow with a cloth, dipped into a basin and passed it to him. 'You could do this. If you just sit there, and hold her hand.'

'I don't want my fucking hand held. I want my hands free...'

Ralph stretched out and took her fist. 'Squeeze my hand, as hard as you like,' and she relaxed again and let it lie limply in his.

'This is agonising,' she groaned through clenched teeth. 'Is it feeble to want some gas and air? I'm sorry, I don't know your name.'

'I'm Mary. No, it isn't. Here all you do is put on the mask and breathe, long deep breaths. Like this,' and she demonstrated. Tina seized the mask and panted into it, sounding, Ralph thought, again incongruously, like a steam train. She relaxed but then, another contraction and the mask was on again.

'Christ, oh Christ, what the fuck. Fucking hell. Bastards, fuck.' She seemed to recover herself. 'I'm sorry. For the language. It's just that...'

'It's all right. Most women are the same,' Mary said. 'Just

let yourself go. I've heard it all before. So, I expect, has your husband.'

No, I haven't, thought Ralph. It's a side to Tina that's new to me, but said nothing. Tina's contractions were becoming closer to one another, and with each, she inhaled the gas and air.

'Oh God, oh God, what have I done to deserve this,' she moaned. 'Bastards, bastards, I shouldn't be doing this. I shouldn't be doing this. Oh fuck, oh fuck. I shouldn't be doing this. Ian, oh Ian, why are you making me? We shouldn't. Fuck, fuck, fuck.'

Her eyes opened, glazed and she turned. 'I can't go through with this,' she said, not looking at either of them.

Ralph had been listening. A cold shiver ran up his spine, angels walked across his grave, and he felt sweat appear on his forehead. He saw the nurse looking at him.

'Don't worry Ralph. She's completely out of it. She's no idea what she's saying.' She smiled encouragingly. Ralph did not know what to do or say and smiled a thin, wan smile that had no humour.

'It's not long now Tina,' the nurse whispered. 'Keep going, you're doing fine.'

Tina did not appear to hear her, she was in the final phase of labour, panting and contracting, mask on her face, eyes tight shut.

'Bastards, cunts, bastards, cunts,' she muttered, over and over again.

'Keep on going. You'll know when you're ready to push.' Mary was imperturbable. 'Keep at it. You're doing great Tina.'

Suddenly to Ralph, the room was full of people, Jenny, Mr Phillips, Mary and another midwife. He could not bring himself to hold Tina's hand, but curious, went and stood to one side at the bottom of the bed. Tina's feet were raised in stirrups and spread out. Who knew a fanny could become so wide, so large, so...and then he saw a pale crescent in the middle.

'Push, push, now push.'

'I'm bloody well pushing. I'm fucking well pushing. Don't go on at me,' Tina shouted, face contorted, and, a vein bulging, a vein that Ralph had never noticed before.

'Fuck,' a long drawn-out cry and then, the baby was there, cradled in the arms of Jenny, passed to the midwife for cleaning, Dr Phillips bending down to look into the yawning chasm, a swift internal, 'Yes another one is on its way.'

'Push Tina,' they chorused, 'keep pushing.'

'I've had my fucking baby. It's out, I know. Why do I have to keep pushing?'

'Because you're having twins, Tina.'

No one seemed at all disconcerted by her language or abuse. Ralph watched, morbidly fascinated, as the procedure was repeated, more quickly this time and, accompanied to cries of, 'Fuck, fuck, fuck' from Tina, another baby appeared, was handed by Mr Phillips to the midwife, Mr Phillips doing an internal examination, standing up taking his gloves off, looking sympathetically at Tina, lying there, eyes closed, gasping for air, hair wet with sweat, bedraggled, gown round her waist, feet in stirrups, and turned to Ralph and said, 'A nice straightforward delivery. You're the father of twins.'

'Are they healthy?'

Jennie turned and said, 'Full complement of everything.'

'Everything?'

'Well not everything in one sense,' she laughed. 'You're the father of twin girls.'

Tina, opening her eyes, smiled. 'Girls. Where are they? Where are my girls,' and started weeping, a flood of tears. Ralph, quietly, moved next to her and kissed her.

His were mixed emotions but he started crying as well, his cheek against hers, and then, the midwife said, 'Here you are,' she having gently removed Tina's legs from the metal fetters, lain her legs on the bed, removed the afterbirth and swabbed Tina, pulled her gown down, and put a cover over her. 'Your two girls. Do you know,' she looked hard at Ralph, 'they've got your mouth.'

At that, Ralph let out a sigh, a long relieved and happy sigh, his earlier doubts forgotten, and started sobbing quietly beside his adored and adorable Tina. He recovered, taking out a handkerchief, mopping his eyes and cheeks and looked at Mary.

'Sorry,' he sniffed. 'I was overcome.'

'Don't worry. It's not every day you get the gift of two gorgeous little girls.'

Ralph finally, all he had seen so far were seemingly blue, little, faceless shapes passed from hand to hand, looked at the babies, each swaddled, lying on Tina's tummy.

He knew that they would change colour as their systems acclimatised themselves to being outside their mother in a new, harsh and alien, environment. He was prepared to accept, without question, the medical assurances that the twins were healthy, and he looked at them, both with his mouth and then at Tina, who was looking at him, brightly and triumphant, and felt as though he had climbed Matterhorn, but without any oxygen.

'Do you think that you would like to try feeding them Tina?'

asked Mary. 'Look, like this,' and she withdrew Tina's breasts, and putting a baby near each nipple, showed Tina what to do. Both babies started sucking without any encouragement.

'Ah,' said Mary, 'they're going to be good little girls.'

Smoothing Tina's brow again, she smiled at them. 'I'll be round the corner if you need me. You'll want some time alone,' and was gone, the door hissing as it closed behind her.

'I'm just coming round,' Tina said. 'Aren't they beautiful? Was I out of it? I can't remember anything. Just the pain and a roomful of people. God. It was awful.'

'I think you were out of it. Completely. Lost to the world.'

'Oh God, I didn't make a fool of myself, did I?'

'No. They said it was quite normal.'

'What was normal.'

'Your expletives.'

'Oh no, I didn't, did I?'

'A bit, but never mind,' he bent and kissed her. 'They're lovely. What shall we call them?'

'I just don't know. I'm so tired. All I want to do is sleep. Ralph, oh God, I love you. Thank you, thank you, thank you for two little girls. I've got everything anyone can want. Do you think they've had enough to eat? Drink I mean. I've no idea. My bosoms feel empty. Do you think you could get Mary, please. Oh Christ, I'm so tired,' and she shut her eyes again.

Ralph went to the nurses' station. Mary was not there, she was now in another room with another mother. A midwife said she would look in soon and Ralph, standing for a moment, outside the door of Tina's room, was asked by another man, 'Has she had it, then?'

'Them actually,' said Ralph feeling proud and a ridiculous,

he knew, sense of achievement.

The man looked at him pityingly. 'Them. Twins you mean? You poor fucker. I hope it doesn't happen to me,' before turning and going into the room opposite.

Silly sod, thought Ralph, pushing open the door.

Tina was lying there, eyes half open, still smiling, still holding the twins to her breasts. 'I think they've fallen asleep. Look. I've been studying them. They're identical. Your mouth, my nose. It's amazing. I just want to cry. I'm so bloody happy and relieved.'

'So am I, so am I,' Ralph said. 'I feel as though I've had them myself. Absolutely drained. Emotionally and physically.'

'Are you going home?'

'I don't know. What do you want me to do?'

'Get the baby stuff. What time is it?'

'I've no idea. I'll look,' and checking his watch, Ralph was astonished to find that five hours had passed since they had come through the door. 'It's 1.15, no wonder I'm hungry.'

'You go and have something to eat and come back later. I'll be all right, Ralph,' said Tina quietly. 'You know, I don't think I'm going to be able to do it for a while. You won't mind will you?' She looked at him tenderly, 'But we'll find a way, I promise,' and smiled, and waved as he left the room after he had kissed her.

He got into the car, feeling an idiotic sense of wonder, achievement and pride and understood totally why new fathers talked of walking on air. He promptly reversed into the wall behind the car and cursing and smiling, got out to inspect the damage. It was minimal, a scratch on the bumper, but this, for him, was so out of character that he switched the engine off, and sat for five minutes, trying to recover his mental breath.

At last, shaking his head and grinning widely, he drove home where he made himself several sandwiches, which he ate hungrily, drank two cups of coffee and went into town to the babyshop.

The owner remembered him and said, 'All's gone well. Happy mother and healthy baby?'

'Yes, except it's plural.'

'Plural?'

'Yes, she had twins.'

'Oh congratulations, sir.'

'No, congratulations to you. You've just sold me two of everything on this list,' and Ralph passed it to him.

He scanned it, 'Yes, I can do all that for you. Do you want to take it now?'

'No, just the clothes, the nappies, the unguents and the carrycots. I don't think we want two prams. I suppose we'll need a double which I'll come back for later, as well as two cots.'

The purchases paid for Ralph, realising that he would have to ask for an increased limit on his credit card before he came back, went and got the Mercedes, parked it on the double yellow lines outside the shop and loaded it up.

A traffic warden approached him.

'I'm sorry I was just loading up. My wife's had a baby, two in fact, this morning.'

'Congratulations, sir, take as long as you want,' and she went on her way, smiling.

Did the whole world smile at babies, about babies, Ralph wondered. Perhaps they did, a subconscious pleasure at the affirmation of life in the face of inevitable death and extinction.

He looked at his watch again, nearly four pm. He'd go back at six pm he decided and went home to telephone Ken, whose reaction was predictable.

'Congratulations Ralph, you must be very proud. Well done.'

Why congratulations and well done? He had done nothing, only the act of sexual intercourse; it had been Tina who had grown them, looked after them and then squeezed them out. For the first time, he understood why women get so annoyed when men congratulated each other on having children. It was a complete nonsense, only designed to boost the male ego, which he considered generally large enough anyway. He resolved to tell Tina of his discovery.

'I'll not be in for a couple of days Ken. Is that all right?'

'Of course. Well done, old chap, bye.'

Tina gave an exclamation of joy as he opened the door. 'I was hoping it might be you. The world and his wife have been to see me since you left.'

'Who?'

'The paediatrician, the midwives, other doctors...' she trailed off. 'What have you been doing?'

'Getting these,' and he opened the suitcase on the chair. 'I think it's called a layette or two. Carry cots are at home etc etc. I've been busy. I've rung Ken and told him that...'

'You're not going to be in for a week or two?'

'No, not exactly. A few days anyway. I haven't phoned anyone else. I thought you might like to.'

'I'm feeling much better now. I have the horrible feeling I made a complete fool of myself, I was so out of it.'

She was seeking reassurance again. Did she have any idea of what she had said? Should he ask her about Ian? Not now, surely. But later, one day later. It had confirmed something that Ralph had suspected for a long time already and he found the thought sickening. Shuddering at the memory, he looked at Tina, who seemed now to be radiant with health. The babies were each in a plastic box, name tags on their wrists, sleeping peacefully.

'Aren't they beautiful, Ralph? You made them. They're yours. Aren't we lucky? Do you want to hold them?' The words came out in a rush.

'No, you can't wake them up just for me to hold them.'

'No, I need to wake them up for a feed. I'm not indulging in demand feeding. They can have regular mealtimes. I'll do six months and then that's it.'

'You've clearly got the whole process planned,' he interrupted.

'But what are we going to call them?' she continued ignoring his comment.

'Have you any ideas?' he countered.

'None whatsoever. Boys are easier. I had an idea or two but two girls. My mind's blank.'

'We've got six weeks to register them. That's plenty of time.' he replied and then sat, as she woke first one, then the other, the expression on her face like a Bellini Madonna, and gave him one to hold and put the other on her nipple.

He held the baby and Tina, catching sight of him said, with surprise, 'You're a natural father, Ralph. You don't hold her like men usually hold babies. You hold her like a woman does.'

He felt absurdly pleased at this comment and then the baby smiled at him and, again as he would later tell people at dinner parties, 'The only phrase for it, I'm afraid, and embarrassing though it is to admit it, my heart melted.'

When Tina judged that the first had had enough, and the baby had obligingly and compliantly delivered herself of a loud burp, she handed her to him and she took the other, who promptly smiled at him as well.

'She's smiling at you.'

'Yes, it's a reflex reaction. They do it to everyone,' he replied coolly, but secretly feeling very pleased, even though he knew his remark was accurate.

'My little flowers,' she said as the second burped. 'They're going to be so well behaved and good little girls.'

'Flowers, Tina, think flower names.'

'What, Holly and Ivy?' she snorted at her joke.

'No, Rose, Daisy, Poppy...'

'Buddleia, Senecio...' she continued,

'No, no the pretty ones. Primrose, Violet...'

'Nasturtium, Lupin. No actually, I like the idea. What about Poppy and Daisy.'

'There are far too many of them already. A bit common if you ask me.'

'Well, I like Daisy. I like Poppy too. What about Primrose and Daisy.'

And thus it was decided.

Ralph left her that evening, both in high spirits and hoping that she might come home in the morning, everyone having told her that she would probably be in hospital not long enough to warm the bed. Ralph slept fitfully again, that night, was it the first he had spent apart from Tina and woke knowing that he needed her body, her warmth beside him, not just physically but metaphysically as well. He went in at 11 am and was greeted by Tina still in bed. He had thought she might have been dressed and waiting for him and his disappointment was evident.

'No, I'm coming home tomorrow. They just want to be sure that everything is all right.'

'Like what? The girls are OK, are they?' She nodded.

'You're OK?' She nodded again.

'Then discharge yourself and let's go.'

'I'd rather do as they suggest. They're the experts. You expect people to take your advice.'

'Yes, but...'

'No I'm going to stay in another night. I've decided. Sorry and all of that. I miss you too Ralph. There's nothing I'd like better than to be at home with you, sleep with you, hold you. I had a terrible night. Hardly slept.'

'Neither did I. I had troubled dreams. About losing you.'

'Silly, I won't leave you. You'd have to get rid of me. Scrape me out of your life.' She kissed him and turned to the babies, asleep, in their cots.

'You know, they've run at exactly four-hour intervals. All they've done is sleep, been woken up, get fed, burp, smile and go to sleep again. If they're like this, then it's going to be a doddle. Knackering making the milk, though. I guess I'll need lots and lots of bed rest.' She stressed the word bed and he felt himself stir, 'But none of that yet. Not for a few weeks at least. God, I'm tired. I think I want to go back to sleep,' and yawned.

Ralph felt torn between staying and just holding her hand quietly and getting on with something. 'I'll leave you now and come back later.'

'Must you?' she said blearily.

'No, but I'll be back later,' and bending, he kissed her, but she was already asleep; a beatific smile and regular breathing.

He knew exactly what he was going to do, went straight to the DIY centre and bought more paint. He worked like a maniac, hardly stopping to eat or drink, and by the late afternoon had finished the walls and done a base coat on the woodwork. He quickly showered, to get rid of the smell of white spirit, and dressed, and then he visited her again.

'I've been on the phone since I saw you last, what have you been doing?'

'Paperwork,' he lied.

'I think Primrose and Daisy. They seem like Primrose and Daisy.'

'How do you tell the difference?' He was looking at them, seemingly identical.

'Primrose has a slightly larger nose.'

'Why is that one Primrose?' he asked looking at the two babies. He was not at all sure either had a nose larger than the other but was not prepared to admit that he had failed to discern this.

'Well one of them has to be. It's fate. Chance. That sort of thing. Or we can go back to the drawing board and start again. You know, Alison, Beatrice, Clara, Diana, Edwina, Fanny,' and giggled, 'Pussy'.

'Oh, Christ, no Tina. Let's stick with those names but let's give them some more so they have a choice later on.'

They spent the next hour discussing girls' names, finally deciding that they could not make a decision, and that they would narrow the choice down to four names each and then discuss it again in the morning.

'I've been told I can leave tomorrow. The doctor's ward round is at eleven am so all things being equal, back for lunch. Can you be here for twelve?'

'Yes, most certainly.'

'I love you Ralph. It's time to feed them. Do you want to get them up?'

He picked up first one, then the other, and then, turning at the door, saw her smile, the same beatific smile as she had worn when asleep the previous evening.

Tina was happy, she started singing them a lullaby as he went, and he wondered how far he would feel emotionally and physically excluded now from her. Would the girls take over life to the extent he and Tina would have no time for one another? They had had, after all, so little time together, by themselves. She seemed to have been pregnant immediately and, whilst he had managed to ignore their presence inside her, she did not have to do anything for them then, now that they were here, with demands, feeding, changing, burping, ailments, might she have to have more time for them than him? He could hardly bring himself to consider the prospect. He took out an instant meal from the freezer, microwaved it and ate quickly. He intended to finish the nursery that evening.

He collected Tina, Primrose and Daisy the following day, after going to the babyshop for expert advice on car seats, having read that the safest place was the front passenger seat, but being sold two rear facing seats that he was assured were more than adequate.

'Is your midwife on duty?'

'Yes, I've seen her this morning.'

'Do you want to give her these or shall I?'

'Ralph, what a lovely thought. You do it. She's probably at

the nurses' station.' Ralph found her and handed her a large box of chocolates. She seemed embarrassed

'No, it's only my job.'

'You made it much more pleasant for us both. Please.'

'Thank you. And forget what she said when she was delirious.' It must have concerned Mary, perhaps she had seen him wince, look pained, hurt, angry even. Ralph did not know, but smiled, 'Of course,' having already worked hard at forgetting but unsuccessfully.

Tina chattered, chattered was exactly the right word, for her stream of consequential and inconsequential stories, how excited her parents had been, when they were visiting, how Frances and Henry had rushed over to see her, how Sylvia was coming over, when were they going to paint the nursery, how had he been, had he eaten, the hospital food wasn't bad, the staff were wonderful, could they, did he think, have Jenny over to dinner, what were they having for supper, until Ralph interrupted and said 'Primrose and Daisy are stirring.'

'Stop the car, I want to check them.'

'Come on, we're nearly home.'

'No, stop the car please.'

'It's stupid, we're here now.'

'There's a good mile to go.'

'And as we speak, we get nearer.'

'All right. Twins, we're nearly home. Your new house. You can't see, you poor little things.'

'Come on, let's get them in, you take one and I'll take the other.'

'Which one is your side?'

'Daisy,' she replied confidently. 'They need a feed and a sleep.

We'll put them in our bedroom for the first few weeks.'

'Can't they go in the nursery?'

'We'll put them so they can't see what we're doing, don't worry, Ralph. But no, don't you want to be able to hear them breathing? To make sure they're all right.'

'Yes I suppose I do,' he said, having had a horror of cot deaths since she announced her pregnancy. They went upstairs and put the babies on their double bed.

'I'll get the cots. I put them in the nursery.'

'I'll help,' and she came with him and shouted when she saw what he had achieved.

'Ralph, it's beautiful. When did you learn to do dragging?'

'I know it's a bit passé but I've always liked the effect.' The room was a soft pastel pink with all the wood work dragged in a cloudy blue.

'The colours are lovely. What a genius. They'll love it.'

Already she had invested them with personalities and preferences. 'I must bring them in and show them.'

'Tina,' he said with affection.

Soon after the birth, Sylvia and her boyfriend had come over for the day. It was a pleasant family occasion,. they all six went out in the Mercedes, a bit of a squash but Robert was happy enough to squat in the boot and Tina sat between the twins in the rear, Sylvia beside Ralph. Walking round the park Ralph found himself between Sylvia and Tina.

'How are things Ralph?' she asked, 'Being a father and all of that?'

'It's wonderful,' Tina answered for him, 'he only goes to his Chambers now to pick up the post and say the occasional hello. Little court work so he's home usually by early afternoon, aren't you darling?'

'Well, I've got to keep an eye on you and the children. Make sure you don't come to any harm,' he joked.

'Well, it's nice having you at home nearly all the time,' Tina said with apparent sincerity. 'He has more time with the children than most men.'

'I'm seeing them grow up. I'll be there during their formative years. Once they go to school, that's it. Poof. They're gone, you've handed them over to society at large. Do you remember what Ratty said to Mole in Wind in the Willows anyone?'

No one did.

'Beyond the wild woods, there's the wide world. Don't go there. I suppose it sums it up for me. The world's a nasty dangerous place.'

'It's only because you inhabit a world that's peopled by criminals and accident victims,' said Sylvia.

'No it's not. The world is a dangerous place. Even in this

town, the one we live in, you can't safely walk down the streets without fear of getting mugged, raped if you're a woman, and when you stagger back to your house, bruised, bloodied and walletless, the chances are that some toerag will have burgled it and trashed the place.'

'It's a gloomy view Ralph,' said Sylvia.

'I sometimes think that Ralph worries too much. You're overprotective in many ways.'

'I'm not,' he retorted with barely suppressed irritation.

'No, I know you're not. You're a loving, caring and considerate husband and father,' and she smiled, stopped for a moment, kissed him and said, 'and that's why I love you. Come on, let's go and feed the ducks.'

Watching Robert and Tina throwing bread on the water, the twins of course far too young to be able to attach any significance to the activity but perhaps aware of the noises and flapping of wings, Sylvia came up to Ralph, 'She's radiant isn't she. Look at her. You'd never think that only a few weeks ago, she was big with child, huffing and puffing. I've never seen her look more content, or happy, not even the day you married her.'

'I think she's beautiful.'

'Thanks for the compliment.'

Ralph coloured; it was true, the two women looked very alike. 'You know what I mean.'

'I'm only teasing you Ralph.'

'Sylvia, she is beautiful. I wonder if I deserve her.'

'Of course you do. What a nonsense. Why do you say that? It's what she's said to me on the telephone. She doesn't think she deserves you. She worships you, idolises you. You can do no wrong. You must realise that.'

'I have such dark thoughts all the time. Did she have many boyfriends?'

To Sylvia it must have seemed an abrupt change of subject, but to Ralph it was a natural question following the mention of his dark thoughts. She looked puzzled for a moment.

'Why do you ask? You're surely not the insecure type. She'd never be unfaithful to you.'

'She was to St John.'

'She left him for you.'

'If it hadn't been me it could have been anyone else.'

'But it wasn't. And no, I don't remember her having many boyfriends at all, but then I was two years younger. I think there may have been one or two before St John. I don't really remember. It's a long time ago.'

How sisters protect one another thought Ralph, but said nothing except, 'It's a funny old world. You must qualify soon,' and, when Sylvia nodded, and said, 'Next June,' Ralph asked, 'What are you going to do?'

'I'm not sure. I'm toying with the idea of lecturing. Going back to University. It would be nice to be Professor Sylvia Bond after a doctorate.'

'Not a lot of money.'

'Well there isn't in being a provincial solicitor, unless you're in a big firm.'

'Become a barrister?'

'No, too many egos around. Too much self-absorbed narcissism. I don't include you, mind. My turn to apologise,' she added hastily.

'No, the funny thing is, I agree with you,' he said as they were joined by Tina, Robert and the hideously ill-designed contraption that was called a buggy.

Later that afternoon, back at their house, Robert cheerfully ensconced in the front of the television and a rugby match, Ralph reading the newspapers, Sylvia and Tina were in the kitchen.

'Tina?'

'Yes?'

'I had a really funny conversation with Ralph while you were feeding the ducks.'

'What do you mean?'

'He asked whether you had had many boyfriends.'

'What did you say?'

'Just one or two.'

'Thanks Sylvia, I'll do the same for you. And by the way, if he ever asks you about crotchless knickers just tell him that you gave me them, would you?'

Sylvia laughed, 'That's what sisters are for.'

The months passed, a routine established largely by the presence of small children and the need to attend to their immediate needs, Ralph still nervously, but metaphorically only, looking over his shoulder and wondering as to the author of the note he had found in his pigeonhole. He could not relax in Chambers, had little social dealings with anyone there apart from Ken, to whom he would speak from time to time, but the fact that there was no further note, no further communication at all, did nothing to allay Ralph's anxieties and about which he confided to no one.

Ralph was quite happy with his paperwork practice, occasionally matters would go to trial but, since most civil cases settle before the parties actually ever reach the courts and then again very often outside the courtroom door, his actual number of court appearances was very small.

He had decided to give up criminal practice after Jim Deacon's case, 'I've no stomach for it any longer Ken,' he had said apologetically, and had refused to reconsider his decision despite Ken's entreaties and this, coupled with the drying up of work from some firms whose partners never forgave him for Virginia's death, meant that his income suffered a terrible drop.

Ralph was unconcerned but being short of money upset Tina, who found herself in an even worse position than when she had been married to St John. Ralph was not ungenerous, but money was definitely, in Tina's words, 'bloody tight'.

Nevertheless, they did entertain occasionally and Frances and Henry had come to dinner. The two couples saw one another on a fairly regular basis, staying the night in each other's houses so that no-one need moderate alcohol consumption. This was usually quite substantial and on most occasions all would go to their respective bedrooms slightly the worse for wear. They had already drunk three bottles of wine before they sat down at the table and Frances, particularly, was giggly and cheerfully uninhibited.

'Do you remember that time when we all went to Alton Towers and you,' nodding at her husband, 'refused to get on that ride?'

'It wasn't me who refused to get on it, it was Tom.'

'No. Tom and Jo were happy to get on it. It was you.' She was vehement.

'That's rubbish, it was Tom.'

It seemed to be developing into an argument, so Ralph said, 'It's a funny thing, isn't it, memory. We all have one but none of us seem to have the same recollections, even about important things, let alone the unimportant. We base our judgments and understanding of events, people, life itself on evidence. Make our judgments based on evidence. But do we always understand that evidence or do we sometimes, maybe frequently, misunderstand it? Misread it and draw the wrong conclusions? And where then can facts lie? What, in short, is true or truth?'

'What do you mean?' Tina asked with interest.

'Well, here's Frances and Henry arguing about something that's important to them at the moment although unimportant in the greater scheme of things. In a court of law, they'd each swear they were telling the truth, wouldn't you?'

He looked at them both and they nodded.

Frances said, 'I swear on the bible that it was Henry who wouldn't get on,' and Henry immediately riposted by saying,

'I swear on the bible it was Tom.'

Ralph continued, 'One of you must be wrong. One of you must be lying. Neither of you has any reason to lie but each of you thinks, or more than that, is convinced that what you say is true or a fact. Can there be such a thing as a fact if the existence or event itself is disputed?'

'Of course there are facts. Things happen. That's a fact,' Tina said.

'Sure, but if neither of you remembers if properly, can it still be a fact for you?'

'We'd agree about the important things, the important facts, wouldn't we Frances?'

'Of course we would.'

'I'm not sure you would, you know,' smiled Ralph. 'Should we try?'

They were intrigued by this proposition and Frances said, 'Go on then, try us.'

'Let's find an evening that was eventful. Important to you both. Where you'd expect to remember everything accurately because, for instance, it was unusual or the first time.'

'You want to talk about our first time Ralph,' Frances said raising her eyebrows and smiling a touch lasciviously.

'No, he doesn't,' snapped her husband.

'Pity,' she said. 'I wouldn't mind. Perhaps we can come back to it,' and giggled at her pun as Henry looked crossly at her.

'No, let's take something a bit less personal. Let's talk about the day that Sam was born. Do you both remember that?' Ralph countered.

'Yes,' said Henry and, 'Particularly well,' from Frances.

'What time of the day was he actually delivered?'

She answered, 'Three in the afternoon.'

'OK, let's start with waking up. Frances, you go first. Did you wake up knowing that Sam was going to arrive that day?'

'No, he was a week early. I had no idea.'

Henry interrupted, 'You'd been saying all the previous evening that you were sure it was going to happen that night or tomorrow.'

'I don't remember saying anything of the kind.'

'Well, I assure you, you did.'

'What did you do first?' interjected Ralph.

'Well, Henry went to work. I telephoned him at about ten to say that I thought it had started. He told me not to be so ridiculous. It can't have done, was what he said.' Henry made to interrupt again but Ralph put his finger to his lips and said, 'You'll have a turn in a moment.'

'I sat there for a time convinced it was happening and then decided to go to the hospital anyway. I telephoned Henry again and told him. He said he'd come back straight away. I told him that I wasn't going to wait and I'd meet him at the hospital.' Henry was by now metaphorically jumping up and down in his chair, he was so indignant.

'Oh go on, speak then,' Frances said to him.

'This is simply not true,' he burst out angrily. 'When she telephoned the first time, I said I'd come home then. She told me not to bother, she'd call me back. When she called me back, she got me on my mobile and I was nearly home already. I was only about five minutes away.'

'You weren't,' she said.

'I was.'

'Don't you think I've proved my point,' Ralph interrupted.

'Do you want to carry on?'

There was general agreement.

'I went to the hospital and checked into the obstetric unit. Henry found me there. I was already on a bed and they had started a monitor.'

Henry cut in again, 'You were sitting on a bed. They brought the monitor in while I was there and put it on you. I remember because it was the first time I'd seen one.'

'I think you're confused,' Frances said. 'It must be the drink.'

'I am not confused. My memory is fine. You're the one whose been drinking too much.'

'Come on, there's no need to argue, you two. Do you think I've made my point. Each of you has a completely different recollection of those events. Each of you believes what you say is true. Which is the truth? Henry's or Frances's account? In a court you might have to choose between them. Where there is a huge variance only one can be accepted. We don't need to decide but the supposition must be that the truth lies midway.'

'No it doesn't. What I said was right,' said Henry.

'It doesn't really matter does it?' said Tina 'but so what anyway?'

'The fact is that there are no real facts shared between them about it. Everything is relative. Existence is mediated only through our personal senses. My reality is different from your reality because yours is mediated through your senses. You maybe ascribe different values, attach more importance to things that I might dismiss as trivial and vice versa. What's important to me might be completely irrelevant to you.'

'Like what?' Tina asked.

'Well, everything. How can you really said to be sharing

anything if neither of you truly understands the other's view? And you can only understand a view if you know what shaped it. The history. I mean.'

Frances interrupted, 'I wonder if Henry remembers our first time?'

The question seemed utterly at odds with the argument that Ralph wanted to develop but he thought it might be amusing if he were to keep quiet and let her continue.

'I bet he doesn't.' Henry looked uncomfortable. 'You don't do you? You don't attach any importance to it?'

'I do and I do remember. I just don't feel it's appropriate to talk about it.'

'It was funny. Really. It was over before...'

'Oh come on Frances, it's a bit personal, isn't it?'

'We're among friends, it doesn't matter. It was better though than the very first time I did it. That was just a joke.'

'We don't want to hear about it Frances.' Henry snorted angrily.

Tina and Ralph were both looking amused. She continued, ignoring her husband's objections. 'The very first time I wasn't even sure it was happening.'

'Drunk, I suppose,' Henry said.

'No, I wasn't. I'd made up my mind that it was going to happen that night. I was ready. He was older than me by some years. I was sixteen. Do you know,' she said with animation, 'I'm still not sure that he was ever fully inside me. I thought he was.'

'Oh God Frances.'

'What on earth is wrong with you Henry?'

Ralph said quietly, 'No man ever likes to think of someone

else doing it to his wife or girlfriend or whatever.'

'Yes, that's absolutely true. We don't. We don't want to think about it, let alone be told about it, let alone discuss it over dinner. I don't like the idea of your being Another Man's Fuck,' Henry said angrily.

'Why not?' asked Tina. 'It happened to us all. Not just Frances and me but you two as well.'

'Was St John your first?' Frances asked suddenly.

'Oh no,' said Tina.

'I thought if this was all there was to it, sex was vastly overrated,' continued Frances. 'Really, wham bam, thank you mam. It was only later, with Henry, that I realised it could be more fun.'

Ralph sat wondering about Tina's first time. Had she bought condoms or had he? Was it planned or spontaneous? Was she drunk? He was interested, not in a prurient way, but she seemed to attach an importance to sex, their sex, such that he found it difficult to believe that it had not always been significant to her. She had dismissed sex with St John as boring. She had told Ralph that she had never had an orgasm through sexual intercourse. He had found that too difficult to credit but was prepared to suspend his disbelief because, he supposed, he wanted to or even needed to. Like Proust and his Albertine, he needed to know, could not let go of the lack of not knowing. Or to paraphrase Proust, in order to get rid of the pain caused by the fact that these things had taken place, to know not only what those things were but also what she felt or thought of what she was actually doing, and then to pass through one's own pain to arrive at some kind of understanding.

Tina's first time had, like that of Frances, been entirely of her choosing. In her last year at school she had been going out with Tim, or at least going out with him as far as could be managed within the confines of a boarding school.

The no touching rule meant that there could be no public displays of affection, even in the town when out shopping or having coffee in the least popular of coffee bars. Going out then became a euphemism for private sexual activity seized when the opportunity permitted. Tim was a prefect and Captain of cricket. He thus had a study and was entitled to at the very least, a knock on the door, before anyone came in. In his study, Tina and he had engaged in all forms of touching, fondling, stimulation, oral and otherwise, but she had never let him go, in their then parlance, all the way.

He had remonstrated, cajoled, persuaded, flattered, bribed, but she was adamant. He had once, when both had been naked and he had been very aroused, lying on top of her tried to insert himself very quickly; his fingers had been holding her open and he had just managed to ensure that his penis was exactly placed for a quick thrust to be successful when she stopped, opened her eyes and said, 'If you do, it'll be rape and I'm serious.'

Crestfallen, he had accepted, had not tried to push it, physically or intellectually and not long afterwards, started to be seen in the company of Joanne, another sixth former whose reputation and sexual appetite was legendary. At the same time, Ian, the captain of the swimming team and head of school, was chucked by his girlfriend, and found himself sitting next to Tina on a coach to a competition at another school.

Although they had both been swimming for the school for a number of years and shared certain lessons, neither had shown any interest in the other, otherwise than on a purely platonic level. They were talking and Tina, when told by Ian that he had been dumped, said, 'Gosh, what a silly girl.'

'Why?'

'I think you're rather nice.'

He slipped his hand across the seat, found hers and squeezed it. 'I think you're rather nice too. Should we be an item?'

It was as simple as that and he and Tina had settled into a similar relationship, such as she had enjoyed with Tim, within only a few days. As Head of School, Ian was better placed for privacy in that he had a study that led to a small bedroom and off this a bathroom. The increased privacy made the sexual activities slightly less furtive and anxiety ridden but Tina still, although he did not seem particularly bothered anyway, maintained her policy of not allowing pelvic penetration as she called it.

Anything else, however, was permissible and they played a dangerous game, but all the more enjoyable for that, of seeing how intimate they could be with one another in the swimming pool and under water. Each would swim up alongside the other and try and wiggle a finger or hand underneath the other's swimming costume for a quick feel. Tina had, on one occasion, managed as they were both at the side listening to the instructor who was addressing another group on the far side of the pool, got her hand down the front, closed her fingers round him and, finding him instantaneously semi-erect, had rubbed him to a full erection, and could hardly contain her laughter when the instructor, turning round, said, 'Right out of the water you two and to the deep end.'

Tina had quickly lifted herself up and out and leaned down to offer a hand to Ian, who blushing furiously, had suddenly swum as hard and fast as he could towards the other end. After that he was a bit more circumspect when Tina came near him.

Quite often Tina would use his bathroom, rather disliking the communal facilities which were all that was afforded to her, and she would then lock both the bedroom and the bathroom doors and enjoy the complete privacy of a relaxed bath, a luxury that was otherwise deemed only appropriate for the Head of School.

Ian and Tina had shared showers together, soaping each other's crevices, but this was only very rarely; it was one thing rearranging themselves or dressing hastily when dry, but quite another if they were both soaking wet.

One afternoon in the summer term Tina had been, with a group of friends, watching the First XI play a match against a neighbouring school. Tina found cricket stupefyingly dull, had nothing better to do, but remarked on Tim's batting.

She had stayed until he was bowled out and then, feeling hot and sticky, decided to have a shower, to cool down and freshen up. She had gone to Ian's set, knocked, received no answer, gone in and into the bathroom. She was standing, shower full on, when she heard someone in the bedroom. She had forgotten to lock the door and all her clothes were on the bed.

'Is that you Tina?' came Ian's voice.

'Yes, do you want to join me?' Tina called quietly as she went and opened the door a fraction.

'Tim's with me,' Ian replied and Tina hesitated.

'Should I join you as well?' It was Tim's voice.

Ian laughed, 'I don't mind if Tina doesn't mind.'

'I don't mind if you don't mind,' she replied and opened the door fully. She was naked but both Tim and Ian had seen her in that state so frequently she thought nothing of it. She giggled when she saw them both looking hesitant.

'It's all right Tina, I was only joking,' Tim said with a apologetic expression.

'I wasn't. Come on, let's have a shower together.' She thought of the occasion when, during her French exchange trip, she had shared a shower and a lot of her body with the twin older brothers of Marie-Rose and how much she had enjoyed the combined attention of the two sixteen-year-olds.

Ian looked at Tim and Tim looked at Ian, both wide-eyed. Ian kicked off his shoes, took off his shirt, undid his trousers and let them fall to the ground. He stepped out of them and utterly unselfconsciously took off his underpants.

'What are you waiting for Tim,' he said pleasantly. 'She's asked us to have a shower together,' and went and locked the bedroom door.

Tim, more diffidently, undid the buttons on his cricket shirt, unbuttoned the fly on his old-fashioned cricket trousers and took his clothing off.

'It's like a striptease isn't it,' said Tina. 'Hurry up,' and went back and stood under the shower. A moment later the two boys joined her and they stood together in silence.

'Have you locked the door?' Tina asked.

'Yes, both of them.'

Tina said, 'Good, we wouldn't want to get caught like this would we now?'

'Oh Christ, what a scandal. What a hoot.'

They all started laughing together, a sudden release of tension.

'What are we going to do now then?' Tina asked.

They were standing very close together.

Tina facing them. 'I thought you both might like to wash me.'

Tim got some soap and started lathering it in her hands.

'No, I meant lick me clean.' She saw them look at one another.

'Come on, you've both done that to me often enough. Don't be shy.'

Tina wanted to see if either or both would become aroused. Tim started licking her neck. Ian dropped to his knees and started on her stomach, moving his hands up and down the insides of her thighs, closer and closer.

Tim moved and dropped his head and took a nipple in his mouth, rolling it round his tongue.

Tina was impatient, she wanted fingers or a tongue inside her, and so she pushed Ian's head further down. She had had no idea what would happen when she suggested both should join her, but now had started to consider the possibilities.

She looked down at Ian, kneeling at her feet, and could see that he had become entirely aroused; she turned and looked at Tim - he was likewise beautifully stiff. Ian was by now licking between her legs and had inserted one finger and was moving this up and down. Tina was squirming with pleasure and gasped, 'Change places.'

The two boys did as they were told and Tim immediately stuck his tongue in her and wiggled it, a trick he had perfected with Tina and which he knew always sent her wild.

'Oh God, I'm coming, carry on, carry on, Tim.' She shuddered at the sudden explosiveness of her orgasm and then, recovering herself said, 'Stand side by side,' which they did, each looking at the other's erection.

Not much to choose between them, thought Tina, and kneeling in front of both boys took one in each hand and started rubbing them simultaneously. She knew Ian had more staying power than Tim so squeezed Ian's a bit harder, before putting Ian's into her mouth and sliding her lips along its length, still rubbing Tim.

Then, pulling away, she turned to Tim. She was enjoying herself and had made a decision. 'Tim.'

'Yes,' he moaned.

'Lift me up, under my bottom.' She stood in front of him, and turned.

'How?'

'So that my bottom is up in the air with your hands underneath it,' and stretched her arms behind, around his neck and clasped her hands together.

He lifted her, reached down and put his hands under her thighs. Ian was now in front, Tina's legs spread wide open.

'Put it in Ian, but gently, and slowly and stop if I tell you.'

'Put what in?'

'You know what. That. Your dick now. I want it now.'

Ian looked shocked. 'Are you sure?' he mumbled.

'Yes, but slowly.'

He stood and, taking it in his right hand, nudged the tip against her, probing.

'Now,' she moaned and he slid in, inch by inch.

'Stop a moment. Lift me slightly higher Tim.'

Tim, a strong boy, lifted, his head over her shoulder he could see everything and Tina said, 'Now, all the way,' and Ian was in.

Tina thought the sensation wonderful and muttered, her

eyes half closed with the intensity of the pleasure, 'Now gently backwards and forward but promise not to come inside me.'

His hips rocked and Tina felt the rippling of her second but slower orgasm, more internalised than the last.

'Now it's Tim's turn. Ian lie on the floor.'

Ian did this and Tina kneeled over him, sucking and caressing him, her legs wide open so Ian could see everything and Tim, kneeling behind her, then too guided himself in. He rocked backwards and forward until, Tina knew the signs well enough, he too was nearly at orgasm, she just having had a third.

'Stand up, both of you' and as they did, she knelt and grasped the two penises, rubbing hard and furiously and then, when Ian came, she sucked, spat a bit and then, as she felt the first hot spurt of Tim on her neck, immediately closed her mouth round him and did the same swallowing a bit, before standing up and muttering 'Wow.'

The two boys stood, with their eyes closed, not saying a word. Tina kissed each of them, taking care to pass some semen into each of their mouths.

'Not a bad way to spend a Wednesday afternoon, having the most erotic experience of my life,' she murmured stretching herself languorously, arms held high and breasts pushed out.

The boys looked hesitatingly at one another and then down at themselves, both now softening.

'An afternoon to remember,' one said.

Faintly embarrassed now, but they took their cue from Tina, who was totally unconcerned.

'We'd better get dry and dressed,' she said simply and laughed.

A few minutes later, sitting drinking coffee in Tim's study, neither boy was yet sure what to say.

Tina said, 'It's not to be talked about, right?'

It did not really matter; they were all leaving that term anyway. A Levels had finished and each, dependent upon results, was going to a different University.

She considered it a triumphant end to her school career; her full sexual initiation had not been the usual teenage fumble; it had been smooth, seamless and successful.

Tina had been sitting at the table with her eyes closed when Frances said, 'What's the matter Tina, thinking about your first time?'

'No, not at all,' she replied. 'Just wondering why on earth you didn't say something your first time. You know, made him think a bit more of you rather than him.'

'I guess I was too young, too nervous. I felt that perhaps that was all there was to it.'

'No, you must have known there was more to it than that. You'd had other sexual experiences hadn't you?'

'Yes, but not that one of course.'

The men had listened to their interchange deep in their own thoughts. Henry still looked uncomfortable and Frances teased him about this. 'You never thought you had married a virgin; why are you looking so glum?'

'It's not a topic that I relish talking about.'

'No, you never have. Perhaps we should have been more open with one another. You know, when we decided to get married, we considered how much to tell each other and we settled on just saying the number of sexual partners we'd had. And that's what we did.'

'Were you tempted to cheat, either of you?' asked Ralph.

'How do you mean?'

'Well, a man might want to exaggerate his 'conquests'.' They could sense he had put inserted commas there. 'And a woman might well want to minimise the number.'

'Why?' Frances looked surprised.

'Aren't men supposed to be more sexually experienced than women and don't women not want to be seen as perhaps as apparently available as the truth might suggest?'

'I can't see how.'

'Well, suppose the man had only had one partner before. And suppose the woman had had thirty. Might not the man feel slightly inadequate, he might have been refused by twenty different girls, and to hear that his, call her his wife if you liked, had had thirty, might it not suggest to him that she did it with every Tom, Dick, Dick and Dick.'

'I suppose it might. But I doubt that's anywhere near the norm,' said Frances.

'The interesting thing is that all the statistics show that women consistently claim to have had fewer sexual partners than men. What does that suggest? The numbers don't add up do they?'

'Perhaps some women do it with many more men than most and most women limit the number. It doesn't mean that most women are lying,' Tina said thoughtfully.

'I wonder if men double count and women don't count certain experiences as full sexual intercourse,' Ralph mused,

'How do you mean?' said Tina.

'Well take Frances here.'

'You take Frances, I'm not tonight. I've been totally put off the idea.' said Henry, glowering.

'We shan't need to change the sheets then will we? After you go,' said Tina brightly.

'What do you mean Ralph?' Frances asked.

'Frances might have said that what she described was not full sexual intercourse for her whereas the man would claim it.'

'Of course it was full sexual intercourse,' Frances said, 'I felt his thing inside me.' Henry winced noticeably.

Ralph was thinking of an occasion many years earlier. It must have been shortly before he met Lucy. He had gone out with Joan for at least four different periods of between six and ten weeks over the previous three years. They had a pleasant intimacy such that, when either of them found themselves between other steady boy or girlfriends, would instinctively pick up the telephone, and if the other were similarly circumstanced, suggest going out. Going out in this sense meant either staying in her bedroom at her parents' house, or his bedroom likewise and necking and fondling one another. They never actually went out anywhere. It was an understanding and pleasant relationship that both knew was going nowhere in particular, but they enjoyed the sexuality and friendship.

They had, for Ralph had in the currency of those three years had full sexual intercourse, talked about doing it together but Joan had never felt the time was right or she was ready.

One day, early in the Autumn term, she had telephoned him to say she was back from holiday and asked him what he was doing. This was their code for, 'Do you have a steady at the moment?' and he replied that he was at a loose end and asked if she would like to come over the following evening.

She had been enthusiastic and, as they sat in his bedroom,

his arm round her listening to music, she kissed him and said he had some news.

'What?'

'I've done it. Properly. On the beach after a party.'

'Did you enjoy it?' Ralph asked with disappointment, for he had hoped to be her first.

'No, not particularly. It was all a bit rushed.'

'Was it safe?'

'Yes, I'd taken precautions.'

'You knew it was going to happen then?'

'Well, I suppose I hoped it might. So, yes, I had. Taken precautions I mean. I'd bought some, you know, condoms.'

He looked at her, somewhat sadly and said, 'I always hoped that you and I would, you know.'

'I guess I always thought it would be with you Ralph but never mind.'

He kissed her slowly, traced the shape of her breast and undid the buttons of her shirt. She lay back and he undid the buckle of her belt, opened the top of her jeans and undid the zip before moving his hand inside her pants. He was becoming more urgent and she moved her legs to facilitate his exploration.

She suddenly sat up. 'Ralph. I've got a free afternoon from school tomorrow. Let's you and I do it together slowly.' She was flushed, eyes glinting with excitement.

Ralph calculated quickly. He could cut his lessons and take the consequences later. 'I'll meet you at the bus stop at one,' he said.

'Yes,' she said, 'but now we'll just do what we usually do,' and lay back, let him fondle her intimately to an orgasm, before she reached for him and deftly and expertly rubbed him until he came into the handkerchief she had thoughtfully placed nearby. The next day, when they met at the bus stop, they were both excited.

Once home, his father and mother both at work, they went to his bedroom. Neither said anything as Ralph undressed her until she lay, much more naked than usual, on his bed and he, also in a state of nearly complete undress, looked at her and said, 'Are you sure?'

'Yes,' she murmured, 'otherwise I wouldn't be here.'

Ralph slipped on a condom and got on top of her. He had just started to insert himself when they heard a car door outside and steps on the front path. He was nearly fully inside, but pulled out and went to the window. He could just see the back end of his mother's car and could hear the front door unlocking.

'Quick, get dressed. It's my mother,' he whispered. Joan, looking horrified, pulled on her jeans and top and frantically did up the buttons. Ralph did the same, pushing their underwear, her bra, his socks, shoes under the bed. Each was red, perspiring and when his mother knocked at the door, at least she had the decency to do that he thought at the time, he was able to utter a strangled, 'Yes.'

She came in and looked at the guilty pair. She must have known or at least guessed something of what they had been doing but made no comment.

'Would you both like a cup of tea?' she asked.

'Yes please Mrs Edwards,' said Joan, 'that would be very nice.'

They had never even kissed again. Neither phoned the other for a week or two. The magic of the moment had gone, both realised, and could not be replaced. It would have been futile to try. Not long afterwards Joan left with her family for the south west of England and he never saw or heard from her again.

He often wondered whether he should count the experience as one of full sexual intercourse and whether she did. If asked, later, how many sexual partners she had had, would his name be remembered as one of them?

Ralph hoped so, not from any conquest mentality, but because he had so enjoyed the teenage rites of passage that they had traversed together, and always regretted that the final one, although it would not have been the first time for either, that final one which he was going to have tried to make so special for both of them, had been such a failure.

'What are you thinking about Ralph?' Tina asked with frank curiosity. 'You seem a long way away.'

'Nothing much. Just first times.'

'You can't have first times. You can only have one first time,' Frances said.

Ralph wanted to turn the subject.

'So did you fib Frances, when Henry asked you, or did you both write them down so you couldn't change your answer in the light of the other's number?' he asked with amusement.

'Do you know, I can't remember,' she admitted after a pause. 'I just remember feeling it was more important for Henry than for me.'

'I think that's the difference between men and women,' Tina said. 'Men get much more het up about it than women. It matters less to us.'

Ralph did not want to pursue the conversation with Tina publicly but was sufficiently interested nevertheless to ask, 'Why? Why on earth should it matter less to women. Women are just as interested in sex, just as capable of feeling, perhaps more capable of feeling let down or used than men. Each sexual relationship, even when the sex was trivial and mechanical, and that in itself says something about the person, must have involved a giving, a surrender, a hugely significant event in one's life.'

'Oh, you over-romanticise it. For most people it's just another bodily function.' Tina replied, smiling at his earnestness.

Ralph suddenly thought of Virginia, to whom it had been just that, albeit a shared one, but it had never seemed of huge, or even any significant, emotional moment to her. He was wearily tired of the subject.

Henry was looking morose, had taken no part in the conversation, cradling his wineglass and staring intently into it. He spoke, a whisper only, regretfully and sadly, 'It's not so much that there was someone there before. It's simply that there is no way of knowing, or even being reassured, because by definition I think everyone says the things that they think the other wants to hear, that it is any better with you. You want it to be the best. You hope it is and you never know.'

Frances glanced at him. 'Men need so much flattery. Poor things. So insecure.'

'Only because women make us so.' He looked at her, 'only because women make us so,' and sighed.

Tina stood up. 'It's late. Should we go to bed, remember we're taking the children to the zoo tomorrow, or have one more, or a coffee?'

'Let's have a coffee,' Frances suggested.

'I might have a glass of whisky or port. Port I think,' Ralph stood. 'Anyone else?' The others nodded and Frances said, 'That would be nice.'

Ralph went out and into the kitchen. He now kept his wines in a store cupboard, no longer cellaring bottles, but buying on a weekly basis. He was bending down, head in the cupboard when he heard someone else come into the room. He stood, turning, bottle in his hand and was surprised to see Frances.

'I came to help,' she said simply, 'Where are the glasses?'

Ralph pointed to some open shelves, thought for a moment and then asked, remembering that Frances and Tina had been at school and University together, 'Did Tina have many boyfriends then?' He tried to inject the question with a light-heartedness that he most certainly did not feel.

She smiled, 'You know, when men ask that question the question they are really asking is whether she put it about a lot? Isn't that true?'

'Not really.'

'Why don't you ask Tina?'

'It seems like prying.'

'Well why ask me then? What's the difference?'

'The difference is that you have no vested interest in being honest or dishonest. You can be truthful.'

'Don't you trust Tina?'

'Of course I do.'

'Then you should ask her,' and she laughed. 'Anyway I can't tell you. We really only became friends in the second year when Tina was already going out with St John; they were an item. She was absolutely besotted with him. I've no idea what she did before then.'

Ralph was disappointed and felt curiously cheated. He had waited for a long time for an opportunity to ask Frances, considering that she would be what he thought of as a reliable witness and this line of enquiry too had come to an end. If he was ever to satisfy his curiosity, which he recognised was now more than just an idle curiosity but was becoming a need to know, he would have to ask Tina directly again.

He followed Frances into the dining room, and was struck by, now that she had lost a lot of weight, how attractive she had become. He had never noticed this before, accepting Frances and her husband as part of the furniture of their lives, comfortable, homely and unappreciated for anything apart from their functionality. He resolved to comment on it at some stage as he poured four glasses, over generously.

After they went upstairs, each couple first disappearing into their respective childrens' bedrooms to check that their offspring were still breathing, Tina went into the ensuite, emerging a few moments later in one of the rather voluminous night-dresses that she now preferred, and got into bed. She looked thoughtful.

'I think it bothers you too much,' she said looking straight at him. 'There's something unhealthy about it.'

'It only bothers me because we've, or you've never talked about it.'

'The past is the past.'

'I don't understand it. It was months before you even told me about the existence of anyone before him,' he meant St John and she knew this, 'and tonight you blithely discuss it publicly.'

'I didn't discuss anything publicly.'

'You said he wasn't your first.'

'Well he wasn't. You know that. I let him think he was the first because it seemed important to him.'

'Why can't you understand it's important to me too?'

'It's completely different. You know you're not the first. I was married.'

But I don't want to be the twenty-first, Ralph thought, but what difference would it make if I was? We're together here and now. He said instead, 'It's only that I want to know all about you. What the lie was you told him. What the truth is. That's all.'

She looked angry, 'There was one other, that's all. There, now you know.'

'One?' He was incredulous. This was not what he had imagined.

'One,' she said firmly, drawing up the bedclothes and turning her back to him.

He got into bed beside her feeling a strange mixture of elation (he finally had an answer) and bewilderment. He ran his hand down her back, nuzzling into the folds of cloth tucked into her bottom and she turned and said, 'I'm tired Ralph. Go to sleep.' Despite the amount he had drunk over the evening, he could not sleep. He tossed and turned until, exasperated, she said crossly, 'Look if you don't go to sleep now, I'm going to take some blankets and go into the twins' room.'

He lay, quietly thinking over what she had said. What she had said, in fact, had been devastatingly simple. There had been one sexual partner before her ex-husband. He knew that she had had a boyfriend called Tim, she had mentioned him once in the context of a cricketing conversation, saying that she had once gone out with a cricketer and how dull the game seemed then and still so now.

Finally, and on this thought, he did fall asleep. He had a

name and a fact. He felt strangely reassured.

The next day they all went to the zoo and spent time amusing the children and not exchanging an adult word, let alone conversation. They did not return to the subject that evening, either talking mainly of children related activities and thoughts, or their education and plans for them, the usual myriad inconsequential matters that preoccupy parents.

A month went by, a month passed like the rest of them, with Tina at home, seeing to the children's daily needs, Ralph walking every morning to the station, doing mainly paperwork - his practice by now involving even fewer court appearances - and upon returning, to find Tina in the kitchen having just fed the twins and preparing an evening meal for them. It was now much more difficult to observe the pleasant ritual, it had become such and one that Ralph valued, of gentle love-making, a shared bath and then supper.

Tina seemed happy, she had the house, the children, the use of the Mercedes, the swimming pool was up and running, and just enough money to buy herself and the children clothes, and food for all of them.

Ralph tried to be as generous as possible with the allowance, not exactly an allowance but a tacit understanding that she should spend no more than was in their joint account which he kept topped up sufficiently for these purposes.

Life was a bit of a financial struggle for Ralph, he had taken on a bigger mortgage than, with hindsight, had been sensible and he often rued his decision, endorsed at the time by Tina, to give away everything from his first marriage.

He was not bitter though; a realist, he recognised that the contentment he felt, and it was contentment, had occurred largely because of that decision although it was one, with painful hindsight, he need not have made.

He knew too, that he certainly was never going to make Q.C. and that the top fruits of his profession were to be denied to him. He was not notably bothered by this either. His practice, whilst it had diminished after Virginia had died, had grown again as memory faded but he was still not yet earning as much as he had been at the time of divorce.

The difference now, of course, that where then he had been earning what was by any standards a comfortable living, so had Virginia and there had only been the two of them. Now it was only his reduced income supporting four people, albeit two very small ones. Neither did he resent the fact that they lived in the kind of house that they did; it was as different from his and Virginia's shared ambitions as any house could be, but there was enough space, an enclosed garden, a swimming pool kept always safely fenced; the rooms were not large but neither were they small. The bedroom, their sanctuary or nest, was even luxurious. He just missed his Bristol.

Nevertheless, his thoughts often drifted to the enigma that was Tina. Perhaps it was not unhealthy or a surprise; after all, the divorce, Virginia's subsequent death and his remarriage with the twins' birth, had been the most momentous events in his life.

They had, together, conferred something approaching happiness but it was still an unresolved one and his appetite for over-intellectualising everything, seeking reasons, explanations and rational connections was left mystified by her straightforward explanation.

If she had been besotted with St John, then surely the sex must have been good? It must have been more frequent than she had ever admitted and she must, you cannot have it otherwise nowadays, have sought and achieved orgasms with him? Yet, and yet, she had claimed that she had never achieved an orgasm through penetrative sex except with him, Ralph. Had she lied to him about that, for a similar reason that she had lied to St John about it being her first time ever with him?

He could understand that lie but surely St John must have suspected? He cannot have been such a self-centred and unimaginative individual not to have thought through the obvious. Tina Ralph thought, and imagined St John must have thought likewise, was attractive and even beautiful. Had St John not pursued the subject, 'Look Tina, I just can't believe you were celibate before you met me? After all you were 19 by then?' Ralph was also bothered by the fact that Tina had commented on the size of his, and this was the word that he now found himself always using, willy and had compared his unfavourably, disparagingly even, with others? Did that not mean she must have seen more than one or two in real life? He could accept that she might have seen others on films or in pictures but in those they were never, unless he supposed it was hard pornography, shown erect.

If she had seen more than two, then surely then she had had sex with more than two? Ralph could not really imagine she could have seen them without penetrative sex taking place. Teenage non-penetrative sex, he remembered, usually took place in the dark and was a matter of grasping and groping; an activity that would usually preclude scientific and detached consideration of the length of a willy.

She had been so, and he realised those words described her, analytic, scientific and detached when she had made the comment.

Then, and this is where another genuine problem was encountered, there was the question of what she had said under anaesthetic about feeling guilty with Ian. He was still not sure that she had not had some kind of relationship with the man in the shop. She had been to London with him, stayed in the same hotel, she had worked with him at a time when Ralph knew that she had been unhappy in her marriage with St John. Ian was, Ralph was never prepared to go in for any kind of self-deception, an attractive man; many women would no doubt have called him handsome.

Perhaps he had persuaded Tina and she had succumbed. She would not have expected him ever to have known and the episode, however long it had lasted, could have been consigned to the past, to the dustbin of experience and he, Ralph, could and would never have suspected let alone known about it. Ralph somehow, and he believed this to be as a result of an intellectually more convincing analysis, favoured this explanation.

Finally there was the question of oral sex? How can she never have received let alone done this? Again it defied belief. Surely, but surely, Ralph reasoned, someone, be it whoever, must have wanted to do this to her.

None of it added up and Ralph found himself completely confused by the whole conundrum. He had married a twenty-eight-year-old who claimed to have had only two sexual partners, never achieved orgasm and denied ever having practised any form of oral sex. He could accept a small white lie, but he found himself more and more unable to accept the truth of the totality and whenever he thought about it, which was often, became angry that he had been lied to by Tina.

Their relationship, founded in a sense on deceit, should, he considered, have been open and honest enough to admit of truth and honesty about the matters that had been so important to him at the time.

The only explanation for the lies must be that Tina wanted to somehow spare him from, what she saw perhaps as the sordid reality of her background, another analysis that Ralph felt was rationally compelling.

He very much wanted to discuss his doubts and views with Tina but, on the one or two occasions he tried to bring the subject up, she simply said 'Oh, you want to talk dirt again. I don't want to,' and he could get nothing more out of her.

It was shortly after this that Ralph and Tina had their first major row.

It developed, as these marital arguments are prone to do, out of nothing. Ralph thought, looking back on it afterwards, that it was probably because he had said something about feeling short of money when Tina had suggested buying herself some new clothes now that she had regained her figure. It was, whatever the comment, clearly the wrong comment that morning.

Tina snapped back at him, 'We wouldn't be short of money if you hadn't bought a Morgan. Which you don't need,' and then added after a moment, 'and hardly ever use. What good is it? You walk to the station most days or I take you if it's raining. And you spent an awful lot of money on our honeymoon, our two days away.'

Ralph wanted to defend both decisions, and undecided which to address first, paused for a moment.

'You know it's true don't you. We would be better off without...'

'Look. You thanked me for the happiest two days of our life at the time and I gave up an awful lot when we got married including my Bristol.'

'You gave it all up voluntarily. You needn't have done.' Her eyes frosted. 'It was just being generous to her.'

'Like you were to him.'

'No. He deserved it. She didn't.'

'Oh God, what on earth is the matter? PMT?'

'What do you mean by that?'

'You know. People Must Tiptoe.'

'That's bloody offensive.'
'You're being bloody offensive.'
'No I'm not. You just happen to have a convenient memory.'
'My memory is perfect.'
'Yes, perfectly wrong. Go to work and leave me alone.'

She went upstairs and Ralph, sighing, decided to take the Morgan into town or the station, he was not sure, just to show her that he did use it from time to time. It was raining and the Morgan leaked but on the other hand, he thought, it would be a pleasant change. He left the house, went to the garage, opened it and to his surprise the car started first time. He backed out, looked round the milk float parked next door, pulled out and set off.

Tina, to whom the sound of the Morgan's exhaust was always annoying, felt livid as she heard the rasp fade away down the road.

'He's just done that to spite me. Bastard.'

She had forgotten that, in effect, she had started the scene and had escalated the insults. She felt so frustrated by his leaving as he had, that she just wanted to drive after him shouting abuse.

She thought that maybe she would phone him at his chambers and say some more. It was in this mood that she heard the doorbell.

She went to answer, still in her dressing gown, and the milkman handed her two pints of semi-skimmed and the bill. She glanced at it and wondered how on earth they could drink so much milk that the total amount was nearly all of her month's child benefit. She glanced back at the milkman who was eyeing her up and down with quite evident relish.

'What are you looking at?' she snapped at him.

'You, gorgeous,' he replied completely unabashed. 'I like the scenery.'

Suddenly she was curious, was this a milkman's come on? She remembered what Ralph had said about the milkman he had represented and wondered if he was in fact right.

'So it's true what they say about milkmen then is it?'

'What's true?' he said jauntily.

'That you're all randy bastards.'

'Oh that's true enough. What do you expect when gorgeous women like you open the door practically starkers like you are.'

She considered him. Young, blonde, quite good looking. She glanced at his hands, his fingernails were clean and well cut.

'And I suppose you let them off their bills as well.'

'I'd let you off your bill.' He was leaning casually against the door post.

'You're not serious.'

'Course I am. Why not. It's my business. I can decide where to spend the profits.' Tina thought for a moment.

'You're thinking about it aren't you?' he taunted.

'Come round the back in half an hour.' She had decided.

She felt eager and alive again. Ralph quite forgotten, she shut the door and tidied up, got the twins dressed and shut them safely in the bedroom in front of their favourite video and then, half an hour later, she was in the kitchen, heard a knock at the window and let him in.

'What's your name? I don't even know that.'

'John.'

'Well, John, what do you want to do?'

He did not reply but grabbed her, not unpleasantly she

thought, but hard enough to make her wonder whether this was going to be what she had heard described as rough sex. He kissed her and she realised his hand had been placed between her legs. She reached down to him. He already had his flies undone and was manoeuvring it out.

'Don't you want to go upstairs?' she gasped as his fingers entered her.

'You're ready enough,' he said brusquely, pushing her towards the table.

'Climb on here with your legs over the edge.'

She did as she was told, and nearly shrieked with pleasure as he entered her, smoothly in one thrust, and started rocking backwards and forwards, standing over her, one hand massaging her breasts and the other her clitoris.

Sexual excitement, the suddenness of her decision, the unexpectedness of the encounter, the sheer abandon, all drove her to a shuddering orgasm within minutes. He followed very quickly afterwards, eyes tightly closed, thinking of goodness knows what, Tina wondered.

He withdrew, tucked himself in, before saying, 'That was nice. Can't afford to do it too often though.'

'You meant it?'

'Oh yes, no bill today, the milkman's had his way,' he carolled mockingly, wrote a receipt in his book before giving her a copy of this and kissing her down there.

She stood up, feeling dizzy. He was already leaving.

'See you. What's your name?'

'Tina.'

'See you Tina,' and was gone, leaving her, panting but fulfilled.

She went to see the children and then had a long soak in the bathtub. She did not feel guilty, although recognising that she should, rationalised guilt away by saying to herself, 'G K Chesterton said that you should try everything once, except incest and folk-dancing. I wonder if he contemplated fucking the milkman? It was an interesting experience though. Perhaps not to be repeated,' and then, after soaping herself carefully in-between her legs, she got out of the bath, dried herself and, feeling much more cheerful knowing that the money saved on the milk bill would pay for a dress, put some clothes on and went to the twins.

Ralph had a dreary morning. He was not in a particularly good humour as he drove back and wondered what Tina's reaction to him would be. Would she still be cross and unreasonable or might it have worn off? He opened the door and was greeted by her, warmly and affectionately.

'I'm sorry about this morning Ralph.' She seemed truly penitent.

'Oh God, Tina, it's all right. It doesn't matter. I'm sorry if I was a bit short with you too. If you want some new clothes you should go and get some.'

'I did. Not much. Look.' She held up a rather pretty dress.
'That's nice.'

'Would you like to see it on?'

Thankful for the return of a more cheerful mood he agreed and she left, returning a moment later wearing the new dress.'

'It suits you. Makes you look younger.' and then, 'How did you pay?'

'I'd saved a little bit up out of the child allowance. You don't mind do you?'

'Why should I?'

They spent a happy and relaxed early evening together and when Tina suggested they go to bed early because she'd like to make love to him, Ralph agreed without demur.

Their lives became more routine, Ralph perhaps not trying so hard at law now that he had been rejected as a Q.C. He knew that he ought actually to be trying harder, working more ferociously, if he was going to achieve that badge of professional success but some of the bite had gone out of his ambition. He sometimes looked back and reflected on whether it had been Virginia who had been the driving force behind him and whether Tina had displaced this but, being fair, he knew that the ambition had long pre-dated Virginia, had been present when he was with Lucy already, and that it was unfair to even try to blame Tina for his loss of professional libido.

Tina seemed, at least to him, content. She missed her job, and the company it had provided, but would often tell Ralph that the twins, the nurturing, their physical demands, just getting them through the day, was more than enough for her. Ralph was happy enough to accept this assurance and they settled into a comfortable, domestic way of living that, whilst lacking the sexual dynamics of Ralph's life with Virginia, he found ultimately satisfying in a way that he could not have predicted.

Ralph made no attempt to pick up on any of his old friends and Tina had abandoned hers to St John. They received the odd invitation, those relating to work orientated matters, be they Bar dinners or from professional colleagues, Ralph turned down politely without mentioning to Tina, and those that were occasionally given to Tina direct were discussed but usually also refused.

They kept in touch only with Frances and Henry, whose child had been born at around the same time as the twins, and who Ralph had increasingly come to like. They were unaffected company, not demanding, and sufficiently similarly financially circumstanced that there was no envy on either side.

Tina's sister and her boyfriend sometimes came to stay and Ralph usually enjoyed those evenings. He found the contrast between the two sisters an interesting one and it amused him to speculate, asking himself whether he would have been as attracted to her as he had been to Tina, had he met Sylvia first. He thought not, Sylvia's character was more brittle than Tina's; she had the intellectual edge on Tina he was sure, having heard them argue different points, but she did not have quite the same warmth and spontaneity that he so enjoyed in his wife.

He sometimes thought back to his wildest nightmares of Ian and whether or not the children were his own or had been fathered by Ian, and, unable to explain to himself why she should have muttered what she did and unable to actually ask Tina, he usually simply dismissed the question.

He recognised, however, that he was becoming very possessive of her but tried to keep this totally hidden from Tina who, he knew, would get cross with him at any suggestion that she might be thinking of other men let alone having an affair. She had opportunity enough however, he knew, all men are prey to such thoughts and Ralph knew that he was not the exception but the rule.

He could not bear the thought that she might be unfaithful and had been staggered once, talking to a colleague in Chambers, who had recently remarried a girl separated in years from Ron by a much greater age gap than that between him and Tina, when Ron had, quite casually, said, 'I don't expect her to be faithful.'

'Why ever not?' asked Ralph with unfeigned surprise.

'The age gap I suppose. It would be nice if she were but, if she strays, so long as she doesn't do it on the doormat so to speak, I won't get too anxious. It's enough that we are together. If it keeps her happy then so be it.'

Ralph found such an attitude of mind difficult to comprehend. It was not that sexual possession was the most important thing to him, it would be the sense of betrayal, the fact that he had given everything up to live with her and she could not even maintain a simple sexual fidelity. He knew that he would go to pieces if it were ever to happen and indeed, illogical though he understood it to be, was irrationally jealous of anyone else she had slept with before him.

He had pangs, sometimes, so deep and intense that they were painfully physical, that she had not waited for him, had given herself to others, had wanted to give herself to others, had panted and groaned and let their hands explore her body, had let them penetrate her, deposit their semen deep inside her, cleaned herself after them, kissed them and looked forward to doing it with them again perhaps, no probably, perhaps even certainly counting the minutes and hours until they were back in bed again.

Unhealthy thoughts that he acknowledged as troubling, ones he wished would not intrude so frequently, but ones that were real and frightening to him.

He dealt with them, most generally but by no means always effectively, by reciting a mantra, 'I met her when she was twenty-eight. She was married. She was bound to have had sex with her husband. She was bound to have sex with others before him. Q.E.D. End of story. Grow up Ralph.'

Occasionally this worked, but usually he remained troubled and preoccupied for what seemed hours at a time. Work forgotten, he would stare sightlessly at his demons whilst sitting at his desk, trying to face them down, hands clenching and unclenching.

He never mentioned these moments to Tina and she, completely unaware of his anguish, when asked once by him what the boyfriend prior to St John had ended up doing, replied carelessly, 'Oh a lawyer I think, like my husband and my ex,' with a smile and no idea of the mass of conflicting emotions stirred in him by the simple, to her throwaway, answer. She did not even ask why he wanted to know. He could not have replied save to say that he wanted to know everything about her, that there should be no secrets between them.

CATHARSIS
CONTINUED

Frances had come over by herself to have supper with her small child. Henry was away, she had told Ralph and Tina had not mentioned anything untoward, so Ralph had accepted this explanation. The children were all in bed and asleep when the three of them sat down to a simple meal of spaghetti and cheap Chianti. Frances was subdued and said very little. Tina was also quiet and Ralph found himself chattering inconsequentially in an effort to keep the evening going.

Finally Tina, yawning, said, 'Look, I'm jiggered. I'm going to bed. Frances wants a word with you Ralph, quietly about Henry. I'll leave the two of you to talk about it.' Ralph looked at her and decided that she was upset about something and did not suggest she stayed.

After she left the room, Ralph turned in his chair to Frances and, noticing again how attractive she had become, asked, 'What's wrong?'

'Henry is having an affair. He admitted it to me yesterday. I phoned Tina and she suggested I come over to you with the children for a day or two while I try and get my head round it.'

'Are you upset?' It was perhaps a rather silly question but he asked because she seemed so matter of fact.

'No, not really. I've suspected for a long time. The sex hasn't been great or often recently.' She looked at him mock-demurely, 'But then you don't want to hear about that do you?'

Ralph was curious though and she must have realised this because she carried on. 'You may not believe it but he was an energetic lover and fun to be in bed with. That all stopped a few months ago.'

Only a few months ago, Ralph reflected. Good God, they had been married years. The fact that it had only stopped so recently was something of a surprise.

'We both enjoyed it,' she added by way of explanation. 'At first I thought it was pressure of work or the male menopause, or mid-life crisis or whatever. But tidying up his suit one day, I found a packet of condoms. I'm on the pill. There was no other explanation but another woman. I asked him and he simply replied that there was and would say no more. I'm considering divorce.'

Ralph was sympathetic. 'I can understand how you feel. Cheated, hurt, let down.'

'Ralph, it's more than that. The fact of not knowing who it is for one thing. It could be his secretary. She's a tarty little thing. It could be a friend. God only knows. But it's not just that. I went to the doctor yesterday.' Her face crumpled and Ralph saw tears in her eyes. She wiped them with the back of her hand.

'What on earth,' he began.

'I've been told I may have cancer.'

'Oh Christ, Frances. Where? What are they going to do?'

She had stood up and had gone to the door. She said very quickly, 'Usual woman thing. Breast. Nobody can say anything at this stage. Test next week as a matter of urgency.'

Ralph went and stood beside her and put an arm round her. She lay her head on his shoulder as they stood side by side.

'The funny thing is that I haven't told anyone yet.'

Ralph was genuinely shocked. 'Not Henry?'

'No, nor Tina, nor my mother. I'm not sure how I feel about everything. Part of me wants very badly to survive. Part of me says I want to survive and spite Henry. Another part says I want to put the clock back and have everything as it used to be. Henry, me, our little boy. Our ordinary lives but happy. And another part of me says fuck it. I'm going to enjoy myself. I'm going to have me a good time.' She started crying but this time the tears were bigger and there were barely suppressed sobs. Ralph was not sure what to do; he had never tried to comfort a person who may be dying. He pulled her a bit closer to him and she turned so that they were facing, and put both her arms round his waist.

'Oh Ralph,' she sighed. 'I don't know what to do. Can you tell me? You always seem to have sensible answers.'

'My first thought is that perhaps you might like a drink.'

'I think you're right. Have you a whisky? I'd like something strong.'

'Come on we'll go in the sitting room.' He turned on the 'real flame' gas fire, an object he always thought of in inverted commas and when she had put herself in an armchair said, 'Wait a moment'.

He ran lightly upstairs to check all the children. Putting his head round the door of his and Tina's bedroom he could hear her soft and regular breathing and he listened at the other door, not wanting to risk disturbing any of the sleeping children, before going down again, getting a bottle and two glasses and going back to where Frances was still sitting, she apparently not having moved at all.

He poured two glasses, stiffish measures, and gave her one. Her hand closed briefly round his before she removed it saying, 'Thank you' and having a large gulp. She had recovered some of her poise and Ralph, sitting on the sofa opposite her, stayed quiet and waited for her to speak.

He noticed, for the first time that evening, that she was wearing a shortish skirt which she had allowed to ride up her thighs, sufficiently for him to see the darker tops of her tights. Continuing his appraisal, conducted in a very non-obvious way, he looked at her more closely. She was a little flushed and one of her fingers was tapping, noiselessly but rhythmically, against her glass.

Her eyes were closed, her shirt had one more button undone than he would have felt happy about had Tina been wearing it, and her other hand was on her shoulder, smoothing the fabric. Her eyes suddenly opened.

'What are you thinking about, Ralph? You're looking at me a bit intently. I can feel it.'

'I was simply wondering what was passing through your mind. What you were thinking about.'

She laughed and got up. In doing so, she moved her legs apart and Ralph noticed she was not wearing tights but stockings. As she straightened up, she pulled her skirt down, walked over to him, and sat down beside him, curling up against his body and putting her head on his chest.

'Would you like to feel the lump, Ralph?'

He paused. An innate curiosity compelled an affirmative but before he could say anything, she had taken his hand and guided it into her shirt, across her breast and round onto the lower part of her shoulder.

'Just there. That's it.'

He could feel what seemed a totally innocent little pad of tissue beneath her skin. She kept his hand there and sighed again. 'That's what might do for me. Funny old world isn't it. It's breast cancer and not even where you'd expect to find it.'

'What do you mean?'

'You'd expect to find it here,' and she moved his open hand round and held it firmly against her breast. 'It's breast cancer. You'd expect to find it here.' She kept his hand in place.

He, considering that it might seem rude or churlish to try and take his hand away, kept it cupped around her. He could feel her nipple and it seemed certain that it was stiffening. He rationalised this to himself by reflecting that she was a woman with a stranger's, maybe not a total stranger's hand, but a strange hand on an intimate bit and despite herself, she might find this arousing. She shifted her position just enough for him to find that he was holding her breast a little more tightly.

'That's nice, Ralph. Can you stroke me a bit? Just gently. I'd like that.'

Ralph squeezed her breast and, as he did so, heard her breathing change, become less measured, more urgent. She moved again, changing position, but keeping his hand in place, his other still resting on the arm of the sofa with a glass of whisky, and looking at her, he saw that, her skirt was now all at the top of her thighs exposing her stocking tops, the whiteness of flesh, a pair of red knickers.

He idly wondered if her bra matched these but stayed as he was, thinking that if Tina were to walk in now there would be some difficult explaining to do. He dismissed the thought. Tina was asleep and once asleep, even with one of the twins crying, was difficult to wake. He could see little wisps of dark pubic hair curling round the edges and also, he fancied, a damp patch just between her legs.

'Do you like what you see?' she murmured and licked his neck. He was not aware that her eyes had been open or that she had been watching him.

'I think Henry is a fool.'

'Why?'

'Because you're bloody attractive and most men would want you.'

'What about you Ralph, would you want me?'

He did not reply, feeling that sensibly he ought to disengage, firmly but courteously, but was not convinced that in doing so he might not add to her general distress.

'I've always wanted you Ralph,' she murmured, still licking his neck. 'And the thought that I might die without doing it with you is a bit depressing.'

He wanted to answer that she was always going to have died at some point without doing it with him, but said nothing.

'Look,' she removed his hand, stood up, elegantly swinging round. 'I'm not bad am I? I tried after I had the baby. I lost weight and tried.' She unzipped her skirt and dropping it round her ankles, stepped out of it, undoing her shirt buttons.

'I'm not bad am I?' she repeated, wide-eyed, bewildered. 'Other men want me. God knows they've tried.' She stood there, shirt undone, in black stockings, matching red knickers and bra, and looked, Ralph thought, as alluring as any woman could.

'I think you're lovely,' he said, disconsolately remembering a very similar situation with Tina early on in their relationship.

She lowered herself to the floor, sat for a moment before reaching for a cushion and, putting it behind her head, lay down, head away from him, feet nearest, one of which she raised slightly and started stroking the bottom of his leg with her toes. Ralph could not deny that he felt aroused, indeed if he stood up, the fact would become obvious. He was not sure that he wanted Frances to know the effect she was having on him.

'Come and lie down beside me Ralph, please.' Her tone was imploring.

He got up, turning away from her as he did so, and sat down, awkwardly, not at all sure of how to deal with the rapidly increasing emotional temperature. She opened her legs, and taking one of his hands, placed it between them. He felt the warmth and, lying down beside her, took his left hand away and put his right hand there instead.

'That's nice Ralph. That's nice.' He rubbed her tentatively. He felt her hand going down to between his legs but did not want her to do this. She grasped him, 'My goodness Ralph, you're big.'

'What?' he said, surprised.

'You feel huge.' He nearly said, that's not what Tina thinks.

'It feels lovely,' Frances murmured and sitting up, she reached over, undid his waist band, unzipped him and pulled it free.

'I knew yours would be lovely,' she said and started licking the end, little dabs of her tongue as her hand went up and down. She stopped, 'You know, I put stockings on especially in case this might happen.'

'How do you mean?'

'I said, I've always wanted to do this with you and I knew you liked stockings.'

'How?' He felt cold inside.

'Tina told me.'

'Really?' He hoped he did not sound too formal.

'Yes. Women talk all the time.' She bent down again and carried on with little licks.

'She said you were a good lover. It made me want you all the more. She doesn't know how lucky she is.'

Ralph was brought to reality. He could not do this. It was so unfair to Tina, if not himself, and he felt angry that things had gone this far. He was also angry with Tina for betraying what he felt were confidences, intimacies of their life together. Frances had not noticed his change in mood, but lay back and wriggled out of her knickers; she caught him looking again.

'Lots of men like hairy women. Are you one?' and so saying she opened her legs wide. 'Come on Ralph. Make love to me. I'm here for you.'

Ralph lay for a moment thinking and then said, 'It's not fair though, is it Frances?'

'What do you mean not fair? I want you and you want me.' She grasped him. 'It's like a ramrod. Lovely. Put it in me. Slide it in slowly.' She had pushed him down so that he was lying flat and was sitting at the top of his legs holding him with both hands.

'We're both married,' he blurted out.

'Henry doesn't think so.'

'But Tina does.'

She looked at him, at once both enquiring and suspicious before bending down and kissing him on the mouth, full, her tongue round his teeth, exploring, sitting up again, raising and then lowering herself onto him. He could feel the gentle penetration, the warm sensation of entry.

'Have you no idea about Tina?' she murmured before he was finally fully inside her and she rolled over, keeping hold and pulling him on top of her. He lay there, she apparently savouring the feeling of him inside her, his mind trying to cope with the implications of what Frances had just said. What did she mean had he no idea about Tina? His stomach tightened, knotted up. He felt sick. She could only mean that Tina had been, was being unfaithful.

The awful enormity of this and the sense of betrayal were overwhelming. He cried out in his anguish and Frances, who mistook his pain for a gasp of pleasure, started rocking her hips, up and down, so that despite his lying there, passive and inert, he could feel himself sliding in and out of her.

'That's lovely Ralph, harder now, oh God, it's filling me right up, it's lovely.'

She maintained a constant stream of murmured comments and it was at that moment that Ralph decided that, if he was doing this, then he would do it properly and enjoy it. If Tina had been unfaithful to him then he could be unfaithful to her. Before this comment, made so knowledgeably by Frances, he had never looked at another woman in any sexual sense whilst with Tina. He had been happy with her, completely requited.

What had happened that evening, before he had been told this by Frances, had been, he rationalised, out of sympathy and kindness and he had been going to stop, not let it get as far as it had. Now he thought of Frances' warm body, her soft, sticky clinginess and, but then his thoughts drifted again. How alike all women are when you are actually having sex with them. The sensations are identical; if they differ, it is in fine points of detail only. The noises are the same; the commentary might be different but the physical noises, the slap of flesh against flesh, the slurping noises, the sound of suction, of air, of breathing and panting, they too are all alike.

If he shut his eyes, he could be with anyone. Tina, Virginia,

Lucy. It was only another orgasm inside another warm, compliant body. The differences could only lie in the intellectual realm, the areas concerning morality, ethics, promises, self-esteem, self-worth, and there, until then, he would have defended himself against any charge of dishonesty either with himself or Tina.

Now, however, he was firmly and deeply engaged in the sexual act with Frances, and he observed to himself dryly, it was rather pleasant. It did not have the same urgency or passion as when he and Tina had first made love that morning, when Virginia was out on call and St John lay sleeping hung-over in his bed but the fact that Frances was so obviously enjoying it, was so aroused and, thankfully, not noisily abandoned, contributed to a sense of satisfaction that he would never have predicted.

He felt around her back and undid her bra strap. Her breasts, larger than Tina's, fuller, more rounded, fell loose and he moved her down and under him, reaching between her legs.

'Oh God, Ralph, that's lovely, just there, slightly harder, softer now, yes again.'

It was, he thought, like listening to a Grand Prix or Wimbledon on the radio, but nevertheless concentrated on making sure that, if nothing else, Frances could look back on the episode and say that yes, he was a good, a considerate and thoughtful, attentive lover.

He took himself out of her and moved down her body and started licking between her legs. She was right, she was hairy, he felt stifled, suffocated even, after Tina's silky softness, but Frances evidently enjoyed it, suddenly exhaling loudly and clamping her thighs against his head, grasping his hair and pulling it so hard that Ralph nearly screamed out loud. Yes, he thought, she's had an orgasm and licked a little more until she relaxed, unclenching her legs and spreading them out on either side of him. He ascended her body, through the thicket of hair, across her lower stomach, a fine down stretching to her navel, up towards her breasts and, finding his mouth beside hers, he kissed her as he inserted himself back inside her, pushing into the now sodden flesh.

'God, Ralph, that was lovely. Is that what I taste like?'

'What do you mean?' he asked her quietly.

'I've never tasted myself before. What you've just done is a first for me. Ah, you're in, you're in. I feel as though I'm going to... it's so big. Christ,' as he thrust in and out.

'I'm having another. God, God,' and at that he felt himself explode inside her, a flood it felt like, an intense, huge orgasm of a kind that he had not had with Tina for a long time. He lay panting on top of her for some moments, thinking of what she had just said. 'It was a first.' Did that mean that she had never had someone go down on her then kiss her? Could he ask her? Post sexual intimacy might allow it.

He realised he was going limp, kissed her again and rolled off. His shirt was still buttoned, his trousers round his knees, shoes and socks on. He sat up, pulling his trousers up and shirt together, and made himself, as he put it, decent again.

She lay there looking, for all the world, like an upper-class whore, dark hair framing her face, bra-less, clad only in a suspender belt and stockings. He handed her her knickers and watched as she put them on, as she found her bra, sitting up to fasten this, finding her shirt, doing this up and then her skirt. Within a couple of minutes they were both dressed and respectable, the cushion back on the sofa, not even a damp patch on the carpet to offer any evidence of their union.

'Ralph, I know that people aren't supposed to say this after sex. Especially not women but thank you. It was lovely. If you enjoyed it half as much as I did then it must have been good for you too.'

He stopped her mouth with a finger. 'Shh. Let's not talk about it. I thought it, and you, lovely. But...' he stopped.

'What?' she asked with an expression of concern.

'Forgive prurient curiosity but, you know, when I licked you.'

'Between my legs. God yes. I had an instant, an immediate, an immense orgasm like I've never had. No-one has done that to me before.'

'Are you serious?'

'Totally. It's never occurred to me to ask anyone, and no-one ever offered.'

'I don't understand that,' he said as lightly as he could.

'Just the way it's been. Never seemed of any consequence. Pop it, you know, the willy thing in, jiggle it around a bit, each have an orgasm and finish. That's the way it is for most people.' Ralph immediately felt sorry for Frances but said nothing. They were drinking their whisky, Frances in little gulps, Ralph ruminatively, sitting beside one another on the sofa again.

'What did you mean about Tina?' he asked, again as lightly as he could.

'Bad form to talk about other women with the one you've just had but I'll forgive you. I didn't mean anything specific if that's what you're asking. It's just that she hasn't seemed herself recently and, well you know, she's attractive to men and they are attracted to her. Think of the way that all men can't resist touching her. And she responds.'

'Does she?' asked Ralph feeling horrified.

'Yes, in the sense that if she gives them a drink or a plate, she'll always brush her fingers against theirs. She's always slightly closer to them in terms of body space than I think really she should be. That kind of thing. Oh come on Ralph. You must have noticed. You're not stupid. Anyway, what am I doing talking about Tina with you, when we've just done what we've done?' She kissed him. 'It was a wonderful interlude. Ralph, don't worry. I shall tell no one. Shall never mention it so long as you make me a promise.'

He seized the opportunity gratefully; he was wondering how she would feel in the morning and whether she would regret her decision and even want to tell Tina.

'I'll never mention it to anyone providing you promise, on your honour...'

Yes, yes, on my honour, or whatever is left of any kind of honour after I did what I did to Virginia and now Tina, Ralph thought but let Frances carry on, 'Provided you promise to do it to me again. One day, when we're completely alone and there's no possibility of anyone disturbing us for at least a couple of hours.' She looked at him, straight in the eyes, a sparkle in hers and a smile on the full lips. 'There's a lot I'd like to try with you.'

'I promise,' he said, at the same time resolving, despite her physical attractions and the enticing prospect of trying out a lot of things with her, never to be left in a room with her alone again.

'I'm tired,' she announced. 'I think I ought to go to bed,'

and finishing her whisky, kissed him again before standing, straightening her skirt and saying, 'Goodnight Ralph.'

'I hope you have sweet dreams. Despite all the business next week.' He had not forgotten about her cancer.

'I certainly shall,' and she was gone.

Ralph poured another whisky, not as strong for it was a drink he did not like, and sipped at it. He had, and had to acknowledge this to himself, enjoyed having Frances and he was sufficiently sure of her to believe her promise that she would tell no one. What concerned him more was Tina and what Frances had said about her. He reflected on this, her observations about Tina, touching and being touched by other men, always being too close to them, and the fact that, well, at least an insinuation that Tina might have been unfaithful to him.

He had misread her to begin with, he understood that looking back, as initially he was sure that she was saying that Tina was having an affair. Subsequently Frances had backtracked, merely saying that it seemed to her a possibility. The reflections awoke all his old insecurities and doubts about her fidelity, her honesty and possibly her capacity for deception.

He cleared up automatically, leaving the kitchen tidy and washing up neatly stacked on the draining board. He decided to have a quick shower and as he went upstairs listened but no one appeared to be stirring. He lathered himself mechanically in the main bathroom letting the spray wash off any smell or trace of illicit sex and went to bed, climbing in beside Tina who moved, whimpering slightly, and then feeling his warmth beside her, snuggled against him. He fell asleep quickly thinking of the satisfying orgasm with Frances and wondering if it might ever happen again, but believing he would do all that he could to prevent this.

He woke to find Tina looking at him rather seriously.

'Did Frances tell you?' she asked with what seemed anxiety.

'Yes.' He had wondered momentarily to what she was referring, Henry's affair or her suspicions regarding Frances but realised she could only mean the one thing.

'She's a bit upset.' He did not mention the cancer.

'She's more than a bit upset. She's distraught. Poor girl. I've told her that if she wants to she can stay with us for a few days. Is that all right?'

'If that's what you want.'

'She said she'd think about it but would probably go home today.'

Ralph was relieved; he did not relish the idea of Frances under the roof for any length of time, certainly not late at night and after they had been drinking.

'Did you advise her? You know, tell her anything she didn't know or ought to know?'

'I advised her in general terms,' he answered as non-committally as he dared.

'What time did you come to bed? I was asleep.'

'Do you know, I didn't look? I don't think it was late. You were sound asleep, didn't move.'

'The children aren't awake yet. None of them. Not ours or hers and I haven't heard Frances move. Come here,' and Tina rolled over, lifting her night-dress, Ralph pulled the covers down and looked at her, neatly trimmed pubic hair, stomach showing no signs of having had children, breasts still as firm as when they had met.

'No, you turn round and we'll do it the way we used to when

you were pregnant.'

'Why?'

'You liked it like that.'

'Only because I had a huge stomach with two babies in it and there was no other way we could manage it physically.'

'I quite like the feeling of being against you and being able to reach round to your front like this,' and he put one hand round her breasts and the other between her legs and eased himself in, rubbing her mechanically and just as mechanically taking her to orgasm which he followed with his own.

'That was quick,' she said. 'But it was nice, kiss me.' She turned towards him.

He was reluctant but did not show this. He was still preoccupied with the thought of whether or not she had had, or was even having, an affair.

This had begun, casually enough, only a week or two earlier. Frances and Henry were coming to supper with another couple from the estate. Tina decided she had nothing to wear, the feminine euphemism for wanting something new. Tina wanted to go out and buy something, but her account was depleted. She was angry because she had to ask Ralph and when she did so, was angrier still when he said that he had no money either and the overdraft facility was too near its limit to permit any extravagance.

'It's only a bloody dress I'm asking for.'

'It's only another bloody dress you don't need,' he had replied and had refused, despite her entreaties, her imprecations and general bad temper, to consider the matter further. She had announced, mid-afternoon, that she was going out anyway, that he was to look after the children and had returned, an hour or so later with a couple of bags carrying the name of the town's most expensive clothing shop. He had ignored her. She had then gone into the kitchen, finished preparing a soup, the casserole and a pudding before taking the children up and putting them to bed. She had still been upstairs when Frances and Henry arrived early, very cheerily and boisterously. Frances had gone up with their child and left Ralph and Henry to have a drink together.

When Frances came down again she turned to Ralph and said, 'My goodness, Tina looks a million dollars tonight.'

Ralph raised his eyebrows.

'She's got a new dress; she's rather pleased with it. Haven't you seen it?'

Ralph was forced to reply that he had not. When Tina came in he had to pause for a moment, he felt so immediately angry. The dress shrieked expense but it was less that than the fact it revealed more than it covered, décolleté, short, buckles and with her bare legs, it was more suited, he thought, to a minor porn starlet than the respectably married mother of two children and wife of a barrister. He tightened his lips and said nothing but wondered how she intended to keep her breasts in; he was sure he could see the edges of her nipples.

She looked pleased with herself and after pouring a drink for Frances and then one for her, sat down, away from him, and ostentatiously made conversation with Frances and Henry, deliberately excluding him. When the bell went again, he went to open the door, performing the rituals of a host, taking coats, seeing their guests, Nick and Christine through, settling them with drinks after making the introductions. He then went into the kitchen to check the food and stood for a moment wondering whether to say anything. He was, he recognised, very cross, and when he found Tina beside him, also checking the food, said nothing.

She looked at him, challengingly, and said, 'Well, cat got your tongue?'

'No.'

'Aren't you going to say anything?'

'What about?'

'My dress.'

'No.'

'Why not?'

'Because.'

'Well, I like it.'

'I expect you would.'

'What do you mean by that?'

'Nothing.'

She came up to him and stuck her face in his. 'I got this one because I knew you wouldn't like it.'

'So be it.'

'You don't, do you?'

'What.'

'Like it.'

'It doesn't matter. Let's just have a pleasant meal. Let's leave it.'

'No.' She was getting angry too. 'I want you to say something about my dress. It cost enough. I put it on our Barclaycard.'

He sighed, 'I'll save up for it then,' and left the room. He rejoined the others and Tina came back in. She was vivacious, her eyes sparkled as they always did when she was angry, and she was making a big effort to be the cheerful, considerate hostess. He tried to ignore her in a way that would not make his distaste evident to the others.

He thought nothing of it when Tina said to Henry, 'Come and give me a hand getting the dishes,' and left the room with him.

In the kitchen Tina bent down to check the oven and turning was gratified to see Henry staring at her.

'You look fantastic Tina. That colour really suits your hair.'

'Do you think so?' She was standing close to him.

'And any shorter and you needn't have bothered.' He was looking at her crotch. 'And any lower it would be a belt,' looking at her breasts. 'Why don't you ask me to kiss you?'

She stopped, thought and remembered. It was Henry who had managed, some years before, nearly to get it inside her, had seized what he had seen as the opportunity and expertly undone his trousers, moved her knickers aside, parted her with one hand and holding himself with the other, was just about to enter her when she had drawn away with a smile and a very polite rebuff. It had never been mentioned again.

'Why don't you ask me to kiss you?' he repeated, his left hand resting on her right shoulder, his right hand just brushing against her breasts before moving downwards. She looked at him, and opening her mouth, ran her tongue across her lips. As he bent down and his lips closed on hers, she felt his hand in between her legs. Then, as his tongue licked her mouth and his fingers, moving her knickers aside, entered her, she sighed with pleasurable abandon. She wondered whether he would try to insert himself again and, on moving his body away slightly, still kissing her, realised that he must be undoing himself with his left hand. She pressed her hips forward and felt Henry's erection, out of his trousers, his hand guiding it towards her. She leant against the units, parting her legs and then, with a gasp from her, and a sigh from him, he was fully inside her, swaying his hips enough to stimulate them both.

That moment, a door opened in the hallway, there was a burst of laughter and she pulled herself away from him. He had heard it too and tucked himself back in, rapidly and proficiently, before the door opened.

When Ralph came in, a moment later, she was bending down at the open oven door and Henry was picking up a pile of plates which he took past Ralph saying, 'Tina would like the other ones through as well,' nodding towards some more plates.

Ralph looked at Tina, straightening up, 'You look flushed.'

'It's not surprising, I've had my head nearly in the oven,' she snapped as she put a casserole on the surface. 'We're ready to eat.'

Apart from the local marital difficulty, which no-one seemed to notice, it was a pleasant enough meal. The conversation was convivial and everyone laughed a lot. Ralph had drunk enough for the initial anger to subside to a feeling of irritation when he looked at Tina. His anger resurfaced, however, when, after cheese, she asked if anyone would like a swim. Their neighbours immediately said yes, they would slip back for their costumes and Frances and Henry, who invariably brought theirs, disappeared upstairs to change. Tina did not switch on the outside lights but only the underwater light of the pool, which glowed eerily blue. She went upstairs leaving Ralph to tidy up and open the door to their visitors, who re-entered in dressing gowns and trainers with towels round their necks.

'Come on through,' he said, opening the patio doors. Frances and Henry had already gone outside and were removing the cover.

Henry dipped a toe in, 'A bit chilly but here goes,' before jumping in, closely followed by Frances. The other two got in more tentatively and all were laughing together when Tina arrived on the poolside.

Ralph had forgotten about the costume she had bought before they had been swimming together that first time, never having seen it since. As she stepped forward, the other four stopped swimming, looking at her and at Ralph. Tina might, Ralph thought, just as well have been naked. He felt a hot flush of embarrassment cover him and was relieved it was dark and no one could see the physical evidence of his discomfiture.

'You look great,' shouted Frances. 'Are you coming in?'

Tina stood on the edge of the pool, turned so that she was facing away from it, positioned herself exactly and then did a backflip, entering the water clearly and beautifully. It was an extremely dangerous dive in six feet of water but when her head emerged, she was smiling. There was spontaneous applause as she swam to the steps.

She started getting out and it was then Ralph realised that she was drunk enough not to have noticed that the dive had displaced her top which was round her waist, and she was getting out of the pool effectively only wearing a thong. The men stood ogling but Tina was oblivious to them. She stood on the poolside again, paused to stretch upwards, drawing attention to her breasts and body, before throwing herself into the water in a racing dive and cut through the water, an impeccable fast crawl, racing turn, back up again and repeating this. The others were all intent, just watching, the men clearly waiting for her to get out again. When she stopped again at the far end, she paused for a moment before she swam to the steps. When she got out the halter neck was fixed properly back in place.

'Aren't you coming in Ralph?' she called to him. 'It's ever so nice.' When he did not answer she came up to him, dripping and looking anxious. 'Are you cross still?'

He felt he could not trust himself to speak. It would be all round the neighbourhood that his wife went skinny dipping in public and that he had stood there stony faced. He managed to say, through clenched teeth. 'I prefer your other costume,' before going in to put on his swimming trunks.

When he came out again the other five were still in the pool. Henry stayed unobtrusively close to Tina, while Ralph swam, hard and severely, backwards and forward.

Henry managed once or twice to get close enough to Tina to tentatively reach out under water and feel between her legs.

Tina was reminded suddenly of the last term at school, after she and Ian had started their sexual relationship. Their last night, they had sneaked into the pool. Ian, as swimming captain, still had the key, and then had spent a gloriously erotic couple of hours, making love in the water, and finally he had his orgasm inside her as they lay on the top diving board.

Afterwards they had stood up, both naked and holding hands had dived together into the water below, a perfectly executed joint dive, that had seen them emerge together, clinging in an embrace that for both was tinged with the sadness of realisation that nothing would ever be quite like that, or that evening, ever again. They had dressed, gone back to his room where, in defiance of all the school rules, she had stayed with him in his bed, neither sleeping, until, when the bell rang to signify the start of the day she said, 'Make love to me once more,' and as the school came to life for the last time that school year, and the very last time for Tina and her contemporaries who were leaving, she had an orgasm that was so bitter sweet she had started crying.

She had not seen Ian in that last school holiday. They had spoken many times on the telephone but each was preoccupied with getting ready for University and of course the A level results which would determine who went where. Ian had called her to say that he had got into Oxford; Tina was not surprised and congratulated him. He was very full of himself and Tina had then thought, decisively, that there was no future for them. She was enough of a realist to know that it would have been practically impossible to maintain a relationship in a first term at two different universities and she also noticed that he had not asked whether she had got into her preferred choice. She interrupted him and said, 'I got in too.'

'Good, where?' He had forgotten.

She kept him guessing. 'My first choice.'

'Oh terrific, well done.'

'And where am I going Ian?

'Uh, I've forgotten. Forgive me Tina. Where are you going?'

She told him.

'That's terrific. Will you come and see me? Or shall I come and see you?'

'Give me a ring towards the end of the holidays and perhaps we'll get together.'

'OK. Take care, Tina. I'll be thinking of you.'

'I'll think of you too Ian. All the best.'

They had not seen one another after that conversation and he had not phoned her. Neither had she phoned him. She did get a letter, forwarded from her parents' house, about three weeks into their terms. It was non-committal, not cool but certainly not impassioned and she thought, ruefully for a moment, of the shared intimacies and their last night at school and wondered with whom he was sleeping now.

She was generous spirited enough to hope that the new one was nice, she had enjoyed her time with Ian but was now preoccupied with her own life at university, making new friends and establishing herself in various clubs and in the swimming team. Not long after that she had met St John at the faculty party.

It was growing cooler now and the swimmers were beginning to tire. The initial excitement had worn off and when Tina suggested that it was perhaps time to call it a day, they assented.

Ralph got out first and went and turned on the patio lights. They looked what they were, early middle age except for Tina, who seemed to glow with colour and energy. She did another couple of fast lengths before getting out and coming over to Ralph.

'I'm sorry,' she said quickly.

'What for?'

'The dress. My top coming off. I didn't mean that to happen. And when it did, I had to show I wasn't embarrassed.'

He was not mollified but simply nodded. The other couple had decided to leave then, to change at home, thanking them for what they described as a super evening. Ralph saw Henry looking thoughtfully at Tina and, as Tina handed him his dressing gown, noticed that her fingers did brush against his, in what Ralph thought a totally unnecessary way.

Frances and Henry went upstairs, Frances saying,

'Goodnight,' Henry talking of having another drink.

Ralph, who had done most of the tidying up already, including the loading of the dishwasher, stood in the kitchen for a moment. Tina joined him there; she had changed into a simple long dress.

'Are you going to have another drink Ralph?'

'No, I don't think so. I might go to bed. What about you?' He felt tired and a bit miserable he realised.

'Henry was talking of having another one. I might keep him company. Are you sure you won't?'

Just then Henry came in. He had been to the dining room and gathered together the bottles of wine that weren't empty. He got some glasses and started to pour some white.

Ralph decided that he had had enough and did not have the energy to talk anymore; in any event he was still feeling cross with Tina and announced, 'Not for me. I'm off to bed. See you in the morning Henry. See you later Tina,' and left the room. He went upstairs, checked the sleeping children, paused at the bedroom door where Frances and their child were and undressed and went to bed. He lay awake for a minute or two, thought briefly of their money worries, Tina's - what seemed to him - exhibitionism and then fell into a dreamless sleep.

Downstairs Tina and Henry were in the sitting room with a glass of by now rather warm white wine.

'That was a nice evening Tina, if a bit interrupted.' He looked at her.

She moved in the sofa, patting the seat next to her. 'Come and sit beside me.'

He got up and, came across, drawing the curtains on his way, before sitting down where indicated. The only light came from a table lamp and the coal effect gas fire; despite it being summer, the evening was now quite cold.

She shivered and he put his arm round her, asking, 'What's wrong?'

'I'm just a bit cold. And nervous.'

'What do you mean?'

'You know. You and me together and alone. Everyone asleep. We could. You know.'

'Nervous about what we may do.'

'And what may we do then?' She looked archly at him.

'This,' he said as he put his hand on her leg and stroked her thigh, kissing her. She did not respond and he stopped. 'What's wrong?'

'I'm not sure I want to do that.'

'You seemed to earlier.'

'You didn't ask. You wanted to.'

'You let me.'

'Yes, I suppose I did. But that was then and this is now.' His hand was between her legs, holding her over her knickers, and she removed it and said firmly, 'No, not tonight. I'm going to bed.'

'Another time? An away day?'

'Maybe. We'll see how it goes. No hard feelings Henry?'

'Plenty of hard feelings,' he said, chuckling at his own crude joke which she had heard before, 'and lots of anticipation. Goodnight then. If you're sure.'

'I'm sure. Hard feelings though? But we could do this quickly...' and she bent down over him, undid his zip and, massaging him until he started to moan, then put her lips round the end, swallowing before saying, 'Goodnight Henry.'

After he had gone, Tina sat for a while before pouring herself another glass of wine, gulping it rather than sipping, staring at the fire and wondering why she was again tempted, thinking of the episode only a few days earlier with the milkman. She supposed that basically sex with Ralph had become rather predictable and thus a bit dull.

He still seemed to want her physically as much as ever but since the children had been born, her energy levels had been less, her libido had been reduced and, she was not reluctant to acknowledge this, it was really nice to be wanted by someone else. Even if it was only Henry, whom she had always liked, but had never really considered as a lover.

Hers was not a bad marriage. They had less money than she had expected. She had got used to the idea that they would probably never have as much as they had talked about in those early days, full of optimism and confidence. She had the twins, the house she had wanted, the swimming pool, enough food to eat, a reasonable social life and, she came back to this, a husband who still wanted her sexually. But she did not really want him sexually. She had gone off sex in a big way during pregnancy. The thought of the life inside her stomach, developing in its sac, being assaulted by shockwaves as Ralph thrust in and out of her was something that occasionally she found unpleasant, at other times, repulsive even.

It was she who had suggested gentler sex, she lying on her side with him penetrating her from behind, facing her back. It was somehow less physical and less intrusive. It was a silly thought she knew, but it seemed less likely to wake the baby. After the birth she had not felt like sex at all. She had assured Ralph that this was normal. He had replied that she was jolly lucky that he still desired her, she ought to be flattered, as being present at births put most men off sex with their wives forever.

He had quoted an old feminist joke to the effect that women had a double edged problem with the presence of their men at childbirth; on the one hand they wanted the men to know exactly what the women had to endure because of him but on the other, and more importantly, they were aware that their husbands were never likely to want to do it to them again.

They had resumed a full sexual relationship about three months after the birth but it had never really been the same for her. She had tried, but knew that Ralph was seemingly always disappointed in her lack of enthusiasm, her tiredness from the unremitting demands of two infants, her sore breasts with their cracked nipples and the fact that, when her head hit the pillow, she went straight to sleep.

They had still occasionally bathed together, had the odd bottle of champagne in their bedroom, but the sex had never again been as uninhibited or as much fun as prior to the children. In addition there was always the risk, and very often the reality, of a child's voice calling from their room, or soon probably at their bedroom door, demanding attention and immediately.

She had often got up to see to their needs, changing a nappy or soothing a childhood anguish to return to find Ralph disconsolate and limp. He had then frequently been unarousable again and this in turn put him in a bad mood, it seemed, with her and the children.

Was she tempted by Henry? Yes, she thought she was, but she could not really see the point of an affair or, indeed, adultery for the sake of adultery. She rationalised the milkman by saying to herself that it had simply felt right at the time. She did not want to leave Ralph for Henry but there was something, a sensation between her legs, which occurred when she thought of Henry and his desire.

She went to bed, going in to check the children turning them, listening to their breathing and thinking of the passionate, animal love she had for them that meant they were more important to her than anything else, the house, marriage, Ralph, everything. She climbed in beside Ralph who was asleep on his back, gently snoring. She touched him under his nose, he sniffed, turned over and the snoring stopped. She turned over and fell asleep.

When she woke, it was to find Ralph, already awake, lying on his elbow looking at her.

'What on earth are you thinking about?' she said, not crossly but with a flash of irritation.

'You,' he replied simply. 'Last night.'

'What about it? I said I was sorry. I am sorry. It was unforgivable, I know.' She was contrite. 'I didn't mean to upset you. Come and hold me.' She reached out for him and he allowed himself to be encircled in her arms as she kissed his neck. Suddenly one of the twins started crying.

'I'd better go,' she said, getting out of bed and putting on a dressing gown. 'I'll see if she settles and then I'll come back.'

Ralph waited, listening to the mother and child noises next door. The child was placated and Tina returned looking cheerful.

'They're playing quite happily in their cots. There's no sound from our visitors. We've got five minutes. Come here.'

'I can't do it to order,' Ralph grumbled. 'Men need to be aroused.'

'Don't I arouse you any more?'

'Yes, but not instantaneously every time.' She stood above him and took off her dressing gown. Then, swaying gently, she drew her night-dress up slowly revealing her lower body and then her breasts. Finally she pulled it over her head and stood there smiling.

'Any more aroused?'

'A bit.'

'I'll do it for you then,' and she bent down over him, started rubbing him, then bestraddled him, moving up and down. When he tried to reach to stimulate her she said, 'No, you have one. I'm OK,' and carried on until he came, eyes closed, lying passively under her.

'There, that was nice wasn't it,' she murmured, kissed him perfunctorily and got up, pulling herself off him, and looking at him lying there still, said absently, 'It's not very big is it?'

'What?'

'Your willy.'

'Why on earth do you say that now?'

'Well, I suppose it just occurred to me.'

'It's not a very nice thing to say to a man. Any man.'

'Why not?'

'If you don't understand that, you don't understand anything.'

'What do you mean, I don't understand anything.'

'Saying that.'

She was getting angry again. 'Are you telling me I'm stupid?'

'No, just that what you said wasn't very nice.'

'That your willy isn't big. Big deal. It works. It's a nice size,' she added.

He suddenly felt quite savage. 'After having twins I guess a baseball bat would rattle about a bit in there.'

'Thank you. That's really nice.'

'No nastier than what you've just said.'

'It's much nastier.'

He stopped, appalled at her unfairness and irrationality and then said, in measured tones, 'Anyway, I suppose you're the expert. I have to hand it to you. You know what you're talking about. You're the one who's seen them all, no doubt felt them, measured them, had them inside you, one after the other. God knows. I don't. No one's ever complained to me. It's always been OK for you. You used to say...'

She interrupted him. 'What are you saying? What are you telling me?' she hissed. 'You know that's not true. You're filthy if you believe that. You know that I was relatively sexually inexperienced when we met. I told you.'

'Yes,' he said bitterly. 'You told me. But you admitted that you lied to St John about being a virgin. Why should I believe you told me the truth? Any more than I should believe you if you were to say that you'd not had an affair with Ian. You know. The Adonis of Mothercare.'

'What do you mean? Ian? What the hell are you talking about?'

'How do I know that you didn't sleep with him?'

'I didn't. Isn't that enough?'

'No. It's not.'

'You are disgusting. You've got a nasty, filthy mind. You should have stayed with her. Virginia. Virgin. Grade 1 A'

'But I didn't. I left her for some tart, absolutely not virgo intacta but certainly virago intacta...'

'Then go back to her if that's all that's important. I'm getting seriously angry. I'm not talking about it anymore.' She dressed and left the room without another word.

He heard her getting the twins up, heard Frances and Henry go downstairs and ordinary domestic noises, interspersed with the screams of children and laughter from the adults.

He got up, rubbing himself as though he had been physically beaten, and he too dressed and went downstairs and tried to be as unaffected by and indifferent to their quarrel as was Tina who, in mother and hostess mode, was busy organising and cooking a large breakfast.

The conversation, as ever with small children present, was inane to the point of banality and, when the children had finished eating and had been put in a play-pen, stayed on the light and inconsequential.

Henry helped Tina clear, Ralph noticing their hands touch seemingly inadvertently, once or twice but Ralph also noticing that Tina made no great effort either to avoid this or remove her hands from any contact with any urgency.

They had gone for a walk in the park, to the swings and roundabouts and, Ralph reflected, would have seemed like any other youngish couples with small children on a summer's day, light-hearted and carefree.

Ralph was smouldering, angry and upset. He found it difficult to avoid the horrible intrusive thoughts of Tina with Ian, Tina with St John, Tina with God knows how many others. The lies she must have told him, the deceit appalled and fascinated him. How, he kept on asking himself, could he have been so comprehensively duped? It was absolutely impossible for him to concentrate on maintaining an appearance of the ordinary Ralph with a devoted wife and two small twins but, steeling himself, he did so and joined in the games with the squealing happy children.

At length, Tina who seemed to have assumed an air of command that morning, suggested they go back and think about lunch. At home, the sun still shining, Frances, looking at the swimming pool asked Tina if they all might swim again.

Why not ask me, thought Ralph. It's my house. My money runs it. Pays to heat the pool and the rest of it, but did not say anything.

Tina nodded an assent and the children started squeaking with excitement. Frances and Henry went upstairs to change again and Tina turned to him and said coldly, 'I'm not sure I can forgive you.'

'I don't think I'm going to forget what you said in any kind of hurry,' he replied as mildly as he could.

He did not swim, he watched the other three adults and the children in their armbands, thought of Tina the previous night, her immodesty and the fact that he had evidently married a complete and utter slut, a little tart who had put it about, who took her clothes off in public, who had the moral finesse of a cat on heat.

He knew that he felt utterly diminished and that it was a nonsense. When she had once previously made a similar remark about size, he had gone to medical textbooks in the library at his chambers, taken them to his room and read around the subject. He had learnt that size varied from country to country, in America even from state to state, but that for a white Caucasian European male he was completely average. That meant he rationalised, that whilst there were at least some bigger than him, another roughly equal amount would be smaller.

The trouble was, and to his mind there was no escaping this, Tina had only obviously ever experienced the larger variety and saw him, no doubt, as some kind of underdeveloped freak in that area. He was well aware that women talked about the size of men's sexual apparatus, that some women said size didn't matter, it was what men do with it that was of moment, but all men liked to think they had a big one and all men with small ones were self-conscious about themselves.

Again, he rationalised this through, and remembered a friend from University who was always talking about the fact that whilst he, Kevin, only had a tiny todger as he put it, he had no end of sexual conquests with girls, he claimed, queuing at his door. Perhaps it was pure fantasy on Kevin's part as to his desirability, but on the other hand, he was never without a girl in tow; true, not the best looking girls but presentable ones who, Kevin assured him, 'banged like shithouse doors.'

He was also aware, and knew this as a fact, and consequently was the more surprised at Tina's assertions, that every girl with whom he ever had sex with the notable, to him, exception of one, had come to orgasm.

He had, in fact been so concerned about it all that he had, after locking the door to his room, masturbated himself to a usual rigidity and then taken a ruler to the length and a tape-measure to the circumference, to establish exactly where he stood, so to speak, statistically. Thus reassured, but not really totally, he had, in his careful, intellectual way, assessed the size of the problem, addressed it to his own satisfaction and forgotten about it completely until yesterday when all his anxieties and insecurities were reawakened.

He could feel a twinge of arousal at the thought of Frances and he looked at her more thoughtfully, when she lifted herself out of the pool, her breasts flattened but rippling under her costume, a more pronounced bulge between her legs than Tina, a more curvaceous body in fact altogether, but stopped himself, deciding he was thinking like a puerile adolescent.

After a light lunch their guests left and Tina put the children to bed for an afternoon sleep before sitting down to watch a film on television. Ralph felt restless and told Tina that he was thinking of going to his Chambers to do some research. She hardly looked up and muttered, 'OK, if that's what you want.'

'Well you hardly seem to want me do you?'

She glanced at him. 'No, I don't,' and he left without saying goodbye.

He drove into the city in the Morgan, with the top down, and enjoyed the feeling of freedom, of being in control of something, if only a motorcar, that he could make go faster or slower at whim, that responded blindly to his commands and wished life itself could be more like that.

He parked and let himself in. It was quiet but, as in any very quiet building, especially on a Sunday, even if there is no noise, the presence of other human beings can be sensed and Ralph was aware that he was not alone in Chambers; who was there too he could not guess, was not really interested in any event, and he thought no more of it after he had gone into his room shutting the door behind him.

He got out a bundle of papers, undid the pink ribbon, ruefully regretting that he no longer dealt with everything on an immediate basis, these papers having arrived at least a week earlier, and started reading.

He found himself unable to concentrate, his mind drifting all the time to Tina. Instead he decided that he might to try and put his thoughts in order and it might help if he were to formulate an indictment. The case against Tina. He started writing. Some time later, when there was a tentative knock at his door, he was surprised and relieved saying, 'Come in,' simply glad to have some human company.

It was Angharad, their new pupil, twenty-six years old, a starred first from a top university, a Bar Finals prize winner and, the Pupillage Committee had concluded, an asset to any set. Ralph, who was a committee member, had voted for her principally because she reminded him so strikingly of his first, what he considered true, love Lucy. Lordy, juicy Lucy, he had remembered and had no hesitation in expressing his endorsement of the decision.

He had met Lucy soon after her family had moved to the area. She was lonely, had been brought to the party by a school contemporary who had already drifted off and, according to Lucy, was either snogging or already worse in an upstairs bedroom. Ralph had been attracted to her immediately, had quizzed her in an amused and amusing fashion, had enjoyed her flirtatious response but was disappointed when she finally said she had a boyfriend back in Lancashire to whom she intended to remain faithful.

'It can't be the real thing already? You're far too young to settle down.'

'It's the real thing at the moment.'

'How long will it last?' he had asked, taking her hand.

She returned his gaze steadily. 'I rather think until you ask me out.'

'Let's leave the party,' he suggested, 'I'm asking you out.'

'I'll come with you.'

They had walked hand in hand through the darkened town, Ralph pointing out some of the more historic sites that were not marked by tourist plaques and telling funny stories about life there, both of the present and the past, and Lucy had laughed so much that she was nearly crying.

'I've so enjoyed being with you tonight but,' looking at her watch,' I'm expected home in ten minutes.'

They had gone back to the house, Ralph saying that he would drive her home.

'Do you have a car then?'

'Yes.'

He had worked every summer that he could remember to save for what was then his pride and joy, a Mini Cooper Mark 3, that went as well as it looked. She got in, he opening the door for her, and drove her back to her parent's house, in a street not that far from his own house, where he had, after deciding not to go for the big clinch, kissed her decorously on the cheek before getting out, opening her door and walking her up the drive. At the doorway where she had turned and kissed him, not decorously but firmly on his mouth, before breaking away she had said, 'Phone me, my number is 269169.'

'An easy enough number to remember,' he had said and when she looked surprised had explained, 'Sorry, it's my dirty mind. Twice rude, once rude. How can I forget it?' She had giggled before going in and turning, touching her fingers to her mouth as she shut the door.

He had sighed and gone back home where he had fallen asleep, but only after first deciding that Lucy was the nicest girl he had ever met, determining to pursue her and masturbating wildly until, with his eyes closed, he had seemed to come in a shower of sparks.

He had phoned her of course, could hardly wait until school had finished before doing so. She had answered, he had asked her out, she asked 'When', he replied 'Tonight?' she said, 'Yes' and he had picked her up in his car. He suggested the cinema, she suggested a drive and he readily acceded. 'Where to?' 'Somewhere nice?'

They talked as he drove and he decided too that they were soul mates. He took her to a well-known beauty spot, a river, a long series of waterfalls. It was a summer's evening but there were only a few people about.

Hand in hand they had walked along the path, through the beech woods, she admiring the setting sun, he preoccupied with thoughts of her body. He had had sex with a couple of girls in the months before and when Lucy turned and kissed him, urgently, voraciously even, he had immediately been aroused. She had felt it against her hips and said, quietly but smiling, 'That must be uncomfortable. It probably needs readjusting,' before putting her hand down his trousers, finding it, straightening it upwards and holding him there, still kissing him.

He took that as an invitation to reciprocate and tentatively ran his hand down her back, round her bottom and felt, through her skirt, the softness in between her legs from behind. He could not quite reach and she, noticing this, took his hand and, taking this away from behind her, placed it in front, in the same area, but where he could massage her to more purpose. She groaned before saying, 'This is no good. Let's get off the path. Where can we go?'

'There are caves nearby?' he enquired.

'Sounds OK to me,' and disengaging from each other, they had gone, arms around one another to a sandstone cave, hollowed out of the hill above the river, where he had taken his greatcoat off, spread it on the ground and they had, kissing, sunk slowly down until both were kneeling. She pulled her skirt up, undid his trousers and then, looking at him, asked, 'Do you want me to do this?'

She, fastening her mouth around him, had started but it was

too much for Ralph, to whom it seemed like minutes but can only have been seconds. 'Stop Lucy, I'll come too quickly,' he had implored.

'Let me instead,' and bending down over her, had lifted her bottom, pulled her knickers down and off, before burying his face in her softness.

'Yes, please, now,' she had muttered.

'Are you sure?'

'God. Yes,' she had replied, and he had entered her, slowly and deliciously, she sighing, until he was right inside. They lay for a few moments like that, clutching one another and looking deep into each other's eyes.

'I can see your soul,' Ralph said.

'I can see yours too'

'I love you.'

'We've only just met.'

'It doesn't matter. I just know.'

'I love you too.'

'We've only just met.'

'I know, but I know as well,' before Ralph had concentrated on holding himself back and ensuring that Lucy had an orgasm that would, in his words then, blow her brains out. She had come, with great wrenching cries before he, suddenly worried as to an unplanned teenage pregnancy, had whispered, 'Should I come on your tummy?'

'No, it's all right. Inside me please, and kiss me while it happens,' and he then had the most deeply satisfying and emotionally moving orgasm in his hitherto rather brief sexual career. He had kissed her, as he lay on top, her legs wrapped round him, and had felt and said that he had never felt so close to anyone before.

'Oh God, Ralph, that was lovely, lovely, lovely.'

They sat afterwards and talked, she of her twenty year old boyfriend she had been going out with for three years, since she was fifteen, and how upset he would be when she wrote saying that it was over between them, he of his limited sexual experience which she did not believe, telling him that he was a liar because he seemed to know exactly what to do, when and how, to maximise her pleasure and both agreeing how lucky they had been to meet.

Their relationship was a sunny one, never arguing, studying for their A levels together, they were each doing French and English, she in addition History, he German and they stimulated one another intellectually as much as physically.

Her parents approved of Ralph and knew of the sexual side of their relationship but Lucy and Ralph kept this quiet and never flaunted this in front of them or in fact anybody else. They spent hours in his car, otherwise walking, talking and read and studied in each other's bedrooms.

Ralph and Lucy both agreed, that when their A level results came out and each had achieved straight A's, that they owed it to the other. It was the best time of his life, talking of the future, marriage, careers, a life together. They had applied to the same university, he to read law, she English. He was determined to be a barrister and a judge in due course. She encouraged him, believed in him, talked of his going into politics, while she would become an author. She had ideas for novels which they discussed and Ralph was convinced she should write.

'You'll be the twentieth century Jane Austen.'

Neither could have been happier or more content; the world

seemed to have been made for them to enjoy and conquer. Out of school inseparable, in those last summer holidays before university always together, only parting to sleep in their respective parents' houses, they looked forward, anticipating a bright and successful future.

They had spent an evening together, revisiting for the umpteenth time the scene of their first sexual encounter where she, sinking to her knees in the cave again, had insisted on trying to recapture that first time, pretending again that it was then and reliving each move and moment.

'God,' she had said afterwards. 'How can anyone be, let alone deserve to be as happy as we are.'

Arranging to meet at lunch time the following day at his house, they had parted, a kiss, a look, a meeting of the eyes, she to go to town the following day with her parents and he to wait for her afterwards at his house.

When she failed to turn up, he was concerned but not anxious. He rang her house but there was no reply. He went round there but it was empty, her parents' car absent from its usual parking place. He was in an agony of indecision and misery. He went home and waited. It was only when his father, on his return from the bank, said that there had been a nasty car accident in town, a bus had careered out of control into a car, that Ralph, feeling sick and empty, had telephoned the police to ask whether they could say who had been in the car.

'A family called Shaw,' the impersonal voice had said. Ralph had started shaking.

'How are they?' he managed to say.

'I don't know. They were taken to hospital. I'm only the desk sergeant.'

Ralph had driven like a madman to the local general hospital, gone into Casualty and asked a friendly-looking nurse about the Shaw family.

'Why, are you a relative?'

'Lucy and I are getting married,' he had said, not feeling that there was anything at all preposterous at the idea of two eighteen-year-olds already having so decided.

'What's your name?'

'Ralph.'

'Ralph, come with me,' and the young girl, with a wisdom beyond her years, had taken him to a side room, before sitting him down and holding both his hands in her hands said, gravely and professionally, 'I'm sorry Ralph. Lucy is dead. Her father is critical, and Mrs Shaw is conscious but has no idea of what has happened. She's heavily sedated.'

Ralph had sat numb for what seemed to him an eternity before letting out a howl, had collapsed, onto the desk, head in his arms, choking for breath, twisting and curling up in anguish. The nurse had sat with him, had asked if he wanted medication which he had refused, and insisted on a doctor seeing him before she would let him leave.

He had recovered enough to ask if he could see Lucy but was told, firmly and compassionately, that it was not possible.

Her father died later that night. Mrs Shaw, with many broken bones and internal organ damage had been kept in hospital for nearly two months and had not been able to go to the joint funeral which Ralph had attended, just another mourner amongst the family and friends.

Father and daughter had been buried in the same grave in the town's municipal cemetery, a melancholy place of ordered graves and ranks of cypress trees, far removed from Ralph and Lucy's romantic vision of lying together for all eternity in a little English country church yard, straight out of the Canterville Ghost, a Garden of Death, with a gentle loveliness touching the old yews, the ancient gravestones and a timelessness that had appealed to them both.

Ralph, in his only suit, the one he had worn to the university interview, stared down at the coffin; he had not been allowed to see her, had been told it would be too distressing, had not insisted, feeling that he had no right. He wanted to make a grand gesture like Laertes, but threw a small bunch of lilies down onto the wooden box, silent tears coursing down his cheeks, so many that his shirt was wet, unchecked, unimpeded and seemingly unceasing.

There had been no wake, no farewell party, the mourners had simply dispersed and Ralph had gone to his Mini, driven up to the special place and had sat there, for the rest of the day, still crying and shaking with an unstoppable grief.

In the remaining three weeks before the holidays had ended he had visited Mrs Shaw every day. She had, of course, been told of her daughter and husband's death but never alluded to them. She had aged, Ralph thought, ten years between his last seeing her and the first time he was allowed to see her again. They sat together, in silence, holding hands, for the duration of the hour, each locked in their own thoughts of loss, the unfairness of life, its transience, its uncertainty, the injustice.

On the last occasion he had visited, the day before he was to go with his car and his worldly possessions to start his new life at university, she had taken both his hands in hers, in an unconscious imitation of the nurse who had broken the news to him, and had said, 'Ralph you've been a great comfort. I know Lucy would want you to go on and try to achieve her and your dreams. Don't forget her but please, don't let it ruin your life. For her sake, please try and do everything you planned. For my sake too. I'll watch the papers for news of you in years to come.'

He had been so overcome all he could say, between sobbing again, was, 'It was my fault, you were on your way to drop her at my house, there can't ever be anyone like her again.'

She had said gently, 'There has to be. Just remember how happy you were with her. You made her the happiest girl I've ever seen. I can only thank you and bless you for that. And you must never, never, never think again that it was your doing.'

He kissed her. 'I'll try Mrs Shaw. I promise,' and had left the ward.

Mrs Shaw was discharged from hospital some weeks later and went, Ralph understood, to live with relatives in Devon but he never learnt of her new address, had not even exchanged Christmas cards with her and she would certainly never have known of his subsequent achievements.

Ralph had gone to university wearing, it was not an affectation, a visible air of tragedy. It was soon common knowledge that he had loved and lost, not through his own fault, but simply a car accident and this, coupled with his dark clothing, his intellectual abilities and the deliberate cultivation of what he considered a poet-like appearance, combined to make him attractive to girls who wanted to mother him, comfort him, believed that they could be the one with whom he could achieve another happiness.

He was sexually promiscuous in a monogamous way but derived no great pleasure from the sex act again. He always thought of Lucy, beautiful, generous, open-hearted Lucy, to whom he always believed he had lost his real virginity, who had taught him how to love and what it was like to be loved.

He had often cried into his pillow when alone and sometimes when making love with another girl, tears had come to his eyes but which he always managed to conceal, usually by breaking away and burying his head between their legs; they didn't notice his tears in their pubic hair. It was in such an emotional state that he had met Virginia in his third year.

'Mr Edwards?'

The voice broke into his recollections. 'I'm sorry to disturb you but...'

He looked round, eyes blinking slightly, the memory of Lucy had been so strong that he had momentarily forgotten time and place, had been transported back nearly twenty-one years and, shaking his head as if to clear his thoughts, said, 'Ralph, please, not Mr Edwards. What can I do for you Angharad?'

She stood there, hesitantly. 'I just wondered if you'd spare me a moment to look over an Opinion I've drafted.'

It was an unspoken rule in their Chambers that any pupil could access any of the more senior members for a view or discussion, if the time were right. Ralph was glad of the diversion.

'Certainly. Is that it in your hand?'

She nodded and gave it to him, and turned to leave. He said, 'No, sit down. I'll look at it now and talk it over if you want.'

She sat down, crossing her legs, in one of his visitor's chairs and he thought again of Lucy. As he did so, she said, 'What's the matter. You look so sad. Sorry. Didn't mean to be personal but...'

'You remind me of someone I was very close to.'
'Who?'
'Oh, just a girlfriend a long time ago.'
'Why so sad?'

He found himself telling her the whole story. She must have known, of course, about Virginia and Tina. It was pretty well common knowledge even though it had all happened nearly two years earlier. She periodically made sympathetic murmurs and when Ralph looked up again, he found to his horror, that there were tears in her eyes.

'You poor man,' she said, getting up and coming round to his side of the desk, bending and slipping an arm around him. 'How very sad. And it still affects you like this.'

'Yes,' he said, 'I'm afraid it does.'

She squeezed his shoulder and stood up again. 'Don't worry; I won't mention it to anyone. It's a bit private. Have you told anyone before?'

'My first wife knew but I've never talked about it since.'

'Your first wife was killed in a car accident as well wasn't she?'

'Yes. And I blame myself for that as well.'

'You can't blame yourself for the first one. What was she called?'

'Lucy.'

'Lucy's death was hardly your fault.'

'Maybe not but I still feel that I could have prevented it And Virginia's.'

'You can't go through life blaming yourself. You've got to escape the past.'

'I can't escape the past. It's with me all the time.' He thought of Tina. Her past and how it intruded all the time on the present.

'It's silly, the past is gone.'

'It influences the present and the future.'

'Yes, but it doesn't need dwelling on. You won't like me saying this but I think it's a bit morbid. Yes. Have the happy memories but don't let the sad ones, the uncontrollable ones take over.'

'You're right of course but don't you have sad or uncomfortable memories that intrude from time to time? You're married aren't you?'

She nodded.

'Do you share the unhappy or uncomfortable ones with your husband? I tend not to with my wife.'

'Oh God, there are certain things you just can't tell each other.'

'Like what?'

'I think complete honesty a recipe for disaster.' She was sitting in her chair again, leaning across his desk, her chin resting on her hands as though she was considering a particularly difficult legal problem. 'Well, for instance, my husband doesn't know I was engaged to someone else before him.'

'Why not?'

'Because I never told him.'

'Why not?' He was fascinated. It seemed to bear so much on his current preoccupations.

'I really didn't want to tell him. It made no difference and might have hurt him.'

'Might it not hurt him more if he found out now? By accident, or just out of the blue. One of your family for instance.'

'They understand that I don't want it talked about. And

anyway, it was only a teenage romance.' He winced. 'I don't mean it like that. I was as fond of him as you were of Lucy, but it was over. I chucked him the expression was, perhaps still is, after I started at university. He was a librarian, older than me, working. I don't even know what became of him.'

Ralph was appalled at her seeming indifference.

'But we were happy together for a time.'

'And you're happy now with your husband?'

'It's still the honeymoon period. We've been married for less than two years.'

The same as me, he thought bitterly, but the honeymoon seemed over.

'No, it's all right,' she continued, 'but you mustn't tell each other everything. You've got to have some secrets.'

'Why?' he exclaimed.

'I'm really not sure. I just feel you have. Look,' she suddenly straightened up. 'I'm taking up your time. I only wanted you to look over this,' motioning towards the unread document.

'I'll do it now.' He concentrated and read it swiftly through, then reread it more slowly. The linguistic analysis, the legal reasoning and the conclusions were all faultless. He handed it back to her saying, 'It's a terrific piece of work. I certainly couldn't do any better.'

She looked pleased. 'Thank you Ralph. It's kind of you to say so. I'll get along now. It's been more than interesting talking to you.'

She was gone. Ralph had almost asked her to go for a drink, had almost wanted to proposition her, wondered how she would have reacted, outrage or a cautiously enthusiastic response? The thought of having her, on his desk, was a pleasant one.

He had not been prepared to try however, had not wanted to, and sat after the door had closed, pondering the enigma that she had presented. Perhaps he was being unreasonable in his enquiries, albeit they were ones he did not pursue out loud with Tina. He looked at his watch. It was well past the twins' bedtime and he decided to call Tina, but hesitated. He drew his hand back from the telephone, not sure of what he wanted to say, and instead, checking that lights were out, Angharad must have gone very swiftly, closed the door behind him, went down the stairs and out into the city evening.

He left the hood down as he drove home, head empty of thought, just concentrating on the motorway and its traffic. When he reached their house, the lights downstairs were out, and only a glow through an upstairs window betrayed occupation. He let himself in quietly, went into the kitchen, found and opened a bottle of wine, noting glumly that all the choice he had was cheap Bulgarian red or white, both at the same temperature, and sat at the kitchen table, glass in front of him, lost in dark thoughts again. Tina put her head round the door.

'You're back then?' She did not seem particularly angry or concerned.

He simply said, 'Yes.'

She got another glass, poured some wine for herself and sat down opposite him.

'What's wrong? Where have you been? What have you been doing?'

'Chambers, reading, working.'

'What's bothering you?'

'You.'

'Why?'

'Are the children asleep?'

'Yes.'

'Tell me what's bothering you?' She seemed genuinely concerned.

'I keep on wondering about you. We know so little about one another. You've never really asked me about my childhood or my adolescence or my university years. You've never told me anything much about yours. Why aren't you interested in my history?'

'Because I wasn't there with you. I wish I could have been your first but I wasn't.'

'No, I wish I had been your first too but I wasn't. Tim was.'

She looked startled, 'No, he wasn't, Ian was.'

'Who was Ian? You've never mentioned him.'

'Ian was my boyfriend after Tim. Ian was my first. I was his first too.'

'You must have been fond of him.'

'I was,' and her look changed to one, he thought, best described as rueful chagrin.

'When was that then?'

'The sixth form, my last year.'

'I'll bet you couldn't keep your hands off one another after that.'

'No,' she smiled, amused at the recollection, 'we only did it once, no twice.'

It was his turn to be startled. 'You only did it twice? That can't be true.'

'It is,' she was still smiling, eyes far away. He felt a gust of relief, not quite believing what she had said but wanting more than anything to believe that she really was telling the truth.

'And with St John?'

'I never liked sex with him. You know that.'

'Good God, you're almost new then.'

She beamed, 'Yes, if you want to put it like that, then I suppose I am.'

He finished his glass and held out his hand. 'Come to bed with me please,' and led her upstairs, she pausing as usual outside the twins open bedroom door, reassuring herself that both were sleeping before going into their bedroom, where, all thoughts of supper cast aside, he drew off her night-dress, pushed her onto the bed, unzipped his trousers to reveal his erection, her earlier aspersions and his morbidity forgotten, and sank down onto her, he deriving more pleasure from entering her that night than on any occasion he could remember since she had given birth.

Afterwards, as she lay there, he beside her, each having had what they assured one another was a wonderful orgasm, she said, 'You're just about back to normal. That's much more like it. Why don't you do it to me like that more often?'

'Because you don't seem to want me to.'

'Of course I do, darling. You've got to make some allowances for being tired, overwrought, children, that kind of thing.'

'I shall, I promise,' and he cradled her head while she fell asleep.

It was only then, in the clearness of the night, when he always felt most lucid, that he considered what she had told him. Could it really be the case that what she said was the truth or was she misleading him totally? He ran the arguments for and against over and over in his head.

Against was the sheer unlikeliness of her assertion. Ralph

found it logically difficult to accept that, having done it once, having surrendered herself, and if she had been nineteen, then she had waited because she felt it important to wait for somebody she had considered important enough to her to do it then, that she did not, or more to the point he, did not want to do it again and again and again.

After all, he Ralph had with Lucy and conversely Lucy had with him. As far as Lucy was concerned, however, she was not a virgin when they met, had actually been fairly sexually experienced and had taught him everything even, before they had learned together. Was comparing Tina to Lucy fair? He was not sure.

For the proposition, was first the fact of its sheer unlikeliness. Ralph had discovered that in life the unlikely was often true and this could well be one such more. Taking that, with what she had told St John, and the fact that presumably he, St John, could have enquired of her old friends, had he wished, then perhaps once or twice only with Ian, was more tenable than scores or hundreds of times. The once or twice might have been more historically able to be hidden, disguised or brushed aside than had she done it more.

He fell asleep wondering if it mattered at all, given the distance that had now passed.

He woke up convinced it did, it reflected on the essential nature of their relationship. He, who had seen himself and Tina as Tristan and Isolde, Abelard and Heloise, tragic but romantic figures destined for one another, although perhaps doomed, could not bear the thought of dissimulation, lying or being misled.

He said nothing to Tina though, wanting to get a further perspective on the whole thing. He at least knew who it had been, had a name, although, thinking about it he realised he had always had a name, Tim, but had never thought about Tim, who he had thought was the first, in the way that he was thinking about Ian whom he had now been told was the first.

It was a fine day, he glanced at his watch. Six fifteen. He got up quietly without waking Tina, put on his trunks, taking a towel and went soundlessly downstairs and outside. He drew back the swimming pool cover and eased himself into the water, checking the temperature of it as he did so. Eighty degrees, a pleasantly invigorating but not too warm temperature and he did his customary fifty lengths, not at high speed but enough to get his heart rate up which is what he understood was desirable.

Getting out he towelled himself down quickly and then, putting on a gown, went back inside and upstairs. In their bedroom he looked at the sleeping form of Tina, and, unpredictably for him, found himself aroused at the sight of her, eyes closed, hair fanned out on the pillow and got back in bed beside her. She was lying away from him and he lifted one of her legs gently and, holding himself with his other hand, started easing himself inside her.

She suddenly exclaimed, 'Christ. Your willy's cold. Can't you go and warm it up a bit?'

'How?' he asked bemusedly. Did it matter whether a willy was hot or cold? He could not be sure but did not want to annoy her so said, 'Wait a moment.' and hopped out of bed and went to their bathroom where he ran some hot water and leant over the sink and doused it with a warm stream. The radiator was on and he rested it against it for a few moments, worried that the, to him, elaborate preparations might make him detumesce, but they actually seemed to make him more rigid.

Tina was lying where he had left her and when he got into bed again, she parted her legs without his asking and he slid gratefully in. 'No, I don't want one,' she said, 'but you go on.'

'Are you sure?'

'Yes, but you have one. It'll be nice. Women aren't like men; we don't need one all the time. Being held and wanted is sometimes quite enough.'

Feeling a bit selfish but sufficiently aroused for this not to matter, Ralph thrust his way to a perfectly pleasant but unexceptional orgasm that left him feeling slightly cheated. He preferred it if she had one first or they had one together.

'There, that was nice, wasn't it,' Tina murmured, turning round to kiss him. 'We'd better get on.'

He watched as she got up, pulled on her knickers, fastened her bra, pulled on a T shirt and then jeans, tugging on the zip and doing up her belt. She bent down facing away from him to pick up her shoes and he looked at her bottom, and the way the line of the join of the jeans disappeared into and around her crotch. She turned just then.

'What are you staring at?'

It was not said unpleasantly so he replied, in kind, 'You, I still fancy you rotten.'

'You know all the right things to say,' she smiled, bent over and kissed him and had gone into the children's' room before he could reply.

He could hear the twins waking up, they were sound sleepers which was a bonus for their parents he knew, and the merriment of their chuckles and laughter, and the low, encouraging noises of Tina, prompted him to get a move on.

He drifted through the early morning tasks as though on auto pilot, making the right noises and responses to both Tina and the children, helping with their breakfast, before going back upstairs to change into a dark suit.

At the door he asked Tina what she was doing that day and she answered, as she had so often already that summer, 'Nothing much. Go to the park, feed the children, maybe have a swim while they're asleep or maybe do some housework and have a swim with them after they wake. Then you'll be home. I'll see. Another mundane day.'

'Well hardly mundane. You wanted children and you've got two perfectly delightful ones and a swimming pool to use. The sun's shining.'

'Yes, I know, but it's hardly intellectually stimulating is it? Not like your day.'

'All I'll be doing is going into Chambers, picking up my post, exchanging good mornings with anyone I see, going into my room, sitting at my desk, for some time and doing anything especially urgent and then come home. I think I'd rather stay at home.'

'Why don't you then? What about e mail, computers?'

'I hadn't thought about it. I know nothing about them. But I suppose I could try and learn if you want me to.' He was suddenly rather taken with the idea.

'That would be nice. The children will be gone before you know it. School. Grown up. It would be nice if you spend as much time with them as possible.'

He kissed her and set off towards the station, walking purposively as ever, considering a change in his working practice. In fact, he thought, if he bought a computer, connected himself to the Internet, he might not even have to go to his Chambers at all. He knew little about computers or the Internet but understood that his clerk could scan in documents and e mail them to him. He need not even physically see them.

If he bought the essential law books, some he owned already, he could probably do much of his paperwork without difficulty. He also recalled that Chambers subscribed to an on-line legal service, he had heard it discussed and had indeed voted for it at a Chambers meeting without any real intention of using it, which presumably he could access from home as well. He resolved to have a word with Ken about it later on, bought a paper, waited for and got into the train and settled himself for the forty five minute journey.

Tina meanwhile tidied up. She had put the twins in front of morning television, Ralph had initially objected to this but had been silenced by the suggestion that they either had a nanny instead or they went to a childminder. 'How else am I to get on with the housework? You like clean sheets and a tidy house don't you?'

'What about while they're sleeping after their lunch?'

'I need to get on with other things then.'

'Like what?'

'The rest of the housework.'

'Reading and swimming.'

'Yes, that too. I deserve the relaxation. But if you'd prefer to pay for someone to look after them, or I'll look after them and you pay for a cleaner, then I'd be quite happy. On the other hand, they're quite happy to sit in front of the T.V. and I can get on with all the other stuff.'

'OK then,' and that was how it had been left and thus it was that every morning, Tina put the two of them into the family room, switched on the T.V. and left them there while she did the routine chores. She did not mind that her days were routine; she complained occasionally to Ralph but, she often said, for the most part she was happy enough. She loved the children, was much better, as most women are than men, with them than Ralph, had endless patience and was endlessly fascinated by them. She could happily lose a day in their company, just playing, singing, talking or reading simple stories. Occasionally she would do just that and Ralph would come home to the breakfast, lunch and children's supper things all still in the kitchen, the house untidy still, but Tina and the children totally content.

Tina did not depart from her plan as outlined to Ralph. She washed up quickly, gathered the children into their double buggy and took them to the park, a twenty minute walk, letting them toddle beside the buggy for the final one hundred yards. At the park the children had evolved their own routine; they preferred to go on the mini roundabout first, followed by swings for some minutes, Tina pushing them alternately, and then onto the slide before finishing on the roundabout again.

They all went home, Tina pausing to buy them an ice-cream from the van at the gates, pushing them all the way back. In front of the television again, usually at this time of the day a video, followed by lunch after which she put them to bed. They were always tired and fell asleep instantly, another routine Tina had encouraged believing that a sleep in the afternoon did them no harm, and allowed her to either have a rest, which she often felt she needed, or to swim or do more housework.

Today the sun was shining and she decided on a swim. She chose her serious costume, rather than the skimpy thong like garment, as she wanted to do some proper swimming and, after checking the front door was dead-locked it, she went through the patio windows and uncovered the pool. Pausing only for a moment, not even testing the temperature, she dived in and had done fifteen lengths or so before, on a tumble turn, she became aware of a man standing at the end watching her. She stopped and took off her goggles, standing in the shallow end.

'Good God, it's you.'

'Yes,' said Henry. 'I just happened to be passing and thought I'd call. Where are the children?'

'In bed as usual at this time of the day.'

'Water looks inviting.'

'Have you time for a swim? Do you want to join me?'

'No costume.'

'You could borrow one of Ralph's.'

'No, I shan't bother. You're not overlooked here, it's private enough,' and so saying, already jacket and tieless, he kicked off his shoes, pulled off his socks, took off his shirt, dropped and stepped out of his trousers and boxers. Totally naked, he walked to the edge, dipped a toe in and jumped, close to Tina. He must have straightened out under water because the next thing she knew was a hand, two hands, running up her thighs under water before he appeared right beside her.

'It's a nice temperature.'

'What is?' Tina enquired. 'Me or the water?'

'You,' and he bent to kiss her. She offered her mouth to him with enthusiasm. Backing off, he said, 'We can take up where we left off on Saturday.'

'But not here,' Tina said.

'Why not?'

'Someone might come round - just like you did. And anyway I want to be comfortable.' His hand was between her legs cradling her, with one finger stroking her through the costume and she was involuntarily moving her hips in response. She felt down and, finding him already erect, closed her fingers round it and started moving her hand up and down its length.

'Take your costume off.' She hesitated. 'Go on. I can't get round the elastic at the bottom. It's too tight and I'll hurt you.' He had been trying to move the crotch to one side but had failed. She pulled her costume down and wriggled out of it, still in the water.

'Here turn round and put your hands on the edge for a moment.'

She did as he asked and then felt his hands part her before he slid himself inside.

'God that's nice. You feel hot in there.'

'I am,' she grunted and then giggled to herself. 'Go on, fuck me.'

He moved rhythmically, backwards and forwards, the water

around them sloshing and lapping against the wall of the pool.

'I'm going to come soon,' he gasped. 'Do you want to go inside?'

She giggled, 'Yes. I want one too. Come inside and come inside me.'

He withdrew himself and she turned to him, put her arms around his shoulders and gave him a long kiss. 'We'll go to the spare room,' and levered herself out of the water. Kneeling on the pool side, she felt his tongue at the tops of her legs before he started between them, long, slow licks that had her writhing with pleasure.

'No I can't stand it. It's too too nice. Let's go in to a bedroom,' and standing up she ran naked towards the door.

He followed, looking somewhat self-conscious about his erection. Inside the house, they went upstairs to the spare room still with the sheets on the bed that he and Frances had used. She pulled the covers down, and then lay on the bed, arms out and legs parted.

'Lick me again,' she said in a whisper. He bent down and started, then put one finger inside her.

'God, that's lovely. Yes, just like that, don't stop,' and he did as he was told until she suddenly had her first orgasm. He stood up then and she, sitting on the edge of the bed, closed her mouth round the end.

'No stop, I want to be inside you.'

She lay back again and opened her legs. 'Here Henry, right here,' and he leaned over her, tickling the edges with his erection before pushing and sliding easily into her.

'Don't stop,' she squealed before nearly shouting, but remembering the sleeping babies muttering, 'Fuck me, Henry, fuck me rigid,' and he, taking her at her word, slammed backwards and forwards when, finally and nearly at the point of orgasm she, realising this, said, 'Take it out and do it over me.'

Understanding what she wanted, he withdrew, sitting astride her hips as she reached forward and rubbed violently until a stream exploded from the end, showering her stomach, breasts and face. She rubbed it into her skin like face cream, licking her fingers afterwards.

'That was nice, worth waiting for. We couldn't have done that on Saturday night, could we?'

'No,' Henry agreed. He was feeling spent. 'That was shattering. Shall we make it a regular fixture?'

'No, let's keep an element of surprise. Just give me a ring if you're in the area.' Tina went into her bedroom to get dressed and came down to find Henry, back in his clothes.

'I ought to go.'

'Yes. The twins will wake up soon. It's been lovely.' She kissed him lightly and watched him as he walked down the road, unhurriedly and seemingly unconcerned, to where he had parked his car. She looked at her watch. Three pm. 'Time to wake the twins,' she thought and went upstairs to get them.

When Ralph came home that evening he was excited. 'I'm going to get a computer for my study so I can work at home. I've spoken with Ken about it today and he sees no problem. In fact, he says it's probably the future anyway. Why pay rent and rates for offices if all we need is a machine in the corner of a room which is connected to a clerk's room? In the future we'll probably only need a library, and even that might be on-line and a couple of conference rooms.'

Tina tried to show enthusiasm but the whole subject of

computers bored her and she was still glowing inside from earlier in the afternoon.

'That will be nice. How often do you think you'll have to go into Chambers?'

'Not often at all. For the first week or two I think I'll go in at least a couple of times but I'll see how it goes. Have you been swimming today? Twins? Have they?' he asked Tina, not getting an answer from them.

'No.'

'I might take them in now. Do you want to come?'

'Maybe I'll join you.'

Ralph changed quickly while Tina changed the twins into their costumes, and then he took them to the edge where he fitted their armbands. He noticed some black material in the pool and jumping in, picked this up and said to them, 'What's this then?' They looked blank and he unfolded it calling, 'Tina your costume's in the pool.' She came out. 'What on earth is it doing here?'

'One of the children must have thrown it in.' The children looked at one another not comprehending anything of the conversation.

'Well, there you are then. Might as well put it on and join us.'

Ralph lifted the children and spent time with each, taking one armband off and encouraging them to swim by themselves. He was determined that they would be competent swimmers before they went to school and they had made enough progress each to be able to swim a width with only one armband provided one of their parents was at the other side to provide reassurance. Tina jumped in beside him.

'Come on, let's see if they can do a length' and the next twenty minutes were spent, each at opposite ends, shouting encouragement to the twins who, both nearly managed this. They got out, the four of them, laughing and Tina went to cook the children's supper while Ralph took them upstairs for a quick bath, dressing himself as they played in the warm water. Putting their night clothes on, he took them downstairs again where they ate quickly and eagerly.

'In many ways they're model children, aren't they?' he asked Tina rhetorically.

'Yes, they're yours. I'd expect them to be,' she answered. 'I hope they have your brains. They seem intelligent enough but you can't tell, can you? I'd like them to grow up like you. Able, confident.'

'In many ways, I'd rather they didn't grow up at all. We can protect them at the moment. The moment they go off to school, you've handed them over to the world. Up until then it's just us, our values, our influence, our teaching them. Then, they're anybody's.'

'They've got to go to school.' Tina was always practical.

'I know but they're lovely at the moment. Innocent, sweet, usually cheerful.'

'Yes, and tired. They can go to bed now.'

'Are you going to read them a story or am I? Whoever doesn't read can make supper.'

'Whichever you prefer.'

'You usually read. I'll take a turn.' Ralph went upstairs with them and, after they had selected one of their favourites, read for half an hour. The children sat, tousle-headed, sucking their thumbs, listening attentively. When he had closed the book, they cried out for more so he read for a few minutes longer before putting each in their cots and kissing them goodnight.

'Mummy will be up in a moment.' He drew the curtains. Tina had had them lined with heavy material so that their room would be dark even in the summer, and said, 'Night night children.'

'Night Daddy,' they chorused and he went downstairs again. Tina was in the kitchen, had laid the table, and was stirring a saucepan.

'What are we having?'

'Spag bol.'

'What happened to the way we used to eat? Spaghetti is for students. It was a staple of mine at university. I'm twice that age now.'

'If you want to eat nicer food, you can do the shopping,' she said as she spooned it onto plates.

'I don't mind. If I'm not travelling for a couple of hours a day, I'll have more time for everything.' The prospect was quite beguiling.

'And what I save on fares, I'll spend on better food.'

'Why don't you spend it on...'

He interrupted. 'No. I'll quite happily do the shopping, or we can do it together. We don't have to have fillet steak every night but it would be nice to get away from basic food.'

'Are you criticising my cooking?' She was smiling.

'No, Just the ingredients. Which I have to use too. I'll come back earlier tomorrow. Unless you want to come with me? I'm just going to pick up the post and buy a computer. We could stop at a supermarket on the way home.'

'Yes, I'd like to do that. It would be fun. What about the

children in the computer shop?'

'I'll leave you in somewhere suitable like...'

'Oh thanks a bunch, I might like to look at computers with you.'

'Then we'll tie them to their buggy and gag them. Not a problem,' grinned Ralph. They cleared up, watched T.V. for a while and then went to bed, Ralph putting his arm round her and lying close up against her back.

The next morning he woke, got up, looked out of the window and decided to swim again. Afterwards, when he came into the bedroom, Tina, who did not open her eyes said, 'If you're expecting the doings, you can warm your willy up. I'm not having that cold thing inside me again. It gave me a nasty shock yesterday.'

Ralph feeling foolish, but also expecting "the doings", went to the bathroom radiator again and pressed himself against it. Judging it now to be warmer, and certainly stiffer, he noticed, he went back into their room and found Tina, lying naked on the bed, arms and legs spread.

'What on earth?'

'Come here Ralph, it's the first day of the rest of our life, let's celebrate,' and he sank down onto her.

'I want a huge orgasm and I'm not letting you go until I've had one,' she said quietly.

Afterwards she kissed him. 'If you don't have to go to work, we can do that every morning. I'm too tired in the evenings. It's much nicer at the beginning of the day, even if your glop does fall out into my knickers later on.'

Ralph looked pained. 'Do you always have to be so biological?'

'Well it's yours, isn't it? I don't mind. It reminds me of you. Come on. Let's get going.'

Driving in the Mercedes, Ralph looked at Tina beside him and the twins in the rear, strapped into their safety seats, and felt content. His family around him and, with the prospective purchase of a computer giving him a freedom that he had never envisaged, he felt as though he had taken charge of his life again. He bounded into Chambers, having left Tina and the children in the car parked in a twenty minute slot, and picking up his post, nodded to Ken and said, 'I'm off to get a computer, Ken. I'll e-mail you later.'

Ken grinned, 'You've had lessons have you? It's a bit complicated you know.'

'OK, I'll e-mail you tomorrow.'

'Yeah, yeah, yeah. Give me a ring if you need help. And I'll bet you do.'

'We'll see,' replied Ralph completely determined to master the machine.

They then drove to an out-of-town shopping mall and went into an industrial sized shed that sold office equipment. The children were temporarily silenced by a lolly each and Ralph stood, feeling bewildered by the choice and variety. A salesman approached, 'Can I help you?'

'Yes, I'd like a computer.'

'Any particular kind sir?'

'No, just an ordinary computer that I can send and receive e-mails on and a printer.'

'It's more complicated than that sir.'

'No, I don't want to complicate it. I just want a straightforward computer. Decent memory. Cables to connect to telephone socket. Doesn't have to have a games capability. It's for preparation and transmission of documents only.'

The salesman seemed put out, perhaps disappointed at not being able to indulge in techno-speak as Ralph called it, but showed them, what he assured Ralph was a suitable piece of equipment.

'Right, I'll take it,' Ralph said having looked at the price and realising he could squeeze it all onto a credit card.

'You don't want to try it? Check it out at all against other ones?'

'No.' Ralph was reluctant to admit, let alone show, that he knew absolutely nothing about the machines and would have to embark on a learning process that as yet did not have any foundation.

Tina looked at him suspiciously. 'Are you sure you don't want a bit of advice on how to work it?'

'No.'

'You're an arrogant sod aren't you?'

'No. It was designed by a human being and my intellect will be just as good as the designers. I'll just follow it through rationally.'

'Let's see,' she said. They took the boxes out on a trolley and filled the rear of the car. There was only just enough room and Ralph had to pack and unpack several times before they were all in.

'Right, supermarket,' he said, 'and then home.'

It was a long time since Ralph had been in a large supermarket and he was quite taken aback at how expensive everything seemed. Nevertheless he enjoyed choosing meals for the rest of the week but was staggered when the bill came to over one hundred pounds.

'Now you know,' Tina said.

'Well, my rail fares were over forty pounds a week. They cancel each other out.'

They loaded the car and Tina suggested going out for lunch. Ralph, however, wanted to get home and assemble the computer.

'Let's eat at home.'

'You just want to play with your new toy.'

'Not at all, but the sooner it's up and running, the sooner I can stop going into town.'

Ralph disappeared into his study having taken all the boxes up there first. After connecting all the components up to one another, which took much longer than he anticipated, he switched on. A reassuring hum and then the computer crackled into life. Ralph spent several hours feeling his way round the machine, patiently trying out various routines and to his surprise found that it was all much simpler than he expected.

Tina brought him some sandwiches but he hardly looked up, rapt in the intricacies that he was trying to elucidate.

She came up again. 'It's five. Would you like a swim with the children?'

'Maybe. I'll just finish this.' He was so engrossed that he immediately forgot about her suggestion and was surprised when she poked her head round the door to tell him that the twins were going to bed.

'I'll come and say goodnight in a moment.'

The next thing he knew, she came to tell him that supper was ready. By then he had run an extension cable to the telephone socket in their bedroom and was about to install the free software for the Internet.

'Right, I'll be right down.' He disengaged himself reluctantly and went to the kitchen. Tina had cooked Wienerschnitzel and there was a bottle of wine on the table. He ate and drank hurriedly, pausing only to say, 'Thank you, that was delicious. I must try and finish,' before going back to his machine.

Tina came in to say that she was going to bed. He replied that he would follow her. He was having difficulty in working out how to use the Internet and e-mail facilities. He had installed an ISP free disc and carried on however, persistently and doggedly, methodically trying things out, retrying them again and again until he understood the system.

At last he was ready to write an e-mail and, manoeuvring his mouse with a proficiency that he knew Ken would find incredible, he accessed the correct area and wrote, 'Dear Ken, here it is. So there! Can you reply with a scanned in document please? Yours Ralph.'

He moved the mouse, pressed send and had great satisfaction in seeing the words 'e-mail sent' appear. He looked at his watch. Good God, he thought, who knew it could take so long? It was hardly worth going to bed and he wondered what to do next. Looking out of the window, he saw that it was already light and thought of a walk or a swim. He found it difficult to decide, so simultaneously was he adrenalised by the learning curve, but also dog-tired, so tired that he could fall asleep in an armchair.

He gave up, closed his computer down, and went to bed. Tina did not stir and he lay, for an hour, quietly, unmoving, on his back, hands behind his head, staring at the ceiling. At about six thirty he got up and swam his customary fifty lengths and came back up, going to the bathroom to dry himself. Tina was stirring.

'Are you warm?'

'Not particularly. The water was quite cool.'

'Warm yourself up and come and cuddle me.' He leant against the radiator in the bathroom for a while, warming himself and it up and then got back into bed. Tina reached for him. 'Come here, put it inside me,' and rolled over.

'That's nice,' she murmured, 'slowly please.' He did as he was asked, judging her reactions and movements until, when she started moaning softly, he permitted himself to let go and they came together, he clutching at her breasts.

Tina, who had been looking forward to seeing Henry again, ever since the last occasion when they had had a swim together, followed by satisfyingly athletic sex compared to Ralph who, boringly to her mind, seemed now to prefer pregnancy mode on their sides, was obviously cross with him. Henry had telephoned to say that he would visit that day, 'if the coast is clear.'

'I thought you were going to Chambers today. You always go on a Thursday for the Chambers meeting and spend a few hours there.'

'God, Tina,' he yawned, 'you've no idea how dull it all is. Yak, yak, yak. New secretary this, new book that. Should we, shouldn't we, twenty-five prima donnas, all with a different point of view, all determined to argue their dreary corner. I thought I might give it a miss and stay at home with you and the twins. If there's any post Ken, or one of his girls, will e-mail me and they don't need me anyway. I've effectively stopped saying anything.'

Tina was panicking. There was no way she could contact Henry, if Ralph was in the house, without the risk of discovery. She could imagine it. 'Who did you phone?' or worse still, he walk in on her and hear her saying, 'Not today, Henry' or even worse still, she suddenly thought, his picking up an extension and overhearing an incriminating conversation. And the fact was she wanted some hard urgent sex with someone else.

'Well, I think you ought to go,' she said.

'Why, have you other plans?' Ralph teased her. 'Is there another man?'

She coloured slightly. 'Of course not. Don't be so absurd. I'm just going to do the usual things. My routine you know, cleaning, tidying, washing, feeding the children.' Ralph knew all about routine, routine clattered about the house, loudly, every day and sometimes the noise was such that he couldn't concentrate on his paperwork and longed for his old way of life.

'I think I might go in after all. I've got some research I ought to do which would be much easier in the library there.' Tina brightened.

'What time will you be back?'

'Oh,' he looked at his watch, 'I'll go in about eleven. Chambers meeting at four thirty. Back, I suppose, about seven. Do you want me to get anything?'

'No. I'll go shopping with the twins. Do you want a quickie?'

'Why only a quickie?'

'Because the twins need their breakfast. Come on,' and she rolled onto her side, felt him enter her, and when he gasped, 'Tina, Tina,' and she felt him ejaculate, simulated an orgasm herself, turning to him and saying, 'That was lovely.'

She spent the rest of the morning, after he had gone, immersed in her routine and precisely at two, the babies having been fed and put in their cots for the afternoon, the doorbell rang. Henry stood there, perhaps a bit shame-faced and self-conscious and clearly wanting to get in the house as quickly as possible.

Once in, the door closed, he put his arms round Tina, pulled her close, kissing her and beginning an urgent exploration of her body. His hand fastened round her fanny, groping and clutching, and Tina said, 'You're hurting.'

'I've wanted you so badly, I've been...'

'Me too.' She relaxed as she said this and he began to undo her zip, unfastening the top button of her Levis, and then putting his hand down, down and, as his finger touched her, she moved so that it slid right in.

'I've got to have you now,' she groaned. 'I can't wait. Quick, upstairs.'

They went to the bedroom again, where each undressed and then, opening her legs, she pulled herself gently apart, before groaning, 'Put it in.'

Henry was on top of her, pounding away, thrusting and grunting until, with an animal-like roar, she felt him come inside her, which, although she had had a small orgasm already as he entered her, was enough to precipitate another longer one which, this time, was not small at all.

As they lay there, panting and sweaty, Henry said, in a melancholy tone, 'I'm back with Frances.'

'Oh, does it matter? We can still have our sessions can't we?'

'Oh God, yes. I was hoping you'd say that but I thought...'

'Look, I've no intention of leaving Ralph, you know that. I told you last time. This is sex, which I like with you.'

'No. But I thought that it might make a difference.'

'It would if either found out. So let's not let them. Are you recovered enough to do it again?'

After he had gone, she pulled the soiled sheets off, leaving them on the landing, meaning to take them to the wash basket later. The twins woke up, distracted her and so she had forgotten about the sheets altogether by the time she had changed their nappies, dressed them, amused them for some time and fed them.

She seemed shocked when Ralph walked into the kitchen.

'You're home early. I didn't expect you for a couple of hours.

'Aren't you pleased? You seem a bit put out.'

'Of course I'm pleased, darling.'

He went upstairs to change and, seeing the crumpled sheets outside the spare room door, looked puzzled. He picked one up, then put it down again and, having changed into sweater and jeans, came down saying, 'Why are the spare room sheets on the landing?'

Was he suspicious? She said carelessly, over her shoulder, 'The children, Ralph, the children. One ran off after I'd taken her nappy off and then the other started crying and I picked her up and then went to find Primrose. Anyway she was on the bed nappyless. You can guess the rest.'

His mouth puckered, his distaste evident, Ralph shook his head. 'How two such sweet and charming little creatures can produce so much excrement is beyond me.'

Relieved, Tina smiled winningly at him. 'Blood, sex and excrement wasn't it? Didn't you say once?'

'Well, not quite that, but that was the gist of it.'

'Anyway why so early?'

'I got fed up. I walked out of the Chambers meeting.'

'Oh no, Ralph, not in a huff surely? You didn't say anything, you know, provocative or outrageous did you?'

'No, I pleaded a meeting. I wanted to come home to you.'

In view of this, perhaps it should not have come as a surprise to Tina when, the following Thursday, he said that he would be staying at home all day. Tina said nothing when he announced his intention and after breakfast asked if he was going to get a newspaper as usual. 'Yes,' his usual routine being a brisk walk to the newsagents half a mile away.

After he had left, Tina picked up the phone and was just about to dial when Ralph came in again.

'Forgot my wallet. Who are you phoning?'

Tina immediately replied, 'My mother, why?'

'I just wondered.'

'I'm not doing anything wrong am I?' she enquired crossly as she put it down.

'No, of course not. Carry on,' and he left again.

Tina phoned Henry's office. He was not expected in until late afternoon. No, there was no way they could contact him. Could they say who had called?'

'No,' Tina had said wearily, hanging up.

At two precisely, the doorbell rang. Ralph was there before Tina and was astonished to see Henry, who seemed equally astonished at seeing him.

'Ralph, what are you doing at home?'

'I live here, remember?' Ralph grinned amiably. 'What are you doing here, more to the point?'

'I was just passing. I thought I'd drop in and say hello to Tina and the girls. I've brought them a present.' He held out two gift wrapped packages. I am their Godfather after all.' Ralph looked at him, the first vestiges of suspicion insinuating themselves into his thoughts.

'Come on in,' he said affably, calling out then, 'Tina, Henry's here.'

Tina came out of the kitchen wiping her hands on a towel. 'Henry. How nice to see you. What brings you here?'

'I had to go past, an appointment, and I thought it would be nice to see the girls. How are they?'

'Asleep at the moment, but they'll be up soon.'

Henry and Tina behaved exactly as if this was a chance encounter, giving nothing away.

'What are you doing at home anyway Ralph? It's a nice surprise to see you.'

'I'm working mainly from home now. I've brought myself into the 20th century and gone computerised. E-mail and all that.'

'How long have you been online?'

'Only a week or two but it's going pretty well.'

Henry looked impressed. 'Did you go on a course? I've tried to teach myself but I think I must be a technophobe. I can't get the hang of it at all.'

'No, he taught himself,' Tina said. 'He's ever so clever.'

'Oh, I know that. Remember, I saw him in action.' He turned to Tina. 'Has Frances phoned? We're back together, I'm pleased say. Let bygones be bygones.'

'I'm ever so pleased, as of when?'

'Last week. I crawled round, on my knees, head in hands, begging forgiveness. And she did. I'm not going to stray again,' he added meaningfully.

'Good. Frances will be relieved,' laughed Tina. 'I hope it works out for you. Listen. There's a child crying. I think it's Daisy.'

They all listened and the sound of one crying was superseded by the sound of both crying loudly.

'Well, that's the end of adult conversation. I'll go and get them.'

While she was upstairs, Henry turned to Ralph and said, 'What's wrong?'

Ralph was putting his own two and two together.

'I was just thinking about you and Frances. I understand from Tina that her illness is in complete remission.'

'Yes, thank God. All we can do is pray and keep our fingers crossed. I wish I'd never done it but, there it is. It happened. Haven't you ever been tempted Ralph?'

Ralph thought of Frances, her black stockings, her red knickers, her pendulous breasts with their dark nipples, the bush of black pubic hair, the sensation of her sliding down onto him and then crying out, 'It's huge,' then thought, realised that she must have been making a comparison between them, and laughed out loud. Henry must have an extremely teeny peeny. Ralph laughed again, 'No Henry, I've not been tempted.'

'Why are you laughing?'

'At the folly of human beings.'

Tina came in with the girls, who looked unnaturally clean and wholesome.

'Look, it's Uncle Henry.'

'Henry, Henry,' they went and toddled up to him to be kissed.

'I've got you a present, my lovely little cherubs. From Auntie Frances, Sam and I. Here.'

They tore the wrapping paper off and each exclaimed with delight at the Steiff soft toys he had chosen.

'Tank you, tank you,' they chorused before toddling off to watch their favourite video for the sixtieth time.

Henry looked at his watch. 'Bloody. I'll be late. I only meant to look in quickly. I must fly,' and standing up, pecked Tina on the cheek, saying, 'I've told Frances you must come over soon, we'd like to celebrate with you both. Our being back together. Frances will phone you Tina. Bye,' and was gone.

Ralph cleared away the cups, moodily and grimly, the inchoate thoughts gradually resolving, forming and reforming themselves.

Tina came in. 'What's wrong?'

'Nothing, nothing at all.' He considered direct confrontation but rejected the idea. He did not want to argue. He was a lawyer, trained to argue, but forensically, skilfully, intellectually, in the polite and procedure-ridden confines of a courtroom. Raw anger and raised voices were not really his scene. So he avoided the issue, making polite conversation with Tina until she decided it was time to put the children to bed and for her afternoon rest.

'Do you want to come with me?'

'No thanks.'

'There's something wrong. I thought we might you know...'

'No, I've got work to do,' and he went back to his study, where he remained, staring at the blank computer screen, trying to make sense of his life.

Frances was on the phone the following day, 'Would you like to come to dinner and stay with us on Saturday night? I know it's short notice but some friends are over from Zimbabwe and we thought you'd like to meet them. Say yes, Tina.'

Tina went up to Ralph with the portable phone in her hand, went into the study and found him sitting, doing nothing, just gazing. She was perturbed but, holding her hand over the mouthpiece, said, 'It's Frances. Can we go to dinner on Saturday? They've got friends.'

'Yes, whatever, sure,' he replied without looking up. 'It seems a bit quick. When did they get...' but Tina was speaking into the phone and ignoring him.

'We'd love to come. See you tomorrow then. Bye. Sorry Ralph, what were you saying?'

'Just checking when they got back together.'

'A couple of days after Frances came here by herself. Why?'

'Seems a bit quick to have people round. You'd think they might like to lick their wounds in peace.'

'Perhaps they've done all of that already and want to try and consolidate a bit.'

Ralph made love to Tina that evening, after the children had been put to bed, before they had their customary bath, without enthusiasm, even wondering if Tina would notice if he feigned an orgasm. She did not feign one and, in the event, neither did he.

They set off early on the Saturday, Tina hoping to get the girls settled before the other guests arrived. Tina immediately went upstairs with the babies, Henry trailing after her with the portable cots, insisting that he would do it rather than allowing Ralph who, leaving the twins strapped in their seats on the floor in the sitting room, went in search of Frances. She was in the kitchen, her hair up, dressed in a long black skirt, slit up the side and a décolleté white blouse. She turned to him and he went to kiss her, politely, on each cheek. She, shutting the door quickly, grabbed him by the shoulders, pulled him towards her, kissing him longingly, probingly and putting her hand between his legs.

He did not respond but waited, until she drew back saying, 'What's wrong?'

'I can't. Anyway I thought you were back with Henry.'

'Yes, I am. But I'm not sure he's given up on the other woman. And you know how I feel about you.'

'You don't think he's finished with her? That's crazy. He told us he wasn't going to stray again. That he'd implored your forgiveness. That kind of thing.'

'I don't know. But I still want you.'

He smiled bleakly; all he wanted was Tina. Anything and anyone else was irrelevant.

'Come on Frances, I'll help you set the table,' and gathering cutlery and plates, he went through to the dining room.

Upstairs, Tina and Henry were locked together, kissing passionately.

'Is there time for a quickie?'

'You can hear every movement in this house and they're downstairs,' Henry muttered, undoing his flies and letting it spring out.

'Yes, I'll bend over here. Quick, quick,' and she leant over the dressing table, stifling her moan of desire as he pulled her knickers to one side and he inserted himself quickly, thrusting hard, harder, quickly, grunting as she suppressed another moan when she came and felt him, now on the short strokes and then coming inside her, she immediately straightening up, adjusting her knickers, pulling down her short skirt and he doing himself up.

'Must be a record,' he grinned at her. She grinned back.

'Teenage sex,' he said.

'No. Simple lust,' she responded as she and he started assembling the cots.

At that point Ralph walked in. 'I thought I heard noises in here. I was in the dining room just below.'

'I was showing Henry how to undo the cots and erect them.'

Did they exchange smiles at the mention of the word 'erect'?

Ralph was not sure but there seemed to be an easy intimacy between them and there was no doubt that Henry looked a bit dishevelled.

Had they been kissing, groping each other, jumped apart when he came in? It would explain the noises he had heard when downstairs.

'Here let me help,' he said, with the horrible suspicion, vision even, dominating his thoughts.

When they had finished, and Tina had made up the beds and had gone to get the twins, Henry, turning to him, said, 'You know, Tina seems to grow prettier by the day. You're a lucky man Ralph.'

'Frances is pretty good looking too you know.'

'Oh, Frances.' He laughed. 'Sometimes I think its just the sex that kept us together and is going to keep us together still.'

'Why?'

'She likes to do it at least three or four times a week,' he said, proudly, as though this conferred distinction on him too.

Ralph laughed; he liked to do it at least once a day. 'That's great Henry. You're a lucky man,' and they, each deluding themselves and the other, went down to the women, who were in the kitchen, children playing happily at their feet.

'Come on girls, bedtime, say goodnight to Auntie Frances and Uncle Henry. Say goodnight to Daddy. Kiss,' Tina said, scooping them both up and holding them for their bedtime kisses.

Henry picking his son up and saying similarly, 'Bedtime for babies, kisses,' and following Tina out of the room.

Why does he always follow her around? Ralph wanted to ask Frances but said instead, very quietly, 'Frances, I didn't know you were a sex machine. Henry's just told me you want it three or four times a week.'

Frances turned to him smiling. 'I don't want it three to four times a week. I'd like it three or four times a day. It's all he can manage. He has difficulty getting it up. Not like you,' and she licked her lips provocatively, drawing the flap of her skirt aside and revealing stockings and the fact that she was not wearing knickers, her pubic hair dark against her pale skin.

Dropping the fabric down again, she said in a slow reflective way, 'You're sitting next to me at dinner.'

Their other guests arrived, some neighbours and a very cheery couple, who, explaining that they were expats, and the others must forgive them but there was nothing else to do but drink there, had brought several bottles of wine with them.

'We always drink far too much so it's only fair to bring our own supplies to top up,' and proceeded to do just that, the others perhaps drinking a bit too much in consequence.

The conversation across the table turned to babies and there it stayed for the first, main and dessert course. Periodically, Frances put her hand under the table and rested it on Ralph's crotch, squeezing him, kneading it, evidently hoping that he would reciprocate, shifting in her seat, showing that her legs were apart.

He did not respond to the very obvious invitation, worked hard at being pleasant to everyone but was especially charming to Frances.

Tina was in the middle of talking about her birth when Wanda asked her, 'Did you have a natural birth, epidural or pethadine? Twins must be awful.'

'No it wasn't too bad. Just some gas and air.'

'Did it blow your mind?' She looked at her husband, 'Do you remember that story about Malcolm and Karen, where he'd broken his leg and I went with them to that little hospital to reset it and they gave him pethidine and the higher he got the more he babbled on about his affair with his secretary. And his wife sitting there, God it was funny. On and on he went, she getting more and more livid. I had to hold her down. I thought she was going to tear his legs off.'

They all laughed, Ralph remembering his thoughts of Ian, inflicted on him during the birth, forcing his mirth he felt, through clenched teeth and asking, 'What happened?'

'Oh, when he came down again, she had a go at him, he poor bugger in plastered leg, couldn't do anything apart from cover his face and ward off the blows. I tried to hold her back but she wasn't having any of it, not until she'd whacked him a couple of dozen times,' and Wanda laughed again. 'The truth will always come out.'

Ralph looked at her grimly. 'And afterwards?'

'Oh they're still together, older and wiser,' and the conversation moved on.

Ralph took little further part but, thinking of Ian, and Henry and God knows who else, suddenly thought, 'Why not?' and dropped his hand down onto Frances' thigh. She looked at him, seemingly surprised and then smiled at him and, moving position, opened her legs so that most of the skirt fell off to one side. Ralph let his hand drift up the inner surface, simultaneously despondent, for thoughts of Tina crowded in, and excited, he had never groped another woman at a dinner table and the novelty of the sensation was quite pleasing. He felt the softness at the top of her legs and then, slipping his hand over her pubic hair, he curled one finger and, moving it along, then downwards, parted her labia.

The others, talking inconsequentially, Tina gazing at Henry in what Ralph considered a particularly rapt and intense way, were all unaware of what he and Frances were doing. Frances bent towards Ralph and whispered. 'Wiggle it a bit, I could have one. It's so naughty,' and he moved his finger, trying to stimulate her clitoris, until she exhaled, turning this into a cough to disguise her shudder of pleasure and picking up her napkin and covering her face for a moment. He immediately withdrew his hand and put it to his cheek, resting his elbow on the table.

'Are you all right Frances?' Tina asked from across the table. 'Ralph you look so judicial sitting there like that. Why don't you pat Frances' back? She's having an appalling cough.'

'Frances, would you like me to pat your back?' She nodded and Ralph patted her a few times, a token more than anything else, before she put down her napkin, smiled brightly and said, 'God, that was unexpected. Who'd like cheese? Would you like to help me Ralph?' and getting up, surreptitiously adjusting her skirt before doing so, gathered the plates. 'We need some more wine too, come on Ralph, do the honours.' Ralph stood up mechanically, wondering where all this was taking him, eyes only for Tina, talking again animatedly to first Henry and then Russell, Wanda and the other two guests.

In the kitchen, Frances put the plates down. 'Bloody hell, Ralph. That was so fucking erotic it was untrue. I had the biggest orgasm of my life. I thought I was going to pass out. I'm sorry I can't do the same for you though. At the table. People might notice it shaking. Pity there's not time for a quickie here. Or is there?' She turned away from him and bent over the table simultaneously lifting her skirt up. 'Quickly Ralph. I want you inside me.'

Ralph felt panic. Doing it with her when Tina was sound asleep and there was no chance of discovery was one thing but here in the kitchen...

'No, we can't, someone might come in...' but she had stood up again and approached him, her hand extended.

'Maybe later then,' she murmured and then her hand was in his trousers and getting him out.

'No, Frances.'

'Be quiet,' she was kneeling, teeth nibbling and then it seemed altogether swallowing him whole, as her head went backwards and forward faster and faster. He was lost now, standing firmly, thoughts of Tina pushed aside, as she administered an expert, textbook, prostitute's blow job, bringing him to climax in less than two minutes and swallowing every drop, before standing up again and kissing him lightly.

'One good sex turn deserves another,' she said picking up the cheese board. 'Bring the wine Ralph would you. It's over there.'

When Ralph went back into the dining room no-one looked up except Tina.

'Hi, Ralph, we're just talking about you. Your ears must have been burning. Henry is telling everyone about that case you won for him.'

He wanted to deflect the subject of himself. 'Wine anyone?' he asked and went round the table filling their glasses. He was drained, physically and emotionally, not capable of any real rational thought, confused and bewildered, the certainties in his life swept away, his infidelity oppressing him but not as much as that of Tina and Ian, or Tina and Henry or Tina and anyone else.

He went onto social autopilot, apparently relaxed and urbane, but underneath a cauldron's brew of seething doubts and torments. He was preoccupied and only dimly aware of Frances beside him, unzipping him under the table and infiltrating her hand into his trousers again. Finding him unresponsive, she eventually left him alone, with a look of disappointment. He did not put his hand up her skirt again, keeping both elbows on the table and cupping his chin with his hands, he remained a combatant in the conversation, part of it, but apart.

When the guests had finally dispersed from the sitting room and left the house, he realised that he was still sober, he had not had any wine for a couple of hours. Henry was slurring his words, Tina was swaying slightly and Frances had to hold on to the side of the door for a moment to recover her balance.

'Goodnight Frances and Henry. I've got to go to bed. I can't keep my eyes open any longer.' Tina kissed them both, Henry lingering fractionally longer than was socially necessary, as his hand touched her shoulder. 'Are you coming up Ralph?'

'In a minute.'

'I'll probably be asleep.'

He was torn between going up and just lying beside her, holding her to him, enjoying her proximity, her scent, the heat of her body, and denying her and himself that pleasure.

Henry got up too. 'I've got to go now as well. I've had it as well.'

Was there an innuendo in that remark, a sexual signal to Tina? He was not sure if he even cared but saw, once more,

Henry stumble, falling out of the door after Tina, to kiss on the landing, he wondered, hardly time for a quickie with him and Frances downstairs and, then thinking of Frances, found her looking at him with frank enquiry.

Parting her legs as the door shut and then, listening to the sound of the footsteps going up, slowly and deliberately lifting her skirt over her long black stockinged legs and opening them wide, revealing herself, peeling her lips apart with one hand, inserting a finger of her other, stirring herself in anticipation of what she was certain was to happen.

Ralph sat, untouched glass in hand, watching her, meeting her eyes, looking down at her finger and murmured, 'You exert a considerable sexual attraction.'

'Why don't you come over and fuck me?'

'I'm enjoying the show,' he said mildly but with a smile, 'I've always thought you rather beautiful but shouldn't we wait for the others to go to sleep?' but thinking that the only person he wanted to fuck, as she had just put it, at that moment or any other, was Tina, doing God knows what with Henry upstairs. Should he go and look, on the pretext of checking the children or going to the lavatory, he wondered, as he listened for noises upstairs?

Frances smiled, a smile of delicious sexual complicity, and standing up, rather unsteadily, drew her skirt round her and said, 'You want a show, I'll show you a show,' went away for a moment only and came back with a silver phallus and, sitting down again, opened her legs and started teasing herself with it, partially inserting the object, drawing it out, only to put it further in each time, shutting her eyes when she had reached what must have been her desired depth of penetration and tempo.

Ralph, to whom this sort of thing was completely new, found himself erotically fascinated by the sight of the attractive woman playing with herself and started to feel aroused.

'I use this when Henry can't manage it.' She opened her eyes and closed them again, dropping the phallus and using one hand to open herself, put three fingers inside saying, 'I've never felt readier or randier. Come here, come in me and over me...'

'Stay there, I'd like to check the children are OK,' he said.

'And that everyone else is asleep,' she asked, raising her eyebrows.

He went into the hall; there was no noise or sound whatsoever. He climbed up the stairs quietly and listened outside each bedroom, the regular sound of Tina's breathing, a light snore from Henry, the twins breathing and Sam, all were asleep, and went down and back into the sitting room.

Frances was there, still in a position of complete abandonment as he had left her, legs spread wide, but her hands were resting on the sofa, the phallus on the floor. She was asleep, snoring very softly, and did not stir as he approached her. He tried shaking her very gently but enough, he hoped, to wake her, for he knew he could not leave her here like this. Even covering her up, if Henry came in and found her, upon any kind of investigation, knickerless, he might jump to unwelcome conclusions.

Then, Ralph, his eyes travelling the length of her body, lighting on her pubic hair, her lips still gaping enough to see the pinkness inside, found himself appallingly aroused.

What was it like to do it to an unconscious woman? Would she sleep through it and never know, or might she wake up and perhaps scream and wake the house?

Ralph felt down and undid his trousers, knelt down in front of her and putting two fingers tentatively inside, found her so moist and sticky that he knew he must try.

Carefully, he put it against her lips and pressed forwards until he was right inside. She did not move, so he started a rhythm, very slowly at first, building up until he came, withdrawing at the last moment as he did not want to leave any evidence, this went into his shirt tails instead, and tidying himself up immediately.

He hid the phallus under a cushion of the sofa and then, going to Frances, whispered, 'Frances, Frances, wake up, come on. It's time to go to bed. Come on,' repeating this with more urgency until blearily she responded. 'What is it?'

'Time to go to bed.'

'I thought you'd never ask,' as her eyes focussed on him.

'No, your bed, can you get upstairs?'

She shook her head. 'Yes, I thought we were going to...'

He silenced her, putting his finger to his lips. 'Not tonight, you're too tired. Come on. I'll follow you up.'

'Christ, my pussy feels excited.'

'I've hidden your thing under that cushion.'

Recollection dawning in her eyes, she grinned, 'I didn't finish the show, did I?'

'No, but there's always another time. Come on,' as she groggily moved forward.

'I'll hold you.' He got her to her bedroom door without incident. 'You'll be all right?'

'Yes, I'm OK now. Sleep well.'

'Goodnight Frances' and he waited, listening carefully as she shut the door, pausing to blow him a kiss, the door clicking shut, her footsteps, imagining the rustle of clothes being shed and then a creak as she got into bed. He went to their spare room and opened the door. Tina was still asleep, and he climbed in beside her, she snuggling back to him, making a small mewing noise as she did so.

Tina woke up with a hangover but was in a good mood.

Ralph woke up without a hangover but had dreamt all night of Tina with her lovers, nightmare after nightmare of Tina laughing at him, moving away from him, ignoring him, Tina, sweat pouring down her face, energetically fucking, being fucked, oral sex, semen bubbling round her mouth, and consequently he did not feel terribly well-disposed towards her.

Tina kissed him 'I've got a thumping hangover. Did we all drink too much?'

'You all did. I didn't.'

'I wonder what Frances and Henry feel like? What time did you and Frances come to bed?'

'About twenty minutes after you.'

'What were you talking about?'

'Reconciliations. How difficult they are.'

'Oh. Are the babies awake?'

'I haven't heard anyone move. It's still quite early.'

'Then you've got time to make love to me.' He nearly groaned with despair as she started to move down the bed with the obvious intention of arousing him orally. Thinking that Frances' smell might still be there, he jumped up and said, 'Hang on.'

'What's wrong with you?'

'I need a pee.'

'Oh well, if you don't want to do it, we shan't.'

'No, I do. I can't do it with a full bladder.'

'Fair enough, I'll be here waiting for you.'

He put on a shirt and opening the door, looked around and went into the bathroom where he washed himself, not with soap as that might make her suspicious, then dried himself quietly, before going back to Tina.

'I've been playing with myself thinking about you. I kept on thinking, last night, at the table, how clever you are and how lucky I am. Come here Ralph, kiss me.' At that moment a child cried. 'That's Primrose. She can wait for a few minutes.'

'It's not fair; we're in someone else's house. We can't leave her crying,' he said, relieved at finding an easy way out of the predicament of lack of desire.

'I suppose you're right. We can always do it this evening,' Tina said as she climbed out of bed and started to dress. 'That's something to look forward to. Let's go and get the babies up,' as she disappeared.

Ralph lay there for a few moments as the house came to life, trying to make sense of everything, and acknowledging this an abject failure, remembering only how friendly, and affectionate Tina had been towards Henry, at the dinner table and in front of him, as though she simply did not mind if he knew.

Ralph had never had to address a problem of a wife's infidelity before and was unsure as to what to say or do.

He got up and went downstairs to what, on the face of it, seemed an ordinary group of three, now four, adult friends and three small children.

'Good morning Ralph,' said Henry, cuckold and cuckolder.
'Hi,' said Frances, temptress and adulteress.
'You're up,' said Tina, whore and adulteress thought Ralph.
'Hello everyone. Sleep well? Hangovers? Big ones I guess?'

'Pretty awful Ralph. Henry's had several painkillers already. I'm probably going to take one. None of us feel up to a big breakfast. Would you like anything?'

'A cup of coffee and an apple would be fine.'

'Do you know, I feel so bad I think I've got to go back to bed?'

'Go on then Henry. I don't think we're going anywhere are we?' She looked at Tina.

'Do you want to go anywhere? We haven't made any arrangements.'

Tina looked at Ralph, who found the idea of spending hours in their joint company anathematic.

'I could usefully do some work at home,' he volunteered.

'Well then,' Tina announced, 'let's get going when you've finished,' and getting up from the table stated collecting plates, before going out of the room, she said, to pack.

Henry followed her again, to Ralph's fury and he struggled to hold a comment in check.

Frances listened as they went up the stairs and, turning to Ralph pulled a mock-sad face, said, 'I'm sorry about last night. I can't remember going to bed but I know that...'

'No, it doesn't matter. Your thing.' He raised his eyebrows, 'is under the red sofa cushion.'

'My thing?' She was surprised.

'Your silver thing.'

'Oh my God. I didn't get that out did I? God. I must have been pissed. What on earth did I do?'

'Nothing.'

'Ralph?'

'Yes.'

'Will we ever see one another properly?'
'You mean by ourselves?'
'Yes.'
'I'm sure we will.'

She seemed satisfied with this and carried on clearing and Ralph went upstairs.

He found Henry and Tina dismantling the cots, not talking, just easing the mechanisms closed but Ralph could imagine what they had been doing.

'I'll take one down if you take the other,' said Henry, giving him one. They put them in the car and Henry said, 'Too much port. I really should know better. See you soon.'

'Thanks for having us,' said Ralph, thinking bitterly, thanks for having my wife.

'Goodbye,' and as Henry ambled towards the front door, out came Frances, Tina and the three children. Tina tucked the children into their seats, did the belts up, put the overnight bag in the boot while Ralph watched, her beautiful face set in an expression of maternal love.

'Right, I'm ready, Frances, goodbye. Thank you for having us.'

Thank your husband for having her, thought Ralph.

'It was a pleasure, a real pleasure,' Frances smiled, kissed Tina and then Ralph, whispering the word, 'Soon?' in his ear as she pecked his cheek.

Starting the car, setting off, both waving at Frances, Henry having gone in, down the drive and out into the road, a silence between them.

'What's wrong Ralph? You seem in an awfully odd mood.'
'Nothing.'

'There is. Why don't you tell me?'

'It's something I don't want to discuss at the moment.'

'OK.'

She thought for a moment and then, 'Do you find Frances attractive?'

'Why do you ask?'

'Well I know she's always fancied you. She told me once. "I bet you have great sex" she said. If he's as good, she was a bit crude.'

'Yes,' said Ralph, 'I can imagine.'

'If he's as good with his dick as he is with his head, then wow.'

'What did you say?'

'I maintained what you call a judicious silence. Has she ever made a pass at you? Did she last night? Even though she's a best friend, I wouldn't put that past her.'

'No.'

'Not even kiss you?'

'What on earth do you mean not even kiss me?' he asked angrily, temper aroused.

'Well, kiss?'

'I don't go around kissing other women. How can you think that?'

'I just wondered.'

Why on earth wasn't she more concerned? Why could she contemplate the fact that he might have been kissing, been kissed by Frances, been aroused, which might have led to more, how could she ask him this, with such utter equanimity, he demanded of himself.

Logic took him to one inescapable conclusion and confirmed

his suspicions; she could only contemplate him doing this with Frances because she, herself, had been kissing Henry.

There was no other sensible, let alone plausible explanation. He took his eyes off the road for a moment, looked at her, she was staring out of the window, a smile, oh that smile he adored, on her lips. She did not see his glance and he returned to his thoughts and driving.

At their house he unpacked the car, did not respond at all to her questions as to his mood and what was wrong, and tortured by the doubts, the horrors crowding in, went upstairs.

Had she? Had they? He went to his study and sat down. Could she? Could he? Could they? He was not sure.

There had been evidence, he rubbed his eyes, what evidence? He remembered her calling out for Ian, when having the babies and then Tina, bare breasted in the swimming pool, in front of everyone. What else? He tried to remember. The bathing costume in the pool. Sheets outside the bedroom. The London trip with Ian. What had she done when she went to see St John? Were the babies his?

The thoughts and suspicions crowded in on him, one after the other. 'Oh God, surely not. I don't want to believe it. I can't believe it. I mustn't believe it.' He sat exerting mental control, breathing deeply, staring at his computer screen.

To distract himself he switched it on, connected to the Internet, and remembering that he had once asked Tina whether she had ever seen any pornography, indeed, on being told that she had not, had gone out and bought a pile of magazines determined to show her what men were like and what they liked, but had been embarrassed and had not wanted to sit beside her while she looked at them, also not liking the thought of her looking at erections without him there, had thrown them away, decided to surf for pornography.

He was not sure where to start so simply tapped in 'porn' on the search engine. He was astounded at what this produced and two hours later, when Tina put her head round the door, had already seen enough pornographic images to last him a lifetime. He had tried other words, crude words, which produced websites of staggering depravity and sickening photographs. He watched video clip after video clip of little jerking puppet like human beings willingly and sometimes less so, to the extent that perhaps the women had been not just coerced but were being raped, engaging in sexual intercourse in a myriad of dismal and different ways. He felt soiled and unclean and perhaps even tainted forever.

He looked up at her, switching off the monitor, and stood up.

'A cup of tea. I've brought you a cup of tea. What's wrong, Ralph? You look ill.'

'Overwork,' he muttered, 'stress,' and took the tea and went and sat behind his desk again, facing her and silent.

'Aren't you even going to say thank you?'

'Thank you Tina. It was a kind thought.'

'Are you sure you're all right?'

'Yes, I'm OK,' he passed his hand across his forehead, 'maybe I'm coming down with something.'

'Why don't you stop now? You work too hard. Have a rest.' She looked troubled and concerned,

'No, I'll finish. I'll join you for supper,' and, when she closed the door, he switched the monitor on again, ploughing ceaselessly and remorselessly through a tide of filth.

He heard her put the children to bed, went and kissed them goodnight, ascertained that supper was in an hour's time and went back, to the screen showing so many different and beautiful women, really beautiful he thought, not just slags, and men, some with enormous, even gigantic organs, others with ordinary ones, on Asian websites even with tiny ones, and was utterly bewildered.

Sex was just a common activity. He knew this. He knew that everyone did it, well all adults in relationships he supposed, but how could so many of them allow themselves to be photographed or filmed doing it? Why was he so concerned about Tina and her past?

He switched off and went for supper.

'How are you Ralph? Do you feel better? You look ghastly.'

'I'm fine.' He picked at his food, morosely, and did not try to make any conversation and when Tina asked him, for the umpteenth time whether he was all right, snapped and said, 'How many men did you say you'd slept with?' with a savage ferocity that made Tina wince.

'I've told you, two.'

'Then who the fuck was Ian? You had an affair with that bastard in the shop didn't you, that you never told me about.'

Tina sprang to her feet. 'I did not, I did not. What are you talking about?'

'I heard you. When you were under pethidine. You were talking about him.'

'What do you mean?' she stared at him, eyes glittering and cold with apparent fury.

'Don't make me do it. Ian, Ian, fuck me, that kind of thing.'

She sat down, 'I did not,' she said quietly.

'You did.'

'You're making it up.'

'You had an affair with him. You lied to me.'

She sat sphinx-like. 'You're quite wrong. I did not.' She knew that he had no way of proving otherwise. 'Ian was my first boyfriend. My first real boyfriend. I've told you that.'

'That's not true. That was Tim, you're lying to me again.' He was shaking with anger.

'You're wrong, you don't know. You weren't there. Tim was the one before that.'

'How many have you had, you slut,' he heard himself shouting.

She, in the face of this, was aghast but remained composed and simply said, 'Pull yourself together. I'm not a slut. I never have been. Ian was my first boyfriend. The first one who,'

'Fucked you,' he shouted again.

'I made love with. OK.'

'Why should you squeal 'Ian we mustn't do this. Don't make me,' in your fucking delirium?' He spat this out.

'Because we only did it twice, once at the end of the term and then again in the Easter holidays after I had started going out with St John. I wasn't sure that I wanted to do it again...'

'Oh, so you were unfaithful to him then. You said you'd never been. You lied to me,' Ralph screamed, his face only inches from hers.

'I had started going out with St John, I was not sleeping with him. I didn't really think I was being unfaithful...Ian wanted to. I was initially reluctant but I suddenly decided that I wanted to with Ian, another time, again. So I did.' She looked at him. 'And I don't regret it.'

He stood up and slapped her, with all the force he could gather, across the face, a blow that threw her out of her chair and onto the floor where she lay, crying, great choking sobs.

'What have I done to deserve this, what have I done to deserve this?' She moaned over and over again as he stood, wordlessly above her, and kicked her again and again.

At last he stopped and, bursting into tears, he knelt beside her saying, 'I'm sorry Tina. I'm sorry, I'm so sorry. I don't know what came over me. I'm sorry. Believe me. Please forgive me. Please, please, please.'

She looked up at him, mute, expressionless.

'Please Tina, I love you. I love you so much,' before collapsing, sobbing over her.

She let him lie there, it must have been at least twenty minutes, before she tried to move. She ached, she wondered if there was any internal damage, she hurt everywhere. She pushed at Ralph who, looking up with red rimmed eyes, said, 'Forgive me Tina please. Let's go to bed. Let's let everything be all right. I've had a nightmare. I'm scared. Hold me, please.'

'Stand up Ralph. You're hurting me.'

He got up and stood against the table as she lifted herself onto her hands and knees, then standing up, with difficulty, straightening, she said to him, 'What have I done to you Ralph?'

'Nothing, Tina.' He wanted to believe it. 'Nothing, I'm sorry. Let's go to bed.'

She shook her head. 'There's no going back. I'm going to have a bath,' and, walking slowly and carefully, left the room.

Ralph, overcome with feelings he could not begin to understand, let alone explain, watched.

'My precious Tina, my precious Tina. She's lied to me. None of it's true. How could she,' and started sobbing again. At last, he went back to his study, having listened at their bedroom door, not going in, hearing the sound of the bath water running, and switched the computer back on.

Ian? Who was Ian then? Tim, he thought he had known about. Who was Ian? The question repeated itself. He did not log onto the Internet again, he felt disgusted at mankind and himself. And Tina. The dirty slut. He had always had suspicions that she was not telling the truth and at last he had the evidence. He thought of Ian. Ian taking Tina's virginity. Tina willingly surrendering it. Not to Ralph but to Ian. Who was he? He was looking at the books in their shelves, lining the walls. Why had Tina so wanted to hang onto what she called her school year books? Silently, thoughtfully, with a mounting sense of anxiety, he found them, placed neatly beside the ISIS publication she had already bought and from which she had been selecting schools for the twins, schools that Ralph knew they could never afford.

He turned the pages of the volume of her last year and alighted on the sixth form. There she was, Tina. T Bond. Member of the school swimming team. And then he saw T Williams, was that Tim? It must have been. Captain of Cricket, and then, and he felt sick, Ian McArthur Rodgers. Captain of School Swimming Team. Head of School. A superhero. A god.

Ralph put the book back, went to the lavatory and was sick, great bruising retches that left drops of yellow bile in the pan. He felt at once devastated and diminished. She had told him he was a lawyer.

No doubt he was a fucking superstar there as well.

Or was that Tim? He couldn't remember.

Ian Rodgers. Ian Rodgers. Tina. Ian rogers Tina. Ian will roger Tina. Ian was rogering Tina. Ian has rogered Tina. Ian. He was sick again.

Tina cannot have heard him, in all events she did not come out of the bedroom. He picked himself up from where he had been kneeling, flushed the lavatory and stood up. And was promptly sick again. Wiping his mouth, he looked at himself in the mirror and was appalled at what he saw.

Flushed, sweaty, with vomit on his chin, he washed his face under cold water and went back to his study and switched the computer on. He went to a search engine, typed in barristers, logged onto the barristers' directory for England and Wales. No Ian Rodgers. He went next to the solicitor's directory and tapped in the name. Ian Rodgers. Partner at a well-known fashionable firm. He logged onto their website and read Ian's biography. A divorce lawyer. Oh what irony, what exquisite irony. There was a photograph of him as well and Ralph stared at this man who had been where Ralph had so desperately wished he could have been.

A smiling, not unhandsome face, regarded him blankly. Did he ever think of Tina? With what memories? Lots of fucking and laughter no doubt.

Ralph then worked out how to use 192.com. He tapped in the name again on the search of the electoral register. There was only one Ian McArthur Rodgers listed. An address in Islington. He did a reverse search. There was another Rodgers living at the same address. A Sally Rodgers. Sister? Probably a wife. There was no way of checking.

Ralph closed the computer down. He went to the bedroom

but stopped when Tina said, 'No, I don't want you near me tonight or ever again. Sleep somewhere else,' and went and lay on the double bed in the spare room, staring expressionlessly at the ceiling before getting up to write.

The children had not woken, had given no sign that they heard anything; he could hear their breathing across the landing, he could hear the sounds that Tina made, the little mewing noises that he so liked and of which she was unaware, not believing him when he told her about them when she woke, he heard the house cooling down when the central heating went off, the tiny noise of his watch and he did not sleep.

At six o'clock he got up from his chair, went swimming and then, gingerly lifting the cover, he got into bed beside Tina. She stirred, turned, still asleep and pressed her back to him. She made no protest when he lifted one leg, and entered her slowly, inch by inch, then gently thrusting himself to an orgasm. She said nothing. She did not simulate an orgasm but lay there like a dead thing.

'I love you Tina,' he whispered. She turned and looked at him.

'Why did you do that?'

'What, I'm sorry, I'm truly sorry.'

'No, I deserved that.' Why did she say that, he thought. 'No, I meant fuck me, just now. Why didn't you leave me alone?'

'Because I love you.'

'You don't. You love an image of me. Not the real me. The flesh and blood me. The me that is me because of the experiences I've had. You don't love a human being. I'm not sure you could ever love a human being. You may not want a factotum but you need a fucktotem,' she said bitterly and started crying.

'I'm sorry, Tina. I'm sorry.'

'So am I. Oh God, you've no idea how sorry I am. I wish things had never happened,' and she turned away from him.

He got up, got dressed in a suit; he had made a decision.

'I'm going to Chambers, Tina. I'll be back this evening. I might be late.'

He bent down to kiss her.

She did not turn her face and did not reply when he murmured, 'I love you.'

He believed he did love her, but he knew also that his love lay shattered, fragmented, in a million cold little pieces and he was doubtful that he could ever put it all together again.

NEMESIS

He drove to the station, caught the train, one more, just another, pin-striped commuter and went into his Chambers where, getting out the Solicitor's Directory from the library, he went to his room and, checking the telephone number, dialled Ian Rodgers' firm. He asked to be put through to his secretary and, a bright London voice answering, asked if there was any chance of an appointment with Mr Rodgers this afternoon.

'Wait a moment, I'll see. It's a bit short notice,' the noise of a diary being leafed through, 'but yes, at four o'clock, if you like.'

'At four o'clock then. Ralph Edwards.'

'Have you a telephone number?' He gave it to her and going through the clerk's room, ignored Ken's cheery greeting, only hearing him say, 'What's wrong with him today,' as he left.

Sitting on the train to London, Ralph had no idea of what he was going to say to him. He found it difficult even to articulate his name. Mr Rodgers.

Mr Rodgers fucked Tina.

He sat blankly in the carriage staring at the Times crossword puzzle, thinking and thinking. After arriving he caught a taxi and decided to go to the National Gallery where he stood for an hour in front of the Bellinis, the gentle Madonna caressing with such love her little infant, all rendered in such exquisite colour with such beautiful exactitude.

He found himself crying again at the betrayal and at his loss.

At length, he caught another taxi to the offices, smart and expensive but Ralph looked part of this world, nothing out of the ordinary, no eyebrows raised at him, he was just another expensively attired suit, another client waiting to be shown to see a solicitor.

The receptionist phoned, spoke briefly to some-one and said, 'Mr Rodgers can see you now.'

He was met at the top of the stairs by a secretary.

'Good afternoon Mr Edwards, come this way.'

It was the same woman he had spoken to earlier. He looked at her more closely. Attractive, very attractive. Did Mr Rodgers roger her too? Across his desk first thing in the morning?

'Here you are,' and he was in, a man in a dark pinstripe suit standing up to greet him, stretching out his hand, his hand that had groped his Tina, that had inserted one, maybe two fingers up her, stretching her before putting his dick in...

'Pleased to meet you Mr Edwards.'

The voice broke into his thoughts. 'How do you do Mr Rodgers.'

'Please sit down.' It was a perfectly commonplace formal and professional exchange.

'What can I do for you?'

Ralph looked at him again saying, 'It's hard to know where to begin. My wife has been unfaithful. I want a divorce.'

A solicitous and professional expression on his face, Rodgers asked him the usual questions. It was easier, Ralph supposed, as he knew divorce law, because he could simply state the facts which justified a divorce. He lied about Tina's name though but otherwise answered the questions.

Had Rodgers been a banking lawyer, a construction lawyer or any other kind of specialist, Ralph could still have woven a convincing story, enough at least to get him through the half hour or hour that he wanted to spend.

Ralph evinced all his charm, Rodgers knew of his Chambers, indeed a university contemporary of his was a junior there and by five o'clock, preliminary advice having been given, explanations as to costs, advice which Ralph had no intention of acting upon, any more than he would have acted upon banking law advice, but Rodgers had been beguiled into thinking that they were already chums.

'Call me Ian,' he had said, and noticing him looking at his watch, Ralph asked 'Do you finish about now?'

'Normally, yes.'

'Let me buy you a drink,' an invitation that was accepted with enthusiasm.

He was not an unpleasant man Ralph decided, although tempered by an irrational and jealous hatred of him, he wanted to know, to finally know, the truth.

In the bar, after some small talk, he deftly turned the subject to sex and how this, or the lack of it, seemed to inform everyone's existences.

'It's astonishing that a small area of skin at the top of a woman's legs, and a piece of erectile tissue between a man's can be the determinant of so many lives, the cause of wars, death, destruction, isn't it?' Ralph asked this with a smile. 'I used to have a divorce practice, in my early days. What made you carry on with yours? I mean specialise?'

'Human interest, I suppose. But yes. If you've done divorce you'll know. The sex thing. It drives and kills marriages. Lack of it. Too much. Infidelity. It's staggering.' He was on his third drink and was visibly relaxing.

'Are you married, Ian?'

'Yes.'

'Happily?'

'Oh yes.'

'I thought divorce lawyers had a high divorce rate.'

'They do, statistically.'

'I came across a divorce lawyer socially the other day who married his first real girlfriend. Now divorced, of course.' He had just made this up.

'How do you mean?'

'The first girl he'd been to bed with.'

'Oh well, mine wasn't my first,' he contemplated his fingers and smirked, 'not by a long chalk.'

'No, nor was mine. But I sometimes think of my first and, I liked her a lot, wonder how things would have been if...' he thought of Lucy and her death and stopped.

'I'm not sure I remember my first,' Ian began.

Ralph felt as though he had been hit in the stomach.

Not sure if he remembered his first? Tina? How could he not remember Tina who had given herself to him for the first time, had... for a moment the world seemed to close in on him, a fog enveloping and he, trying hard to concentrate, said instead, 'Everybody remembers their first time. I remember mine distinctly. As though it was yesterday.'

Ian sat, eyes closed. 'Yes I do remember. Tina she was called. A pretty thing. It was her first time too.'

'Memorable was it?'

'Not terribly. A sticky rite of passage,' and he laughed at the crude joke. 'I ought to be getting back.'

Ralph had checked the underground stations, and knowing where Ian lived and assuming that he would use the tube, lightly said 'I'm going to Holborn Tube Station.'

Ian replied, as he drained his glass, 'That's a coincidence, that's where I'm going. We'll walk together.'

Ralph also knew which platform Ian would use and, telling him that his hotel was in a street two stops up, Ian was not surprised when Ralph accompanied him.

They had just missed a train and were standing alone in the dark, green lit chamber close to the edge.

'Your Tina,' Ralph began.

'Yes?'

'Did she moan or did she mew when she had an orgasm?'

Ian did not seem surprised at the question, and considered for a moment. 'Neither. She didn't have one. I did though. Three of them. In quick succession.' His face broke into a broad grin. 'Christ, what orgasms. I still remember them...'

The platform had filled up and they were being pushed from behind, the weight of people, a dense mass.

'Did you do it often with her then?'

'No, only once again,' as the noise of an approaching train began to reach a crescendo, 'But I was jolly glad to have got there first. Why?'

Suddenly puzzled, he looked Ralph in the face.

Perhaps he guessed, perhaps he did not, but as he leaned towards him, Ralph whispered, 'Because I married her, you bastard,' saw Ian's eyes widen in terror as Ralph pushed him, as hard as he could, over the edge and into the path of the train, which of course could not stop and, as Ralph merged, melded, one more pin-striped suit amongst all the other pin-striped suits, all he could hear was the sound of screams.

He walked quickly and purposefully through the station and boarding another train was soon in Euston. Where he caught a train back.

Only a few hours later, he was in their kitchen. There was a note on the table which simply said, "I have taken some sleeping pills. Do not wake me." Tina was in bed. She did not wake, did not stir, heavy breathing, sighs, the sounds of the tiniest gentle snores were the only noises.

Ralph carried on writing until dawn broke, and then went for a swim.

He came back, towelled himself dry, and then warming it against the radiator, he went into the bedroom, Tina did not move, was still asleep. He gently parted her legs, shut his eyes, inserted it an inch or two.

Then pulled the trigger. The sound the shotgun made seemed deafening and, opening his eyes again, he looked. And was sick.

Fragments of love. Fragments. Fragments.

He was sick again. When he finally stood up.

He turned and went out of the door and down to the kitchen, where he sat at the table and put his head in his hands and wept.

OBLIVION

Which is where I am still.
          Now, finishing writing this. The indictment. The case against her.

I've taken the rest of the pills. Enough to kill me as well. Lots of them. But am now struggling, fighting to retain the intellectual rigour of thought, clarity, that I have so desperately required over the last month. Oh God, I know it all finally.

I have been writing this for some weeks.

For I am Ralph Edwards and intelligent enough to see behind the deceptions, the facades, the nonsense. I understand people. I can read them like a book.

I am a barrister, a seeker of truth, a lawyer, a seeker of justice.

Her lies were not enough to deceive me. How could she expect to when I guessed all along. I have no doubts any more.

Writing this has shown me what happened.

Claiming that I was the only one she ever asked in the kitchen I should have known then

Only twice with Ian And then that husband of hers

I know what they were like I know what Henry was like From the noises Milkmen are all the same I knew Frances too Alas, I knew her too well A lass I knew her

I have had to flesh out the details flush out the flesh

but I am Ralph Edwards and know

Did she think I was a total fool

The twins have not stirred I should have had them DNA tested

I began writing this when I suspected Tina my lovely lovely faithless wife

I kept on seeing the evidence.
But I killed my Lucy my juicy juicy Lucy and my Virginia died too
My Virgin Grade 1A
She shouldn't have killed her though
Why did she have to kill her
Why did she betray me
I shall never know now
Anymore than I shall know the details of her affairs
I only know what she told me
Which was little In fact nothing
Why did she not tell me more
It is only by filling the gaps that it makes sense to me
To me To me
She told me nothing
Faithless woman
Frailty thy name is woman
Frailty thy name is Tina
My lovely loveless loving lovely Tina
Lucy Virginia Tina
I am Ralph Edwards scourge of the faithless
it was meet right my bounden duty so to do the peace that passeth understanding the pieces that are past understanding may the peace of the lord go with you may the pieces
RIP
Requiescat in Pieces
it all makes sense finally
Lucy in the Sky with Diamonds They are forever
What of life is left when the loving has to stop
What of love is left when the living had to stop

this is the final chapter
In the beginning was the word and these words are my ending
In my beginning was my end
who of us who knew our endings would want our beginnings
I can hear the twins crying waking
its morning
morning all
mourning twins
I am finishing
finished
now I have to go and see to the children.

AFTERWORD

The police were diligent in their investigations after what the newspapers called "the gruesome tragedy" had been discovered. A young woman detective superintendent was assigned to the case who, determined to try and understand the motivation, interviewed all the principal and many of the peripheral witnesses after she had finished reading Ralph's manuscript.

St John denied any sexual contact with Tina from a date that actually preceded their meeting Ralph. He became very angry at the suggestion that he was 'into kinky sex, rubber bras or vibrators'. He accepted that he and Tina had met at his house after separation - so she could collect her things - but was emphatic that there had been no sexual relations between them then and most certainly never at his Chambers. The very thought was 'outrageous'. As for the 'naughty knickers' he had never seen these let alone given them to her. Sylvia, although very ill with a reactive depression, was able to confirm that they had in fact been a gift from her and had been a joke between the two sisters.

Ian, the assistant manager, had scoffed at the suggestion that he and Tina had any sexual relationship or that anyone, let alone Tina, had climbed onto the photocopier. They had all gone their separate ways after the meal in the restaurant and, he pointed out, his girlfriend had in fact accompanied them that night and that, against the rules, she had stayed with him in the London hotel while he was on the management course.

The same detective had even tracked down Tina's friends at the time of her wedding and had established that Tina's hen party had been a rather sober affair in a wine bar. No such person as Stella existed.

She also interviewed a number of St John's and Tina's male friends. All were uniformly aghast at any suggestion of impropriety on their part or hers, in the kitchen or elsewhere.

Frances acknowledged the episodes with Ralph, believed that she 'had led him on' but could not forgive herself, she said, after she had been told that Ralph had probably started his account, his indictment as he had called it, within a day or two of their liaison beneath the sleeping Tina. The policewoman had shown Frances Ralph's manuscript and had pointed out how so much of the material describing Tina's sexual experiences and her past had been interpolated; it was in a more hurried and scrawled handwriting, most of which, it is thought, was written and added in the day or so before the murders, and while Ralph was still lucid but psychotic. Frances, when she realised that this meant after her dinner party, her seduction of him in the kitchen and then, understanding that she had been effectively raped by him, albeit consensually, collapsed and had to be taken to hospital.

Henry, who had never understood why Ralph had apparently not told Tina of Virginia's death, Tina having found out from them and saying that she thought Ralph would talk about it in his own time and that she did not want to distress him, acknowledged that there had been an affair, but it was with his secretary and very definitely not Tina. He subsequently moved in with his former girlfriend and, at the time of writing, is seeking custody of Sam.

The milkman scorned the policewoman's suggestion, saying, 'I'd have had as much chance with that one as with the Queen Mother.'

Tim, after he had read the relevant sections, and who had remained friendly with Ian, was too distraught at first to say anything but finally confirmed that the episode describing them and Tina in the shower was nonsense. The last night at school, as related by Ralph, had simply never taken place. Tina had been with a group of ten or so, including Tim and Ian, who had spent the night together reminiscing and looking forward with excitement to their lives and their bright futures.

The general consensus among the psychiatrists was that Ralph suffered from Delusional Jealousy Disorder, a well-documented condition characterised by the psychotic belief that the sufferer's spouse or lover is unfaithful. The belief is without foundation and is based on incorrect inferences and supported by small bits of 'evidence', eg disarranged clothing or spots on the sheets, which are collected and used to justify the delusion.

Onset can be difficult to explain, even when the circumstances are known. Perhaps the sudden overwhelming sexual attraction Ralph felt for Tina, the fact of his leaving a happily married wife, her violent death, which was, there seemed little doubt, certainly suicide – Jane reluctantly admitted that Virginia had said, in the weeks preceding the decree absolute, that life without Ralph was not worth living - any of these might have been the precipitant. The sufferer from this condition can follow an apparently normal existence, seemingly functioning on their usual, sometimes high, intellectual level. In addition, as one textbook (*Clinical Psychiatry*, Slater E. and Roth M., 3rd Edition 1969, London: Bailliere Tindall and Cassell) states, 'delusional states of jealousy whether arising from stressful experiences or out of a clear blue sky tend to pursue a chronic and intractable course uninfluenced by environmental events.

The symptomatology may be bizarre with an elaborate delusional system, falsification or fabrication of evidence against the spouse, pseudo-hallucinatory experiences and aggressive behaviour which may culminate in murder.'

There is no cure.

FRAGMENTS
AND PIECES:
THE TRUTH

She did not want to let him go and said, 'No, stay there.' He noticed she was biting her lip. He had seen her do this before. She opened her eyes and there were tears.

'Why are you crying?'

'It's never been like that before. Nobody has done that to me. I just feel so relaxed and happy.'

He wondered why it had never been like that for her but dismissed the thought quickly. It had been special for him too he acknowledged.

*

They talked little but Tina, catching sight of both herself in the mirror and Ralph watching her, asked, 'What are you thinking about?'

'You,' he answered truthfully.

'What exactly?'

'Who are you?' He was aware that he had reached a decision but was completely unsure as to how to tell her or move anything forward.

'I'm me. Tina. The girl you've just ravished, satisfied and who is extremely, extremely happy. I've left my husband. I'm on the brink of a new life. I'm with you in a lovely hotel. I'm happy. That's who I am.'

Ralph had meant the question in a much broader sense. He wanted to know all about her. He was on the point of committing himself, throwing away an old life, including Virginia, and needed to know more. 'I really wanted to know more about you, your background, your likes, your dislikes, your fears, your happiness. Everything about you. I want to understand you.'

'All I've ever wanted is someone like you.'

'What do you mean?' Ralph felt flattered.

'Someone who wanted to bathe with me, who took the trouble to satisfy me sexually, who looks at me the way you do. Who strokes and touches me and says nice things. Who cares and wants me,' and she smiled. 'Thank you.'

*

In his car, a little later, driving out on the motorway, in the dark, her face illuminated by the glow of various dials, like an aircraft she had said the first time they had got in the car together, he looked at her profile. He felt he at least knew this well, and said, 'I know nothing about you. But I love you. Is that inconsistent or simply stupid?'

'You don't need to know everything about anyone to love them. You can love them for what they are,' she smiled.

Or for what they seem, he thought with a lawyer's realism. 'Should I know anything about your parents before I meet them?'

'Not really. They're like me or I'm like them. Uncomplicated. A bit disappointed in me. They made sacrifices to send me to school and I don't think I've repaid them. They'd hoped that I'd be more successful. I used to want that as well but it seems less important now that I've met you.'

What had she told them about him? He asked her.

She did not answer immediately then said slowly and carefully. 'I've told them that you are the most important thing in my life. That I think that I have found real happiness,' smiled at him, that smile which he so liked. 'That's all.'

*

Really, you never tried?' Ralph asked. He was relieved.

'No, I've told you. I know I was his first. Funny, thinking back on it. It seemed important to him that he was my first as well, so I let him think he was.'

'Wasn't he?'

'No. But it seemed to please him to think so. I had no serious sex life with him at all. Only the occasional Friday night shag. That was his delicate term which I always loathed. As I did the sex. I think he did it only because you were supposed to when you're married. He was almost asexual, looking back.

*

When she saw him she broke into a run, looking a little undignified, but she ran towards him, threw her arms around him and kissed him eagerly.

'Oh God, Ralph, I've missed you so much. I've been so looking forward to seeing you again. It's been weeks it seems since we lay next to one another.' She was still clinging to him. He held her tightly as well.

'Oh God, I've missed you. You've no idea how much I need you.'

'I'm never going to go away again. I'd rather lose my job. I want to be with you, Ralph. Always.'

*

'I can, but I like to think about other times as well, like the car, you know. I've told you. I had a really dull sex life before I met you. You seem to have switched me on. You're smiling.

I know it's a cliche but it's all so different. I feel as though I've discovered what sex is about, that it can be nice, pleasant, fun, satisfying. Not wifely duty stuff.' She kissed him. 'And I've got you to thank for that.'

*

She started sniffing and then she sobbed, as she stood beside the bed, holding a pair of knickers up and then, wiping her eyes with them, she gave a wan smile. 'I'm sorry.'

'What's wrong?'

'I'm crying with happiness and regret. I just wish I'd met you sooner. First. I'm crying for all the years we didn't have together. The years when we could have... Oh, I don't know. Done anything and everything.'

He walked over to her, cradled her in his arms, kissing the tears in her eyes and said, 'We've got each other now,' and undressing her, slowly and carefully, he helped her into bed, where she lay, curled up and eyes closed.

*

'Because I wasn't there with you. I wish I could have been your first but I wasn't.'

'No, I wish I had been your first too but I wasn't. Tim was.'

She looked startled, 'No, he wasn't, Ian was.'

'Who was Ian? You've never mentioned him.'

'Ian was my boyfriend after Tim. Ian was my first. I was his first too.'

'You must have been fond of him.'

'I was,' and her look changed to one, he thought, best described as rueful chagrin.

'When was that then?'

'The sixth form, my last year.'

'I'll bet you couldn't keep your hands off one another after that.'

'No,' she smiled, amused at the recollection, 'we only did it once, no twice.'

It was his turn to be startled. 'You only did it twice? That can't be true.'

'It is,' she was still smiling, eyes far away. He felt a gust of relief, not quite believing what she had said but wanting more than anything to believe that she really was telling the truth.

'And with St John?'

'I never liked sex with him. You know that.'

'Good God, you're almost new then.'

She beamed, 'Yes, if you want to put it like that, then I suppose I am.'